Karyn's Memory Box

STEPHANIE GRACE WHITSON

Publishers Since 1798

THOMAS NELSON PUBLISHERS
Nashville

To Bob,
my leader, my example,
my beloved, my friend.

In loving memory of B. Celest Higgins (1947–1996).
Her faithful friendship, loving care, caring love,
encouraging words, sweet wisdom,
pure heart, perfect visits,
understanding spirit,
knowing thoughts made
her all it means to have a friend
of like mind, and her departure left a void
in my life that will remain until we meet again.

Copyright © 1999 by Stephanie Grace Whitson

All rights reserved. Written permission must be secured from the publisher to use or reproduce any part of this book, except for brief quotations in critical reviews or articles.

Published in Nashville, Tennessee, by Thomas Nelson, Inc., Publishers.

Scripture quotations are from the Holy Bible, KING JAMES VERSION.

Library of Congress Cataloging-in-Publication Data

Whitson, Stephanie Grace.
    Karyn's memory box / Stephanie Grace Whitson.
        p.   cm. — (Keepsake legacies)
    ISBN 0-7852-7186-4
    1. German Americans—Nebraska—Fiction. I. Title. II. Series:
Whitson, Stephanie Grace. Keepsake legacies.
PS3573.H555K37   1999
813'.54—dc21

                                                            98-46782
                                                            CIP

Printed in the United States of America.
3 4 5 6 QPK 04 03 02 01 00 99

Prologue

I hope this is worth it," Reagan muttered to herself as she sipped the last of her lukewarm coffee. She had been on the road since before dawn that morning, determined to be one of the first antique dealers to arrive at what had been billed as one of the largest estate auctions held in Custer County in years.

Pulling off the interstate, Reagan headed northwest on Route 2, but not before stopping to fill both of the pickup's gas tanks. Leaning against the truck while the gas pump clicked off gallon after gallon of gas, Reagan reached into the cab and pulled the auction announcement from where she had tucked it between the sun visor and the roof of the cab. As she read through the long list of items to be sold, she thought, *Daddy and Mother would surely have loved this one.*

Reagan smiled to herself, remembering the moment she became "hooked" on auctions. She had been only fourteen, and she and her father had driven the light blue Volkswagen "Beetle" to an auction. When a beautiful antique love seat and matching chair came up for sale, Daddy raised his hand. "Just starting the bid for George, Reagan," he whispered when Reagan looked at him in surprise. But "just starting the bid" for their auctioneer friend George backfired that day. No one else bid on the furniture.

Daddy had looked down at Reagan with his easy grin. "Well, now. Your mother's been wanting some new furniture. Guess the Lord just gave her some." They strapped the furniture to the roof of the little car, and drove home not sure which was more fun—the looks from other motorists or the look on Mother's face when they drove up the driveway at home.

Well, it was a good buy, anyway, Reagan reasoned. She still had the love seat and the chair, and no amount of money in the world would make her part with them. Recovered and refinished more times than Reagan could count, those two pieces of furniture and the story of their acquisition were now a permanent part of the Bishop family legacy.

The chair and love seat had been only the beginning. Nearly every Saturday after that, when the weather was good—and some Saturdays when the weather was abominable—the little blue Volkswagen took Reagan and her dad to some estate sale or country auction, "just to look things over." Reagan developed an interest in Depression glass. She began collecting a pink pattern called "Mayfair." Her mother soon followed suit, although she preferred the green "Rose of Sharon" pattern. With Mother along, the adventure was even more sweet. The two women chided Daddy for buying rusted tools and broken chairs, and he complained about hauling boxes of glassware to the car. Soon, they had to stop driving the Volkswagen in favor of "the big car."

By the time her mother and dad passed away, Reagan had begun to dabble in buying and selling antiques. She rented small booths in two antique malls. Neither booth made much money, but being a dealer justified Reagan's attendance at auctions.

She discovered that she had an uncanny knack for buying things just before they "caught on." Once everyone else wanted something and the bidding at auctions became frenzied, Reagan's strict budget usually made her stop buying. However, even when other dealers began to show interest, Reagan's passionate fascination with antique textiles never waned. She had been known to stand in the hot sun for hours, just to procure one small set of quilt blocks stashed in the bottom of a box of towels. She had paid five dollars for a pile of oil-stained rags out of a rickety garage just to retrieve a used-up gold-and-green quilt that had been thrown out with the rags.

Once a casual boyfriend had asked, "What are you going to do with that?" when she excitedly showed him a hand-pieced quilt top.

"Well," Reagan said laughingly, "I'm going to *have* it."

"But what exactly is it *for*?" the young man wanted to know. "I mean, it isn't even finished."

Reagan had looked at him with pity. Their relationship didn't last long.

Over the years, she had driven thousands of miles to auctions that advertised patch quilts or quilt tops. More often than not, the patch quilts were tied comforters, and the quilt tops were stained beyond repair. Still, something drew Reagan to the old fabrics. She didn't bother to philosophize about why she felt such a link to other women in other times. She simply enjoyed the wondering as she held their handwork and asked herself why it had never been finished, or what the woman was like who made it.

And so, as the sun peeked over the horizon in the rearview mirror of Reagan Bishop's pickup, she fingered the auction announcement that promised a "large amount of quilts, linens, etc." and thanked God aloud for the clear blue sky and the cool spring air. Added to the verbalized prayer was an unspoken hope that Helen Stapleman would not drive this far just to check out a few quilts.

Reagan was only a few miles northwest of Grand Island when she began to wonder if she had taken a wrong turn. She had seen only two other pickups—and they had been headed in the opposite direction. Just when she was thinking she might need to turn around and retrace her route, she saw the small sign at the side of the road. "Auction" it proclaimed, with an arrow pointing to the northeast and a gravel road that was barely more than two tracks through a pasture.

Reagan followed the road for over half a mile until, at the top of the next ridge, she could see a weathered white frame house surrounded by ancient cottonwood trees. A few vehicles were already parked in the pasture. Reagan swung in next to them. Stuffing her long red hair up into her "auction hat" and grabbing her driver's license, she hurried across the pasture to a small trailer with a sign that read "Bidding Numbers Here."

A few minutes later she pinned her bidding number to her hat and set off on the quest for treasure. Looking up toward the house, she saw that this would, indeed, be a huge sale. Row upon row of folding tables in the front yard groaned beneath piles of glassware, cookware, and tools.

It was going to be a wonderfully long day. It would likely be long after midnight before she made it home. She recognized another dealer, nodded hello, and feigned interest in a blue granite roaster on the table before her. As soon as the dealer turned his back, she made her way around the side of the house, wondering if the "large amount" of quilts and linens that had been promised in the auction ad would turn out to be a half dozen rotten comforters pulled out of the barn loft.

Well. I guess not. Hanging on the clotheslines on the east side of the house were some of the most glorious quilts Reagan had ever seen. Her hand almost trembled as she reached out to touch a blue-and-white Ocean Waves quilt. She walked between the clotheslines, inspecting quilt after quilt, bemoaning her limited budget and praying that Helen Stapleman had either not seen the ad or, if she had, was too busy or too sick to come. *Not really sick, Lord,* Reagan thought guiltily. *Maybe just a mild headache.*

Of course God in His wisdom often responds to prayers with a resounding NO. And thus did He answer Reagan Bishop. Helen Stapleman, the woman with the silver hair and the bottomless wallet, the woman who held her bidding number high and never, ever gave up on something she really wanted, was just now striding confidently across the lawn toward the quilts.

All right, Helen, Reagan thought even as she nodded hello and flashed a friendly smile, *but you can't have them all. I'm going to have that Ocean Waves; I don't care what you bid on it. It's mine. It's going home in my truck to live at my house.*

But hours later, when the auctioneer walked along the clothesline, selling quilt after quilt, the Ocean Waves went to Helen Stapleman. Reagan fought back tears of frustration when the quilt was taken off the line, folded, and passed across the crowd and into Helen's waiting arms. How could she have known that Helen would give nearly a thousand dollars for it? In spite of her disappointment, Reagan also felt a glimmer of relief. She had bid over eight hundred dollars that she really could not afford. Reluctantly, Reagan had to admit that it was a good thing that God had saved her from her own stupidity.

As the last quilt sold, Reagan turned away. *I ought to go.* But she had stood for an entire day and dropped out of bid after bid in order to save her money for that quilt. Now she faced the antique dealer's ultimate defeat: a drive home in an empty truck. She followed the auctioneer down a slope to where a kind of shed jutted directly out of a ridge that ran along the back of the house. A few crocks and half-rotten barrels and about a dozen orange crates had been dragged out in the sun. For some reason, one of the crocks drew Reagan's attention. It had been a water-cooler, but both the spigot and the lid were missing. Some-one had used it to hold empty burlap bags. When no one bid on it, Reagan raised her number and paid fifty cents for the crock and fifteen orange crates.

"But I don't want the orange crates," she protested.

"Sorry," the auctioneer insisted. "That's the lot that sold. You want me to resell it?"

Reagan shook her head. "No. It's all right. I've got room in the back of the pickup. Maybe I can find a use for them."

Someone stepped forward who had missed the sale of the orange crates. "If you don't want the crates, I'll give you a buck for them."

Reagan nodded. "Great. Take them all." She pocketed the dollar, congratulating herself on having earned a free cup of coffee on the deal.

The auction ended. By the time Reagan had paid her bill and retrieved the crock, the auctioneer's own truck was the only vehicle still parked in the pasture. As Reagan lifted the crock into the bed of her pickup, he teased, "You sure must have wanted that crock bad. You got a stash of old spigots and lids at home? It's probably worth nearly two hundred dollars complete."

Reagan grinned, talking as she lifted the tailgate and walked around to the driver's side of the cab. "Actually, I wanted the burlap bags. Couldn't care less about the crock. I heard yesterday that they're making curtains out of burlap bags on the coast. It's as big a craze as the fifties' look was last year. Why, they're willing to pay five dollars a piece for seed bags if they've still got farm dirt on 'em to prove their authenticity." She opened the door, got in, and rolled down the window, laughing as she concluded, "And if you believe that . . ." She began to sing a familiar country-western song, "I've got some oceanfront property in Arizona . . ."

They both laughed again. Reagan waved, started the truck, and headed across the pasture, down the gravel road and out onto the paved highway, completely unaware that, had Irene Peale's grandmother been present at that sale, she would have paid more than the entire farm was worth to have retrieved what lay in the bottom of the broken crock in the back of Reagan Bishop's pickup.

Reagan left the broken crock in the back of her truck for several days before even bothering to unload it. When she did, she just set it by the back door of her bungalow and ignored it. Then, one day when she was planting geraniums along the front walk, she thought of a use for the old crock. *I always buy too many flowers for that little bed out front,* she scolded herself. Walking around the back of the house, she pulled the burlap bags out of the crock, intending to shovel in some dirt and use it for a planter. But the crock held more than just bags.

With a little "Oh" of surprise, Reagan lifted a box out of the crock. In the light, the box elicited an admiring "Ohhhhhh." It was covered with dark fabric, which at one time had been sculpted green velvet. Even with the velvet pile nearly worn off, the box was beautiful. There was an oval beveled mirror set in the lid. The corners were protected by ornate brass protectors, and an exquisite hinge held closed what proved to be a photo album. Carefully lifting the lid, Reagan was delighted to hear the tinkling of a music box. A tiny latch was attached to the hinge, so that whenever the photo album was opened, music played. Reagan sat and listened, trying to identify the tune. When she could not, she carefully pushed in the latch to silence the music and began to study the top two photos. From the left smiled a young, dark-eyed woman with a beautiful lace kerchief knotted about her throat. Her dark hair was almost entirely hidden by a crushed velvet hat. On the right was a full-length portrait of a very handsome, dark-haired man. He was standing beside a chair, and as Reagan peered at the photo she realized he must have been very, very tall.

He had the largest hands she had ever seen, and startlingly pale eyes. *Hello, gorgeous.*

There were other photos as well: a golden-haired woman, with curled hair, sparkling eyes, and a mischievous smile, and an older couple, obviously husband and wife. There were two young men with drooping mustaches seated at a table with a bottle of beer or wine between them. Reagan chuckled, thinking they must have caused some trouble in their day.

The last photo in the album was of a farmstead. Looking closely, Reagan recognized the farm where the auction had been held. Written in pencil across the bottom of the photo was "Mikal Ritter, 1914." Reagan recognized the gigantic windmill in the center of the farmyard and the huge barn with two cupolas that had housed the refreshment stand on the day of the auction. But the photo showed at least half a dozen other outbuildings of varying sizes that must have been torn down since the photo was taken.

The box was more than a photo album. A second compartment beneath the section of photos held an odd assortment of items: a pressed flower, a Belgian lace handkerchief with the monogram "C," knitting needles, a lock of someone's hair, and what Reagan guessed was a rattlesnake's tail.

Reagan took the items out one by one and spread them on her picnic table. Intending to wipe the years of grime away from the bottom of the box, she found the greatest treasure of all. The box had a false bottom, and in the hidden compartment was a leather-bound book. Reagan opened it with trembling hands, revealing line upon line of beautiful handwriting . . . in German.

Her heart pounding, Reagan laid the book aside. Once again opening the photo album, she peered at the photos, wondering, *Who are you?* Turning to look over the things spread across the top of her picnic table, she wondered who had kept such an odd array of things . . . and how they had come to be in the bottom of a broken crock in an old shed.

Reagan went inside and rummaged through the pile of papers on her desk until she found the auction bill. She dialed the auctioneer's phone number. "Tom, this is Reagan Bishop. You remember that old crock I bought at the end of the Ritter sale? Yes, that's the one. The huge sale out in Custer County. Well, I've found something the family might want to know about. There was something in the bottom of the crock. It's really unusual—a photo album with a music box, and then a compartment below it. And there's what appears to be a diary. I've never seen a combination of a photo album and a music box like this before. It's probably fairly valuable, but I'm more concerned about what's inside it. The family really should have it back if they want it . . . Yes, well, just let them know." Reagan provided her phone number and went back outside to gather up the treasures and return them to the box.

Nearly ten days after her phone call to the auctioneer, Reagan answered her doorbell and ushered a tiny, white-haired woman named Irene Peale into her living room. The box was sitting on the cobbler's bench Reagan used as a coffee table. At the sight of it, the little woman clasped her hands before her. "I can't believe it! After all this time. I can't believe it." The woman reached for the box with trembling hands. At Reagan's invitation she sat down.

Ever so carefully, she opened the top section. "Oh, it still works!" she exclaimed softly as the music began to play. Then, with tears in her eyes, she studied the first two photos. Finally, she looked up at Reagan. "I cannot begin to tell you how very grateful I am that you called about this."

Smiling softly she tapped her index finger next to the photograph of the man. "This is the only known photograph ever taken of my grandfather, Mikal Ritter. We have others of my grandmother," Irene explained, "but there was only the one of Opa Mikal." Irene looked up at

Reagan. "Do you speak any German, dear?" When Reagan shook her head, Irene explained, "*Oma* is the endearing term for Grandmother. And *Opa* means—"

"Grandpa?" Reagan offered.

Irene nodded. "Oma Karyn* told me about when she insisted Opa have that picture taken. He was quite put out with her, but he did it." Irene's eyes clouded with tears. "We always intended to have copies made, but Oma wouldn't part with it for even a day. We thought we could do it after she was gone . . . but then the box was lost." She looked up at Reagan. "Thank you so much for getting in touch with me."

"I wouldn't have dreamed of keeping it until I was certain no one was interested." Reagan hesitated before asking, "Would you like a cup of coffee?"

"Oh, you don't need to do that," Irene said, starting to get up. "I've already been enough of a bother to you. I should be going."

Reagan shook her head. "Really, it's no bother. If you have time, I'd love to hear about the box—and your grandparents. Do you have any idea why such a beautiful thing would have been in an old crock?"

Irene thought for a moment before asking, "Where did you say the crock was at the auction?"

"Just outside a caved-in shack of some sort. I suppose the auctioneer dragged it out along with the orange crates and barrels."

"The dugout!" Irene exclaimed. She smiled. "Things are falling into place at last." She looked about the room. "You seem to like antiques."

Reagan chuckled. "I can't afford real antiques. But I sure do love 'old stuff.'" She explained, "Neither of my parents knew very much about their family history. They

*A note to the reader: Karyn is pronounced Kah´-rin, not the American Karen.

grew up very poor in a rural setting and were kicked out to fend for themselves early in life. We didn't have any family heirlooms, so I've begun collecting my own." She nodded toward the end table by Irene's chair. An array of sepia-toned photographs seemed to deny her lack of family history. "My friends think I'm crazy, but I frame some of my favorite auction finds."

She reached for one of two barefoot, very cross-eyed children. "Doesn't your heart just go out to these poor kids? Imagine how they must have been teased." She shrugged, slightly embarrassed. "My friends joke about my 'ancestors for hire,' but I don't care."

Suddenly Irene changed her mind about staying to visit. "I believe I would like some coffee, if it's not too much trouble."

Irene followed Reagan through the dining room and to the kitchen door. While Reagan made coffee, Irene stood in the doorway. Reagan told the story of the acquisition of the love seat and chair. She told the story of the day her father had bought her a sterling silver thimble with an elegant border of birds. "It was in a half-rotten sewing basket. He bought it for only a dollar. The sewing basket is in a corner by the front window. That's it with the gangly philodendron growing out of it."

Reagan handed Irene a cup of coffee. As they walked through the dining area and back toward the living room, Reagan pointed out the window to a backyard flower bed. "Recycling broken things is fun. Just look at what a beautiful planter that old watercooler from your grandparents' homestead made."

Irene looked outside. The cooler was filled with blooming geraniums and asparagus fern. "Well, you picked the perfect flower. Geraniums were Oma's favorite." The two women settled in the living room as Irene continued, "She said she was welcomed to America with a small geranium. The pressed flower in the box is from a geranium, although it's hardly recognizable after all these years. Oma used to talk about how they bloomed on the ledge of her sod house window all winter long."

"She lived in a sod house?" Reagan said, amazed.

Irene smiled. "Yes. She and Opa lived in a sod house for nearly twenty years before building the house you saw at the auction."

"There was a sod house on that land?"

Irene laughed. "Not at first. Actually, Opa lived in the dugout you thought was just a caved-in shed before there was a real house. It's bigger on the inside than you might think. Over the years he dug far back under the ridge to enlarge it. But he had built the sod house before marrying my grandmother. When the time came to build the farmhouse, Oma insisted it be exactly on the same site as the soddy, so they both moved back into the dugout while Opa razed the soddy and built the frame house."

"I didn't realize history was so—so near," Reagan murmured.

"My own mother was born the year before the new house was built. In the soddy," Irene said. She set her coffee cup down on the cobbler's bench and took up the treasure box. Sitting down, she opened the lower compartment and inspected the contents. "After Opa Mikal died, Oma used to sit in her rocking chair in her room with this box on her lap. She would lay her hand on the lid and gaze out the window with the most contented smile on her face."

Irene reached into the box and withdrew a small wooden cylinder, pulled it apart, and smiled as she withdrew a rusty needle. "These things each had some special significance for Oma Karyn. When I was a child and I visited her, she used to let me select one thing from the box, and she would tell me a story about it." Irene put the lid back on the needle case and returned it to the memory box. She sipped her coffee absentmindedly.

The two women sat quietly for a moment. Reagan finally broke the comfortable silence between them, murmuring, "What a wonderful legacy."

Irene nodded. "Yes, Oma was a dear, dear woman. She was quite a character for her day. Independent, strong-willed. Even so, I don't remember ever hearing her say an unkind word either about or to another person. I don't think I ever saw her really, really angry. Except once."

Irene chuckled. "One day after Opa died, my parents tried to persuade her to come and live with us. I was supposed to be playing in the orchard, but I sneaked up under the kitchen window and peeked in. There Oma stood, her dark eyes flashing with anger. She had her hands on her hips and her feet planted."

Irene explained, "Oma spoke fluent English, and she always prided herself on the fact that she had almost no discernible accent. But that day her German resurfaced. She shook her finger at Mother and Father and came the closest I ever heard to shouting when she said, 'Never I live so long that I am told by my own *kinder* what I can and cannot do. If I die all alone on this place, what is so bad? Hundreds of times I could have died alone on this place when your father was away. Is not bad, to die at home. Don't you worry. God knows when I will die, and God knows how I will die. As long as God knows where to find Karyn Ritter when she is dead, you don't worry.'"

Irene sighed. "As it happened, Oma had a stroke not long after that confrontation. She managed to get to the telephone and call for help, but before anyone got to her, she had slipped into unconsciousness. She never woke up." Irene reached out to touch the box. "This was the first thing we all thought of when we had to plan her funeral. We wanted to make a little display of what was important to Oma. But we couldn't find it. Mother and Dad thought perhaps she had lost it on one of her long walks. I was hoping it would turn up when we sorted things for the auction, but my brother supervised everything." She sighed. "He isn't as attached to the place as I am. When I tried to sort through things he became angry. In the end we just tossed items into boxes."

Irene sat back. "Oma must have gone down to the dugout to reminisce just before her stroke. When she wasn't feeling well, I'll bet she secreted the box in the crock where it would be safe. Maybe she was a little confused . . . maybe she thought she was back living in the dugout those weeks when Opa was building the new house. Then, she headed for the big house . . . and the treasure box was lost."

"It's an interesting collection of items," Reagan offered, not wanting Irene's visit to end. "Do you know the names of the other people in the pictures?"

Irene nodded. She opened the lid. "The couple are the Delhommes.* They were older homesteaders who befriended my grandparents as soon as they arrived in Custer County. And the two young men are their sons. Evidently they were real characters." Irene went on to point out Sophie, Karyn's younger sister, and a young girl named Tilda Stoddard, who had taught Karyn to speak English. "The sour-faced old woman is Amalia Kruger. Oma had a lot to say about Amalia. She's the woman whose biscuit recipe is in the box, although Oma always suspected that Amalia left out one ingredient when she copied it. Oma said she never managed to make biscuits quite as good as Amalia's."

Reagan listened, fascinated. When it appeared that Irene was thinking of leaving, she asked, "Is that really a rattlesnake's tail in the box?"

Irene hesitated. Then, with a wry smile, she asked, "Young lady, are you asking me to tell you a story?"

Reagan blushed, gave a short laugh and admitted, "Yes, I suppose I am."

*Pronounced De-lum with the accent on the second syllable.

Irene picked up the diary and opened it. "I always wondered how much of the stories Oma told me were true. She never wanted to give that away. At least not while she was living."

"Well, now perhaps you can discover the answer to that mystery," Reagan said. "Do you read German?"

Irene shook her head. "No, I'm afraid not. I was around Oma enough to learn a few everyday words, but that's all. Oma was well-educated. This is probably beautifully written. Do you know anyone who might translate it?"

Reagan nodded. "Yes. I think so. When you didn't call right away, I hoped it meant I'd get to keep the box. I made a few calls to the university. There's a professor there who seemed very interested. He said he has two graduate assistants who need a new project." Reagan stood up. "I've got the information on my desk. I'll get it for you."

When Reagan came back into the living room, Irene was standing by the front window looking out at the blooming geraniums. She held one of Reagan's "purchased ancestors" photos in her hand. She set the photo down. "I should be going," she said, taking the piece of paper that Reagan offered and bending to tuck it in her purse. She picked up the box and turned to go. "It's very refreshing to meet someone young who still cares about the past."

When Irene had climbed into her car and started the engine, she rolled down the window and called out, "I'll be in touch, Miss Bishop."

Reagan watched as Mrs. Peale backed out onto the street and drove away.

A few days after their first encounter, Reagan returned home to a message on her answering machine from Irene Peale. Irene wanted to go to lunch. It was only their second meeting, but in an odd way, Reagan felt that they had known one another for years. She found herself telling Irene about her own family, her varied employment experience, her love of history. As they rose to go, Reagan said, "I hope you'll call again soon. This was really fun."

Irene grinned. "Do you like Cary Grant?"

"I've seen *Charade* twenty-seven times," Reagan said. "And I still laugh at the shower scene."

"Then, how about joining me for your twenty-eighth viewing Friday evening?" Irene asked. "Unless, of course, you have a date."

Reagan shook her head. "No dates. No prospects. *Charade* sounds wonderful. I'll bring the popcorn."

"Twenty-one thirty-five B Street," Irene said. "Seven-thirty."

"You live in the *Dressbach Mansion*?" Reagan exclaimed.

Irene laughed. "Tell me how it is that you recognize the street number of my musty old relic of a house."

"My first apartment was over the carriage house just across the street. I used to lie in bed and absolutely lust after that house!"

"Well, now you'll get to see the inside. You probably won't be quite so enamored when you see the old albatross close up."

"I'll adore it," Reagan insisted.

Reagan not only adored Irene Peale's "old albatross," she grew to adore Irene Peale. The two women were, indeed, kindred spirits. They agreed to forgive one another's "brash youth" and "doddering old age." They watched old movies, haunted antique malls, and made an incredible mess in the kitchen one rainy afternoon trying to make authentic rye bread from one of Oma Ritter's handwritten recipes. Occasionally, Irene shared a story about her grandmother, but rarely did the stories seem connected to anything in the box.

All the while Irene Peale and Reagan Bishop were growing closer, Karyn Ritter's diary was being translated. Finally, nearly a year after her discovery, Reagan received a phone call from Irene about the diary. The translation was complete. Irene was offering to share it with Reagan.

"I think you have a singular gift that will enable you to cherish what it says almost as much as I do," Irene said over the phone. She paused and added, "There have been a few surprises for me. Things I thought that Oma was just making up to entertain me have turned out to be true. It's really quite a story. You won't believe why that rattlesnake's tail is in the box. And I never knew the reason for the piece of rose-colored silk. Now I do. I understand so much more." Irene's voice trembled. "I don't have any children, Reagan, and no one else in my immediate family really cares about the past. If you have the time, I'd like for you to know the story."

But entering into the lives of Karyn and Mikal Ritter was to be much more for Reagan than just a way to enjoy a good story. The finding of Karyn Ritter's diary was to change Reagan Bishop's life.

> I've not been called to tell the tale
> of prophets, priests, or kings,
> But oh, the things that I have learned
> observing simple things.

CHAPTER 1

1880
A Pressed Geranium

---

*How shall we sing the LORD's song
in a strange land?*
Psalm 137:4

Dirt. He expected her to look at dirt and call it home. Disgust flickered in Karyn Ensinger Ritter's great, dark eyes as she stood before the miserable hovel he expected her to inhabit.

Home meant crisp white curtains flapping in the summer breeze and bright flowers growing in window boxes. This house of dirt had one very small, very bare window. There were no curtains, no flowers—nothing but huge slabs of earth piled up like bricks, with dead grass sticking out between the layers.

Home meant a door that opened just off a cobblestone street to welcome visitors onto spotless wood floors that were scrubbed daily. In place of a door, this soddy had a tattered quilt. Stepping toward the doorway, Karyn pushed the rag aside. The corners of her mouth turned down. She pressed her lips firmly together and swallowed hard, barely succeeding in smothering her favorite German swearword. *Wer hatte es geglaubt! Not even a floor to sweep. And he expects me to call this home?*

Home meant a nightly climb upstairs to a tiny room to

1

laugh and giggle with her sister Sophie until Mama shouted, "Karyn! Sophie! *Ruhig*!" Stepping farther inside the sod house, Karyn saw that it was only one cavernous room. At the center of the room, a lifeless tree trunk stretched upward from the earth to help support the roof. Karyn looked up. There was no upstairs, not even a loft to escape to. She wondered how much rain would seep through when a storm flung itself at the pathetic shack.

Her vivid imagination created a dripping roof and a sea of mud inside the house, mud dripping onto everything about her, staining the hem of her soft green calico skirt, ruining the lace tablecloth Mama had worked so hard to finish.

It seemed that the walls were closing in on her already, and she had only been inside for a few moments. What would it be like to actually try to live in such a place?

She had to get outside—to breathe. She turned to go, but the expanse of sky and grass stretching away as far as she could see from the doorway of the tiny hut offered no relief to the sick feeling in her midsection. *Oh . . . why did I ever leave Brandenburg?*

At the age of twenty-one, Karyn Ensinger had been eager to leave Germany. Just over a year ago she had lost her beloved Hans. His enthusiasm fueled by his older brother's tales of victory in the Franco-Prussian War a few years before, Hans had volunteered for the army in spite of his wealthy father's protests. He had died of pneumonia during his first winter of duty. Karyn had shown no interest in marrying anyone else, beginning her own sewing business in a back corner of her father's store. Telling herself that she would be an old maid now, that love was not for her, Karyn had waged war daily with her emotions until she believed that she had won.

But then Hans's father, Anton, began to patronize the store. Karyn welcomed him politely. He spoke of Hans in reverent, loving tones, brushing away tears of grief. Karyn listened willingly, finding solace in the memories that she could share with Hans's father. As his visits became more and more frequent, the subject of his ramblings broadened. He spoke less of Hans and more of his own loneliness. He began to ask Karyn's advice, complaining of the difficulties of running an estate alone.

While her father looked on Herr Gilhoff's visits with approving nods, Karyn grew increasingly uncomfortable. Ever so subtly, she began to change her appearance. She took less care with her hair, appearing not to care when dark strands of it fell out of her formerly neat coiffure. She didn't look up when Herr Gilhoff first arrived. But her efforts to offend only served to attract. Herr Gilhoff dreamed of the dark strands of hair that framed Karyn's face. He interpreted Karyn's ignoring him as maidenly shyness.

Karyn had been trying to avoid Herr Gilhoff for over a year when, one afternoon, he reached out to touch her dark hair with a tobacco-stained finger. Revulsion washed over her, and Karyn reached up to push his hand away. But he grabbed her hand and squeezed it. Karyn looked up at him, furious. She pulled her hand away forcefully, stood up, and turned away. But Herr Gilhoff misinterpreted the passion that flickered in Karyn's eyes, the color that flushed her ivory cheeks. Karyn was furious. Herr Gilhoff was in love.

The next day, Ida Gerstenschlager brought news into the store of the invitation from single German farmers in America to German women who would come and build a future. The rules had been laid carefully. The girls would be escorted across the United States by a bilingual guide. They would meet their prospective husbands at a church. There would be a meal and conversation, and if couples so desired, they could be married right away. They would have to remain in Grand Island for twenty-four hours, after which any marriage could be annulled. Ida said that she was going.

That evening at home, Karyn announced that she was going to America. Mama said she was terribly impulsive. But Papa had five other daughters to feed. He made it clear that he thought it time for his eldest daughter to make her own way. If she would not marry Herr Gilhoff, if she wanted to go to America, so be it. Perhaps they would all go to America if Karyn wrote that things were good. Perhaps then little Sophie's health would return.

And so Karyn had come to America. Surrounded by other German girls, Karyn found the trip to Nebraska exhilarating—a grand adventure. The escort who met them in New York was bilingual. She lectured them often about the new customs and the new land to which they had come, painting a charming picture of life in America. It was March when they arrived, and unseasonably warm weather made the journey comfortable. Newborn lambs skipped in the fields they viewed as their train lurched across the country. Other than to tell the girls that there were no forests in Nebraska, the escort had been some-what vague about the countryside where they would live, but Karyn didn't mind. Gentle breezes blew, and she breathed deeply of her new freedom, rejoicing that she was far, far away from Herr Anton Gilhoff.

Grand Island itself was a disappointment. There were no gentle breezes on the day the young women arrived. The dust kicked up from the street by wagons seemed to hang in the air, and Karyn had her first premonition that things in America might not be as she had imagined them. But she buried her fears beneath a veneer of confidence. She ate a hearty supper and then organized the girls into teams to help with the ironing of dresses and the curling of hair in preparation for the next morning. The evening ended with a rollicking pillow fight that very nearly got them all thrown out of the hotel. Long after the girls finally tumbled into bed, Karyn lay staring out the win-dow at the Nebraska moon, wondering what the morrow would bring. She glanced toward the opposite side of the narrow bed where Ida Gerstenschlager lay curled up like a kitten and shivered with the realization that the very next time moonlight shone through her window, it would probably not be Ida's form lying next to her.

During the first few awkward moments of the awful next morning, the young women had stood in a tight group, whispering and smiling as men filed into the church. When a very tall man with startlingly pale blue eyes came in, the girls tittered and whispered admiring comments about him. In spite of his beauty, Karyn had thought him rather frightening. He came in alone, spoke to no one, and leaned against the back wall of the room, openly inspecting the girls. When he finally removed his hat, revealing a thick mane of unfashionably long, black hair, Karyn thought he looked like some wild animal, only recently tamed and brought to town to be tested in civilization.

Karyn found herself wishing that she could shrink back and not be noticeable. *Why couldn't I have been petite, like Sophie?* Sophie could have slipped into the middle of the little group and disappeared. But Karyn was tall, with square shoulders and an almost-regal bearing that precluded her from ever "shrinking back" in any setting. Long ago she had learned to hide her fears behind a thin veneer that looked like self-assurance.

Much to her dismay, Karyn's ruse attracted the wild-looking giant. After a brief look at the other girls, he had bent to set his hat on a chair at the back of the room and walked straight to where Karyn stood next to Ida. Without a glance at Ida, he extended his hand and said in a surprisingly gentle voice, "*Mein name ist Mikal Ritter.*"

Even Karyn's large hand was swallowed up in Mikal Ritter's grasp. Taking a deep breath, Karyn returned his firm grip, lifting her chin so she could meet his gaze. "Karyn Ensinger."

Herr Ritter offered his arm. "Would you sit with me,

Fräulein Ensinger?" He spent the morning describing a good farm with a promising future. They dined together, parted for the evening, and were married the following morning. Karyn was relieved the first night when Herr Ritter left her alone in the hotel room and went to sleep in the livery. In the thirty-six hours since they had met, he had proved himself a complete gentleman. Karyn began to feel positive about her decision to come to America.

But that had been before the interminable ride over increasingly barren land, seated alongside a stranger she must now call her husband. Standing in the doorway of the one-room house made of dirt, Karyn wanted to cry.

While Karyn was inspecting the interior of the soddy, Herr Ritter lifted her trunk from the back of the wagon and to the ground. He waited outside, growing more and more nervous. When she finally reappeared at the doorway, her face revealed what he had most dreaded.

He took his hat off and shook his head. His long hair fell about his shoulders. His voice shook a little as he said, "I visited Brandenburg once. I remember a beautiful little village in a forest that came right up to the banks of a river." He hesitated, clearing his throat before continuing. "This must seem like a horrible place to which you have come." He paused. "I knew you wouldn't like it at first. Still, I hoped you might—" He stopped abruptly and bent to hoist her trunk back up into the wagon. Then, he seemed to think of something. He straightened up, towering over Karyn. Before speaking again he leaned against the wagon as if to make himself smaller.

"Even though it is not at all like Brandenburg, it is a good land, this Nebraska in the United States of America. I have a timber claim, a preemption, and a homestead. That's 480 *morgen*—'acres' they say in English. And unlike those who are coming now into this land, all three of my claims are together." He nodded toward a line of scrub trees a few hundred feet away. "The creek provides

6

water for the fields and the livestock, and I have dug a good well just behind the house." He smiled faintly. "I—we—have neighbors." He nodded toward the southeast. "A little over twelve kilometers that way. You won't be so lonely as some of the wives." He stood away from the wagon. "I need to water the team and feed my livestock." He led the team away, disappearing around the edge of a rise of land that jutted up directly behind the soddy.

Livestock? Karyn wondered. There was no sign of a corral or a barn. *How could he have much livestock?* Curious, she walked in the direction he had gone, surprised to find a good-size corral tucked just around the edge of the bluff not a hundred feet from the house. An obviously pregnant cow stood next to the corral fence, which was made of strips of earth piled up to create a four-foot-high wall. On the opposite side of the corral there was a small pen containing a very large sow. It, too, was "fenced" with sod. Herr Ritter didn't see Karyn. He had unhitched the team and was leading them to the creek.

Karyn turned to head back for the house but was brought up short at the sight of a crude porch. She went under the porch to the opening of a cave cut perpendicularly into the side of the low bluff. Stepping inside, Karyn waited for her eyes to adjust to the dark. Gradually, the room came into focus. On the left there was a single sleeping bunk, then a rough board table and a small stove. On the opposite side of the cave were two stalls. Evidently this room had been kitchen, dining room, parlor, and barn. Karyn wondered for how long.

Herr Ritter's voice sounding from the doorway made her jump. "This is where I started. Two winters I spent here. Alone." He bent down and stepped inside. The space seemed to grow smaller with his giant frame blocking the doorway. He nodded toward the stalls. "Last winter was the worst. Early in the winter there was rain. Just when everything was completely wet, the cold set in. Everything froze into a solid mat of ice. Then came the first snow. Two meters of it. Next there was more rain followed by two meters of snow. The temperature stayed below zero for weeks at a time. Ordinarily the winds blow the snow off of the hills, exposing the grass. The grass here is called buffalo grass, and everyone tells me that livestock wintered on buffalo grass are in better spring condition than cattle fed on the best wheat. But last winter the wind had no effect at all on the thick layers of ice and snow. It covered the whole country in a thick, solid blanket of white. Thank God I had no cattle that winter and only two horses to feed. Breaking through the snow bruised and cut their legs so badly I ended up tying them in the dugout and hacking through the snow with my ax to get grass for them."

He smiled. "And with such talk I have now given you another reason to think that coming here was a mistake."

"You saved your team," Karyn said with admiration.

He nodded. "Yes. We formed a partnership. I saved them from starving to death, and they saved me from freezing to death." At Karyn's questioning look Mikal explained, "I had not spent nearly enough time collecting fuel that fall. When I ran out, I hung my comforters around the stalls to try to trap a little warmth."

Karyn tried to picture the huge man before her huddled in this cave while a blizzard raged outside. She felt the cold, imagined the walls closing in as the wind howled outside. She clutched her arms to herself and shivered. "How did you stand it?"

With a wry smile he answered, "I vowed not to clear one more *morgen* for planting until I had built a house." He leaned against the opening of the cave. "In my head I paced off the dimensions, cut the sod, arranged windows, built furniture." His blue eyes looked at Karyn intently. "Then I realized that no matter the size of the house, it would still be just me through the next winter of storms."

He stepped back outside, under the porch where he

could straighten up. He explained, "The ranchers farther west lost thousands of cattle. Many of them gave up and moved away. Cay Miller—he is another German who just started his own town about fourteen kilometers southwest—says it is a good change. He thinks that more settlers will come now. That there will be fewer problems with the ranchers."

Herr Ritter nodded toward the cow in the corral. "I am hoping that Cay is right. Her calf is to be the beginning of a respectable herd for the Ritters."

After a brief silence, Herr Ritter continued. "This is a good start, Fräulein Ensinger. The land here is rich, and in a few years I will have a good farm." He broke off and looked down at the hat in his hands. "But when I look at it now, through the eyes of someone just arriving from Brandenburg—well, I can see that it must be a terrible place."

When Karyn did not disagree, he took a deep breath and plunged ahead. "I made it through the worst winter in a dozen years. I am strong and healthy. I work hard. We could make a home here."

You cannot make dirt into a home. Karyn wanted to say it, but kindness prevented it.

He looked at her earnestly. "I have been saving money for a new team. The Irvine brothers have imported some English shires. I had a pair of bay mares reserved, but the money could just as well be used for passage back to Germany." He managed a faint smile as he said, "Stay for one month. See about it. See about me." His face turned crimson as he added softly, "I promise you that we will be husband and wife in name only. After one month, if you want to go back, I will take you to Grand Island. The marriage can be annulled, and I will buy tickets for your return to Brandenburg."

Karyn took her eyes from the cave and its contents and put them on the man who stood before her, his hat in his hands. She focused on his hands. They were the largest hands she had ever seen, prematurely aged by hard labor. It seemed impossible that such hands could belong to the young, handsome face that was Mikal Ritter. Studying those hands, Karyn was struck by the likelihood that they would indeed succeed in wrenching a good future from the land. Karyn reminded herself how unlike her darling Hans this Mr. Ritter really was. Hans had had fine, delicate features, gentle brown eyes, the beautiful hands of a musician. But Hans was gone. If she went back to Brandenburg, to what would she be going? Papa would take her in, but then he would marry her off to old Anton Gilhoff, with his perpetually stained shirtfront and his nasty habit of spitting tobacco at the can on the floor beside his chair.

"I still have to feed the animals," Herr Ritter said. Nodding toward the cow he added, "She will calve soon. Then there will be milk." He ducked from under the porch and walked toward the well.

Karyn forced the picture of refined Hans Gilhoff and his father from her mind. She made her way back to the front of the soddy. She sat on her trunk, contemplating the dirt house that Mikal Ritter had labored alone to build. It seemed to challenge her: *You can't do it. You can't make dirt into a home.*

In her mind, Karyn hung starched white curtains at the window. She took down the tattered quilt that hung in the doorway and washed and patched it. That would do, until Herr Ritter could be convinced to haul in lumber to make a proper door. Karyn spun about on the trunk to contemplate the treeless sea of grass rolling into the distance as far as she could see. And how far would he have to go to get the lumber for a door?

She spun back around and looked inside the doorway at the dirt floor. It mocked her: *You can't do it. You can't make dirt into a home.* Suddenly, Karyn remembered.

Papa had once told her of mixing straw and clay to make a surface that hardened like a brick when it dried. She looked about her. *If there is one thing that there is plenty of in this land, it is grass. I wonder if grass would work as well. I wonder if there is any clay. I wonder if Mr. Ritter could be convinced to delay his farming long enough to help me make a floor I can sweep.*

Getting up, Karyn stepped inside the house. Outside the sun was blazing, the seemingly ever-present wind blowing. Inside, it was surprisingly cool and still. Karyn looked up. Herr Ritter had spent some money on that roof. She remembered him describing how he had cut sod for a neighbor to earn the money to buy planks, then tar paper to serve as an underlayment before he put on the layer of sod that would insulate the house so well. He had looked at her matter-of-factly and said, "I could not expect a woman to come to live in a house where the roof drops huge clods of mud on everything inside whenever it rains." Hearing Herr Ritter speak of lumber, Karyn had imagined a frame house, perhaps with green shutters at the windows. She smiled at her own naïveté.

Karyn heard footsteps outside. Herr Ritter ducked under the doorway and came in. He was carrying something half hidden in one hand. He held it out to Karyn. "From our neighbors." He nodded toward the east. "Celest Delhomme grows them. Her window ledge is full of them. When I said I was going for a wife, she said I should take this as a welcome gift from her." He set a small pot with a sprig of green peeking just above its rim onto the twelve-inch-wide window ledge. When Karyn said nothing, he laid one huge hand along the wood that framed the opening in the sod wall, explaining, "I cut it away at an angle like this so it would let in more light. You can grow flowers right through the winter. Celest's geraniums bloom into February."

When Karyn still didn't say anything, he sat down on

11

the window ledge, the tiny potted geranium at his side. Finally, he shrugged his shoulders and stood up. He did not hide his disappointment as he said, "I'll get the team. We can leave right away."

He had bent to go back outside when Karyn surprised even herself by saying, "That will not be necessary, Herr Ritter. Perhaps I was impulsive in coming here, but to return to Brandenburg so soon would be just as foolish. A month does not seem so much to ask."

Turning around, Mikal Ritter displayed the first whole-hearted smile Karyn had seen. It revealed fine, straight white teeth. Anton Gilhoff's tobacco-stained teeth flashed in Karyn's mind, giving her at least one reason to be glad she was not going back to Brandenburg right away.

Herr Ritter walked over to the bed and collected his bedding. "There is not much furniture yet, but if you want anything changed, I will do it as soon as I come back."

Karyn nodded. She followed him to the doorway. He seemed happy to be returning to the dugout where he had been so lonely. He was halfway down the slope when he turned and called out, "Fräulein Ensinger . . . Would you call me Mikal?" Karyn nodded, and he smiled his beautiful smile again.

Karyn opened the lid of her trunk. Even Mikal Ritter's beautiful smile could not prevent homesickness from flooding in at the sight of the trunk's contents. Karyn shook her head, wondering what Mama would think if she saw the lace tablecloth that she had crocheted gracing the stack of empty fruit boxes that served as a table in the soddy. Karyn draped the tablecloth over the side of the trunk. She pushed her hands into the folds of a feather tick and withdrew Oma's fine porcelain teapot. It, too, was set aside.

In the end, it took only a few moments for Karyn to unpack. She hung two cotton dresses and three crisp white aprons on hooks that protruded from the tree trunk positioned in the center of the room. She put on a fourth apron and prepared to make up her bed, which was little more than a shallow box laid atop two long poles stuck into adjacent walls of the soddy. The corner of the box, which stood out into the room, was supported by a stump.

Retrieving a bunch of broomcorn suspended from the ceiling near the door, Karyn did her best to sweep out the bed-box before unrolling her feather bed and pushing it into place. She covered the feather bed with two woven coverlets and stood back to survey her work, blushing at the mental image of Mikal Ritter's massive frame crowded into the bed alongside—*husband-in-name-only. He had promised.*

Karyn had gone outside and was repacking her best things into the trunk when Mikal strode up. He bent down and handed the lace tablecloth to Karyn. "You have fine things, Fräulein Ensinger," he offered.

"Thank you, Herr—" She corrected herself. "Thank you, Mikal. And you must please call me Karyn." She reached out to take the lace tablecloth from him. Something in his expression made her want to comfort him. "I fear I was foolish in bringing such things. They are not very practical." She laid the tablecloth in the trunk and closed the lid.

"If God had intended life to be filled with only practical things," Mikal said, "He would not bother to paint the colors in a sunset." He bent to pick up her trunk, saying over his shoulder, "I will build a beautiful home someday, where a woman's lace tablecloth and a china teapot are needed."

Karyn followed Mikal inside the soddy. He set her trunk down beside the bed.

"Are you hungry?" Karyn asked, crossing the few feet to where several wooden crates had been stacked on their sides to form a cupboard. "If you will kindly show me where you keep your rolling pin and cake cutter—oh, and the eggs, please—I see the flour here—I can—"

Mikal cleared his throat. "I have no eggs. As for a rolling pin and cake cutter—" He smiled sheepishly.

"Oh," Karyn said. "Well, then. Sausage. I can just fry some sausage."

Mikal shook his head. "I have no sausage. Would you like me to show you how I make pancakes?"

Karyn arched one eyebrow. "I do not think that I need cooking lessons, Herr Ritter. What I need is a proper kitchen." She turned toward the stove. "If you would bring in some firewood, I will manage something for supper."

"There is no wood, Karyn."

Of course there is no wood, idiot. Karyn chastised herself. *Did you see some huge forest on the ride to this miserable sod house?*

Karyn stood a little taller. "Then what do I burn in the stove?" Her face was hot with embarrassment.

"Hay and corncobs after harvest. Now I am using chips."

"Chips?" Karyn asked.

Mikal nodded. "Come outside. I will show you."

She followed him outside and to the opposite side of the house where a small mountain of "chips" lay drying in the sun. Mikal explained, "The buffalo are gone now, but they left enough fuel for many winters to come, free for anyone who picks it up. Fortunately, one of their old trails leads right along the edge of my tree claim, so we have chips in abundance."

Dear Sophie . . . America is a wonderful land, where the settlers live in dirt houses and burn buffalo droppings for fuel. There are no eggs just yet, and trees have yet to be invented. My husband is Mikal Ritter. He is tall with black hair and blue eyes and he sleeps in a cave.

Looking at the disgusting pile of dried manure she was supposed to use to cook a supper without eggs, Karyn gave in to homesickness. The emotions of the day rushed in. Abruptly, she turned away. She blinked and tried to will her emotions back under control, but she could not stop the flow of tears.

Seeing the tears streaming down Karyn's cheeks, Mikal contemplated all the toil of the last two years of his life and counted it meaningless. *Mein Gott,* he asked heaven, *for what have I been striving if a woman looks upon my labor and weeps?* He started to walk away.

At the sound of his footsteps, Karyn rubbed her cheeks briskly and called him back. "Oh, please, Mikal," she said through her tears. "Forgive me. I do not mean to be unkind. I was just—" She bent down, hiding her disgust as she put some chips in her apron. "I am so very ignorant of your ways here in America." She looked up at Mikal, forcing herself to smile. "I am afraid that you are going to be very disappointed in me. I know nothing about cooking without milk or eggs—or of using chips for fuel."

Mikal was quick to answer. "I can show you how I have been cooking." He added, "I am certain you will be able to improve on my methods, but it is a place to start. We will visit the neighbors tomorrow. Emile and Celest Delhomme have been here the longest of any other settlers. Celest is Belgian, but she speaks fluent German. Her cooking is a little different, but you will like her."

As if angels had borne a summons to the Delhomme homestead, a voice called out, "Mikal! Mikal Ritter!"

Mikal smiled and looked down at Karyn. Relief sounded in his voice as he exclaimed, "Emile and Celest!"

Karyn dropped the vile chips from her apron and followed Mikal around the side of the house to see Emile and Celest Delhomme riding up on matching gray horses. Karyn hid her amazement that Celest did not ride sidesaddle. She wore a calf-length black divided skirt and knee-high riding boots. Her thick gray hair was tied back loosely with a scarlet ribbon. As slim as a young girl, she dismounted quickly, removed her hat, pulled off her riding gloves, and tossed them into the crown of the hat.

15

Unaware that her own cheeks were streaked with the trails of homesick tears, Karyn extended her hand to greet Celest. "*Es freut mich, Sie Angenehm.* Thank you for the kind gift of the geranium, Frau Delhomme."

But Celest would have nothing of such formality. Looking severely at Mikal, she shoved her hat into his hands. Holding Karyn momentarily at arm's length, she inspected her new neighbor with cool gray-green eyes. Then, she abruptly engulfed Karyn in a hug, kissed both her cheeks, and wiped away the traces of Karyn's tears with her hand.

"So this is the young woman Mikal chose in Grand Island." She spoke flawless German. "Such a lovely girl." Barely pausing to take a breath, she began to shake her finger at Mikal, scolding him. "I suppose you have no eggs, little flour, and no firewood and yet you are expecting your supper soon, *ja?*"

Mikal grinned sheepishly.

Celest opened her saddlebags and pulled out a sack. Taking Karyn's arm, she headed inside the soddy, calling over her shoulder, "Emile, bring in some chips. And see that they are good and dry. Then you men go busy yourselves somewhere. Karyn and I will call you when supper is ready."

Inside the soddy, Celest took charge. From her sack she produced two small jars, one of cream and one of butter. "God has blessed us with a cow that gives enough milk for us to have butter and cream all we want. And enough to share. My boys could not locate a single egg from my worthless hens, or I would have brought eggs. But I can show you a trick for pancakes—"

Rolling up her sleeves, Celest went to work, talking all the while. "Stoke the stove. Now, nearly a teacup of sugar . . . about half so much of cream, and then another half of water. You are so blessed that Mikal found water so close to the house. Now a lump of butter and a little soda." Celest paused. "Stoke the stove again, Karyn. Chips burn quickly. Now, add just enough cornmeal to make the batter stiff." She looked up. "You are probably accustomed to always having flour, but here cornmeal is more common. You may not like it at first, but really it is not too bad." She stirred the mixture. "See how stiff it is? That will make the best pancakes. Now, you see you do not need eggs after all. We stoke the stove again, and then we can cook. I brought you some molasses and my last jar of chokecherry jelly."

Celest smiled. "I can show you chokecherry bushes later this week. There is a good stand just halfway between our homestead and yours. And there are plum trees. It is only April, of course, so things are just beginning to bloom, but we have wild fruit in abundance. At night, when all is quiet and the breeze blows, you can sometimes catch the sweet scent of plum blossoms." She smiled. "We can pick fruit together and make jam. Oh, it will be wonderful to have another woman so close by!" She rummaged for a spoon and offered some jelly to Karyn. "Taste. I wonder if Mikal has any coffee."

From the doorway Mikal called out, "In the tin on the top shelf." He carried a bucket full of fresh water in and poured it into the waiting coffeepot. He picked up both of the wooden chairs from the kitchen and headed back outside, explaining, "There is shade on the side of the house. We can eat there."

Karyn took a coffee grinder and Mikal's tin down from the shelf, happy to at last have a task assigned that she could perform. After grinding nearly a cup of coffee beans, she added them to the pot of already warm water on the stove. Returning the grinder and the tin of coffee beans to their shelf, she made a mental note—tomorrow the shelves would need to be scrubbed.

While Karyn made coffee, Celest filled a basket with tin plates and cups, the jelly and molasses, talking while she worked. "You will want to live outside as much as possible, Karyn. Mikal has bought a very good stove, but when summer arrives, using it will transform this entire house into an oven." She explained, "Three-foot-thick walls hold in whatever air is inside. If you do not cook in here, it will be blessedly cool even on the hottest day. And in winter, just as wonderfully warm. Last winter even in the worst blizzard, water in a bucket did not freeze inside our house."

Emile appeared in the doorway. He growled at Celest in mock anger, "Have you no supper cooked yet, woman? The men are about to starve."

Celest shoved the plate of cakes at him. "Tell the men to be polite or they just might find themselves without a cook!" She kissed her husband just above the line of his gray beard.

Emile chuckled and headed outside, followed by Karyn and Celest. The men had erected a makeshift table at the side of the soddy with a plank and two low sawhorses, and now stood waiting by two upended orange crates. They made quite a ceremony of drawing out the two kitchen chairs and seating the women.

As soon as everyone was seated, Emile said, "Let us join hands," and spoke a simple blessing,

Komm herr Jesu, sei Du unser Gast, Segne uns,
un alles was Du uns bescheret hast. Amen.

Reaching for a pancake, Emile smiled kindly at Karyn and explained, "I had a German nurse. It has been over forty years, but I have never forgotten the simple blessing she taught us to say before every meal. Welcome to America, Karyn Ritter."

Thus began the friendship of Karyn Ensinger Ritter and Celest and Emile Delhomme, a friendship founded upon the cornerstone of loneliness, joined with the mortar of chokecherry jelly, and sealed with a simple German blessing.

The Diary
April 1, 1880

My name is Karyn Ensinger Ritter. I am twenty-one, and I have just come to Custer County, Nebraska, from Brandenburg, Germany. I begin this diary as a way of sharing my heart when I cannot speak it. My husband is Mikal Ritter, and he seems to be a kind man. He is handsome in a wild way that is sometimes almost frightening. The "house" is a pile of earth, and the "farm" is nothing but a few scratches in the earth made with something called a "breaking plow." But I have determined to do something with the house, and although I may be only a woman, I have no less resolve than Herr Ritter displays in his struggle to transform a barren land into a farm. Today I met Celest and Emile Delhomme, our Belgian neighbors. Thanks be to God, they speak German. What they must think of me, coming so far to marry a stranger! Indeed, I am asking myself what I was thinking to do such a thing. But I am here, and I will not flee before the adventure has begun. If only Herr Ritter will keep his promises regarding our marriage, and if only God grants me courage, I will manage. I have agreed to stay one month. Then we will see.

CHAPTER 2

A Silk Ribbon Nosegay

Behold, how great a matter a little fire kindleth!
And the tongue is a fire, a world of iniquity.
James 3:5–6

Only seven days after her arrival in Custer County,
Karyn lay in her bed one night listening to coyotes howl,
reviewing things as she had imagined them and things as
they were.

Of course the labor was tiring, but Karyn's good health
and inborn physical strength met the challenge of hard
work willingly.

Of course the absence of trees was disturbing. But in the
absence of trees Karyn looked more closely at the grass
and found an ocean of variety. Besides, trees could be
planted.

Of course the eternally blowing wind was sometimes
annoying. But Karyn watched the way the wind tossed the
grass and decided it created a wild kind of beauty. Besides,
she could always retreat inside the thick-walled soddy.

Yes, things in Custer County of Nebraska in America
were different from Germany. There were no forests, no
great, deep rivers, no picturesque villages.

Yes, Mikal Ritter was different from Hans Gilhoff. He
was not musical, not refined, not genteel.

Still, as Karyn lay beneath her thin coverlet listening to the coyotes howl, she consciously resolved to like both Custer County and Mikal Ritter. She felt her cheeks grow warm as she admitted that liking Mikal Ritter would probably require minimal effort.

But then, at the end of the second week, in spite of all the reviewing and resolving; in spite of Mikal Ritter's kindness and blue eyes; in spite of Celest Delhomme's friendship; in spite of the dread of Anton Gilhoff, Karyn was struck with a desperate longing for home. Like thousands before her in thousands of different times and places, she considered her choice and called herself a fool. But unlike thousands before her, Karyn's homesickness had little to do with her physical surroundings. Her homesickness was caused by neither the wind nor the heat nor the loneliness, but by the words of Frau Amalia Kruger.

It was the fourteenth day of Karyn and Mikal Ritter's residence together when Mikal said at breakfast, "I need to have the plow sharpened. Perhaps you would like to see Millersburg." He smiled. "The post office is in Cay Miller's store. You can send your letter home." Seeing the delight that shone in Karyn's dark eyes, Mikal added, "We can go on from Millersburg to visit the Delhommes. I promised Emile to help plow a firebreak around his homestead."

Karyn thanked him, trying to control the trembling excitement in her voice. Millersburg! Finally, she would get to see the little village to the southwest. The Delhommes! She had suppressed her loneliness these past two weeks, but the prospect of communion with Celest Delhomme was sweet.

Karyn hurried through her morning chores, drawing water, feeding livestock, washing dishes, working on mending the tattered quilt that served as a door to the soddy. When Mikal drove up the slope from the barn, she was waiting, her first letter home secreted in the pocket of her fresh apron.

Karyn fairly leaped onto the wagon seat, reaching behind her to settle the basket that held their lunch into the corner of the wagon box. When Mikal climbed up beside her and reached for the reins, their shoulders touched. He did not move away. Karyn blushed. Telling herself that it would be rude to offend her husband, she did not move away.

They headed southwest. The wagon had covered nearly two kilometers before Mikal said, "It is not far to Millersburg. Only about fourteen kilometers. We should get there yet this morning." He paused. "Cay Miller has great plans for the town he has named for himself. But at present it is only his store and a few other sod buildings."

Karyn's vision of a nice excursion to a little village where she would go from shop to shop while Mikal attended to the sharpening of the plow died. As she had done dozens of times in the past two weeks, Karyn resolved to make the best of the difference between her expectations and reality.

"Do you know Herr Miller well?"

Mikal nodded his head. "As it happens, I do. Cay rescued me from myself one night when I had had far too much to drink." He hastened to explain, "I do not drink anymore. But when I first came to Custer County . . ." He paused, choosing his words carefully. "I was in a dangerous frame of mind one night. I stumbled into Cay's store hoping to buy more beer. Cay convinced me to talk instead of drink." He paused again. "Some people laugh at Cay behind his back and call him a foolish dreamer. But he is a good man."

As the wagon made its way across the open prairie, Mikal began to tell the story of Cay Miller. Karyn willed herself to listen, all the while wishing that Mikal would return to the night when he had been drinking too much.

Cay Miller had begun his adult life as a bank clerk. Small of stature, unremarkable in appearance, Cay was not the kind of man whom people took very seriously. But then he lost an eye in what the Americans called their "War of the Rebellion." Aware that he was very average in appearance, Cay had always taken special care to be well groomed, to wear the latest fashion. Looking in the mirror one morning after his release from the hospital, Cay Miller made a decision that changed his life. He decided that an eye patch was much more stylish than the ill-fitting glass eye provided by his government. Around that eye patch Cay Miller created a persona. Not long after he began wearing his eye patch, he succeeded in turning a small savings account into a small fortune. Suddenly, everyone began to take Cay Miller very seriously. They sought his advice. They even imitated his taste in clothing. The eye patch became a badge of honor, a symbol of sacrifice, a tangible reminder that here was a man who had *experience*, a man to be listened to, a man who knew whereof he spoke.

And then Cay did something that amazed even the closest of his friends. Having won the respect of his fellow townspeople, having been invited to be on the board of the First National Bank, Cay Miller headed west. He rode the Union Pacific Railroad to Grand Island, Nebraska, where he disembarked and headed northwest into Custer County. He looked the county over before returning to Omaha where he spent a considerable amount of money fraternizing with railroad officials and surveyors. What he learned from the railroad men, he applied at the land office.

And so Cay Miller, a second-generation immigrant from Ohio, purchased a homestead on Lillian Creek, built a sod house, and raised a red flag declaring the presence of a "store."

"Now he waits," Mikal concluded.

"Waits? For what?" Karyn wanted to know.

"For the railroad. He says it will come, and when it does he is perfectly positioned to make a fortune."

Karyn had been quiet for so long, that Mikal finally apologized. "I am sorry, Karyn. I did not mean to bore you."

She answered quickly, "But I am not bored, Mikal. I was just thinking that now I know more about a man I have yet to meet than I know about Mikal Ritter." She asked boldly, "Just why is it that you were drinking so much? More important, what made you stop?"

Mikal turned to look her full in the face.

Something in his expression made her wish she could take her questions back. She looked away. "Please forgive me, I have been too bold."

He leaned forward, resting his foot on the edge of the wagon. "I was eighteen when I took part in the Franco-Prussian War. Then, I was witness to the civil war in Paris." He paused, seeming to grope for words. "I was dissatisfied and restless. Sick at heart. There seemed to be no hope of a good life for me anywhere. I began to doubt that I would ever accomplish anything at all in life. It was a dark time for me. Then I met someone." And then Mikal made a grievous error. Months before he had decided that he would not tell whomever he met in Grand Island about Marie-Louise. Not right away. After the trial period he had planned, if it appeared that things were going to work out, then he would mention her. That would put things in proper perspective. God had healed his grief, and raising the specter of a dead wife was no way to welcome a new one. And so, when it would have been only natural to speak of Marie-Louise, Mikal spoke instead of her brother. "I met someone who had traveled in America. He made it sound so wonderful, so promising, that I came. That was in 1872."

"Just so?" Karyn inquired. "You heard of it and you came?"

He nodded. "Not so unlike one Karyn Ensinger. I was far to the south of Nebraska in Kansas at first, but"—he stopped again, hesitating before continuing his story—"well, Kansas was no good for me. I had some difficulties and I grew to regret having settled there. Sometimes I am a slow learner. It was five years before I finally admitted that I could never be happy there."

"But why not?" Karyn wanted to know. "Is Kansas so different from Nebraska?"

Once again, Mikal avoided speaking of Marie-Louise. "Well, for one thing, I did not come to America to build another Germany. In Kansas everything was German—Volga Germans, Black Sea Germans, Catholic Germans, Mennonite Germans. Many of the Germans there did not even want to learn to speak English. I am not like that. My homeland is precious to me, but America is my home now. I have worked hard to learn English." He glanced sideways at Karyn. "I think in English now, not German." He paused before adding, "And I want my children to grow up speaking English."

"How long did it take you to learn?" Karyn asked. "Of all the languages I heard on the ship and on the way here, English seemed the most difficult."

Mikal nodded and smiled. "Yes, I know. But it will not take you so long as it did me. I was surrounded by Germans for so long, there was no need to learn right away. Here there are settlers from many different countries. Learning English together has drawn us all closer." He teased, "Perhaps I should speak only English from now on. Then you would learn more quickly."

Karyn felt a sudden flash of panic. Would he really do it? After bringing her so far out into a wilderness, would he now remove even her ability to communicate?

Mikal looked down at her. "I was only joking, Karyn. I would never do such a thing to you." He hesitated, then said, "I know loneliness. When first I came to Nebraska, I

25

was miles away from the closest human being for nearly two years. Eventually I discovered that God was here. Now I believe He brought me here, to a lonely place where I would be forced to settle things between God and Mikal."

He lowered his voice and continued, "There was much bitterness in my heart when I came to Nebraska, but" he gestured toward the horizon—"there is a strange sort of power in all that. Power to remind a man that he is very, very, small." He smiled. "I began to realize that Mikal Ritter and his problems were not quite so monumental, after all."

Suddenly, he turned to look at Karyn. "You are too polite, Karyn. Your gracious listening encourages me, and I talk too much."

Karyn protested, "Not too much. At home I had voices about me all day long." She hesitated before adding, "It is one of the things I miss."

Mikal frowned, wondering how he could have been so stupid as to not realize how lonely she must be. Having been alone for so long, Mikal had had some difficulty adapting to the constant presence of another human being in his life. Even though he and Karyn actually spent little time together other than at meals, he was continually aware of her presence. At the slightest sound from "up at the house," he would look up sharply from whatever he was doing and then laugh at himself for forgetting that he was no longer alone, that the sound was not some errant wildlife wreaking havoc in the doorless soddy. It was only his wife.

Just last evening some sound had made him glance up toward the house to see Karyn bending far down to immerse the entire length of her hair in a bucket of water balanced on the seat of one of the kitchen chairs just outside the soddy door. He had watched as she reached up to scrub her hair and rinse it. When she stood up water streamed off her hair in a silver sheet until she reached out to wring it like a towel. She had continued to bend over while she rubbed the long tresses nearly dry. Then, with one motion she had tossed her hair back over her shoulder and stood up straight. Her back was to Mikal, and he caught his breath at his first sight of her luxuriant hair spilling down her back past her waist. He was struck anew by her regal bearing. She was not in the least delicate, and yet her broad shoulders tapered in a very pleasing way to her waistline.

Remembering, Mikal realized that he had enjoyed getting used to hearing the sounds of another human being. But he had been so busy adapting to her presence that he had given no thought whatsoever to the monumental adjustments Karyn was making—adapting to the absence of rather than the presence of other humans.

He apologized, "I should have driven you to Millersburg days ago, Karyn. And I should have taken you to visit the Delhommes. I am sorry. I should have thought." He grinned. "I hope that letter in your pocket does not tell of how your husband ignores you. Your father will be coming to rescue you."

Karyn laughed. "Have no fear, Herr Ritter. My father is more likely to send two or three more of his daughters to Nebraska than to come to take one back!"

Just as Mikal prepared to ask Karyn more questions about her own home, the wagon reached the crest of the hill that had hidden Millersburg from view. Karyn looked down at it, barely hiding her disappointment. There was one small building with a sign above it. They were too far away for Karyn to read the sign, but she noted wryly that it appeared to be almost bigger than the store itself. Next to the store there was a sod hut, and then a larger, more substantial building. As they approached the fledgling town, Karyn noticed that what appeared to be a private residence across from the store boasted not one but two glass windows. A stack of antlers adorned the roof. A few other nondescript buildings had risen up along what was meant to be the street. Perhaps someday it would be a street, but on this April morning in 1880, it was no more

than a path through virgin prairie that had yet to be trod-
den into a dust trail.

Watching Karyn inspect Millersburg, Mikal did not ask
her to voice an opinion. Instead, he drove straight to Cay
Miller's.

Cay emerged from his store to meet Karyn, presenting
her with a tiny nosegay of silk ribbon roses. "Welcome to
Millersburg, Frau Ritter." Cay turned his patched eye away
from her and stared openly with his one good eye. "Well,
Mikal, I would say you filled the shopping list quite well."

"Be quiet, Cay. You will embarrass Karyn."

"What list?" Karyn wanted to know.

From his pocket Cay produced what appeared to be a
page torn from some sort of pamphlet. "This Emigrant
Guide was written in English, but for Frau Ritter, I will
translate . . ." Clearing his throat dramatically, Cay said
in German:

> *The Emigrant Adviser here lists the qualities neces-*
> *sary for a woman to be successful in the American*
> *West. Men planning to be married and homestead are*
> *advised to select their partner with particular atten-*
> *tion to the list which appears below.*
> *—a strong, resilient body*
> *—robust health*
> *—a resilient soul*
> *—strong nerves*
> *—a great lack of consideration for herself*
> *—friendly obligingness to others*

Karyn teased, "But, Herr Miller, it is not possible for
you to know if a woman meets those requirements when
you have just met."

Cay joked back, "Ah, but I know you must have them
all, or you would never have agreed to let this brute bring
you into the wilderness."

Mikal turned to Karyn and said, "Herr Miller suggests that one shop for a wife as one would for a piece of livestock. Which is why Herr Miller remains unmarried."

He looked toward Cay. "I would suggest that you add one qualification for your wife, Cay. She should be very, very short."

In mock anger, Cay Miller blustered back, "Listen, my dear friend. One giant in this community is quite enough." He tapped his temple. "The size of the brain is what matters, Mikal, the size of the brain." He looked at Karyn and then back at Mikal. "And now that I have had the pleasure of meeting the new Frau Ritter, I have hope for you yet, Mikal. Perhaps there is a brain beneath all that shaggy hair, after all."

Mikal was finished with joking. He hoisted his plow out of the back of the wagon and lifted it to his shoulder, then turned to Karyn. "The third building down there." he pointed at an unimpressive soddy. "I will not be long."

Cay led Karyn inside the store. While the room wasn't large, it was surprisingly well-stocked. To the left, a counter stretched down the length of the room. Except for a small space near a cash register, the counter was stacked high with bolts of cloth. Karyn's eyes took in at least a dozen calicoes as well as bolts of heavier cloth and something with an open weave she was to learn to use for making carpets. Below the counter a glass case displayed lace and gloves, earrings and silver rings.

Behind the counter, shelves were cluttered with jars of candy, tins of biscuits and coffee, rolls of ribbon, and countless other "necessities." Opposite the dry goods department, various farm tools and garden seeds were displayed along with boxes of nails and balls of string. An attractive display of pipes and tobacco dominated what appeared to be the "men's department" of Miller's store.

Cay said, "It has been very quiet this morning, Frau Ritter. Feel free to rummage about. There is coffee and a few biscuits on a table in the back corner. I keep the Wards Catalog back there. I can order anything you want." He bowed low. "Now, if you will excuse me, I am going to follow your husband down to the blacksmith shop and try to convince him to join me in a business venture. I will be back shortly."

But both Mikal and Cay were gone too long. As Cay headed up the street after Mikal, old Amalia Kruger watched from the window of her home across the street. She waited until Cay was out of sight and then hurried across the grassy street and into Miller's Dry Goods Store.

Karyn was admiring Cay Miller's bolts of calico when she heard Amalia grunting her way up the stairs. She turned about with a smile, but something about the bent old woman standing by the door made Karyn feel self-conscious. The woman shuffled across to where Karyn stood. She made no effort to hide the fact that she was inspecting the newcomer. Pursing her thin lips, she squinted her watery gray eyes as she looked Karyn up and down. She made an odd clicking sound with her tongue before finally saying, "So. This is the girl from Germany that Mikal Ritter brings to Millersburg." She tapped her cane on the board floor and shook her head. Making her way to the back corner of the store, she pulled out a chair and sat down heavily.

Karyn followed her and graciously held out her hand. "My name is Karyn. Mikal didn't tell me there were other women living in Millersburg."

Amalia smiled briefly, revealing two spaces in her upper row of teeth. She motioned toward the stove. "Let us have a cup of coffee and visit, Frau Ritter." While Karyn looked for clean coffee cups and stirred the fire in the stove, the old woman introduced herself. "My name is Amalia Kruger."

Soon the women were seated opposite one another with steaming cups of coffee before them. Amalia hunched over her coffee, noisily sucking it down while she inspected Karyn. Finally she asked, "Tell me, Mrs. Ritter, what do you think of Nebraska after two weeks?"

Karyn answered honestly. "It's very different from Brandenburg. But I think I can make adjustments."

"Do you have family in America?"

Karyn shook her head. "No. Only I came to America. My sisters remain at home with Mama and Papa."

"Sisters." Amalia repeated the word with a satisfied air. So that was it. Too many girls and not enough husbands.

"Will your sisters be coming to join you?"

Karyn relaxed a little. "Oh no," she said, laughing. "They are good, obedient daughters. They will stay at home and do as Papa tells them." She sighed dramatically and tried to include Frau Kruger in a joke. "I am the only evil child who must have her own way. I hope you won't tell Herr Ritter what a bad choice he has made."

But Amalia Kruger had no patience with chatter and joking. She set her coffee cup down with a thud. And then, with one sentence, she colored what Mikal had intended as kindness in an ominous light that would threaten to build a wall of distrust between Mikal and his new wife for weeks to come. "I hope Mikal has had sense enough to pick someone more suited to the situation this time."

This time? Karyn wondered.

At the surprise on Karyn's face, Amalia smiled. Karyn thought the smile looked triumphant.

"So," Amalia said. "You didn't know." She snorted softly. "Just as I thought. It has been five years, and still he cannot speak of her." She thrust her thin, wrinkled face forward, peering at Karyn as she continued, "But whether Mikal Ritter thinks so or not, you should know." Amalia scooted her chair back from the table and took a deep breath. "You should know so that you can make—what did you call them?—'adjustments.'"

Getting up to pour herself another cup of coffee, Amalia

waited until she was again seated before she continued. "I knew Mikal Ritter when he first came to America. He had been in France, with the army of occupation. And there, in Paris, he met Marie-Louise Jacquot. Marie-Louise's father was a baker. She herself told me that her parents were horrified at the thought of their own daughter consorting with Germans at the very moment the Germans were occupying the French countryside. Still, she ran off with Mikal, and against all laws of nature they married outside their own people."

Amalia's eyes narrowed as she looked at Karyn. "It is quite a romantic story, is it not? Like a fairy tale." She frowned. "But it does not end like a fairy tale. On the ship Mikal and his little French wife met other Germans— Mennonites from Russia—a peace-loving people with no difficulty welcoming Mikal and Marie-Louise into their circle. They crossed the country together and settled in Kansas. Mikal built a dugout. Marie-Louise used to stand at the doorway of that dugout and stare off to the south across the creek, across the valley, and beyond. She tried to adapt, but she lived in constant fear. Fear of wolves, fear of snakes, fear of Indians."

Amalia paused and shook her head. "I knew the minute I met her that there was sadness in her future." She sighed. "Poor Marie-Louise. She was like a jewel. A beautiful, sparkling jewel." She snorted. "Young people are such fools, thinking love can overcome everything against them. Well, it can't. Marie-Louise Ritter tried with all her might, but she was never meant to live a hard life. Love is not enough. *Das ist es ja eben!*"

Karyn wished someone would come in and stop this wretched woman's talk. *She is making it all very dramatic, but you do not know her and you do know Mikal—a little. Do not overreact before you know the facts. Do not allow her to make you suspicious of Mikal. He probably had a good reason for not mentioning all of this.*

Amalia pointed her finger and shook it at Karyn. "Some things need to be known. I know this is a shock. But you need to know the truth."

Karyn didn't want to hear any more, but her pride would not let her betray how she felt. *You can ask Mikal about this later. Do not give this horrid old woman the satisfaction of seeing she has upset you.*

"My own daughter was a good friend to Marie-Louise. The last winter was mild, and we saw her often. She was trying, poor thing, but we could see that she was slipping away from us. She seemed to have taken up residence somewhere far away. When Mikal was present, she managed to find her old self. But more and more often, even Mikal could not bring her back.

"On Easter Sunday, Marie-Louise seemed better than she had been in weeks. Mikal mentioned a trip to Lawrence to buy flour, and she seemed content. She assured him she would be fine staying behind. She promised to come spend the night with us. But at four o'clock in the afternoon, the wind changed from the south to the northwest. Clouds flew in and the air was filled with dust. It turned cold and began to mist and rain. Then sleet and snow filled the air, driven along by a furious wind. Mikal turned around to come back home. Facing the driving wind, he was almost frozen. But he persevered. By God's grace he located the fence of woven willows that he had put around his wife's garden. He followed the fence to the door, but to his horror he found that the ridgepole of the dugout had broken from the heavy load of dirt and snow. Marie-Louise was nowhere to be found."

Amalia's hand trembled slightly as she raised it to her lips and pressed against them, shaking her head from side to side. "Even though it was nearly dark, Mikal rode to our home, beating on the door, shouting for Marie-Louise." Amalia's eyes filled with tears and she continued. "He was half wild with fear and grief. He would hardly believe us when we told him that she was not there. We all hoped that perhaps she had gone to Koukle's. We convinced Mikal that to go searching in the night would mean certain death for us all. Surely, we thought, she was at that very moment huddled next to the fire at Koukle's."

Amalia's voice lowered and she half whispered, "But it was not to be. The next morning Mikal and my Jacob found her about a mile south and east of the dugout. She was on the open prairie, barefoot, dressed only in a thin nightgown." Amalia paused dramatically. "If she had only stayed in the dugout, protected under the fallen roof, she would have survived the storm."

Her cold gray eyes met Karyn's as she concluded the tragic story. "I can still remember that day. Mikal carried Marie-Louise's body to our home in his own arms. He made a coffin from the boards of an old wagon. There was no cemetery, no minister to hold a proper service. He buried his little wife only a few feet from the door of the caved-in dugout. He stood by the grave as a dead man while my Jacob read the Shepherd's Psalm. The moment Jacob concluded the reading of the Scripture, Mikal climbed into his wagon and drove away. Two weeks later he returned with a tombstone. He must have gone all the way to Independence for it. He came to tell us after he had set it in place. It was the last we thought we would ever hear from Mikal Ritter.

"That spring we were so disheartened, and the news from the north was so promising, that Jacob decided we would come and cast our lot with the settlers of Custer County." Amalia took a deep breath. "My Jacob died before we reached our destination. I had no choice but to continue on with my family." She snorted. "Of course, they did not really want me, but they could not just leave me sitting alongside the road, could they?"

She sighed and then returned to the topic at hand. "Imagine our amazement when we arrived here in

Millersburg and recognized Mikal Ritter. Cay Miller told us he was living like a wild man, dug into the side of the bluff on his new claim, that he rarely came to town, that he stayed to himself. That was two years ago. Then, suddenly, he built a sod house and left again. And, just like that, he returns with a new wife. Well," Amalia said, her eyes narrowing, "it's a wonder, that's all I can say. Anyone who had seen Mikal Ritter stagger into our log cabin with Marie-Louise's body in his arms would never have expected him to go for another wife."

Amalia stood up stiffly and tapped her cane twice before concluding, "He must have finally realized. *Wo Keine Frau ist, da fehlt's am besten hausrat.*" (Where there is no wife, the best household utensil is missing.) She looked Karyn over critically. "I will hope for your sake— and Mikal's—that you have the good sense to dispense with the romantic notions that destroyed Marie-Louise." With a final tap of her cane on the rough board floor, Amalia turned to go. "Good day, Frau Ritter. I have told you what you need to know to adapt to this God-forsaken place. I hope you can do it."

Amalia left, grunting her way across to the door and outside. For several minutes after she had gone Karyn sat motionless, trying to absorb what she had just been told, fighting the temptation to accuse Mikal of lying—or in the very least, of purposely misleading her. Oh, why had he not spoken of Marie-Louise? Her hands shook as she mechanically lifted the coffee cup to her lips. She put the cup down and rubbed her hands together, wondering if it was anger or hurt that made her tremble so. Or, was it fear . . . fear that she had come thousands of miles to be nothing more than a convenient replacement for a dead loved one?

Karyn had no time to settle her thoughts before Mikal and Cay came back from the blacksmith's. She could see them through the door as Mikal set the newly sharpened plow in the back of the wagon. When he turned to come inside the store Karyn hurried to the door and stepped outside. Forcing herself to smile, she called out to Cay, "Thank you for the coffee, Herr Miller."

Cay smiled up at her. "You are welcome to my coffee any time, Frau Ritter. Is there anything you needed help with?"

Karyn shook her head and made her way around the wagon. "No, thank you."

Mikal looked across the wagon box with surprise. "What about mailing the letter?"

"Oh, yes." Karyn took it out of her pocket absent-mindedly and handed it to Cay.

Then, without a word, she climbed up to the wagon seat.

Mikal looked at her carefully. His gaze went to the little soddy across the street from Cay's store.

"Are the Krugers at home, Cay? I should introduce Karyn to them."

Karyn reached up to adjust her bonnet as Cay replied, "I saw the wagon head out this morning. Isaac said he was going to Kearney to get a shipment of lumber."

"Well, then." Mikal climbed up next to Karyn and with a parting nod to Cay, urged his team forward. As they rode along, he explained, "We can be at Emile's in time for a late lunch. My homestead is almost directly to the north of town. The Delhommes are north and east." Mikal stole a glance at Karyn. It was clear that something had happened to upset her.

"Are you certain there wasn't something you needed? We could have given Cay an order. It sometimes takes a few weeks, but Cay is very resourceful."

Karyn shook her head. "No. You were right about his store. It is very well-supplied."

Mikal pulled his hat down over his eyes and clucked to the team. As the wagon jolted away from the store and toward the northeast, he said, "Isaac Kruger's announcement that he is hauling in some lumber spurred Cay to want to enlarge his store. I think it bothers him to think of someone else progressing faster than he is. He plans two stories—a larger store below with rooms above. He wanted my help with the building."

Mikal cleared his throat. "To haul the lumber from Kearney is more than a week. Then there would be the time to do the building." He paused uncertainly before concluding, "I told him I did not want to leave you alone for so long."

Angered by what she perceived to be Mikal's lack of confidence in her, Karyn swallowed hard and said coldly, "You do not have to worry over me, Herr Ritter. Just because I said that I miss the chatter and noise of my family does not mean that I will be in despair if left alone." She paused before adding, "If you must go away to take advantage of this opportunity, then go. I assure you that I can make the necessary adjustments."

After an uncomfortable silence, Mikal said, "Well, then. I will go. It will pay for all the seed for spring planting and more." Out of the corner of his eye he watched Karyn. They had seemed to be getting along so well this morning. They had had a pleasant drive together. And she had been so good-natured about Cay's joking. Mikal frowned. Her sudden change of mood troubled him. Marie-Louise had begun to act like that not long after they came to the wilderness in the heart of America. Days of contentment would be suddenly interrupted by fits of tears and temper. At first Mikal was angered by what he interpreted as a willful refusal to accept the challenges of their new life together. But as time went on and the cycle repeated itself over and over again, Mikal had begun to wonder if Marie-Louise was truly unable to cope with the life to which she had come. Finally, something happened that convinced him that his beautiful little wife was slipping away from reality, that he could not stop the tide of her insanity.

It was after a rare week of normalcy when Marie-Louise had risen each morning and made Mikal's breakfast. On the sixth day of happiness, Marie-Louise went outside after breakfast to weed the garden. Mikal was lingering over a cup of coffee when he heard her shrieks—an unearthly sound that sent chills down his spine. He bolted out the door and found her crouched in horror, white-faced, staring at a fat bull snake curled up around a cabbage. The snake had raised its great head and was hissing at Marie-Louise. She seemed to be in a trance of horror.

Mikal had reached out to touch her shoulder. "It is only a bull snake, Marie-Louise. Remember? They are harmless." He reached around her and grabbed the snake, hoisting it up and tossing it away from her.

She covered her hands and began to moan. "Kill it. Kill it. Kill it."

"But it is harmless, Marie-Louise. And they eat rats. We should be glad such a huge fellow stays near the dugout. He will keep more harmful creatures away."

"Kill it! Kill it! Kill it!" She stood up, clenching her fists, screeching at him.

Mikal wrapped his arms around her, trying to comfort her in French. "Come now, *mon petit chou . . .ce n'est rien . . .*" He tried to comfort her, but she began to laugh, pushing away from him, dancing in the garden, shouting and singing in a mad, horrible display that immobilized Mikal. She danced, bending to pick up a clod of mud, smearing herself with it as if it were rouge. When she finally stopped, she walked up to Mikal and said sweetly, "Would you rock me now, Papa? . . . I am very tired."

Mikal had led her inside and sat down in the rocking chair recently purchased in hopes that rocking would somehow calm her nerves. Marie-Louise slid into his lap, laid her head on his shoulder, and fell asleep. When she woke, she seemed to have no recollection of the incident. She didn't mention the snake and was horrified by the dirt smeared on her face. For a few days, she was better . . . and then, another downward spiral began. Mikal came to be haunted by the specter of his own future caring for a woman who would no longer be any kind of wife, but rather a child requiring his constant care.

Mikal's thoughts were interrupted by Karyn's abrupt demand, "If you will slow down a little, please, I would like to walk alongside the wagon for a while."

Surprised, Mikal pulled the team up. Karyn slid to the earth almost before the wagon came to a stop. She began to walk along briskly, and Mikal pulled back on the reins, holding the team to a slow walk. He let Karyn get a little ahead of the wagon seat and watched as she trudged along, newly aware of the pleasing line of her figure.

While Mikal was watching, Karyn was thinking back over the two weeks since her arrival in Nebraska. It had been quite a shock when she saw where she was expected to live. But she had risen above the disappointment. She was rather proud of herself. She had to admit that she was also rather proud of the fact that a handsome man wanted her. Of course, he had shown no sign of *wanting* her, but the habit of replacing the memory of Hans with the very real Mikal Ritter had borne the smallest hope that some-day—her mind whirled. Still, try as she might she could not argue away Amalia Kruger's wrinkled face telling her firmly that while she might have come hoping for love, she would do well to adjust her expectations.

Karyn glanced back at Mikal. *My, but he is a handsome man.*

The Diary
April 15, 1880
   My first trip to Millersburg. There are six buildings. Cay Miller is the founder of the town and proprietor of the store. I met Amalia Kruger, a rather unpleasant woman.

CHAPTER 3

A Monogrammed Lace Handkerchief

A friend loveth at all times, and
a brother is born for adversity.
Proverbs 17:17

Karyn walked nearly two miles before finally tiring and agreeing to ride in the wagon again. The walk settled her emotions, and she was glad that Mikal appeared willing to allow whatever it was that lay between them to remain dormant. As they drove along, Mikal explained, "Now we are going north and east to the Delhommes'. Between here and the route we came this morning is the Tappan Valley. There are no settlers between Millersburg and the Delhommes yet. You cannot tell, but we are slowly going uphill. The Delhommes live up on a great tableland called the French Table." He continued to describe the land for her, helping her to see in her mind that from Millersburg, north to his homestead, and then southeast to the Delhommes', then southwest back to Millersburg, formed a great triangle. The distance between each point of the triangle was almost equal. "Only twelve or four-teen kilometers." Karyn smiled, thinking that within the space of such a triangle in Germany, there were several villages nestled in the forest.

At last the team descended a low hill toward what

40

Mikal called Clear Creek. As the wagon forded the creek, birds flitted in and about the thick undergrowth.

Mikal nodded toward the bushes. "A lot of wild fruit grows along the creeks here. Gooseberries, currants, chokecherries, buckberries, wild grapes, and plums."

"Celest said we could harvest them all together. She promised to show me how to use them all," Karyn offered. She wondered if Mikal had caught the hint that she might decide to stay longer. "Which do you like best, Mikal—jam, jelly, syrup for pancakes, or pie?"

"*Ja!*" Mikal answered. When Karyn laughed, he joined her, glad that the tension between them was finally gone.

Karyn asked, "Do you think any of the seedling trees would transplant? We could try some around the house."

"I want to do that, but I have been so busy tending and replanting trees on the timber claim that I have not managed it." He explained, "To finally get title to my tree claim, I must plant ten acres of timber, with trees no more than thirty-five meters apart, and keep them in growing condition for ten years. If I lived on that section, the requirements would be less, but then I would have had to give up on the homestead. So I just keep replanting trees there." He added, "Now that you are here"—then corrected himself—"if you decide to stay, we can certainly put some around the house. Perhaps even some fruit trees. Emile and Celest have an entire orchard of seedlings."

As the wagon pulled up a long, steady hill on the opposite side of the creek, Mikal said, "Already you have seen that Emile Delhomme is a very gracious man. He is also ambitious. Of his five sons, two already have their own homesteads on the opposite end of French Table from Emile's. Each one has taken a preemption, a homestead, and a timber claim. That means that between the three men, the Delhommes own over a thousand acres of America."

Karyn thought for a moment. "Can women get a preemption?"

Mikal looked at her, surprised.

"Don't seem so amazed," she shot back. "Since you have no sons, perhaps your wife could add to your holdings. Is it possible?"

Mikal shook his head. "Part of filing for the land is promising to live on it for five years."

The team was pulling them up a steep incline. At the top, they gave such a mighty heave that the wagon lurched and nearly threw Karyn off the seat. Mikal grabbed her, teasing, "One of the most basic skills of homesteading, Karyn, is not breaking your neck falling out of your wagon."

Karyn smoothed her apron and laughed with him. But the talk of preemptions and timber claims was interrupted as they drove up onto the plateau known as French Table. When Karyn said something about the unbroken distance, Mikal took the opportunity to mention a common phenomenon. "You might think you see a vast sea or a great city. Once I could have sworn there was a river with huge trees along its banks. It was only a mirage."

Shielding her eyes, Karyn pointed into the distance. "Is that what you meant? Is that castle a mirage?"

Mikal laughed. "No. That's very real. That is Emile and Celest Delhomme's home." While Karyn exclaimed over the size of the house, Mikal told her, "Cay handled the materials orders. He said Emile spent five hundred dollars on that house."

Karyn was speechless, contemplating the incredible expenditure of five hundred American dollars on a home. The closer she got to the house, the more she began to envy Celest Delhomme. Of course, it was made of sod, but such a mansion! Two stories tall, it had a wood, shingled roof from which protruded a brick chimney. The front boasted no less than six windows, a beautifully carved front door, and rounded turrets at each corner. It did, indeed, resemble a small castle.

"Karyn! Mikal!" Celest's voice called out through one of the windows. Turning to look for her, Karyn noted that Celest not only had six windows, she had windows with screen coverings.

Celest came hurrying out the door just as Emile and two of his sons rounded the corner of a huge barn nearby. Celest introduced her sons. Sunburned almost the color of his auburn hair, Remi bowed low, kissing the back of Karyn's hand. Celest rolled her eyes and laughed. "My son, the actor." She put her hand on Serge's shoulder as she introduced him. Not to be outdone by his brother, Serge clicked his heels and bowed low. He whispered something into Mikal's ear, and Mikal shoved him playfully.

"Boys, boys!" Celest intervened, scolding in French. Then, she turned to Karyn, switching almost in mid-sentence to German. "Who would believe they are all in their twenties! They behave like such children!" She appealed to Emile, "Get these young thugs to work, husband. There is hardly time before supper to get half the firebreak plowed."

Karyn and Celest headed for the house just as a huge black dog came tearing around the edge of the barn in hot pursuit of a yellow cat. "Frona! *Platz!*" Celest ordered. The dog dropped to the ground as if someone had shot her. Her chin in the dust, she looked up apologetically at Celest, stirring up clouds of dust as she beat the earth with her tail.

"All right, Frona. You are forgiven." Then Celest said to Karyn, "Do you like dogs? When Frona has puppies, you must have one. She protects the livestock as if they were her very own, but for some reason she has decided the house is her holy habitation. She won't let the cats set foot inside. She kills mice and rats herself—and I have no worry of rattlesnakes when Frona is here."

"Are rattlesnakes a problem?" Karyn asked.

"Not to frighten you unduly, but yes, you must always be watchful." Celest shook her head. "They wreak havoc among our sheep." The women paused just outside the front door of the house while Celest explained, "The first few warm days every year, the snakes come up out of the prairie-dog burrows where they have spent the winter. They bask in the warm sunshine for hours before slithering off. The men all congregate and have contests to see who can kill the most. This year they had their contest while Mikal was in Grand Island. Over one hundred rattlesnakes were killed." Celest nodded toward Frona. "That wonderful dog killed several on her own."

She pulled Karyn across the threshold and into the house. "Come in, come in. I chatter on and on. I am just getting ready to bake bread. You can help me knead it. Wait until you see what a huge mound of dough I have made up."

Celest glanced back at Frona, who had remained in her *platz* by the door. She didn't move, but she did continue to watch Celest hopefully. "*Komm,* Frona," Celest ordered. The dog rose and followed the women into the house. Celest led Karyn into the large kitchen, promising a tour of the other rooms as soon as the bread was kneaded and shaped.

Karyn removed her bonnet and sat down at a small table beside the kitchen window to catch her breath. Frona walked up slowly and laid her massive black head in Karyn's lap.

Celest nodded with approval. "Not everyone receives such a welcome. Obviously she approves of our neighbor's choice for a wife." Celest made her way toward the opposite wall of the kitchen where she checked the fire in the largest stove Karyn had ever seen. As the stove lid clattered back into place, Celest pulled a huge crock down from a shelf and scooped flour from one of three large barrels positioned underneath a row of shelves lining another wall. She set the crock beside a huge mound of dough on the table.

Frona had not moved. She waited patiently while Karyn scratched her ears. Without warning, Karyn began to cry. When she leaned over to hide her tears, Frona licked her. Karyn laughed, crying all the more in spite of herself.

Celest frowned. "What is this, dear Karyn? You must tell me." She crossed the kitchen to Karyn's side. Patting Frona on the head she pushed the dog gently away. "Frona. *Geh Weiter.*" The dog padded away, curling up in the corner of the kitchen from where she watched the two women carefully.

"It's nothing. Just homesickness, I guess." Karyn wiped the tears away and tried to get up. "Your bread. We must get to the kneading."

Celest pulled a wooden chair up beside Karyn. Handing her a beautiful lace handkerchief, she sat down and put one hand around Karyn's shoulders. "Not until I know the reason for these tears. What has suddenly made you so homesick?"

After studying the kitchen's spotless plank floor for a few moments, Karyn said softly, "Did you know that Mikal was married before?"

Celest didn't hesitate. "What of it? You should be happy that he is so open to tell you." She patted Karyn's hands. "Why worry over the distant past when the future holds such promise?"

"Because," Karyn choked out, "because Mikal is not the one who told me of another wife. I learned it in Millersburg today."

"Amalia Kruger!" Celest nearly spat the name out. "Oh, I should have warned you about that woman!"

Karyn shook her head. "Don't be angry with her, Celest. I think she had good intentions." She sighed. "You know, when I first saw the house Mikal expected me to live in, I wanted to get right back in the wagon and demand that he take me back to Grand Island. But he seemed so lonely." Karyn blushed. "He convinced me to stay for one month.

He promised he would send me home if I did not want to stay after a month." She paused, moistening her lips before continuing. "Only—"

Celest interrupted. "—only now you see that Mikal has a good beginning on an excellent piece of land. You see that he will be a successful farmer some day." Celest added with a little laugh, "And I suspect that two weeks of living with that mane of black hair and those blue eyes have tempted you to do a little romantic dreaming."

Karyn looked down at her hands. "I am no fool, Celest. I do not expect that a man would fall in love with me in only two weeks." She blushed. "But I will admit that I have been doing some 'romantic dreaming,' as you call it." She swallowed hard. "I want to believe that he did not speak of Marie-Louise out of consideration for me. But after hearing what Mrs. Kruger had to say, I wonder if Mikal offered only partnership because he cannot offer more—because he will never be able to offer more." She took a deep breath and said, "I have been disappointed once in romance. I do not want to put myself in a situation to be hurt again."

Celest grasped both Karyn's hands and shook them as she said firmly, "Mikal offered partnership and demands nothing more because he is a man of integrity, Karyn. That kind of man does not take unless a woman offers with her whole heart." She released Karyn's hands and said, "Why did he not tell you about Marie-Louise? I do not know. Even after twenty-five years of marriage to Emile Delhomme, I would not presume to say that I understand the way a man thinks." She looked out the window to where the men were plowing. Then, her eyes overflowing with kindness, she said, "From what I know of Mikal, I do not think you should read anything sinister into this. I suspect that he wanted to avoid the possibility that you might feel threatened by his past with another woman—which is exactly how you have reacted. And he probably wanted to see how things go with the two of you. Why should he open old wounds and speak of the past if you decide not to stay?"

"Mrs. Kruger said that Mikal will never belong to me. She said that he belongs to the past."

Celest leaned forward. "Amalia Kruger is a very unhappy old woman who must live with a son and daughter-in-law who are not very kind. She is the one who belongs to the past. Listen to me, Karyn. She clings to the old ways as if they were holy. She was very happy living in Kansas in a little Germany where nothing American was forced upon her.

"Before Cay Miller came to begin his city, the post office was here in this house. I thought Amalia would choke the first time she was forced to actually come into my home and try to speak English to a Belgian regarding the American mail system. I know that she only spoke to me because there was no other way. She said as much to her son one day in my presence. I must confess that her attitude had already galled me so that I gave no hint of speaking German. I am sinful enough that I enjoyed making her struggle to speak English—and understanding her comments to her son without her knowledge.

"I could see her shake the dust from my yard off her heels—literally—every time she left. Of course after the post office was moved and she discovered that I speak German—" Celest broke off. "Well, that is another story. Let us just say that Amalia and I do not have tea together on a regular basis."

Taking a deep breath, Celest continued, "The Krugers came here after terrible disappointments in Kansas. Their only daughter, Ida, ran away to marry a man of whom they did not approve. Then Amalia's husband died on the way north. She is a bitter old woman who seems to take special delight in squelching other people's happiness. But you must not allow Amalia Kruger's gossip to ruin what you have begun with Mikal Ritter. And you must not assume the worst of Mikal. He deserves better. Give him time to tell you about Marie-Louise in his own way. Keep your heart open. You just might be rewarded with a friendship that blossoms into love."

Celest stood up. "Now. To work."

The two women began to punch and knead Celest's mound of dough. They shaped a half dozen round loaves and six dozen rolls and left them to rise in the kitchen while Celest showed Karyn the rest of the impressive house. They went upstairs first, where a central hall stretched the length of the house. Off the hallway to the left was Emile and Celest's room and a bedroom converted into an office for Emile. Along the other side of the hallway were three more bedrooms, each one furnished with sturdy, handmade furniture, each bed adorned by a lovely woven spread or quilt.

Celest was almost apologetic about the size of the rooms. "I told Emile we didn't need anything nearly so fine, but once he began building, he seemed to get such joy out of the process, I could not refuse him."

Celest told Karyn about each of her sons. Thierry and Pascal were both married and had their own homesteads. "You met Serge and Remi." Love for her boys shone in her eyes. "They are incorrigible, but they are good boys. Their younger brother Luc is staying with Thierry for a few weeks. He is my baby. Only nineteen. Very quiet. Completely unlike his older brothers."

Having inspected the upstairs bedrooms, the women made their way downstairs. The dining room boasted beautiful rag rugs over polished wood floors. When Karyn commented on the rugs, Celest explained, "Cay Miller carries the warp. Keep all your worn-out clothing. You tear it into strips so wide"—Celest held her fingers apart to show the proper width of the strip—"sew those strips together, and then roll them into balls." She bent to pick up a ball of strips from a basket in the corner. "Then, the strips are woven through the carpet warp. This makes sections about a meter wide. Once the sections are sewn together, you have a beautiful rug created out of worthless old clothes! That is the American way. Everything is used, and used up, and used again."

"It will be some time before we have enough worn-out clothing for a rug," Karyn said. "But of all the things about that house I dislike, the floor is the worst. I have been wondering . . . do you know if anyone has tried mixing clay with straw to make a hard floor? My father once described some process like that, but I have forgotten exactly how he said it was done."

"I don't know anyone who has done that," Celest said thoughtfully. "But the clay we used for plastering these walls would surely work as well for a floor." She was suddenly enthusiastic. "I can help you. When Luc comes back from Thierry's, he and I will come over. The boys can get a load of clay from the buffalo wallow."

"Oh, no," Karyn protested. "I didn't mean—"

Celest interrupted her. "Now you listen, Karyn. You must get used to how we do things here. We help one another. You help me with bread-baking; I help you with a new floor. You help me with harvesting and drying wild fruit; I help you with sewing. Do you need any wool?" They were near the back door of the house, and Celest led the way outside and into a lean-to attached to the house. Karyn wrinkled her nose at the strong odors emanating from the room. In the corner stood two gigantic spinning wheels.

Celest grinned, picking up a thick wool pelt. "The shearing this spring yielded a wonderful supply. I have managed to wash only a part of it. There is wool to be washed, wool to be carded, spun, dyed." She held out a wad of wool to Karyn. "Perhaps you can help me experiment with some of the local plants for dyes. Do you need wool for knitting? You can have as much as you want if you will knit a pair of socks for the boys once in a while." She leaned toward Karyn and whispered, "Don't tell Emile, but I despise knitting. And since he brought home a sewing machine, I really cannot seem to make myself knit."

Celest led the way out of the lean-to and back into the house. In the parlor, a sewing machine stood just inside the largest window at the front of the house. But Karyn gave the sewing machine only a cursory glance, staring instead at a walnut reed organ that stood against the opposite wall from the doorway. "I never expected to see an organ so far away from—"

"—civilization?" Celest chuckled as she finished Karyn's sentence. "Well, our son Luc seemed to have music inside him from the day he was born. Emile thought an organ would be a nice addition to the community. He was right. The boys often haul the organ into the wagon and take it to dances. Emile plays the violin, and he is finally beginning to learn the American music so that he can play the dances. He and Luc play very well together."

Through the window Karyn caught a glimpse of green. Celest said, "Would you like to see the garden?"

The two women went through the kitchen, out the back door, and around the lean-to where Celest had planted a huge garden inside a wall of sod. She explained, "It isn't a very attractive fence, but it keeps the tiny shoots safe from marauding wildlife and the relentless wind. Has anyone told you what they say about the wind here?" Celest chuckled. "Hang a log chain outside your window. If it stands out at a forty-five-degree angle, there's a mild breeze. If the chain is horizontal to the earth, the wind is blowing."

Leaning on the top of the fence, Celest reminisced. "One of the most difficult things for me when we first came here—besides the wind—was simply dealing with the space just outside my door. As far as I could see there was grass and more grass, sky and more sky. Some days,

I thought I would get crushed between them. I felt that there was no place for me to simply *be*. After a while, I began to notice that there were ways to divide the space in my mind. A buffalo trail divides the north of the tableland from the south. Clear Creek divides the table from the valley. My fence divides the prairie from my garden. And," she said, pointing to the horizon where the men were working, "the firebreak divides the yard from the prairie."

"Have you seen a prairie fire?" Karyn asked.

Celest nodded. "It's terrifying. The flames race along, destroying everything in their path. But then out of the ruins comes lush, new growth." Celest smiled. "Another one of God's lessons. Sometimes what seems ruinous to our human eyes is only God burning away the weeds so that new life can begin."

She touched Karyn's arm and nodded toward the barn. "Let me show you the rest of the homestead." She led Karyn toward the barn and a small chicken house. As the two women stood outside the wire enclosure where a fine flock of hens was kept safe from coyotes, Celest shared, "Emile and I have been here only three years, Karyn. It will not be that long before you have your own flock, your own herds, your own garden. Even your own sewing machine. Did I hear Mikal say that his cow is due to calve soon?" When Karyn nodded, Celest suggested, "Cay Miller will buy all the butter and cheese you can take him. I think he pays almost fifteen cents for every pound of butter and as much for a dozen eggs."

Karyn said, "At home I earned extra money by sewing for women who frequented Papa's store."

Celest finished Karyn's thought. "You can be as busy as you like sewing for other women. Cay can order you a very good machine from Montgomery Ward for less than twenty dollars. He has the catalog in his store. And you are welcome to use my machine until you have your own."

Karyn looked back toward where the men were plowing. It looked as though they were making very slow progress. "Is it really necessary to have such wide furrows?"

"In the fall, when things are dry, lightning, an ember from a campfire, sparks from a train—anything can start a fire. They can burn for days. And believe me, when twelve-foot-high flames come roaring toward you faster than a running horse, you thank God—and the men who plowed—for those furrows with burned earth between them."

Karyn was horrified. Celest encouraged her. "No prairie fire can burn through three-foot-thick walls of sod." She smiled wisely.

"But Mikal's roof is wood, as is yours."

Celest laughed. "Well, then, I suppose we would have to hide in the cistern!" She hastened to reassure. "Don't worry, Karyn. We always get a warning. From your house high on the ridge, you could see a big fire coming for three nights before it reached you. The flames light up the night sky in a wonderful, terrible golden light." She added, "A very wide and deep creek separates Mikal's home from any potential fire. With the creek and a firebreak, you have no cause to worry." She changed the subject abruptly, nodding toward the men. "Mikal seems to be enjoying our new team."

"They are magnificent," Karyn agreed.

"English shires. The Irvine brothers have just begun importing them." Celest laughed softly. "I was afraid to ask Emile what he paid for them." She sighed. "Let's get the fire going for supper. I'll bake some potatoes."

As night fell, Karyn lay on her back atop the beautiful quilts that adorned Celest's guest room bed, staring at the ceiling. She was trying her best to relax the knot in her stomach, but it would not go. At the sound of footsteps coming down the hall, she clutched her hands nervously.

When the footsteps stopped outside the bedroom door, Karyn leaped to her feet.

Mikal ducked and entered the room. He tossed his hat on the chair just behind the door and closed the door before saying, "Thank you."

"Thank you? For what?" Karyn asked.

As he talked, Mikal was spreading a quilt he usually carried in the back of his wagon on the floor beside the bed. "Thank you for giving no hint of our agreement in the presence of Remi and Serge. They would never have let me hear the end of it." He stretched out on the quilt and put his hands behind his head. "Remi and Serge fancy themselves Romeos, and they were quite vocal about their opinion of my signing that letter to Brandenburg. Of course"—he lifted his head enough to see her over the edge of the mattress and smiled—"now that they have met you, they are probably wishing they had joined me in the adventure." He settled back on the floor. "Thank you. And good night."

Karyn lay back down on the bed. Presently, she moved toward the center of the mattress and peered down where Mikal lay. He had turned on his side and tucked one arm beneath his head. "For heaven's sake, Mikal. Take a pillow." She dropped a pillow on top of him. Then she got up and pulled the top quilt off the bed. Walking around the foot of the bed she spread the quilt over him. "And a quilt."

"Quiet, you two newlyweds!" someone shouted as they pounded loudly on the door.

There was uproarious laughter and then Celest's voice could be heard whispering intensely in French. Serge answered in an apologetic tone, but Celest repeated herself angrily and then closed her door. The boys' footsteps retreated down the hall, but not before there was a good deal more snickering and whispering just outside Mikal and Karyn's door.

As soon as the boys' voices quieted down, someone knocked softly on the door. It was Celest, with another blanket. She whispered, "Use this on the floor, Mikal. I am sorry I do not have another feather bed," and then crept back across the hall.

Mikal settled on the floor while Karyn lay back on the mattress, unable to relax, horrified by the realization that she was going to have to sneak out of the room and "out back" before the night was over. She waited for a long time, until Mikal's breathing grew even. Then, she picked her way around the end of the bed and made for the door. She prayed that the floorboards would not creak and awaken Mikal. The floorboards didn't creak, but Mikal was awakened anyway when Karyn tripped over his feet and nearly fell on top of him.

"What?!" Mikal started up. "What is it? What's wrong?"

Karyn could barely control her embarrassed laughter. "It's nothing. Except that I forgot you are so tall and I failed to allow for your feet sticking out at the end of the bed. I just need to—" She couldn't say it.

Mikal understood immediately. He bent his legs at the knees. "My feet are out of the way now. Go along."

Completely mortified, Karyn made her way downstairs and "out back." When she returned, Mikal had turned over in a vain attempt to get comfortable.

"Mikal," Karyn whispered as she closed the door. "This is ridiculous. I am used to sharing a bed with three of my sisters. I can certainly share it with you. Please. Come up off the floor."

Mikal hefted his frame up and onto the very edge of the bed. He turned his back so that Karyn would have as much privacy as possible.

"You must be very tired. I am sorry I insisted on walking alongside the wagon today. We could have arrived here earlier and perhaps the plowing could have been completed. You could have slept in your own bed tonight."

"Do you mind telling me what happened in Millersburg to make you so angry with me?"

"It was nothing important," she lied. "Things are very different from what I expected. Very different from the railroad booklet I saw at home. Different from the letters sent to Brandenburg about America."

Mikal asked, "Tell me more about Brandenburg. I only marched through it on the way to France. And tell me more about your family."

Lying on her back in the dark, Karyn told Mikal about her life in Germany. "We live on a small farm just outside of town. But the farming is really only something Papa does for amusement. He is a merchant with a store in Brandenburg. I am the oldest daughter. Then comes Sophie. When she is well she is lively and fun, but unfortunately she is often sick and unable to work in the store. She sews beautifully, and together we used to make garments for the women who shopped in Papa's store. After Sophie is Jette, then Vroni. Jette is engaged to be married. Vroni says she is coming to America as soon as she can, but not to get married. Vroni wants to teach music." Then, Karyn surprised herself by describing Anton Gilhoff.

"So you came to America to escape one husband and ended up trapped in a dark room with another."

Karyn wasn't certain, but she thought Mikal's tone was teasing. She bantered back through the darkness. "With one little exception. This husband agrees to let me have some say in my future. Anton Gilhoff would never be so considerate."

"Which brings me to the matter of my working for Cay Miller. Our agreement was that you would stay one month. If I go to work for Cay, I must leave in a few days to get the lumber in Kearney. Then there is the time to help Cay with the building. It is hardly a way for us to get to know one another. And I will probably still be away when our agreement expires."

"I am not afraid to be alone, Mikal," Karyn said, hoping she sounded more certain than she felt.

He sounded relieved. "Cay Miller has offered to buy as many cedar posts as I can cut. That requires a trip to the cedar canyons west of here. But once I have the money from Cay for the building and for the cedar posts, then I will need to go to Kearney—or perhaps even Grand Island—to get provisions for the spring and summer."

"Does the wife always stay behind?" she asked.

"Someone must care for the livestock."

"I will be fine, Mikal. There is no need for you to worry over me."

"Does that mean you have already decided to stay past a month?" Mikal asked abruptly.

Even in the dark, Karyn could feel her cheeks growing red. "It means that I see no reason for me to abandon you when I can be of help."

Mikal mumbled, "Good." Presently his even breathing indicated he had fallen asleep. Karyn turned on her side. Mikal had drawn his knees up to keep his feet from sticking off the end of the bed. Moonlight coming in the window made his long black hair shine. Karyn watched him for a long time before finally closing her eyes and falling asleep.

The Diary
April 15, 1880

Mikal is to be gone. I have agreed to stay past the month. It will be strange to be alone in my own home. I do not ever remember that happening before. It appears that women here are often alone. I will adapt. I must learn to speak English as soon as possible. Celest promises me one of Frona's puppies. Already she is a good and wise friend. There are poisonous snakes in this area. I pray to God that I never see one.

CHAPTER 4

Knitting Needles

She looketh well to the ways of her household,
and eateth not the bread of idleness.
Proverbs 31:27

Eager to show her self-reliance and to banish any possible comparison between herself and Marie-Louise, Karyn sounded almost angry when, on the ride home from the Delhommes', Mikal expressed renewed doubts about working for Cay Miller. Impatience sounded in her voice when she insisted, "I can certainly feed and water a cow and a pig, Mikal."

Mikal looked at her soberly. "I know that. But being alone here—you don't know what it's like."

"Planning the garden will take some time. Then I can walk to the creek and dig up some seedlings and plant them around the house. I have promised to do some knitting for Celest. I will be so busy I will hardly miss you— except to be grateful that I do not have to cook so much." Mikal seemed to be weakening, so she continued, "And besides that, I will not be alone. I will have Ella and the sow." She teased, "I shall give the sow a name, and if I get desperate I can walk to Celest's."

Mikal expressed doubt about her visiting without him. "You are too new to the country. It is very easy to get lost."

57

Karyn tossed her head. "From our doorstep it is not so difficult to follow the valley for the first few kilometers. Then there is that huge ridge of boulders sticking up out of the earth. After that, there is a clump of trees right on the edge of a canyon. Then down to cross Clear Creek, and up the long grade onto the tableland. From the tableland, you can see the house—like a mirage—in the distance. And if I make a mistake so that I cannot see the house, I will wait until sundown and look for the lantern shining from the top of the cedar pole right in Celest's front yard."

Mikal was impressed. "You paid attention."

Karyn forced herself to sound much more confident than she felt. "You said that you could earn enough from Cay to make a good down payment on a pair of horses like Emile's. I will not be carried about like an uncooked egg in danger of cracking. If my presence here is a hindrance to your doing what needs to be done, then you should send me home." Hearing herself express such an independent attitude encouraged her. She finished her speech with bravado, "Go do the work for Cay Miller, cut your fence posts—and I expect to see a beautiful team of shires pulling this wagon when you come back."

Finally, Mikal was convinced, although he made an unspoken promise to himself to have Emile check in on Karyn from time to time.

When the day came for him to leave, Mikal spent the morning repeating instructions he had already given several times before. He reminded Karyn about the lantern. "Be certain you light it and leave it in the window. Someone lost on the prairie will know where to get help." Then he handed her a rifle. "And keep this beside you. Any strangers needing help are welcome to sleep down in the dugout. Just make certain they see the rifle. And make them think you know how to use it."

Karyn reached for the rifle, checking to make certain it

was loaded. When Mikal looked surprised, she said simply, "We do have guns in Brandenburg, Mikal. Papa liked to hunt."

So it was that Karyn Ritter (in name only) stood one morning barely two weeks after her arrival in Nebraska, watching as the distance swallowed up the last trace of Mikal and his team. In only a few moments she washed the dishes from their simple breakfast and made her way outside to the spot just northeast of the house where Mikal had said they would have a garden. Karyn leaned against the side of the house, inspecting the area. She made a mental list, imagining rows of beets, tomatoes, potatoes, melons, cabbage, cucumbers, carrots, muskmelon, turnips, and beans. She imagined sod walls like those around Celest's garden, and stepped off the space where she would ask Mikal to build them. Rummaging about in the dugout, she found a pile of stakes. She marked the fence line by forcing a sharp spade through the sod and inserting a stake in each slit.

Standing up to survey her efforts, Karyn smiled to herself. *Only two weeks ago you agreed to stay no longer than one month. Now your husband is to be gone for at least two weeks, and you are planning a garden.* She made her way back down the slope and to the corral, where Ella the Jersey cow stood patiently chewing her cud. At Karyn's approach, Ella thrust her head through the fence, waiting to have her ears scratched. When Karyn lingered near the dugout barn, Ella protested. Karyn laughed. "All right, Ella. I come." She scratched the heifer behind the ears. Next, she hauled a few buckets full of fresh water from the well behind the house.

For the remainder of the morning, Karyn wandered aimlessly about the homestead, from the soddy to the dugout barn, into the barn to contemplate living there, and back to the soddy. She took up a rag and dusted the rough-hewn furniture inside the soddy. Looking out the window, she was inspired to open her trunk and withdraw what was supposed to be another feather tick. She had packed it, imagining that geese would be plentiful in the countryside. Chuckling at her ignorance, she measured the little window where the tiny geranium from Celest sat. It had new sprouts along both stems, and Karyn found herself looking forward to the day when her own window would be filled with blooming plants. The afternoon was taken up with the transformation of part of the empty feather tick into curtains for the window.

Evening came on. As the sun slipped below the horizon and twilight sent shadows across the landscape, Karyn became newly aware of her aloneness. She slipped down the slope to the corral, fed and watered Ella and the sow, and hurried back up the slope to the soddy. She lit the lamp and placed it in the window. She didn't feel hungry, but she wasn't tired either, and it was too early to go to bed. Far off to the northwest, wolves were howling. A breeze made the quilt hanging over the door swing to and fro. Karyn dismantled part of her cupboard and weighted the bottom of the quilt down with two crates. For added security, she braced a chair against the crates. She looked nervously about her.

Finally, she settled by the lamp in the window and took up her knitting. Celest had given her a basketful of yarn with the promise of more to come. Once she started knitting, Karyn relaxed. She began to hum. Having added several rows to the knitted sock in her lap, she looked about her, thinking with longing of the organ in the Delhommes' parlor. Her fingers moved soundlessly over an imaginary keyboard for a few measures. Then, she returned to her knitting.

Karyn spent the morning of her first full day alone on her homestead transplanting seedlings from the creek bed to the yard around the house. With a basket in one hand

and a shovel in the other, she headed for the creek. Extracting even twelve-inch-high seedlings from the sod required a surprising amount of effort. Time and again, she failed to get enough roots to ensure successful transplanting. But finally she had about two dozen promising seedlings in the basket. She spent the afternoon planting: two cottonwoods a few feet from the front door of the soddy; a row of what she hoped were elms along the path down the slope toward the corral; and hackberry trees for the opposite side of the corral.

In the corral, Ella had been moving about restlessly for quite some time. "What is wrong, Ella?" Karyn worried. She drew fresh water, offered more grain, but Ella could not be appeased. She continued to pace about the corral until suddenly, she went down on one side. Karyn was nearly frantic, until she realized what was happening.

Totally ignorant of what to do, Karyn looked about her for a reason to stay nearby. She found it in the dugout barn. She hauled Mikal's bedding out into the sunshine, draping the blankets and a quilt over the fence to air. Pumping more water, she hauled a bucketful into the barn and began to scrub every square inch of wood inside. She emptied ashes from the small stove and polished it until it shone. She spent the rest of the morning pretending to work, when in reality she was continually poking her head out the door to check on Ella. Finally, after what seemed like an eternity, Karyn watched as a perfectly formed calf slid into the world.

Instantly, Ella was on her feet, mooing contentedly, licking her calf. Karyn laughed with relief. "Good work, Ella. You can be very proud of yourself." At the sound of Karyn's voice, Ella looked over her shoulder and flicked an ear as if to agree with her. Then, she turned back to nuzzle her calf.

Karyn watched happily as mother and calf got acquainted and was delighted when the calf rose on spindly legs, searched and found her target, and nursed greedily. Karyn went back to work in Mikal's dugout, with visions of milk and butter and cheese dancing in her head. As soon as she finished her cleaning, she walked up the slope to the soddy, intending to drag the churn out into the yard and ready it for use. But she had just wrestled the churn to the door when a wagon drove up. Celest sat beside the driver, a young man about Karyn's age.

As Celest introduced her son Luc, Karyn nodded and reached up to shake his hand even as she announced the birth of Ella's calf. "Can you make certain everything is all right?" She started down the slope, followed by Luc and Celest. With a few quiet words to Ella, Luc stepped into the corral, checked things over, and assured Karyn that all was well. "That's a good-size calf," he offered in German. "You will have some good steaks from him."

"You have been planting trees," Celest observed, nodding toward the seedlings around the corral.

"Mikal said he meant to plant some last year, but he was too busy on the tree claim to have the time to water them. I thought I would try." Karyn was uncomfortably aware that Luc had noticed the bedding airing along the corral fence. She said vaguely, "I found these old things in the dugout. I can put them back now."

"Come and see what we have brought you today," Celest said, walking back up the hill toward the house.

Karyn hastily folded Mikal's bedding and restored it to its place inside the dugout. When she came out, Luc was pouring water into a gigantic wooden tub just outside the door. Smiling at Karyn, he climbed up into the wagon box and began to shovel gray clay into the tub.

Celest explained, "We've brought your plaster. This clay and the sand toward the back of the wagon, mixed with water, will make a good plaster for the walls. With all three of us working, it shouldn't take long. Then we can try your mixture on the floor. Emile and the boys will meet us at the buffalo wallow again in the morning to shovel more clay. If we work hard, we might be finished by tomorrow night."

"I cannot ask you to spend so much time away from your own home," Karyn protested.

"You didn't ask. I offered to help you. Emile and the boys are perfectly willing to have me gone. They are grown men. I left plenty of fresh bread. They can have scrambled eggs for breakfast and whatever game they can shoot for supper. They will be fine."

Luc reassured Karyn, "We grew up learning to fend for ourselves, Mrs. Ritter. Mama is often called to tend to a sick neighbor." He smiled affectionately at his mother. "She has been the only doctor in this part of the county since we arrived."

Luc ducked inside the soddy and emerged with the crates Karyn had used to block her doorway the preceding night. "Mikal already smoothed the walls," he said to his mother, "which saves us a lot of time." He set to work without giving Karyn any further opportunity to protest.

Together Celest, Karyn, and Luc hauled the few pieces of furniture out of the soddy. Luc mixed sand, clay, and water to just the right consistency. Then, he hauled bucketfuls of the mixture inside for Celest and Karyn to smear on the walls. As the walls were gradually covered with plaster, Karyn began to feel excited about the improvement. *What a difference this makes!*

When it came time for Karyn to feed the animals, Luc insisted she and Celest rest. He handed them both a cup of water and made his way down the hill.

"What a fine boy," Karyn said. "*Er kann gut Deutsch.*"

Celest nodded. "Yes. He does speak good German. Luc is unlike his brothers in every way. He has applied himself well as a student." She smiled. "I poured all of my schooling into Luc. Latin, German, the classics . . . and he eagerly absorbed everything I could give him. Now he is counting the days until he can leave and learn even more. He hopes to study music. After this year's crop, the money should be there," Celest explained. "His father offered to help, but Luc insists he will pay his own way. He is raising his own beef and hiring out to his married brothers and anyone else who needs help. If all goes well, he will be at a conservatory in Philadelphia this time next year. He hopes to teach."

As Luc headed back up the hill and began to mix more clay, Karyn asked Celest to accompany her around the back of the house where she had dug a little opening in the hillside. Inside, she had started a fire and now only glowing coals remained. With an iron poker, she raked the coals out of the space. "I want to see if this will work like an oven." She placed a pan of corn bread into the hole, then put a piece of tin over the opening and raked the coals over the improvised oven door. In an hour, Celest and Luc and Karyn were feasting on fresh bread.

"And soon," Karyn mused, "there will be fresh milk! Life is good."

As the sky changed from orange to dark violet, Luc spread a blanket under the wagon. Celest and Karyn headed for the dugout.

Early the next morning, Luc drove off in the direction of the buffalo wallow. While he was gone the two women mixed up the last of the clay and began plastering. They were hard at work, when Luc returned with the wagon full of fresh clay. Celest rushed outside while Karyn continued smoothing plaster around the corner where the bed-box jutted out from the walls of the soddy.

At noon, when Karyn headed down the slope with a pail of fresh water, she was amazed to see a bay pony trotting around the corral. Luc and Celest came up behind her.

"She's a gentle little thing," Luc explained. "She won't give you any trouble."

Celest added, "She is worth about ten dollars, Karyn. I

hope you will accept her in payment for the knitting you agreed to do for my men."

Karyn looked from the pony to Luc to Celest and back again.

Luc spoke up. "Perhaps we should have asked if you know how to ride."

"Not very well," Karyn admitted.

"Then she is the perfect pony for you," Luc said. "She has not one evil bone in her little body. Thierry broke her himself for his children to ride. He mentioned trading her for something a little more lively. The timing was perfect."

Celest asked, "You did say you don't mind knitting for the men?" When Karyn nodded, she offered, "Cay Miller charges a dollar for a pair of good German socks and fifty cents for mittens. What do you say we agree that you will knit a pair of socks and a pair of mittens for each of my men?"

Karyn nodded, swallowing hard. "Thank you." She was embarrassed by the tears that sprung to her eyes. "You are so kind, I hardly know what to say."

Luc grinned at her and said, "The truth is, Mrs. Ritter, our motive is not completely unselfish. We are having a dance next Friday, and you must come. If you ride Sugar, that saves us from having to pick you up, which means more time for dancing!"

Karyn smiled back at him. She asked Celest, "What is *danke* in English, please?"

"'Thank you,'" Celest answered.

With a thick German accent, Karyn said to Luc, "Thank you." Her cheeks blushed crimson with embarrassment. Luc nodded and smiled.

The Delhomme men made two more trips to the buffalo wallow, and Celest, Karyn, and Luc worked a day longer than they had anticipated, but at the end of Karyn's first week without Mikal, she stood at the doorway of the soddy and surveyed the plastered walls with pride.

Serge and Remi had arrived one day to teach Karyn

how to saddle Sugar. They demonstrated her gentle nature by crawling under the little mare several times, pulling her tail, and lifting her feet. Karyn was reminded of a circus horse she had seen at home that patiently allowed a trained monkey to scamper over the entire surface of its body without budging. When the Delhommes finally headed for home, Karyn kissed each one on both cheeks, using her new English vocabulary to thank each one personally. She watched as their wagon disappeared into the distance, her heart filled with gratitude.

It was nearly dawn before Karyn managed to get to sleep. She blamed her insomnia on the insistent howling of coyotes. As soon as the morning light illuminated the interior of the soddy well enough for Karyn to see, she opened her trunk. Pulling out the lace tablecloth and the china, she set them aside. Then, ever so carefully, she brought out the object of her night's musings. She held it to her, wishing for a mirror like the one in Mama's room at home, a mirror before which she could stand and pose. She had had no thought of wearing it until Luc had mentioned that Mikal might surprise them all by returning in time for the dance. Anticipating Mikal's homecoming, Karyn had spent the greater part of the night imagining the look in his blue eyes when he saw her in her rose-colored silk ball gown.

The Diary
April 21, 1880
   What a blessing good friends are! The walls of my
   house are plastered, and I have a floor I can sweep. I
   have planted trees. Cottonwood (I think) by the
   house, elm and hackberry (I hope) by the corral. Ella
   has a new calf. I have begun to learn English. There is
   to be a dance at the Delhommes' next Friday. I will
   wear the rose ball gown, hoping to see M. The week
   ahead looms before me as vast and empty as the
   prairie around my little house.

CHAPTER 5

Rose-Colored Silk

For jealousy is the rage of a man.
Proverbs 6:34

"Ouch—that was my ear!" Celest giggled like a girl as she reached up to touch the red spot on her ear. She and Karyn were in the kitchen of the Delhomme home, alternately heating a slate pencil and then using it to curl their hair.

Karyn already had a fringe of curls about her face. "I apologize. I am so nervous my hands are shaking."

"There is nothing to be nervous about. It's a party. You will have a wonderful time."

"So many new faces, so many new languages." Karyn asked, "Will everyone speak English?"

"Well," Celest responded, "everyone—except of course Amalia Kruger—will try. Really, Karyn, you have no reason to be so worried. There will be a few other Germans. And everyone, but Cay Miller and Emile and I, is fairly new to Custer County. Many are still learning English just like you. Everyone will be anxious to visit and get to know one another—to get to know you." She reassured Karyn, "Good food and dancing do much to cross language barriers."

Dancing! Karyn had not contemplated that. Here was a

new reason to be nervous. She began to reheat the slate pencil in her hand before asking, "Will they do any German dances?"

Celest nodded. "Of course. German, English—at least one Danish trekant. But if Fred Smith is there, we will have a caller, and that means many, many good American square dances. You will love it. It's very lively."

"A 'caller'?" Karyn asked dubiously as she wrapped another bunch of Celest's gray hair around the pencil.

"Oh, you will see," Celest answered. She stood up and took Karyn's hand. "Come now. It's time to get dressed, and I want to see my foolish old self in a mirror."

The two women ascended to Celest's bedroom, where what the mirror revealed of her new hairstyle made Celest blush with pleasure. She reached up to touch her curled bangs. Peering into the mirror, she squinted and turned her head from side to side. "I wonder if Emile will even notice."

The women turned their backs to one another as they donned an array of petticoats and undergarments. Then, there was the rustle of black and rose silk as they pulled their best dresses on. Reaching for a cameo that lay atop her dresser, Celest turned toward the mirror. "Oh, Karyn," she exclaimed softly. "How lovely you look! That color makes your skin glow."

Standing before Celest Delhomme's full-length mirror, Karyn smoothed the bodice of her rose-colored silk gown. "Do you really think so? I hope it is not overdoing to wear it. When you said that Cay Miller would certainly leave a note for him, I hoped that Mikal might come, after all." She smiled softly. "I wanted to surprise him."

Celest raised her eyebrows. "Has he never seen you in this gown?"

Karyn shook her head. "No. I had planned to wear my other gown the day we met, but then—" She told how she had given the dress to Ida. "And then there was no time to press this one. So I met Mikal wearing a plain green calico."

"Well, it obviously made no difference to Mikal. And it will make this evening more special if he does, indeed, arrive." Celest smiled warmly. "Every young husband should see his bride in such a beautiful gown, with the glow of anticipation on her face. It is a vision he would cherish."

Karyn smiled hopefully. "Do you really think he would come all this way for a dance after such a long journey?"

"Look in the mirror again, Karyn," Celest insisted. "And tell me which you think Mikal would choose—unloading lumber or seeing you."

Karyn inspected herself again in the mirror. She turned sideways, admiring the way the gown draped softly down the back with a fullness that served to accentuate the cinched-in waistline. Her eyes met Celest's in the mirror, and she smiled. "But he probably won't be back in time."

"In that event, my three boys will keep you busy dancing." She motioned to Karyn. "Come. I want to make certain Serge and Remi made enough lemonade."

As Celest and Karyn emerged from the house and headed toward where the men had erected a bowery over the dance "floor" in the front yard, Emile stopped tuning his violin and gave full attention to his wife. Early in the Delhomme marriage, after only a few unhappy drives home, Emile wisely realized that telling his wife she was already beautiful, that insisting she needed no improvements, was totally unsatisfying in light of her careful preparations for dances and literaries. In the interest of marital harmony, he decided it would be worthwhile to make a study of his wife. Thus, the moment Celest arrived at his side, Emile kissed her on the cheek and said, "I have always loved the natural waves in your hair, dear, but these new curls are most attractive. I shall have to watch that old bachelor Fred Smith very closely, or he will be stealing you away from me."

Blushing with pleasure, Celest pushed him away. "Don't be silly, Emile. It's nothing. Karyn insisted I let her try to give me a few curls. I feel rather foolish." She reached up to touch the curls. "Do you really like it? You don't think I'm too old?"

"You, my dear," Emile said softly, putting his arm about her, "will never be old."

Celest patted his hand on her waist and held it there for a moment before turning her attention back to the party. Wagons were beginning to come into view from several directions. Just as Celest said, "The boys had better get the organ out here," Remi and Serge heaved the instrument through the doorway. With Luc's help, they positioned it near the bowery. Luc sat down at the organ, and Emile finished tuning his violin.

Karyn stood next to Celest, surprised at how excited she was as she peered at a wagon approaching from the direction of Millersburg. *It's only Cay,* she told herself. *Mikal told you the drive to Kearney and back would take at least a week. There is very little chance he will be back. And even if he is, he will be too tired to drive so many miles just to see you.*

Even as Karyn Ritter was peering toward Millersburg, Mikal was making his way to his homestead. Unaware of the social at the Delhommes', anxious to know how Karyn had fared for an entire week alone, he had decided to bypass Millersburg completely in favor of a brief stop at his homestead. He drove his team only a half mile to the east of Millersburg, but he missed meeting Cay Miller's buggy heading toward the Delhommes', and he missed reading Cay Miller's notice regarding the dance. Mikal arrived at his homestead near sunset.

When Karyn did not come outside to greet him, a lump rose in his throat. Thinking of Marie-Louise, he called Karyn's name and jumped from the wagon seat. Hurrying down the slope to the corral, he took notice of Ella's calf with a flicker of satisfaction. He stood with his hands on his hips and called for Karyn again and again. Ella walked across the corral and poked her head through the fence. Mikal ignored her, hurrying back up the hill. Finally, he noticed the row of hackberry seedlings by the corral and the cottonwoods near the house. The knot in his stomach relaxed even more when he saw Karyn's new "oven" and the results of her garden plans. *She wants a sod wall like Celest has,* he reasoned, walking along the row of stakes toward the front of the house.

At the doorway of his house, Mikal stopped short. *Plastered, whitewashed walls.* He stepped inside and stopped again. Bending down, he felt the textured surface of the floor. *She mixed clay with straw.* Where had that idea come from? And how had she accomplished so much in such a short time? Examining the walls carefully, he realized that Karyn's inexperienced hands could never have accomplished such an excellent result. A flash of color made him turn his head, and he looked toward the window, smiling at the windowsill now crowded with potted geraniums. Obviously Emile Delhomme had done significantly more than just "look in on" Karyn. The Delhommes had hauled clay in from the buffalo wallow and stayed long enough to plaster the interior walls.

It would be like Celest to insist that Karyn come home with them for a visit. What better time for the two women to get to know one another? What better time for Celest to teach Karyn more about frontier living? Perhaps she would even help with Karyn's English. Heaven knows he had had little opportunity for that. Looking down at the floor, Mikal smiled at yet another example of Karyn's ingenuity. *She may not realize it yet, but she is exactly the kind of woman this county needs.*

As Mikal considered that Karyn was also proving to be exactly the kind of woman that he needed, disappointment set in. He really had been looking forward to seeing her. He stepped outside the sod house and looked toward where Ella lay in the corral, contentedly chewing her cud. Walking to the well, he drew a bucket of water for the team. Then he noticed an extra rope tied to the windlass, running over the edge of the curbing and down into the well. He drew up a bucket containing two well-wrapped rounds of butter. His stomach rumbled, and he took one round out, lowered the bucket back into the well, and headed for the grub box in the wagon. There was still half a loaf of stale bread in the box. Mikal slathered it with butter and ate with relish.

After he had eaten, he watered the newly planted seedlings. Wandering into the dugout barn, he was met with another surprise when he realized that the crude furnishings had been scrubbed. Even the bedding seemed fresh.

His disappointment at Karyn's absence growing, Mikal considered driving to the Delhommes' even as he realized the lunacy of having the team haul a load of lumber such a distance when they had already come many miles farther than necessary. He considered unhitching the team and leaving them overnight while he went to see Karyn. Cay Miller could certainly wait an extra day for the lumber. But his sense of responsibility to Cay finally won out. Going back inside the soddy, he pulled the packets of garden seed he had bought in Kearney out of his pocket and laid them on the table where Karyn would see them. Then, he went back outside and climbed up onto the wagon seat. With a last glance of regret at the empty soddy, he headed back toward Millersburg.

Luc Delhomme claimed the right to the first dance with Karyn. She shook her head. "But I know nothing of these American dances."

"Half the people here will get confused in the middle of Fred's calling and then all will be chaos. But we get better at every dance. I won't let you get too far off." He grabbed her hand and pulled her onto the dance floor. "Come, Karyn. I have to play the organ most of the night. Just one dance."

There was no time to escape. Fred Smith called out, "S'lute ye pardners," and the dance began, with Emile fiddling and Fred stomping and clapping out a rhythm while, with his head thrown back and his eyes closed, he sang in a droning monotone, "J'ine hands and circle to th' left."

Karyn relaxed a little. She understood nothing of what the caller was saying, but by studying the movements of the other dancers she thought she might be able to keep up.

But then Fred called out, "Right hand to yer pardner an' gran' right and left." Luc held out his right hand and pulled Karyn around, where another man took her hand, and thus she and the other women dancers were "passed" around the circle.

Another woman went first when Fred called out, "Lady in the center an' three hands 'round; min' yer feet, fellers, don't tromp on her gown."

Karyn was all set to imitate the first woman, when Fred changed the call to something about "hoe it down" and "caper 'round." She was hopelessly lost, but by then so was everyone else, and the dancers collapsed with laughter.

Fred finally opened his eyes. Surveying the chaos he never missed a beat, but concluded the call of the first dance with, "Ringtailed coons in the trees at play; grab yer pardners and all run away."

Karyn followed Luc's lead and tromped off the dance floor, laughing and gasping for breath.

When Luc went to join the musicians, Karyn rejoined Celest. That was when the trouble began. In spite of the fun of the first couples' dance, the beginning of the Delhommes' social saw Karyn Ritter perched on the very brink of a chasm of feminine rejection.

Frederica G'Schwind and Anna Ohelsberg greeted her cordially in high German, but had to excuse themselves to check on their children. During the first dance, they had both agreed on one thing: Celest Delhomme was expected to have a silk dress. She was, after all, the wife of one of the leading citizens. Karyn Ritter, on the other hand, had no right to flaunt a rose-colored silk gown in the presence of women who did well to manage a clean, unpatched calico.

Neither Julia Ross nor Lizzie Spooner spoke German. But they both spoke "fashion." After Celest translated a few pleasantries, both Julia and Lizzie remembered that they had promised Serge and Remi a dance. As they walked away, Karyn saw them whispering to one another and assumed that she was the subject of some none-too-friendly remarks. She was correct. In spite of the fact that Julia and Lizzie had never been close, they were agreeing on one thing: There were Germans and there were Germans, and apparently that nice Mikal Ritter had chosen an "uppity" German in the vein of Amalia Kruger. Poor Mikal.

Time after time throughout the next few minutes women nodded introductions and then excused themselves. Karyn despaired of her minuscule English vocabulary and grew increasingly frustrated by her dependence on Celest to translate. She took notice when Amalia Kruger looked her up and down and leaned over to whisper something to another elderly woman seated beside her.

When Emile took a break from fiddling to dance with Celest, Karyn escaped and went inside the house and back upstairs. She was struggling to undo the tiny buttons at the back of her gown when Celest found her. "I should never have worn this gown. They think I am a snob." She paused, blinking back tears of frustration.

"Give them time," Celest said, putting a hand on Karyn's shoulder. "I apologize, Karyn. I knew there would be a stir. But, like you, I was hoping that Mikal would come."

Sitting on the edge of the bed, Celest motioned for Karyn to sit down beside her. She took Karyn's hand. "The pleasure of your new husband is much more important than the opinion of other women. You will win the women over. When you can speak better English, they will see for themselves how charming you are. And, in time, they will get over their jealousy. Right now, it is more important to win your husband."

Celest stood up, pulled Karyn up beside her, and began to refasten the myriad tiny glass buttons that ran down the back of Karyn's gown. "Our socials last until dawn. He may yet come." As she fastened the last button, Celest said, "I think God has some very special plans for you and your Mikal, Karyn. Just let Him work." She added, "You have a real man, Karyn. A man after the heart of God. Thank God for him. Cherish him. And win his heart. It will be worth the effort . . . and well worth putting up with a little jealousy from the Julia Rosses and Lizzie Spooners of Custer County."

As the two women got to the bottom of the stairs, people began pouring into the parlor, piling their plates high with generous helpings of potatoes, fried fish, roasted prairie chicken, bread and jam. When two women next to her crowded in and conversed pointedly in English, Karyn filled a plate and slipped out the back door of the house to sit down alone on a bench just outside the door of the lean-to.

"There you are," Luc said from the back door. "Remi and Serge have been looking for you. They want you to try another dance after supper." When Karyn didn't answer, he asked, "Do you mind if I join you?"

Karyn slid over, making room for Luc.

He plopped down beside her. Instead of attacking the plate of food before him, he said quietly, "You may not believe me right now, but most of the people here really are good and kind at heart."

Karyn looked up, surprised, and Luc smiled gently. "I heard Julia and Lizzie talking about you. It seems they cannot see past their jealousy over a silk ball gown." When Karyn didn't say anything, he added, "I do not mean to excuse their behavior, but it probably is difficult to be reminded of all the lovely things they no longer have."

"But I never intended to—" Karyn protested.

"Of course you didn't," Luc said. "And when they have the chance to know you, they will understand that."

"I was hoping Mikal would come."

"And he may yet," Luc said, attacking the chicken leg that lay atop the mound of food on his plate with relish.

For a few moments, Karyn and Luc sat together without speaking. Luc ate heartily. When Karyn feared that he would get up and leave her alone, she asked abruptly, "Did you teach yourself to play the organ?"

When he nodded, she said, "One would never know. Your fingering and sense of timing are excellent. I wish I had had such talent all those years when Mama and Papa insisted I play."

"You didn't tell us you play the organ!" Luc exclaimed.

Karyn shook her head. "I don't. Not as well as you. I took lessons for years and years, but I never sounded half as good as you." She offered shyly, "I had more aspirations with singing."

"You must sing something for us tonight," he insisted. Standing up he said, "I am going for cake. You should get a piece of Mother's beroggie before they are gone. It's the best dessert on the table." He leaned down and whispered, "Russian. It is a family mystery where she learned to make them." He headed for the house. At the door, he turned around to suggest, "Sing a German hymn. That should warm even old Amalia Kruger's cold heart."

It was nearly midnight before Mikal arrived at Cay Miller's. He unhitched his team and led them into the sod stable behind Cay's store, where he found a note tacked to the harness rack: *Dance at Delhommes'. Karyn is there. Ride Buddy. Two new extra-large shirts on bottom shelf behind counter. Choose one.*

It took Mikal about twenty minutes to restock his grub box, scrub himself clean, don the new shirt, and saddle Buddy. If he galloped most of the way, he could get to the Delhommes' shortly after 1:00 A.M. Grateful for the pioneer custom of dancing all night and returning home at dawn, Mikal urged Buddy forward. He envisioned the bowery, the dance floor, the tables laden with food. Supper would already have been served. Mikal didn't really care. He was hungry for only one thing, and that was the sight of Karyn Ritter smiling with pleasure at his surprise appearance. He would commend her work on the homestead, and then—well, he would stop imagining anything beyond that. After all, it had only been a month. But she had agreed to stay longer than a month . . . and she had plastered the walls . . . and planted trees . . . and planned a garden. That could mean anything.

With tremendous effort, Mikal refused to let himself presume the meaning of plastered walls and planted trees. Instead, he made himself think about the next two weeks of work awaiting him in Millersburg. He spent the rest of the ride to the Delhommes' thinking through each step of building Cay Miller's new store.

The supper hour had extended a little past an hour when Emile strode to the bowery, picked up his violin, and began to tune it. When people began to filter back to the dance floor, he played a few measures and then stopped. "Before we begin to dance again, we have the privilege of hearing from our newest citizen, Karyn Ritter."

From where Karyn stood by the door of the house, she could see several women exchange glances.

From behind her, Celest whispered, "Luc has trapped you, Karyn, and it is a good idea." She gave her a little shove. "Go. Sing."

Her heart pounding, Karyn went to stand by the organ. Luc sat down and played an introduction.

Her midsection so tight with terror that she could scarcely breathe, Karyn warbled out a few notes. But then, she closed her eyes, envisioning herself standing among the choir members in the old church at home. She relaxed. The beauty of the music took over. She could breathe, and with the renewed breath, her voice took on its usual richness. She sang out in such a beautiful, clear soprano that even old Amalia Kruger wiped away homesick tears.

Mikal had pulled Buddy to a walk as he approached the Delhommes' house. It was quiet, and he realized that supper must be going on longer than usual. As he dismounted behind the barn, he heard a beautiful female voice singing. Sneaking around to the back of the house and up the stairs, he stood in the shadows of a bedroom peering down at the circle of people gathered about the organ.

As he listened to his wife sing, the excitement he had felt at surprising her came rushing back. Suddenly the organ accompaniment stopped, and there was only Karyn's hauntingly beautiful voice. Mikal looked toward Luc. He was sitting on the little organ stool, his hands on his knees, his eyes on Karyn, drinking in every note. His eyes never left her face. Mikal frowned.

Whatever it was that Mikal saw on Luc's face sent him out of the room, down the stairs, and out the door of the house. He intended to hurry across the yard and make his presence known, but before he could get to the bowery, Karyn had finished singing. People seemed to have decided that "that new German woman" was all right, after all. And who were they to begrudge a pretty girl an evening of dancing in a lovely gown?

Luc pulled Karyn onto the dance floor, fiddles began playing . . . and then Mikal appeared. At the sight of him, Karyn's face flushed with pleasure. But then Mikal grabbed her hand, pulled her away from Luc, and strode off the dance floor, half dragging her behind him. Luc Delhomme shrugged his shoulders and cut in on Serge, finishing the dance with Julia Ross.

The moment they had rounded the edge of the house and reached the backyard, Karyn jerked her hand away from Mikal. "What do you think you are doing?" she demanded, her dark eyes flashing.

"I am your husband, and I will not be humiliated in public while you flirt with Luc Delhomme!"

He's jealous! Hoping it was true, Karyn suppressed her own anger. "I wasn't flirting. Luc encouraged me to sing because he thought it might be a way for me to make amends for wearing this." She rustled her skirt.

Mikal frowned. "What?"

"I wore a silk dress. It made the women jealous."

"The women?" Mikal said stupidly.

"Yes, Mikal, the women." *Good. Now we can both calm down a little.* She tried to explain. "Women compare themselves to one another constantly, and nothing good ever comes of it. Either we end up feeling hopelessly inferior, or we conclude that we are better than others and become prideful."

"What does that have to do with you and Luc?"

"Everyone thought I was trying to show off by wearing a fancy dress. They were not very friendly. Luc and Celest thought that if I sang, it might soften their hearts a little."

"Did it?"

"How could I know? You stormed the dance floor like a jealous schoolboy and dragged me out here before I had a chance to find out."

"I am not a jealous schoolboy! I am your husband!" He gestured angrily, defending his childish behavior. "I think you might be lonely. So I ride for hours to check on you at the homestead. But you are gone. I return to Millersburg, and find the note about the dance. I think you might be happy to see me, so even though I am tired from a long journey, I come. I think you might like to be surprised. But it is I who am surprised. Instead of a wife who misses her husband, I find a woman having a wonderful time with another man."

Karyn stuck her chin out stubbornly. She abandoned her plan to humor him. She began to tremble with emotion. "Apparently you expected to find me at home, pining away for loneliness. If that is your expectation of your wife, Mikal Ritter, you married the wrong woman." She lifted her chin proudly. "Did you see Ella's calf? I can make butter and cheese and sell it. Did you see that I staked out the garden? Did you see your clean bedding? The plastered walls in the house? The new trees? I worked hard for you while you were gone, Mikal." She took a deep breath. "We had an agreement, and I have more than kept it. I thought you would be pleased."

Karyn threw her shoulders back. She stared fearlessly up into Mikal's cold blue eyes and said firmly, "You do not ever have to love me, Mikal Ritter. But you do have to respect me. Never, ever treat me like that again."

She strode away. At the back door of the house, she whirled around and said, "And, for your information, your friend Luc Delhomme gave many hours to the plastering of your home, when he could have been earning money for himself."

Karyn's resolve to not show any more emotion broke down. Hurt tears flooded down her cheeks, and she blurted out, "Also for your information, Herr Ritter, the only reason that I wore this gown was so that I would look nice for you." In a flash of rose-colored silk, she was gone.

Mikal took a deep breath. He called her name, but Karyn had already fled into the house. She didn't come back.

Mikal sat on the bench by the lean-to shed for a long time, impervious to the joyous sounds of music and dancing wafting through and around the huge sod house. Weariness settled over him. He knew that he should find Karyn and apologize. With a sigh he went inside the house and upstairs. From the window of the bedroom he surveyed the dancers below. Nowhere was there a rose-colored dress. Dawn was beginning to light the sky. A few wagons were heading across the prairie.

"She left a little while ago," Celest said, when Mikal finally went outside and asked her. "She didn't want the calf to get all of Ella's milk."

Mikal frowned. "I don't like her being out alone."

"Oh, she didn't go alone," Remi said, walking up behind Mikal. "I thought you went with her, but I guess it must have been Luc." He looked soberly at Mikal and his mother and walked away.

Totally dejected, Mikal saddled Cay's horse and rode southwest toward Millersburg where he would build Cay's new store. He needed time to think. He had to find a way to convince Karyn to stay longer. It wouldn't do to have her leave when things were in such a muddle. He laughed at his own naïveté. He had expected that sharing the workload of homesteading would simplify his life. But there was nothing simple about being husband to a woman he barely knew.

The Diary
April 30, 1880

The disappointment I felt upon my arrival here has been replaced by a determination to succeed. Every day there are improvements. The plastered walls look so clean, and now the inside of the soddy is not so dark. I have a window filled with geraniums. And I have planted a garden. All is work and more work, but I do not mind. I am beginning to understand why those who have come wish to stay. It is very satisfying to know that your days are meaningful. If only accepting disappointment regarding certain people were as easy as adapting to a new house.

CHAPTER 6

Sewing Machine
Needles

Let all bitterness, and wrath, and anger, and
clamour, and evil speaking, be put away from
you, with all malice: And be ye kind one to
another, tenderhearted, forgiving one another,
even as God for Christ's sake hath forgiven you.
Ephesians 4:31–32

During the two weeks following Karyn and Mikal's disagreement at the Delhommes', Karyn began each day by
talking herself out of riding to Millersburg to "settle
things with Mikal." She told herself she was not really
avoiding him, but that she was simply too busy planting
the seeds he had left on her kitchen table to even consider
a ride to town. If Mikal took the initiative and came home
to talk, she would be glad to discuss things.

Her resolve usually weakened early in the afternoon,
but by then she was too tired to ride nine miles. Stabbing
hundreds of holes in the virgin sod had left her with
aching arms. Kneading dough and failing again and again
to create acceptable bread often reduced her to tears.
Milking and churning, and making butter and cheese kept
her so busy that by early afternoon she hoped sincerely
that Mikal didn't come home, because she was too weary
to think.

It was several days before Karyn tried to think through the situation. One evening she settled in her chair beside the kitchen window to knit. As her hands mechanically added row after row to the sock in her lap, she tried to sort things out. While she liked to imagine herself an independent woman, she knew that, in reality, coming to America had not been evidence of an independent nature. Rather, it had been a way for her to run away—from the memory of Hans, from the reality of Anton Gilhoff, from her father's hints about marriage, and from nursing Sophie's varied ailments. *If I were really independent, I would have begun my own business. Instead, I took the first road to America that opened to me.* She laughed at herself. *You wanted to escape the memory of one man and the attentions of another . . . and how do you go about it? By binding yourself in marriage to another man—and a complete stranger, at that!*

Karyn sighed, thinking back to the day when she had first caught the attention of Hans, the youngest son of a wealthy landowner. She and Sophie had been sent on an errand. They were to deliver a precious package of imported spices to a nearby village. They were just outside their own little village when Sophie began to complain.

"Stop, Karyn," she gasped, staggering slightly and slumping to the ground. "I have to—to rest."

Karyn frowned impatiently. "If you didn't want to come, Sophie, why didn't you just tell Papa you didn't feel well back at home?"

Sophie looked up at her with a puzzled expression. "But I wanted to come. I like being with you. And so many interesting people come by on the road—"

At that moment, an exquisite carriage approached from the north. It was drawn by two perfectly matched black horses. Karyn noticed that the horses lifted their snow-white socks in perfect harmony. As the carriage came near, its driver pulled up. He tipped his hat and then removed it before saying, "Could I be of help?" His blue eyes smiled warmly.

Sophie blushed. "Thank you, yes . . . perhaps if you could take us—"

But Karyn interrupted her. "Thank you, sir. Sophie often has these little spells. After she rests for a moment, all will be well. I can walk her home and then complete my errand."

The young man protested, "But you were headed up the mountain, and it will soon be growing dark. Please, let me help you."

Sophie jumped up with surprising energy. "Thank you, sir. You are very kind. If you could perhaps assist me to my home—I am Sophie, Gottlieb Ensinger's daughter. Do you know his shop?" When the young man nodded yes, Sophie blushed prettily and ducked her head. "Well then, if you could perhaps see me home, my sister could complete her errand."

Karyn was horrified by Sophie's boldness and not a little angry at her once again succeeding in simultaneously escaping work and inspiring sympathy. The young stranger jumped down to help Sophie. He took charge of the situation, smiling brilliantly at Karyn while he introduced himself, helped Sophie into his carriage, and headed off toward the village, but not before learning where Karyn's errand would take her.

Karyn smiled, remembering that Hans had delivered Sophie home, refused her invitation to tea, and made his way back up the road to retrieve Karyn and insist that he help her finish her errand before night fell. Arriving at home, Karyn had alighted from Hans's carriage and gone inside, dreading her father's wrath for her brazen acceptance of the attentions of a young man without proper introduction. But to her amazement, her father had seemed pleased when she told him of Hans Gilhoff's kindness. He had silenced his wife's timid protests. "She is nearly a woman, Anna. We must allow her to grow up. To make decisions."

Remembering her father's words, Karyn wondered what he would think of her decision to come to America if he could see the tiny sod hut in Custer County to which she had come. And what would he think of Mikal Ritter in comparison to Hans Gilhoff? Karyn found herself defending Mikal against her father's imagined criticism. Mikal Ritter might seem little more than a rough peasant in comparison to Hans Gilhoff. Still, many good things had resulted from her marrying him.

Karyn stopped answering her father's imagined criticisms and began a mental list of the things she liked about America. There was her friendship with Celest Delhomme. And there was a new sense of accomplishment. At home, she had worked hard executing her mother's plans, meeting her mother's goals. In her own home, she could make decisions and improve things to please herself.

Mikal had given her free rein to do as she pleased about the house and garden, and she liked it. Hans Gilhoff would have expected her to play a preordained role. He would never have let her make so many decisions on her own. Even changing the flowers in one of the many gardens on his estate would have required approval from Anton and the cooperation of the gardener.

Karyn's mind wandered to Celest's comment that God had special plans for her and Mikal. In spite of regular church attendance and confirmation classes, she had spent very little time thinking about God's part in day-to-day life. Still, she liked the idea that God had followed her to Nebraska and was interested in what happened to her.

All the while that Karyn was thinking, she was knitting. Her hands worked mechanically, adding row upon row of stitches while she contemplated her new life. She convinced herself that any difficulties she and Mikal faced could be talked out. Once he came home, she would have calmly assessed the situation, and they could discuss their disagreement and live peaceably.

Karyn sighed and paused in her knitting. The altercation with Mikal at the Delhommes' was probably just because he was tired from his long drive. Yes, they would discuss their disagreement reasonably. And they would live peaceably.

Karyn continued to knit for a few moments when an unwanted memory raised itself to challenge her peaceful view of the future. Looking out into the darkness she remembered a night long, long ago, when Hans Gilhoff had caught her hand and drawn her back toward the carriage. He had given her the sweetest, gentlest kiss. The memory of that kiss created a new knot in Karyn's stomach as she assessed her situation with Mikal Ritter. He seemed to be having no difficulty at all keeping the "husband-in-name-only" part of their agreement. And yet, Karyn knew that Mikal Ritter could not possibly be expected to spend the rest of his life living in the dugout. And she also knew that she could not possibly spend the rest of her life sleeping beside a man who loved someone else. Karyn laid aside her knitting and went to bed.

While Karyn was justifying not riding to Millersburg, Mikal was justifying not driving to his homestead. He told himself that he was too busy. He convinced himself that he owed Cay Miller his every waking moment. But while he was hauling boards and hammering, planing doorways and installing floors, Mikal was thinking and praying about the situation with Karyn.

His motive for going to Grand Island had been to find a suitable partner, a sensible girl with a physique that would hold up to hard work and, if God so willed it, to child-bearing. He congratulated himself on having found a resourceful woman with both the will and the strength to work hard. Karyn had plastered the walls, even thinking of a way to rid herself of the despised dirt floor—and without asking him to spend any money. There were curtains at his window and geraniums blooming in his house. There was fresh butter for his bread, and he had no doubt that Karyn would raise abundant produce in the garden.

He had given little attention to the idea of romance. After all, he reasoned, was it not romance overcoming reason that had resulted in the tragedy of Marie-Louise? Marie-Louise's passion had swept him into a seven-year odyssey of extremes. After days of bliss, something would unexpectedly plunge her into emotional darkness. God forbid that that ever happen again.

But at the Delhommes' social, Karyn had looked so incredibly beautiful. And she sang like an angel. Thinking about it, Mikal forced himself to remember Marie-Louise. He must pray for more self-control in the matter of romance. A steady friendship was a much more sure foundation for a meaningful life.

After days of both mental and physical hard work, Mikal grew eager to get back to his homestead and clarify things with Karyn. They could have a good life together, if she wanted it. And he, Mikal Ritter, was going to make her want it. He owed her an apology for his behavior at the Delhommes'. He would convince her to stay longer. And it was time he told her about Marie-Louise. It might help her understand.

Mikal had the building framed out and was nailing the last floorboard into place when Luc Delhomme rode up.

Luc grinned. "I thought I'd let you calm down before I showed up for work. Cay hired me at the dance. The sooner I can earn money and get to school in Philadelphia, the better I'll like it. Remi and Serge will join us tomorrow. You'll be back with your wife in no time."

Mikal looked at him soberly and thrust out his hand. "Shake my hand and tell me you forgive my stupidity, Luc."

Luc shrugged. "There is nothing to forgive, Mikal. Perhaps I was flirting a little. Can you blame me?" He grinned again. "And by the way, I don't think you have anything to worry about. I only rode back to the homestead with Karyn because I thought I could calm her down. She let me come, but she had absolutely nothing to say, other than to ask a thousand questions about you." He picked up a hammer and a bag of nails as he teased, "I assured her you only experience brief moments of insanity. I think if you show up with a significant peace offering, she may just let you in the door."

Looking up at the sun, Mikal said, "Let's get to work. With you here, maybe I can get home a couple of days early."

When Mikal finally drove into the yard at home, Karyn was inside the soddy wiping down the insides of the crates she used as a pantry. She heard him call her name, but she didn't go to the door. After all her reasoning and logic, she had been ready to begin again—after she asked about Marie-Louise. But then, Mikal had been delayed for another week, and he hadn't even cared enough to come and check on her. He had sent Luc Delhomme to tell her. Luc had been on his way home to visit his mother. But Mikal could not spare a few hours to check on his own wife.

Mikal called her name again. She rattled pans to let him know that she was there and that she was angry. She heard him jump down, heard the sound of something scooting across the bed of the wagon. She rattled her pans more loudly, pretending not to hear. It made her even angrier when she thought she heard him chuckle. She heard him walk to the back of the house. Peeking out the window, she watched him water the team. His broad back was toward her. The veins stood out along his muscular forearms as he lifted a full bucket of water from the well.

She went back to her scrubbing, expecting to hear the wagon headed down to the corral. But the wagon was still standing just outside the doorway. What was he waiting for? Try as she might, Karyn could find nothing else to do inside the little soddy. She went to the door, planning to scoot along the front of the house and disappear from sight. He could look for her if he cared to know where she was. And why should he care? Had he cared that they had parted angry with one another? Had he cared to do something about that?

Karyn stood in the doorway blinking in disbelief at the back of the wagon. Tears stung her eyes. From where he stood at the head of the team, Mikal saw her. He finished watering the horses and took the bucket back to set it on the curb of the well. Then he returned to the wagon, pausing to run his hands across the broad neck of a beautiful bay shire mare. He played with the mare's mane, pulling at imaginary tangles while he waited for Karyn to speak.

It seemed like hours, and Karyn said nothing. Mikal frowned and asked gently, "Is it not a good model, Karyn? Cay Miller said that Celest's machine was a Singer. He thought it was the right one to order." He cleared his throat before explaining, "I sent Luc out here to tell you we had to work a few more days, hoping you wouldn't suspect. The machine didn't come until this morning. Luc offered to come by with an excuse. Then he rode home to check with Celest to make certain Cay had ordered the right one. Luc didn't give away my surprise, did he?"

When Karyn still didn't speak, he worried aloud. "I should have asked you if a Singer would be all right. I thought it would be a good surprise." He walked to the bed of the wagon and began to cover the sewing machine with a tarp. "I can take it back. Cay said that Amalia Kruger was very angry when he told her that I had already bought this one for you. We can let Amalia have it. You can order what you want."

Karyn raised both her hands to her face and burst into tears. "*Ach,* Mikal. *Danke.* It is wonderful." Mikal left off covering up the machine and turned toward her as she said, "I was so angry with you, Mikal. So very angry."

Mikal nodded. "Yes, I know. First I make a fool of myself at your first social here, and then I seem to ignore you for three weeks. I don't wonder that you are angry." He climbed up into the wagon bed. "Let's get the machine unloaded. Then I think we must talk."

"You got your new team," Karyn said, nodding toward the horses. "They are magnificent."

"Yes." He pointed to the mare on the right. "That is Lena. The other beautiful lady is Grace. With their help, I hope to plant double the corn crop I did last year. We can plant melons and pumpkins in with the corn. Emile said it would help keep the deer and antelope out of the fields." He nodded in the direction of the garden. "But first, I will build your sod wall about the garden."

He hoisted the machine to the ground. Karyn opened the lid, running her hand lovingly over the graceful curved arm of the little black machine that popped up into place. "Now I can sew for others. Already Celest has asked that I make her a dress. She was going to have me use her machine, but now that won't be necessary. And knowing Celest, she will let it be known if I do well. Celest said that on your Fourth of July, there is quite a celebration. She thinks I can be very busy making new dresses."

Mikal laughed. "And with all that money you will buy—?"

"Hens. Cay pays almost fifteen cents for each dozen of eggs."

"And with the egg money you will buy?"

"Geese. Then I can make you a fine feather bed." She blushed at her reference to Mikal's bed, which was not also hers, hastening to repeat a German proverb. "*Eine sorgliche Frau fullt das Haus bis unters Dach.*" (A thrifty wife fills the house up to the roof.)

After he had unhitched his new team and turned them into the corral, Mikal positioned the wondrous new sewing machine just outside the front door of the house. When they parted to do their evening chores, Karyn baked bread in her improvised oven and made potato soup. After supper, Mikal went to bed down the team in the dugout. Karyn had just carried a chair outside and positioned it where she could watch the sun set while she knitted when Mikal walked up the hill, his hands in his pockets.

"*Was darf es sein, bitte?*" Karyn asked, starting to get up. "What can I get you?"

"*Bitte setzen Sie sich!*" He waved her back into her chair. "Sit. I thought I would have another cup of coffee. Would you like some?"

"I can get it."

"No. Keep to your knitting. I can make coffee." He made the coffee, then carried another chair outside. Instead of sitting, he put one foot up on the chair and rested his coffee cup on his knee. He sipped coffee for quite a long time before finally saying quietly, "I want to make things right between you and me."

Karyn spoke up. "Thank you again for the wonderful gift. And for the surprise of the garden seeds. It was very thoughtful of you to include some flower seeds. Celest suggested I throw those up onto the roof. She said they would grow and bloom there. Is that true?"

"What?" Mikal asked stupidly. "Oh, the flower seeds. Yes, now that you mention that, I have seen flowers blooming on other roofs." He took a sip of coffee then took a deep breath. "I think it is time that I tell you about something. I could have done so before now, but I didn't want to make more of it than necessary." After another moment of silence, Mikal said quietly, "I told you that I had difficulties in Kansas. Everything I told you was true.

What I did not tell you was that I was married when I lived in Kansas."

Karyn didn't look up from her knitting as she said quietly, "Yes. I know. Amalia Kruger told me about it."

Mikal was dumbfounded. "Amalia Kruger? When?"

"The first time you took me to Millersburg."

"Cay said the Krugers were gone."

"Well, Amalia wasn't. She came into the store while you and Cay were at the blacksmith's and told me all about Marie-Louise."

Mikal sat down. He set his coffee cup in the dirt beside his chair and leaned forward, his elbows on his knees. "But why didn't you say something?"

Karyn shrugged. She didn't look at him, but concentrated on her knitting as she said carefully, "As you said, why make more of it than is necessary? You don't owe me an explanation of your past life."

Mikal leaned back in his chair. "I can imagine what you heard from Amalia Kruger." He tapped his foot. "You deserve to know the truth." After a brief pause, he began, "I met Marie-Louise Jacquot in Paris when I was serving in the army of occupation. Against the will of her parents and the advice of my fellow German officers, we were married in secret and fled together to America. On the ship, we fell in with a wonderful group of people called Mennonites. Even though my family was not religious and Marie-Louise was a devout Catholic, we were both drawn into their circle of love. When we landed in America, it was only natural that we stay with them."

Karyn gave up all pretense of knitting as Mikal spoke. He told her exactly the same story that Amalia Kruger had whispered—without emphasizing his emotional despair. She detected no emotion at all in his voice when he recounted the details of Marie-Louise's death. Only once did he pause in the telling, and that was to refill their coffee cups.

"After Marie-Louise died, I fled north into Custer County and filed on my three claims, never intending to be anything but a hermit for the rest of my days. I lived very much like a wild animal for the first year. The second year, I ventured into Millersburg more often. Cay Miller took great pains to be kind to me. Eventually, I grew to think of him as my friend. One day, he introduced me to Emile Delhomme."

Mikal chuckled and rubbed the back of his neck. "My hair was past my shoulders, and I hadn't bothered to wash or comb it in weeks. I don't imagine I smelled very pleasant. But Emile put his hand on my shoulder and looked into my eyes with such kindness—" Mikal's voice wavered. He cleared his throat. "Two days after I met him, Emile came riding up to my little dugout with Luc. I was, to say the very least, not a very good host. But they didn't seem to notice. They brought me a pie from Celest. Then they lured me to their house for dinner with the promise of more pie." He laughed softly. "Even an animal can be lured with food. They didn't ask me to talk. They just fed me and sent me home. After that, I slowly came back to life. Then came the long winter I have told you about. It was at once the most difficult and the best winter of my life."

Karyn had been trying to avoid looking at him, but when he paused she finally gathered courage to look up at him. He was staring toward the horizon, and the golden light of dusk reflected in his blue eyes, giving them an unusual warmth. Karyn looked away just as he glanced at her. She bent to set her own coffee cup on the earth and took up her knitting as Mikal continued.

"Right before the first blizzard I had been to the Delhommes'. Celest succeeded in getting me to let her cut my hair. When I left, I had a German Bible tucked under my arm. When the blizzard hit, I had nothing to do for days on end but sit out the storm. Tending the fire in the stove was a constant job. And as I tended the stove, I began to read. It changed me." He pointed to his heart. "In here. I began to feel alive in a new way. I read that God loved me. I began to make a mental list of questions to ask Celest and Emile as soon as I could get to their house." He laughed. "Of course, it was weeks at a time between visits with them. But they answered many questions. Many they could not. Still, I found a new peace. I began to feel human again and to want something to end the desperate loneliness." He paused and looked at Karyn. The sun had set. She was listening attentively, her knitting needles lying in her lap.

Mikal stepped toward her and put his hand on the back of her chair. "You can't see to knit. Let's go inside."

"No," Karyn said softly. "Let's just stay out here. The stars are so beautiful."

From where he stood behind her chair, he apologized. "I'm sorry you had to hear about Marie-Louise from Amalia Kruger. I didn't tell you sooner because it is part of a past I have put to rest." His voice was sincere as he half whispered, "I can imagine that Amalia spoke of Marie-Louise in very glowing terms. Amalia was very fond of her." He paused before saying, "But life with Marie-Louise was not always the symphony of joy that Amalia probably described. Living with someone who is mentally unbalanced is its own kind of hell. In some ways, it was a blessing that Marie-Louise was taken when she was. I think she would have gone completely mad if she had not died that day."

"Mikal," Karyn said quietly, turning to look up at him, "I have been angry with you about something of which I myself am guilty. I was not married before. But there was—someone. His name was Hans Gilhoff. He died in the army."

"I see." That was all Mikal said. He took his hand from her chair and sat down again opposite her. It was dark now, and Karyn found herself wishing that she could see his blue eyes more clearly as she explained. "I didn't tell you any lies. There really is an Anton Gilhoff, and my father really did want me to marry him. And that really is why I came to America."

"This Hans Gilhoff," Mikal asked softly. "He is still in your heart?"

Karyn answered firmly. "*Nicht im geringsten.* I have a new life here in America."

"Then I don't need to wonder about Hans Gilhoff, and you no longer need to wonder about Marie-Louise. Now, about my behavior at the Delhommes'—"

Karyn interrupted him. "I'm sorry if I appeared to be flirting, Mikal. Regardless of whether or not we continue as husband and wife, I would never do anything to dishonor you before your friends. It won't happen again."

Mikal put his hands on his knees and pushed himself up. His voice was almost playful as he said, "I know. I made it clear to Luc that unless he knows how to play the organ with broken fingers, he will remember that your last name is Ritter." He said good night and stepped away from her. Karyn could hear him whistling softly as he walked down the hill to the dugout.

The next morning, Karyn was awakened by an unfamiliar sound just outside the soddy. She got up and dressed quickly. Going to the doorway, she saw Mikal drive a posthole digger into the earth. He explained, "The wind I cannot stop, but the sun—that I can manage a little." He spent the next two days erecting a large porch to cover both the doorway and the spot where Karyn had said she would like her sewing machine.

The weather was unusually cool the evening that Mikal laid the last piece of sod on the porch roof. Karyn said they would eat inside. When Mikal finally came in for supper, the rough-hewn table had been covered with a fine lace tablecloth on which sat two china plates with matching cups and saucers. The small tabletop was crowded with two platters, one piled high with blina pancakes, the other with sausage. There was even a pie. Karyn had donned her best apron. She stood waiting to pour his coffee from the fine china pot that had been repacked into her trunk the day of her arrival.

Mikal paused at the doorway. He looked down at his filthy overalls and back at Karyn. Without a word, he hurried off to the dugout. Karyn waited for only a few moments before he reappeared, his face scrubbed, his muscular frame crowded into a rumpled suit.

As they sat down at the table to eat, Karyn sighed happily. It already seemed that she had lived a lifetime on this treeless prairie where even the smallest things, like a nice dinner, required exhausting effort. Looking across the table at Mikal Ritter, she thought to herself, *This is my husband . . . mein mann.* And she decided that the exhausting effort that brought Mikal to her table looking so handsome was quite worth it.

Her new sewing machine expanded Karyn's world far beyond Emile and Celest Delhomme into the varied ethnic groups who conducted their business in the growing settlement of Millersburg. As soon as Cay Miller let it be known that a seamstress resided only nine miles away, women began making the drive out to the Ritters' to visit. Karyn soon learned that visiting and socializing were quite common, even when "dropping in" required a few hours' drive across the prairie.

Most of her visitors wanted Karyn to sew for them. If they didn't speak German, Karyn communicated with smiles and gestures. She nodded and sketched, and the women smiled back at her, refusing to allow such a little thing as a language barrier stand between themselves and a new dress.

Karyn was paid with everything conceivable except

actual money. In addition to many new phrases in English, she acquired two cats, several yards of shirting, more flower seeds, some blood sausages and cheeses, and an extra feather tick. By mid-June Karyn had learned to measure in miles and inches instead of kilometers and centimeters. She had acquired a basic understanding of simple English and orders for eleven dresses to be made before the Fourth of July celebration in Millersburg.

Cay Miller delivered a letter from home (they had celebrated her birthday and hoped that she had had some chocolate) and expressed interest in having her make shirts for him to sell in his store. Karyn insisted that he stay and eat supper with her and Mikal. After Cay left and Mikal went down the hill to the dugout, she took time to sit down and answer the letter from home. She took a kerosene lamp outside and used her sewing machine as a desk.

I did not have chocolate. In fact, I did not tell Mikal it was my birthday, so the day passed unnoticed. But save your pity. If we had everything all the time, we would not know how good things were. Really, I am having the best time in the world. I have progressed with my English. If my customers speak slowly and use simple words, I understand. But I must learn more. It is so annoying to be in Millersburg and to stand like a clockhead and be unable to answer when the women try to include me in their chatter. I think I may ask Mikal and Celest to speak only English so that I am forced to learn more quickly.

I can earn $1.50 in American funds in only one day with my sewing machine, all of which Mikal insists that I keep for the needs of the house as I see them. When we get a fine house and one hundred acres under cultivation, I would not trade with anyone. Mikal is kind. He is very tall, with black hair and blue eyes.

97

Karyn looked up from her letter and stared off toward the horizon. Pondering Mikal's blue eyes reminded her of the thing she was learning to suppress. It had been raising its head more and more often of late, and Karyn was growing impatient with herself. It was obvious that Mikal Ritter had selected a wife to be his partner in achieving a successful homestead. He had not chosen for love, and he had promised that they would be husband and wife in name only. He appeared to be having no difficulty keeping that promise.

Karyn scolded herself for lapsing once again into a state of contemplating Mikal Ritter's considerable physical attractions. She finished her letter home, reporting on Nebraska with glowing terms, stating that, if only Sophie had had the strength to accompany her sister to the new land, she would undoubtedly find herself enjoying vastly improved health.

The Diary
June 5, 1880
   Mikal has come home now and things will be better between us. We have had a good talk. Oma would be pleased to know that I have used her teapot. And Mama's tablecloth as well. Even in a soddy, one can enjoy nice things.

CHAPTER 7

A Methodist Prayer Book

She stretcheth out her hand to the poor; yea, she reacheth forth her hands to the needy.
Proverbs 31:20

Karyn was inside the soddy one afternoon when she heard the now-familiar cadence of Sugar galloping up to the house. Mikal had made a hurried trip into Millersburg to have the blacksmith repair a harness ring.

"Do you want to ride along?" he had asked pleasantly.

Karyn had declined. "No, if I have time I must get Frau Zoerb's dress finished. I still have seven to make before the celebration. But you can bring me two spools of thread. And there are four pounds of butter in the well for Cay."

Later in the day, Mikal came galloping back. He reined in Sugar and slid down, speaking hurriedly, "Karyn, I have brought you some sewing. But this customer is very proud, and we must be unusually creative in finding a way for him to pay. He has nothing. His wife is gone, and he has two children. They are dressed in rags, and there is no money. Cay Miller made one of his mathematical errors when he prepared the bill. This resulted in him owing the customer the price of a bolt of cloth, but—" Karyn smiled as Mikal described yet one more example of Cay Miller's generosity.

Mikal had no more time for explanations, for just outside the soddy, Karyn could see a thin young man climbing down wearily from a wagon. As Mikal introduced her, Karyn stared at the wagon, wondering how it had possibly held together for the nine-mile drive from Millersburg. The wonder of the wagon was exceeded only by the wonder that the two nags pulling it had not collapsed. But it was the sight of two pairs of eyes peering at her over the wagon box that almost made Karyn cry. When their father called to them, the children slithered over the edge of the wagon box and stood barefoot, looking shyly at Karyn.

As the young man introduced himself, he put his hands affectionately on each child's shoulder, "Sten, Tilda. Greet Mrs. Ritter." Sten and Tilda nodded at Karyn and mumbled something she took for a greeting.

Karyn smiled back at them as their father explained, "Their Ma died last winter. We're headed back east. Can't seem to make a go of it on my place, not without Anna. You can see the children are kinda' poorly. I traded in my tools at Miller's. Got a couple sacks of flour, some coffee, a bolt of calico. Miller said you might be able to make a new dress for Tilda. A shirt or two for Sten. Something fittin' for the trip back east." He swallowed hard. "I got to get them better fixed up before I take 'em to see their ma's folks. They didn't like her marryin' out of the clan." He smiled bitterly. "I thought they was just bein' proud Swedes thinkin' they was better than a boy born and raised in good old Kentucky." He looked at the dirt as he mumbled, "Maybe they was right." He swallowed again, then looked up at Karyn, his eyes pleading. "Their Anna died having their third grandchild."

Karyn understood almost nothing of the stranger's words, but seeing his hand placed gently on the shoulders of the too-thin children, hearing the brave desperation in his voice, she understood all that was necessary.

Without waiting for Mikal to translate the details of the

stranger's speech, Karyn took the bolt of cloth from the man's hands and nodded. "*Ja.* I sew. For Tilda. For Sten." She smiled down at the children. "My name is Karyn." She urged the stranger, "Come. Eat. Sleep. Tomorrow I sew."

The stranger spoke up. "I can't pay money for—"

Karyn shook her head. "No pay."

The man turned to Mikal. "You got any work I can do?"

Mikal looked perplexed. Certainly there was no lack of work on the homestead, but the stranger's team was in no condition to be plowing. Indeed, the stranger himself appeared near the end of his own strength. Mikal hesitated.

Inspiration struck. Karyn knelt down before the girl. "Tilda?" The girl nodded, managing a shy smile. Karyn asked, "You speak English, *ja*?"

Tilda giggled. "Of course I speak English. My ma was a schoolteacher. She grew up speaking Swedish, but she knew English better than most Americans."

Tilda's father said proudly, "I never had time for learnin', but my Anna was a real scholar. She taught the young'un's real good."

Karyn looked up at him. "You have English. I want English." She pointed to the girl. "You teach." She pointed to herself. "I sew." She looked up at Tilda's father. "Is good trade. *Ja*?"

Tilda pulled at her father's sleeve. "We still have Ma's Bible, Pa. I could use it to teach Mrs. Ritter, just like Ma did when she taught Sten and me. I remember how she did it."

Sten spoke up. "Me, too. I'll help."

Tilda's father looked from Karyn to Mikal, who nodded and winked at the stranger. He accepted the arrangement. "That's fair. Sten and Tilda will teach you as much as they can."

Karyn stood up and laid the bolt of cloth on her sewing machine. She held out her hands toward Tilda and Sten. With a glance toward their father, the children took Karyn's outstretched hands and followed her inside the soddy where they overwhelmed Karyn with their willingness to help and their eagerness to impart fluency in English before the evening meal was fully prepared.

The sun had barely sunk below the horizon when a well-fed and well-scrubbed Tilda and Sten Stoddard slithered between two thin blankets that had been spread over a thick layer of hay, which their father laughingly called "prairie feathers."

Through Mikal, Karyn tried in vain to convince Doane Stoddard to move the sleeping children into her bed. He insisted they were already accommodated in a far better fashion than they expected. Karyn relented until the men bid her good night, Mikal to the dugout and Doane to his own bed of "prairie feathers" in the dilapidated wagon bed. She watched the men disappear into the darkness. Then, she went inside and folded back the two quilts that covered her feather tick. She was amazed at how light Tilda and Sten were. It took little effort to lift them into her bed. She took great satisfaction in watching as, fast asleep, they snuggled into the depths of the feather tick.

The first morning of the Stoddards' stay on the Ritter homestead, Mikal took Karyn aside. Nodding toward Sten and Tilda, he whispered, "They are too thin. They need rest and good food. Their father and I are going hunting. There is no hurry with the sewing." The two men departed on a hunting excursion that day.

That first day, Karyn washed Sten's and Tilda's hair. It took the greater part of the morning to gently untangle and de-mat Tilda's waist-length, thick brown hair. When it was finally done, Karyn presented a wide-eyed Tilda with two lovely ribbons for each of her long braids. The child was speechless with delight.

After lunch, it was Sten's turn. He shuddered when the cold well water was poured over his head, but sat patiently while Karyn washed and cut his shaggy hair. What emerged from the session were two quite attractive children.

By their second day on the homestead, the children were accompanying Karyn everywhere. When she weeded her garden, Tilda and Sten each took a row. When Karyn fed the livestock, Tilda and Sten shoveled manure out of the corral. Karyn learned words like *garden, hoe, horse,* and *cow.* But even with the children's help at chores, Karyn found no time for sewing their new clothing that day. Patting the bolt of cloth, she shook her head and sighed with mock regret. "Maybe tomorrow."

That evening, Tilda produced her mother's Bible, opened it to Genesis 1:1, and began to instruct Karyn in the reading of the English language. With the dust in the yard as a blackboard and a stick for chalk, Karyn learned to read and write, "In the beginning, God created the heaven and the earth." Long after Sten and Tilda were asleep that night, Karyn sat by the lamp turning the pages of the Bible and searching for words she could recognize.

Mikal and Doane were gone for several days. By the time they returned, Doane's horses had begun to regain their strength. He was thrilled to see them trotting about the corral, neighing loudly as he and Mikal rode up. The trip had also had its effects on Doane. He climbed down from Mikal's horse, laughing with delight as Sten and Tilda ran up and embraced him.

Karyn watched the children greet their father, her face wreathed in smiles. She called out in English, "You have good children, Mr. Stoddard. They teach me to talk like real American." Having spoken the two sentences she had practiced over and over again, Karyn found herself once again fumbling for words.

Karyn greeted Mikal in German. She blushed with the realization that she had almost followed the children's example. She had almost run to Mikal, almost thrown her arms about him. She reached up to swipe her flushed cheeks with her open palms and turned to go inside and begin preparations for a feast of wild game.

Mikal and Doane worked most of the next day oiling and repairing harnesses. Karyn unrolled Cay Miller's donated bolt of cloth and began to plan her sewing for Tilda and Sten. Lessons in English continued throughout each day. Karyn added words like *sewing machine, calico, scissors,* and *dress* to her ever-expanding English vocabulary.

At the end of the week, Mikal announced that he and Doane would be going on another trip, this time in search of fence posts to replace the sod wall around the corral. While they were gone, Karyn took apart one of her own skirts, which she insisted was worn beyond repair, thereby managing to create a brown calico dress with pink trim and a pink calico dress with brown trim for Tilda. She teased Sten, threatening to sew pink cuffs onto one of his shirts.

When Mikal and Doane returned ten days later with their load of lumber, they dug postholes and fenced the corral. They moved the sod from the corral and built the wall around Karyn's garden.

The men drove into Millersburg. On their trip they had used deer meat to lure and poison three wolves. Mikal insisted that since Doane was the one who devised the successful scheme, he was the rightful recipient of the bounty, which amounted to $2.50 for each pelt. The money provided lumber to repair Doane's wagon and supplies for the drive east.

Karyn grew less shy about speaking English. She was fanatical about pronunciation, wanting to rid herself as much as possible of any accent.

Finally, Doane Stoddard announced that they must leave. "Do you think you can have Sten's shirts finished soon?"

At mention of the sewing, Karyn admitted, "Oh, except for a few buttons, the sewing has been finished for a while." She looked at Mikal for support. "Can you not stay for the Fourth of July celebration? I want everyone to meet my English teacher." She grinned at Tilda and tugged at one of her long braids.

Doane was resolute in his insistence that they leave.

Karyn smoothed her apron and said softly, "I can do the buttons tomorrow morning." She fought back tears as she looked at Tilda and Sten. "We will miss you."

Doane stood up. "And we won't never forget you." He cleared his throat awkwardly. "We stayed on longer than we planned. And now we're mended." He held out his hand to Mikal. "You done us all a heap of good and we thank you."

The next day came too soon. Tilda climbed up beside her father on the newly constructed seat of their repaired wagon. Their meager supplies had been added to by Mikal, who insisted that Karyn's sewing was not ample pay for all the work that both Doane and the children had done during their stay.

Finally, Doane clucked to his team and the wagon pulled out of the yard. Karyn, who had determined not to cry at their departure, complained to Mikal about the dust in her eyes and headed for the well to rinse them out. She turned her back as the Stoddard wagon faded into the distance, only to hear Tilda calling her name. When she turned about, Tilda was running toward her, something clutched in her hand.

"We—all of us—we want you to have this. Please. It will help with your English." She lowered her voice before adding, "And it will help you to remember us." Impulsively, Tilda kissed Karyn on the cheek, thrusting something into her hand. She was gone in a flash of brown-and-pink calico. As the Stoddard wagon disappeared into the distance, Karyn stood in the yard of her dirt house, crying softly and clutching a prayer book, the inside cover of which identified it as the property of "Anna C. Stoddard."

The Diary
June 30, 1880

I am speaking English like a good American now, although I will continue my diary in German. It feels more comfortable. Two dear children who stayed with us for a few weeks taught me. They left this morning, and how I miss them. They gave me their mother's prayer book, my first book in English. My garden is fenced. How odd that I have been here now for weeks and weeks, and yet I know my husband no better. We see one another in passing from one chore to the next, but there is little time to talk. Perhaps now that the Stoddards have left us, things will be different.

CHAPTER 8

A Photograph of Four Girls

Withhold not good from them to whom it is due,
when it is in the power of thine hand to do it.
Proverbs 3:27

Sophie. Karyn could not believe it. The very morning that Doane Stoddard headed his wagon off toward the southeast, Cay Miller drove in from the southwest bearing fragile cargo in the form of Karyn's younger sister Sophie. Even as Cay jumped down to help Sophie, Karyn blinked in disbelief. Even with Sophie sitting at the breakfast table, delighting Cay and Mikal with her spirited account of the long trip from Brandenburg to America and across America by train to Kearney, Karyn could scarcely believe it.

"So there I was in Kearney," Sophie was saying in nearly flawless English, "alone and feeling completely lost. No train. I think, *What shall I do?*" She smiled brightly. "But then along came Mr. Hawks."

Cay nodded and looked at Mikal. "And can you believe it? She actually convinced Judson Hawks to bring her, even though he didn't have a full load of freight yet."

Sophie winked at Mikal. "We women have our ways of getting what we want." Sophie's soft accent changed the *w*'s to *v*'s as she spoke. Still, Karyn was amazed at her seeming ease with English.

Karyn rose from the table and slipped outside. She drew water for coffee and set the pot on the fire. It was a good way to get the time to collect herself, for Karyn was less than delighted by Sophie's sudden appearance. Sophie was petite and fragile-looking. Men had always been attracted to her golden hair and sparkling blue eyes. She had a way of affecting childish innocence that made them want to protect her. And now, her soft accent made her seem even more vulnerable. Sophie had flawless skin. Karyn regretted having forgotten to wear a bonnet the day before. She was sunburned, and freckles had begun to break out on the backs of her hands. Sophie had a dimpled smile and charming self-assurance that made it easy for her to talk with anyone. Why, already her storytelling had so fascinated Cay and Mikal, they had taken no notice at all that Karyn was outside alone.

As she stood over the fire in the front yard, listening to the sound of Mikal's laughter, Karyn admitted to herself that she had always resented that dimple in Sophie's cheek. Oh, just a little bit, to be sure. But resent it she did.

"Karyn." Sophie stood in the doorway of the house, coffee cup in hand, looking very stern.

"Yes, Sophie. What is it?"

"You are doing the work, and you have not asked for help." She stepped outside, followed by Mikal and Cay.

Karyn ignored Sophie, nodding instead toward Cay. "Thank you for bringing Sophie to me, Mr. Miller. America has held many surprises for me, but to have my little sister arrive in such a way—that is the greatest of all surprises." Wiping sweat from her brow with the back of her hand, she drew the coffeepot off the fire. "Your coffee is ready now."

Cay looked honestly regretful as he said, "Thank you, but I must be getting back and open my store, or the people of Millersburg will be gossiping. Amalia Kruger saw me driving out of town with this lovely girl at my side." He chuckled. "I can imagine the rumors she has begun already."

Sophie thanked Cay, offering her pale, tiny hand even as she looked up at Mikal and said, "I must apologize to you, brother-in-law, for arriving unannounced." She looked behind her at the soddy, barely hiding her disdain as she added, "I will only require a tiny corner of space for a very short time. I hope to begin a dressmaking business in Millersburg."

"Nonsense, Sophie," Mikal insisted. "You and Karyn will share the house. I have plenty of room in the dugout."

When Mikal pronounced *dugout*, Sophie glanced toward Karyn with a questioning look. It was not a word that her language instructor at home had included in her lessons.

Cay snorted. "You'd better get busy building onto the house, Mikal. I remember how you were the spring after that second winter of blizzards." He looked toward Karyn, smiling wisely. "If you want a sane husband, Mrs. Ritter, you will talk him out of taking up residence in that dugout." He turned toward Mikal. "I will provide a window and lumber for the roof on credit—as a welcome gift to our newest citizen." He helped Mikal haul Sophie's massive flat-topped trunk into the house and then, with a flourish, kissed Sophie's hand and left.

The moment Cay drove off, Mikal headed toward the corral.

"Where is he going?" Sophie whispered, slipping back into German.

"When did you learn English, Sophie?" Karyn asked.

Sophie smiled. "You must know that I could never go for long without my dear sister in my life, Karyn. As soon as you left for America, I badgered Papa until he agreed to hire an English tutor. I knew I would be coming to America soon, and I worked hard to learn as quickly as possible."

Karyn nodded. "You always were a good student,

Sophie. And now that we are in America, we will speak English."

With a slight frown, Sophie nodded and answered in English, "All right. As long as you are here to explain new words. This word *dugout*. What is that?"

"I'll show you in a little while," Karyn explained. "Look down the hill and you can see the edge of the corral. Just around the edge of the bluff there is a barn—well, a dugout, actually. In the side of the hill." She led Sophie inside the soddy. "We don't have a word for it in German. You will see. But first, you must unpack."

Sitting on the wooden edge of the box-type bed, Sophie surveyed the inside of the house with mournful eyes. "Oh, Karyn, it isn't at all like you wrote. I should never have come. Do you think Mikal will build another room soon?"

Karyn was defensive. "It is different from Brandenburg, but we have a good start. I would never think of asking Mikal to leave off his work right now. We manage just fine, and you will, too. Why, in ten years—"

"In ten years you will be a dried-up old woman. Just look at your hands, Karyn. Why, they used to be as white as mine, and now—"

Karyn retorted, "Mikal says that in ten years he will have the finest farm in Custer County." Karyn's brown eyes flashed. "He has faith in God, faith in himself, and faith in his Nebraska soil. And so do I. I'm not afraid of hard work."

Sophie's beautiful blue eyes narrowed a little. "You know, Karyn, you were not really truthful about things in your letter. Your house is not at all what I imagined. You said it was small . . . but I never imagined this—this house of—"

"Sod, Sophie. The house is called a soddy. The men use something called a breaking plow. They slice up the top layer of earth and then lay the slices atop one another. Just like a brick house, only better for Nebraska."

Sophie pronounced the word *soddy*. Lifting her eyes to the rafters above she shook her head gently. Then, her expression changed as she teased, "Your house is not at all what I imagined. Nor is your husband." She smiled slyly. "Although that part of your little deception is better in reality than in your letters. You wrote that he is tall, and you mentioned black hair and blue eyes. But you said nothing of how handsome he is." She turned around to smooth the bed pillows. "I can see exactly how it is that you have managed to bear it here. And I do not think it is because of the hope of a nice home in ten or so years."

Karyn shook her head. "Mikal and I are friends, Sophie. Partners." She looked away, feeling her cheeks turn crimson as she said, "He would never take advantage."

Sophie pondered for a moment. Her eyes widened. "I see," she half whispered. "Then you haven't . . . you don't . . ."

Karyn turned away and opened Sophie's trunk, surveying the contents with disapproval. "Didn't you read any of the immigrant guides, Sophie?"

"Of course I read them." Sophie added, "But I also read your letters about the wonders of America and your homestead. I read about the dances and your good neighbors, the Delhommes, and about the beauty of the spring flowers."

"I also mentioned gardening and soap-making, Sophie. Did you expect to do those things wearing these?" Karyn asked, lifting the third silk dress from the trunk.

Sophie drew her bow-shaped lips into a pout. "Of course I know you can't wear silk every day. But I thought there would be a department store here for everyday things. I thought they might not have nice silk, so I brought that and planned on buying whatever else I needed. Papa sent a generous amount of money to get me started. I thought you would be pleased." She whined. "I even brought you a new silk dress. The blue one is for you."

Karyn thanked her. "It's lovely, Sophie. But, really, didn't you bring any practical clothing besides your traveling suit?"

"I brought my best apron," Sophie offered hopefully. "And a shawl, and felt boots for when it gets cold. And Mama sent two fur mitts for winter."

Winter, Karyn thought. *She speaks of winter when Mikal has not even asked me to stay through winter.* Karyn shook her head in dismay. "Well, perhaps we can cut down my plaid dress enough to fit you."

"But that's too much work for you, Karyn. And besides, plaid doesn't suit me. That golden stripe will make my skin look green. Tomorrow we can go to Mr. Miller's store and buy some dress fabric." Sophie hesitated. "I realize he has no finished goods for women, but surely he has fabric."

Karyn shook her head. "Calico is thirty-five American cents a yard, Sophie. It would cost nearly four dollars to buy buttons and cloth for a new dress. We don't have means to go to Miller's and buy dress fabric."

"But I do," Sophie argued. "I told you Papa was very generous."

"You also said that you are hoping to start a business. How much do you have?"

"After I paid Mr. Hawks for bringing me to Millersburg, I still have nearly twenty dollars."

"To rent a room in Millersburg—if you can find one—to buy a sewing machine and a few sewing supplies—this will take more than twenty dollars, Sophie."

Sophie looked up, enthusiasm shining in her eyes. "Oh, that won't matter. Cay Miller offered a window and lumber on credit for an addition to this miserable hut." She raised her blue eyes to meet Karyn's gaze. "Surely he would extend credit to pay for one new dress." Her mouth was set. It was a familiar expression. Sophie Ensinger was going to get her way, and that was that.

Karyn shook her head, determined to be just as stubborn as Sophie. "No. We do not buy things we don't need, Sophie. Cay Miller's generosity allows credit sometimes. But Mikal is determined to reserve credit for emergencies. He would feel responsible for your debt, too. He is my husband, and I will obey him. We are not going into debt to buy you a dress."

Sophie's lower lip protruded in the severe pout that had always succeeded in bringing matters her way. But instead of giving in and finding a way to grant Sophie's wish, Karyn was rankled by the attempt to manipulate. She said firmly, "In another week or so, I will have enough butter and eggs to afford fabric for a dress. Until then, you can wear the plaid dress. If we work together, I think we can finish the alterations tomorrow."

Sophie wheedled, "But you only have three dresses, Karyn. I can't ask you to make such a sacrifice for me." She reached for her little bag, and withdrew a small roll of bills. "Please. Just this once. Can't we go into Millersburg—"

"I have been in America for three months, Sophie. I have been to Millersburg twice. Once when I arrived, and once with Mikal. We do not go to town on a whim. Besides, I am making dresses for several of the women for the Fourth of July celebration. I have too much work to do to take an entire day to go to Millersburg."

"The Fourth of July?" Sophie asked.

Karyn explained, "The day when the Americans celebrate the beginning of their country. Mikal says it is the biggest party of the year. Even bigger than Christmas."

Somewhat mollified by the prospect of a party so soon after her arrival, Sophie calmed down.

Karyn had continued to unpack the trunk as they talked. With the exception of Sophie's hair combs and apron, a feather tick and a few books, her possessions were, like Karyn's, not suited to life in a soddy. Karyn ran her hands lovingly over one of the books. "I'm glad you brought this," she said softly. "I will enjoy reading it again."

Sophie teased, "I remember you sitting on the front step pretending to read that book. What you were really doing was waiting for Hans Gilhoff to drive by."

Karyn sighed. "Yes, poor Hans." She surveyed the pile of things on the bed. "We must repack these things. Then you can see the dugout where Mikal spent his first two winters." Karyn smiled. "And you will realize that our little sod house is an improvement."

When the trunk was once again nearly filled with Sophie's treasures from Germany, Karyn asked, "Could we use your trunk for a table over by the stove?"

Sophie was hesitant. "What if the wooden slats across the top make things tip? Something might seep inside and ruin my things."

"I'll make a flat cover out of some crates Mikal has out back," Karyn explained. "The trunk will just be a base." She was already positioning the trunk near the stove. She stood up and smiled happily. "In fact, this will also make a good cutting table. I won't have to move my sewing so often. I can leave the kitchen table outside."

"But then we will have to eat outside," Sophie protested.

Karyn nodded briskly. "Of course. It was cool enough this morning when you came to eat in the kitchen. But most of our eating and as much cooking as possible is done outside. It keeps the house cooler." She smiled. "Did you notice that even my sewing machine is outside? Sophie, you will get so much good, fresh air here, I am certain your health will improve. You will be the owner of your own business in Millersburg in no time." Enthused by the thought of Sophie living in Millersburg, Karyn added, "You won't regret coming to America, Sophie."

Karyn rolled up her feather tick and headed for the door. "Come and see the rest of the homestead." On the way down the slope to the corral, Karyn pointed out her seedling trees. "Mikal was gone for three weeks. He hauled lumber from Kearney and then built Cay's new store.

While he was gone, the Delhommes helped me plaster the inside of the house and make a floor that I can sweep. I transplanted seedlings from the bank of the creek." As she spread the feather tick on the corral fence she said proudly, "Mikal was very surprised when he got back and saw what I had accomplished."

Sophie was amazed. "You mean it looked even worse than this when you first came. And you stayed here? Alone? Weren't you frightened?"

Karyn shook her head. She leaned against the corral fence for a moment as she spoke. "I was a little nervous the first night, but I soon became accustomed to the sounds of the various night creatures. The nights really are lovely here. The sun goes down and the sky is a rainbow of peach, then apricot, then there is the most stunning violet . . . and then the moon and the evening stars appear. The air is cooled, and more stars appear overhead like a vast garden of diamonds." She joked, "Of course, I was reassured by having Mikal's rifle with me."

Sophie nodded. "Then he knew not to worry about you."

Karyn grinned mischievously. "Oh, I didn't think it was necessary for him to know everything about me right away. I told him Papa likes to hunt, and I left it at that."

Sophie laughed. "Well, I hope I am there when he discovers that you are probably a better shot than he is."

Karyn led Sophie inside the tiny dugout.

"He lived in here for two entire winters?" Sophie looked about her in disbelief. Karyn nodded proudly.

Sophie shivered. "I would have gone mad." She headed for the doorway and the sunlight, promising herself that she would have her business established in Millersburg long before winter.

"Tell me more about the Delhomme family," Sophie asked as they walked back up the slope toward the soddy.

Karyn recounted the details of her meeting with Celest

and Emile. She told Sophie about the dance they had hosted, concluding with, "I see Celest as often as I can. She is our nearest neighbor. Only a few miles away."

Sophie sighed. "I'm glad you are so happy, Karyn." She looked about her. "I can see that you and Mikal are working very hard, but"—she stopped short, then plunged ahead—"I thought it would be a good joke on you to arrive unannounced." She looked towards the soddy and sighed. "But I should have waited until Papa was ready to come." She smiled. "He believes all the stories about people coming to America and having their health restored."

"Have you been very ill, Sophie?" Karyn asked, heading back up the slope toward the house.

"Oh, nothing really serious," Sophie said quietly. She reached up to lay one hand at her throat. "It just seems that I never have energy." As if to illustrate her point, the moment they arrived at the door of the soddy Sophie sank into the chair beside the sewing machine, breathless. "I'm always so tired." Her blue eyes grew dark and serious. "Sometimes I think I won't live long, Karyn."

Fighting her resentment of Sophie's dramatics, Karyn patted her on the shoulder and said, "Don't be discouraged. We will visit Celest. She knows about remedies from the Indians. I'm sure you'll feel better soon."

Sophie looked up, frightened. "Indians?"

Karyn laughed. "There haven't been any Indians about that I know of, Sophie. Mikal says they are all farther to the west now." She shielded her eyes and glanced toward the sun momentarily. "Come now. You take a nap. Mikal has forgotten his lunch, and it's time I take it to him. Then, I must get to my sewing."

Sophie followed Karyn inside the soddy and sank onto the bed with a sigh. Karyn put half a loaf of bread, a chunk of butter, and a sausage in a sugar sack. While she worked, she explained, "Mikal is plowing the northwest quarter of our section. I won't be gone too long." There was no answer from the bed. Sophie had fallen asleep.

Mikal was waiting with a big smile and a hearty thanks when Karyn rode up and handed him his lunch. He took off his hat and wiped his brow. "I wouldn't have blamed you for letting me go hungry, but I'm glad you didn't. I brought water for the horses, but in all the excitement I forgot about feeding myself." Mikal opened the sack with his lunch in it. He took a bite of bread and then set the sack on the ground.

"Sophie's arrival was quite a shock, wasn't it?" Karyn said quietly. Frowning a little she said, "I'll do my best to see that she is not a burden to you."

Mikal protested, "How could such a little thing as Sophie be a burden?" He looked up at Karyn. "She will be good company for you and good help with the sewing, too. I'm glad she came. In fact, I was thinking as I plowed this morning that it might be better for you if she stays with us for a while instead of moving into Millersburg. Although I am certain Cay will be eager to rent her the rooms over his new store." He asked abruptly, "Can you stay while I eat?" He didn't wait for Karyn to answer. Reaching up he put his hands about her waist and lifted her to the ground. In the process, he bumped against the broad brim of her bonnet, pushing it back off her head.

Blushing, Karyn turned away from him and fumbled with untying another sack containing a corked jug full of fresh water. She left the bonnet as it was, draped about her shoulders, unaware that Mikal was admiring the way the sun put red and gold highlights in her rich brown hair. When she handed the jug to Mikal he took a drink. Then, stepping away from Karyn, he removed his hat and poured the cool water over his head. Water plastered his flowing hair to his head, ran down the back of his neck, and soaked his shirt. He shook his head like a horse.

Drops of water flew in all directions as he clamped his hat back on his head.

After Karyn had put the empty jug back in its bag and tied it to the saddle horn, she raised her hand to her brow and squinted toward the far end of the line of broken sod. "The new team is making a difference, yes? Already today you have much plowed."

Mikal lowered his voice and cleared his throat. "Do you think—I mean, now that Sophie has come, it should be easier for you here. Not so lonely." He took his hat off and wiped his damp brow with his forearm before continuing. "I was hoping that the planting of the garden meant that you were thinking of extending our agreement. But I haven't had the courage to say anything. It seems we never have opportunity for talking—just us two."

Looking up into Mikal's blue eyes, Karyn felt her heart begin to pound. Self-consciously, she bent to retrieve his lunch from where he had set it on the ground. As she handed it to him she said, "I have been thinking about harvest. Celest speaks of our working together to can and dry our garden produce."

Mikal seemed to have forgotten about eating his lunch. He held the sack in one hand, but his blue eyes never left hers as he said, "I don't think I can manage to build another room onto the house this year. Do you think you and Sophie could stand a Nebraska winter in the soddy? You remember my tales of my two winters here. It will be much colder than Brandenburg . . . much more severe." He quickly added, "Of course I can manage in the dugout."

He wants me to stay through the winter. Karyn straightened her back and answered firmly, "I'm not frightened by tales of blizzards and cold, Mikal. We can manage just fine. With or without Sophie." *Please, God, without Sophie.*

Mikal took note of Karyn's reference to "we" and nodded happily. "Then it's settled. I promise never again to hint that you might not be able to persevere, and you promise not to speak of leaving Nebraska."

Karyn nodded. She gathered up Sugar's reins and mounted, preparing to leave. Mikal thanked her again for bringing out the lunch, which he still had not eaten. Karyn urged Sugar forward, but the little mare had taken only one step when Mikal called Karyn's name. She pulled Sugar up.

Mikal reached out and put one giant hand over Karyn's. He squeezed gently and said, "I don't say much, Karyn, but it's good to have you here in Nebraska. In my life."

Looking down into Mikal Ritter's gorgeous blue eyes, Karyn was suddenly filled with happiness. She said, "And it's good to be in your life, Mikal."

Mikal nodded. Clearing his throat he pulled his hand away and said, "Sophie will be wondering what has become of you."

"Yes," Karyn said. "I should be getting back to Sophie." She urged Sugar forward and rode off at a smart gallop.

Karyn had unsaddled Sugar and turned her into the corral, picketed Ella in a lush stand of buffalo grass, watered each seedling tree, and was seated at her sewing machine before Sophie woke from her nap.

When Sophie appeared yawning and blinking against the bright sun, Karyn said, "Bring a chair outside, Sophie. I want to hear everything about home. You can hem this dress for me while I set in the sleeves on another. You always could do the hemming so much more quickly than I."

Sophie came outside. "I brought something for you." She handed Karyn a photograph of herself with Vroni and Jette. Sophie joked, "We wanted to make certain you didn't forget us now that you are a rich American." She sat down and began to stitch and chatter about their friends and acquaintances in Brandenburg while Karyn pushed the ornate foot pedal on her sewing machine faster and faster.

"Does it disturb you to hear me speak of the Gilhoffs, Karyn?" Sophie asked suddenly.

Karyn stopped sewing. She leaned back in her chair and stretched, bending her neck from side to side and reaching up to rub her shoulder before she answered. Finally, she said, "Hans is not coming back to this earth, and I have a new life here in America. I intend to make it a useful one. Mikal is a good man. He's very different from Hans, but he is suited to this life." She turned her head and looked across the vast tableland that stretched toward the east. Remembering Mikal's hand on hers only a few hours earlier, she said sincerely, "I'm content."

"But what of love, Karyn? Have you given up thoughts of love?"

Karyn considered the question, looking soberly over the shiny black top of her sewing machine. "I thought I loved Hans. But I was just a foolish girl play-acting a romance: Handsome Boy Goes to War and Swears Undying Love." She looked down at her hands. "Celest Delhomme says that true love is standing by someone in sickness and trouble as well as in happiness." She began to stitch very slowly. "Mikal Ritter is the kind of man who stands by his friends in sickness and in trouble and in happiness."

"Well," Sophie blustered, stabbing the dress hem energetically, "if I were in your place, I would want to be much more than his friend."

And I do. Karyn blushed and changed the subject. "Mikal says he knows many men who have come here from the east because of poor health. Most of them find that the hard work and the good air improve their health." She smiled. "We must hope that you find the same result, dear sister."

Sophie tied off her thread and looked towards the horizon. After a long moment, she murmured, "There is not even a thing one can hide behind." A moment longer and Sophie's face brightened. "Well, Karyn, until I can find a little room in Millersburg, perhaps I can be of some use to you. Heaven knows I have been too ill to be much help to our dear mother. But if what you say is right about America, things will improve."

Karyn finished setting the sleeves into the dress in her lap and stood up. "I must get to the weeds in the garden, or my poor little cucumber patch is going to disappear and die."

Sophie jumped up. "I can help."

The two sisters walked together to the garden. Karyn recited what she had planted, teaching Sophie the words for each plant. "Tomatoes here. Cucumbers there. Cabbage here. Turnips and beets over there." She handed Sophie a hoe. "When I first came, this was only a square of tall grass. You would not believe the work it is to plant in virgin sod. I did it while Mikal was gone." She straightened up for a moment. "And then he put the sod wall around to keep wildlife out. I never imagined things would grow so well the first year. Mikal says the soil is unbelievably rich. We won't hoe along like we do at home. Only chop out the tall weeds."

They had finished only half a row when Sophie stopped to wipe the sweat from her brow. She leaned heavily on the hoe, shaking her head. "I am sorry, Karyn, but I fear I am too weak—" The words were barely out of her mouth when Sophie crumpled to the ground.

Karyn ran to the well. Soaking a cloth in cool water, she ran back to Sophie. Cradling her head in her lap, she wiped her brow, shading her from the sun with her own body.

Sophie opened her eyes and smiled softly. "You see, Karyn, how the old ways have followed me even here." She sat up and looked about her, blinking her eyes.

"You had better get out of the sun, Sophie."

Sophie nodded. "Yes. I am afraid you are right."

"It's cool in the house. Go in and rest for a while. If you feel better, you can finish hemming the blue dress."

Karyn helped her up, and Sophie made her way to the sod house, weaving uncertainly as she walked. As she disappeared inside, Karyn grabbed the hoe Sophie had been using and tossed it toward the garden wall. Then she returned to her own work, striking at the offending weeds in her cucumber patch with unusual vigor. *So. This is how it is to be.*

The Diary
June 30, 1880
Sophie arrived today. Such a surprise! She speaks— in English—of a dressmaking business. May God grant her renewed health. Mikal asks that I stay through the winter. It will be strange having Sophie in the house. Mikal says the dugout is fine, but I wish it did not have to be this way. How I have changed, from longing to have people around me, to longing for time alone. But no, not really alone.

CHAPTER 9

Red, White, and Blue Ribbons

----

*For the lips of a strange woman drop as an
honeycomb, and her mouth is smoother than oil.*
Proverbs 5:3

"But you *must* wear it, Karyn," Sophie begged, holding
the blue silk gown up for Karyn to inspect. "I brought it
all the way from Brandenburg." She wheedled, "You'll
look so pretty. It will be a wonderful surprise for Mikal to
see you in a new gown. He won't be able to take his eyes
off you."

Karyn stubbornly shook her head. "No. I appreciate
your bringing it. It's truly lovely. But I cannot wear it."

"Why not?" Sophie actually stamped her foot. "Surely
you can see it's much better suited to your coloring than
that old green thing you brought with you."

"As it happens, Sophie, I don't have 'that old green
thing' anymore. But even if I did, I wouldn't be wearing it."

"What do you mean you don't have it anymore?"

"I gave it to Ida the night before the meeting in the
church."

"Karyn Ensinger! You didn't! Why, Ida Gerstenschlager
never had a silk gown in her life!"

"She deserved to feel just as pretty as the rest of us,
Sophie." Karyn smiled, remembering Ida's shy smile when

she saw herself in the hotel mirror the morning of her meeting with her prospective husband. While Sophie fumed, Karyn went on to recount her experience at the Delhommes' social. She concluded, "I absolutely cannot arrive in a new silk gown. Not one of the dresses I made for this celebration was silk. I will not have the women thinking I purposely tried to best them. It would be cruel. I will be much happier in the red calico." She pulled some red, white, and blue ribbons from a box on her trunk and held them up. "I am going to braid these ribbons you brought me into my hair. I will look just like the American flag!"

Sophie sniffed impatiently. "Well, *I* am wearing a silk gown, and I will *make* them like me whether they want to or not."

Indeed. Karyn reached for her red calico dress. She sighed a bit wearily. She had risen almost in the middle of the night and spent the entire morning baking and cooking. She had two baskets each of corn bread and rye bread. Mikal had shot half a dozen prairie chickens and a particular prize—a wild duck. Karyn had spiced their last treasured crock of dried apples, adding vinegar and the last of her white sugar to create *eingamachcte Apfel,* something Mikal had once mentioned that he missed from his homeland. There was a platter of blina pancakes, to be served with sausage and beet syrup, the latter to be provided by Celest. As they loaded the wagon, Karyn blushed with pleasure at Mikal's praise for the bounty she would add to the tables at the celebration.

The closer they got to Millersburg, the more excited Sophie became. She moved her slippered feet in a little dance as they rode along, exclaiming happily as they approached Millersburg and saw that the little hamlet was already crowded with wagon after wagon. Children dressed in fanciful costumes ran everywhere, and small clutches of women moved up and down the street complimenting one another's new dresses and trimmed bonnets.

Cay Miller and Luc Delhomme had erected a dais on the front steps of Miller's store. The store itself was bedecked with red, white, and blue bunting. Lacking a cedar pole long enough to serve as a flagpole, Cay had unrolled a huge American flag from the second story roofline of his store. Loud popping noises came from behind the blacksmith's shop where a group of young men had gathered to fire their guns and pound powder on the blacksmith's anvil.

Across the street from Cay's store, a long row of tables stretched along the entire length of the Kruger house. There were massive quantities of fried chicken, potato salad, sandwiches, something Celest later identified as "brownstone front cake," and gooseberry and raspberry pie, a testimony to the diligence of both women and children in gathering wild fruit from creeks and canyons.

There were four huge barrels of fresh lemonade. Someone Karyn didn't know was producing a precious chunk of ice from a gunnysack. Wiping off the strands of insulating straw that had kept it frozen since the previous winter, he began to chip it into four chunks. Seeing the ice, Karyn wondered if the rumor was true that there would be real ice cream at the dance that night.

Karyn was carrying her platter of blina to the tables when Celest caught up with her. "Already I have heard from six women who tell me that you made their dresses." She squeezed Karyn's arm affectionately. "See, I told you you would have all the work you desired."

Karyn set down the platter of blina. "I have news, Celest. My sister has come."

"What? Which one?"

"Sophie. There." Karyn pointed across the street to where Sophie was standing next to Mikal. As Celest and she watched, Sophie smiled and shook Emile's and Luc's hands. Something was said, and Remi and Serge pressed forward, laughing and shoving one another. Sophie lifted her hands and waved them toward the boys, then turned and headed for the wagon where she retrieved a basket of biscuits and headed toward Celest and Karyn.

"You must be Celest," Sophie said. "Already I have met the charming men in your family," she said, nodding back over her shoulder. She set the basket of biscuits down on the table and turned toward Karyn. "Mikal says that we are to leave him to get the rest of the food. He has our chairs unloaded, and they are to begin the speeches soon." She leaned toward Celest and whispered, "And I do hope the men in America are not like the long-winded orators in Brandenburg." She stepped between Karyn and Celest, tucked one tiny hand under each woman's arm, and pulled them toward the chairs.

Every family in the surrounding area had brought chairs from home. There were rockers and straight-back chairs of every imaginable style. While some left their chairs in their wagons and sat at a distance from the podium where Cay Miller was just announcing the first speaker, others, like the Delhommes and the Ritters, arranged their chairs in theater fashion before Miller's store. In only a few moments, Germans and Danes, Irish and Swedes, English and Easterners, sat side by side, listening reverently as Cay Miller read the preamble to the Constitution of the United States. When he finished, the crowd stood to sing *America* and *The Star-Spangled Banner,* and then once again settled in their chairs for an afternoon of speech-making by various county dignitaries. Speeches were interspersed with songs. Women fanned themselves while their husbands smoked. Children alternately sat in their mothers' laps and trotted away to filch biscuits from the supper table.

When the speeches were finished, the afternoon of contests began. There was a horse race pitting Cay Miller's thoroughbred against Emile Delhomme's favorite saddle horse, followed by a baseball game in which the Millersburg Nine played the Olive Creek Gang. The

Delhomme family contributed over half of the Millersburg Nine team. Luc Delhomme convinced Mikal to pitch. "With that arm," he said hitting Mikal playfully, "we'll be sure to win."

Mikal grinned. "Well, that's a strong arm, all right"—he pointed to his head—"but I don't understand that American game at all."

"You don't need to understand it, Mikal." Luc laughed. "Just throw the ball as hard as you can. We'll tell you what comes next."

Mikal threw the ball as hard as he could. Unfortunately, his control was lacking, and the Millersburg Nine nearly lost the game. But Remi and Serge saved it in the last inning with colossal hits judged to be home runs by virtue of the fact that each baseball landed in a patch of switch-grass just behind the blacksmith's shop.

Sophie kept her promise to make the women like her in spite of her silk dress. Had she not been Sophie's sister, Karyn would have been tempted to think Sophie's behavior a bit contrived. Still, her mention of having been ill so much, her sighs for home, her exclamations of humility when women admired her gown, all seemed to endear her to the community.

In Karyn's eyes, Sophie's charm, which had worn thin as the day advanced, became positively annoying by the end of the baseball game. Mikal was coming toward her, his face wreathed in smiles, when Sophie felt faint and Mikal hurried off to get her a glass of lemonade. Karyn scolded herself for her lack of concern for her sister.

When Mikal encouraged her to join Celest and another group of women inspecting the new bolts of calico that Cay Miller had just received, she obeyed him. Looking through the window of the store, Karyn could see that Sophie had made a remarkable recovery. She was standing on tiptoe, wiping the sweat from Mikal's brow with a lacy handkerchief.

Finally, the sun set and the music began. Everyone moved their chairs from the front of Miller's store to the bowery where dancers could rest and talk between numbers. Cay Miller danced with Sophie for nearly half an hour before reluctantly allowing Serge Delhomme to cut in. Emile and Celest Delhomme waltzed beautifully to a rendition of "The Blue Danube." But much to Karyn's disappointment, Mikal gave no sign of interest in dancing with his wife. He joined the conversation with the new settlers, seemingly impervious to the music.

Mikal had just sat down by Karyn when Luc joined them. "Mikal," he said, "knowing you as I do, you are at this moment wondering how to tell your lovely wife that you dance with all the grace of a bull. So I have told her for you. And now I ask your permission to dance with your wife."

Mikal looked sheepishly at Karyn. "I'm afraid what he says is true." Obviously embarrassed, he nodded toward Luc. "Thank you, Luc."

"But everyone loves to dance, Mikal," Karyn insisted.

He shook his head. "Not me."

"But—" Karyn started to argue when Luc interrupted.

"Save yourself, Karyn. Believe me, you do *not* want to entrust yourself to this man. He'll break you with one giant step forward right onto the top of your foot." Luc grinned. "Sometime you must ask him to tell you about the evening my mother insisted that she could teach anyone to dance."

Mikal shook his fist at Luc and growled with mock ferocity.

Luc ducked away, defending himself with, "I promise I won't tell her the details, Mikal. But really, you should have let her know before she agreed to come out here, that while we have many, many dances, there is absolutely no possibility that she will ever actually dance with her husband!"

Caught between Mikal and Luc's easy banter, Karyn felt a surge of happiness. It was obvious that the two men were once again friends, and that any jealousy between them had been resolved.

"It's all right, Mikal," Karyn reassured him. "To tell the truth, Sophie is the dancer in our family." She turned toward Luc. "Why don't you find her, Luc. She's a much better partner than I." She longed to reach out and hook her hand in Mikal's arm, but something held her back. She could not bring herself to make a public display of something that did not exist in private.

Luc pulled her gently toward the bowery. "Just one dance, Karyn," he urged.

"Oh, all right then," Karyn agreed. With a glance at Mikal, who was nodding his encouragement, she followed Luc onto the dance floor.

Karyn danced with Luc, with Emile, with Serge, with Remi, each time returning to stand beside Mikal. He seemed content to have her dance with his friends, and she was content to bask in his gaze as he watched her move across the dance floor. It was nearly midnight when Karyn realized that Mikal had disappeared.

She went to look for him. She thought she saw shadows in the moonlight behind Miller's new store. Thinking that some of the older boys might be up to some mischief, she went to investigate. But instead of mischievous boys, Karyn discovered Sophie in Mikal's arms.

No, she reasoned later, *they were not really embracing.* She could hear what Sophie was saying. She was instructing him in a dance. Karyn was devastated. She had done everything in her power that night to convince Mikal to do even part of a dance with her. He would not concede. *How is it,* she wondered, *that Sophie, so recently arrived, has such power over him?*

"Karyn!" Sophie called happily. "See how I have convinced Mikal that he can dance, after all."

The moment Sophie spoke, Mikal wheeled about to face Karyn. He said sheepishly, "I thought perhaps I could learn, after all."

"Yes," Karyn said. "I see." She backed away. "Well, I think I'll be loading up the remains of our supper. Perhaps there will be enough that I won't have to cook so much tomorrow." She wheeled about and headed toward the outdoor tables. In the moonlight, she covered the plates. Mikal appeared beside her. Without a word, he took things from her hands and returned them to the wagon. When they had finished, he spoke up. "She said she could teach me. I thought I might surprise you by asking you to dance before we go home."

"It is all right, Mikal. Please don't make such an issue of it."

When Mikal finally suggested it was time to go, Karyn pleaded a headache and went to lie down on the feather tick she had originally put in the wagon for Sophie. By the time the wagon pulled into the yard in front of the soddy, Sophie had fallen asleep on Mikal's shoulder.

The Diary
July 4, 1880
My first Fourth of July in America. Such a celebra-
tion they have! Speeches and food, games and more
food, dancing and more food. We ate until our eyeballs
ached. Almost everyone is learning English, and listen-
ing to the chorus of voices and the accents made me so
proud of this country, which offers an equal chance to
all who will work hard. I have much for which to be
grateful, and I must dwell on this rather than being
tempted to worry over things of no consequence.

CHAPTER 10

A Rattler's Tail

Thou shalt not be afraid for the terror by night ...
nor for the destruction that wasteth at noonday.
Psalm 91:5–6

A faint light in the east promised the coming dawn by the time the Ritters arrived at home. "What a wonderful time!" Sophie exclaimed as Mikal lifted her down from the wagon. He took a step toward the wagon box, but Karyn jumped to the ground from the opposite side of the wagon. Reaching for a basket of leftover food, she headed for the house.

Sophie lingered in the predawn light, looking up at Mikal with shining eyes. Mikal didn't notice. He was looking toward the house even as he lifted the chairs down from the wagon box. He carried two chairs inside, setting them down near where Karyn stood with her back to him, unloading the contents of the basket. When she didn't turn around, he took a step toward her. He was about to put one hand on her shoulder when she wheeled about briskly and, brushing past him, went back outside.

Mikal heard Karyn saying to Sophie, "I'll get the other basket of food. You must get to bed. You are exhausted, and you don't want to be ill."

Sophie giggled. "An evening of dancing could never make me ill, Karyn!"

From the doorway Mikal watched as Sophie whirled around happily. She said, "Wasn't it wonderful? Serge and Remi promised to help me with that American dancing soon. I don't know if I'll ever be able to keep up with the calling."

She looked past Karyn and at Mikal. "You must help me with my English. I want to learn to speak without such an accent."

Mikal stood to one side to let her go in, then he went to the wagon for the other chair, which he set beside the sewing machine outside. "There was talk of a literary meeting this Friday, Karyn. I have never cared to go alone, but perhaps we could attend together."

Yes, now that Sophie is here he finds time for such things. Karyn answered coldly, "Whatever you wish, Mikal. Good night." Thus dismissed, Mikal turned to go.

Inside, Karyn slipped out of her dress and into bed.

"Karyn—Karyn, listen. What is that?"

Karyn ignored her, but Sophie was persistent. She reached out and jostled Karyn's shoulder. "Karyn, wake up. I don't like the sound of that."

"It's only a cricket, Sophie. Go to sleep."

Sophie was quiet for a few moments, then she whispered loudly, "I think I hear someone talking. Is someone outside?"

Lifting her head from her pillow, Karyn listened carefully. "Coyotes. They look like small wolves. They will do us no harm, and Mikal will guard his sow and Ella and the calf. Now go to sleep."

"Who can sleep? That may be coyotes *outside,* but I still hear something *inside,* and I do not think it's a cricket." Sophie shivered. "What if something crawled in through the doorway while we were gone?" She muttered, "I cannot believe you live without a front door." She slipped out of bed. "I am going to get Mikal."

Karyn sat up abruptly, managing not to shout but still letting Sophie know that she was very angry. "Don't be ridiculous. We cannot be bothering Mikal every time we hear a little sound. You must remember that *he* cannot sleep late tomorrow." Motioning for her sister to get back in bed she said firmly, "He deserves at least one hour of sleep before his day begins."

"And do we not deserve to sleep, too?" Sophie insisted. She hurried outside while Karyn lay in bed fuming.

Mikal appeared at the doorway, his shirt half buttoned, only one strap of his overalls fastened. "What is it, Karyn?" he asked wearily.

Karyn didn't even turn over to look at him. "I told Sophie not to bother you. I will take care of it in the morning."

But Sophie persisted. "Something came in while we were gone. I am sure of it. I could hear it"—she pointed to the corner of the room—"over there."

Holding his lantern before him, Mikal dutifully inspected the corner Sophie had pointed out. "There's nothing there." He reassured her, "Everything seems louder at night. I'm sure it is nothing. Even with such fine housekeeping as Karyn's, unwelcome guests visit. Go to sleep. It's too dark to look anymore tonight. Tomorrow is Karyn's cleaning day. You can solve the mystery when the sun comes up."

Mikal left. After perching on the side of the bed for a moment, Sophie relented and snuggled under the quilts again.

While Sophie snored, Karyn lay awake replaying the evening's events. She wrapped herself in a cloak of self-pity for as long as possible. For nearly an hour she managed to justify her feelings. But then she considered Mikal's response to Sophie's pleas for him to look for a mere cricket. He was exhausted, but he had come back up the slope with his lantern. Instead of scolding Sophie for her silliness, he had inspected the soddy. He had been patient and reassuring. He had even complimented Karyn's housekeeping.

Over and over again Karyn thought through the awful thing that Mikal had done at the dance the evening before, but try as she would, she finally had to admit that she was the author of her own misery. When Mikal had been jealous over her dancing with Luc, she had been angry. And now she was guilty of the same offense!

But she could not admit that to Mikal. Why, she would have to admit that she always felt clumsy and plain around Sophie, that she had to fight against resenting Sophie's charm. Worst of all, she would have to admit to feeling possessive about Mikal—even jealous! Admitting that would include revealing that she was beginning to have feelings for him, which went far beyond their spoken agreement to be partners in the business of creating a successful farm. Mikal had said that he was glad that she was in his life, but he had given little indication that he had plans for them to ever be more than good friends. He was a forthright man. Unlike Hans, he was not given to flirting and to clever, romantic speech. If she raised the issue of feelings about Sophie and Mikal, he might well take the opportunity to say that he found Sophie attractive. No, she definitely could not talk to Mikal about being jealous of Sophie.

Lying in the dark, listening to the rustling of something that she knew was not a cricket, Karyn decided that tomorrow she would clean the soddy, she would clean Mikal's dugout—and she would find a way to apologize to him without words.

By the time Mikal emerged from the dugout the next morning, Karyn was bent over the outdoor fire pit cooking his breakfast. By the time he fed the livestock, she had disappeared. He went up the slope to look for her, but stopped when he saw a steaming cup of coffee and a plate of cakes sitting on one of the stumps beside the fire. Beside the stump a sugar sack held his lunch. Obviously, Karyn had no intention of discussing the previous night's events. With a sigh, Mikal settled down to eat. He had downed nearly half a plateful of pancakes before he saw Karyn making her way toward the creek with a basket over her arm.

As soon as she saw Mikal drive the team out of the corral and head toward the tree claim, Karyn began cleaning the dugout. She pulled his feather tick and comforter outside and stretched them across the corral fence. She was careful to put the comforter bright side down so that the relentless sun could not fade the colorful fabric used for the top. She swept the floor vigorously, sneezing amid the clouds of dust and thanking God that her house had a hard floor. She wiped down the few pieces of furniture in the room and cleaned the little stove in the corner. Then, she put a bouquet of wildflowers where Mikal would see them as soon as he returned from the tree claim.

Karyn was on her way up the slope toward the soddy when she heard Sophie shriek, "Karyn! Karyn, where are you! A snake! It's a snake!"

Karyn ran to the doorway of the soddy where she stopped, staring with horror at a huge brown snake coiled up at the foot of her and Sophie's bed. It was a hideous thing with an odd diamond pattern running down its back. Its tail rattled.

"Don't move, Sophie."

Without taking her eyes from the snake, Sophie whispered, "I can't move, Karyn. I'm too—too—" She didn't finish; she just sat wide-eyed, staring at the snake.

Karyn took a step backward and whispered hoarsely, "I'll get—something—" She wanted to scream for help, but she knew that even if Mikal heard her, he was too far away to get there in time to stop that hideous thing from striking out at Sophie.

The thought of defending Sophie melted the last vestiges of resentment over her flirting with Mikal. It also spurred Karyn to action. She hardly knew what she was doing, but one moment she was backing out of the soddy and the next she was headed back inside, walking calmly toward the snake and grasping a hoe poised to strike it.

Sophie's eyes grew wider. "Karyn—what if you miss?"

"I won't—miss." In the seconds she had paused between the words, Karyn struck at the snake. Miraculously, she pinned the ghastly head of the creature against the quilts. It thrashed about with deadly force, flailing the three feet of its length about in a vain attempt to escape the pressure of the hoe against its neck.

Terrified, Karyn bore down with all her might. What seemed like hours passed before the snake was finally dead, its head partially severed. Karyn reached down to pick it up by its tail. It was a meter long, but she laughed nervously. "Not so big." She dragged the dead snake out of the house, tossed it aside, and went back inside to comfort Sophie.

Sophie cried for a long time, clutching desperately at her sister. "How did you do it, Karyn? Weren't you afraid?"

Karyn hugged Sophie. "I couldn't stand idly by and watch my Sophie be hurt, now could I?"

"Well, I couldn't have done it. I would still be sitting there staring at that hideous thing or suffering from the effects of the poison. I heard the men talking about rattlesnakes at the celebration. A child was bitten last week. He suffered horribly before he died." Sophie, who had begun to calm down, began to cry again.

"Come now, Sophie. Don't let it make you ill. Get dressed. We don't have to look for an intruder anymore, but I still want to clean. We must wash the shelves in the

kitchen, air the quilts and the feather tick, sweep, dust—"
She smiled. "Work will take our minds off our little ordeal."

Sophie got dressed and went through the motions of
helping Karyn clean, but it wasn't long before she pleaded
weakness and had to sit down. Karyn was not to be
deterred. She accomplished her tasks alone, humming
happily to herself while Sophie sat on a chair just outside
the door, pretending to sew.

When at last Mikal arrived home, he was greeted by the
aroma of cabbage soup cooking over the fire. With renewed
vigor, he turned the horses into the corral and made his way
up to the house.

Karyn emerged from inside with a plate of biscuits in her
hand just as Mikal bent over to inspect the dead rattlesnake.

"You did not tell me that Nebraska has this variety of
cricket, Mr. Ritter."

Mikal was speechless.

Karyn continued, "The ungrateful creature was willing
to share the warmth of our bed, but quite unwilling to
depart without threatening violence to poor Sophie."

Mikal looked toward where Sophie was sitting. At the
question in his eyes, Sophie nodded. "I awoke this morning to the specter of that creature coiled at the foot of the
bed, preparing to strike me down." She described Karyn's
performance with the hoe. "She saved my life, Mikal. She
saved my life." Sophie burst into tears.

He frowned. "I should have warned you, Karyn. It is
one of the bad things about Custer County. We wage a
constant war against the rattlesnakes."

"You mean," Sophie cried out, "you mean there are
more—nearby?" She clutched the dress she had been hemming to her breast in a dramatic show of horror.

Mikal shook his head. "Probably not many now. I
killed thirty-five during spring plowing. Emile and the
boys killed more earlier, when they had just come out of

their burrows. They've scattered now." His voice shaking, he added, "Thank God you weren't hurt."

Was that tenderness in his voice? Karyn blushed. "Yes, thank God and"—she looked down at the plate of biscuits—"and have a biscuit." She thrust the plate at Mikal and hurried toward the fire where she began dishing up soup.

"Come, Sophie," she called. "You've had the entire day to recover from our excitement over the snake. Come. Eat."

The morning after her introduction to the prairie rattlesnake, Karyn awoke before daylight to the sound of the wagon being driven out of the yard. Hurrying to the door, she watched in dismay to see Mikal headed toward Millersburg. In light of the previous day's excitement, she would have expected Mikal to invite her to ride along.

"Sophie, wake up!" Karyn called over her shoulder. "Mikal has gone to town without us. What do you say to a visit with the Delhommes? If we take our time, we can ride double on Sugar."

A few hours later Karyn and Sophie rode up to the Delhommes' house just in time to help Celest prepare lunch. After a meal during which Sophie once again exercised her dramatic talents recounting the story of the rattlesnake, the women made their way across a pasture to a small thicket of chokecherries. They collected the deep red fruit until their baskets were brimming. The rest of the day was spent washing and pitting chokecherries. They made four pies for Friday's literary meeting, then canned the remaining fruit. Shortly after supper, Mikal rode up on one of the draft horses.

"You didn't leave word where you were." He was obviously upset. "I was worried."

"Well, you didn't leave word where you were going, either," Karyn retorted. "I didn't think we needed to wait meekly for your permission before going to help a neighbor harvest chokecherries."

Mikal grinned. "Of course you don't need my permission." With a look toward the horizon, he said, "Those clouds may be here before we can get back, but I'd like to try and beat them. I have a surprise for you at home."

He was obviously quite pleased with himself. Karyn's heart beat a little faster when he said, "You ride with me, Karyn. Sophie can manage Sugar."

Mikal pulled Karyn up behind him, and they set out for home. When they finally rode up to the soddy, it was dark enough that Karyn saw no evidence of Mikal's trip to Millersburg. Mikal kicked one leg over his horse's mane and slid to the ground, and as he did so, Sophie, who had jumped down first, squealed with delight. "A door, Karyn. Mikal has given us a door!"

Karyn laid one hand on her husband's arm. She took her hand away, blushing. "It's so good of you. I hope you didn't feel pressure from us." She frowned. "I would never want you to have to go in debt for anything so—"

Mikal interrupted her. "I made a very satisfactory arrangement with Cay. Don't be concerned. When I told him what had happened, he dropped the price of the door. I will have it paid for by next week. In fact, he threw in a large bell, which I will position at the top of a pole here in the yard." He leaned toward Karyn. "And the next time there is an emergency, you will be able to ring the bell for me."

From inside the house Sophie called good night, leaving the two of them alone. Karyn said hopefully, "Would you like some coffee, Mikal? It won't take long to stir up the fire."

He thanked her. "Just let me take Lena down and turn her into the corral. I'll be right back."

It wasn't long before the two of them were seated

around the fire. Mikal sipped coffee and said, "Thank you for the flowers, Mrs. Ritter."

Karyn blushed and spoke once more of the debt at Miller's store. "How much do we owe, Mikal? Cay mentioned wanting me to make shirts to sell at his store. If you can get me the cloth he wants me to use, I can help with the bill."

"Really, Karyn, it's no problem. Cay offered a very satisfactory solution." He chuckled softly. "When I asked for credit, he answered, 'Credit I would gladly give you, Mikal. But you don't need credit. If you will arrange for me to sit by Sophie at the Literary Society meeting, I will consider it a fair trade for the door. In fact, if you can get Karyn to invite me to dine with you sometime soon, I will include that large bell so that Sophie and Karyn have a way to summon help in future emergencies'."

"So that's how it is," Karyn said softly.

"Yes, that's how it is." After a brief pause, Mikal said, "You know, Karyn, as the founder of Millersburg, Cay has a very promising future. Once the railroad comes, he will be able to relax and enjoy life. He has enough investments already to provide him with a good income. He only lacks a wife to share his future." He added pointedly, "And one thing is certain. Cay Miller's wife will have an easy life."

Karyn and Mikal drank coffee and talked until long after the little fire died down. Mikal finally said good night, unaware that Karyn was watching him retreat down the slope. He lay in bed looking at the wildflowers Karyn had put on his table for a long time before finally getting up and going back outside, where he leaned against the corral fence. He heard the hinges of the new soddy door creak and looked up to see Karyn come outside. A faint golden light from a lamp illuminated the back of her silhouette. She had taken her hair down. Dressed in her nightgown, she stood under the porch for a few moments, looking up at the sky before turning around and going back inside.

Standing in the dark, looking up toward his house, Mikal thought of Cay Miller and smiled. Perhaps, just perhaps the way had been provided for him to once again have the life he longed for, the privacy he and Karyn needed.

The Diary
July 6, 1880
I killed a rattlesnake. Horrible creatures. God pro-
tect my Mikal from them. He said that he has killed
thirty-five already this year. Sophie and I helped Celest
can chokecherries and make pies for the literary. We
have a new front door. I will use the old quilt to stuff
another comforter for Mikal. There is a plot between
Cay Miller and Mikal regarding Sophie. I must invite
Cay to dinner soon.

CHAPTER 11

A Literary Society Programme

----

*God thundereth marvellously
with his voice; great things doeth he,
which we cannot comprehend.*
Job 37:5

On Friday, Karyn decided to roast six prairie chickens for the supper preceding the literary society meeting. Since only three hens would fit into the roaster she used in her outdoor oven, Karyn fired up the indoor stove. Firsthand, she learned the excellent insulating properties of sod walls. Not only the hens, but also anyone inside the soddy, roasted. Even Sophie spent the day outdoors.

After lunch Karyn went to tend the garden. Sophie, who could not bear the hot sun, meandered down the slope of the hill to where Mikal sat outside the dugout mending harness. At sight of her, he smiled and nodded. He didn't look up from his leather-working when he said, "It's about time Ella was moved to fresh grass." He nodded toward where the heifer had been picketed between the creek and the corral.

Sophie sighed. "I'm sorry, Mikal, but I'm afraid of cows."

He looked at her levelly. "Some say that the best way to overcome fears is to face them. Ella is very gentle. She'll follow you like a puppy." He nodded back up toward the garden where Karyn was hard at work. "It would help us both if you could take charge of Ella. I can teach you to milk. Perhaps you and Karyn could work out a way to share the butter-making. Then you could begin to save money toward your business in town." He paused meaningfully. "It shouldn't tire you out too much. Try it."

Sophie marched off to move Ella, indignance evident in the tilt of her head and her unusually energetic gait. She snatched up Ella's picket rope, screeching when Ella tossed her head to flick away the flies. When Ella's calf butted her playfully, Sophie was caught unawares and sprawled on her back. She lay there for a few moments, waiting for someone to help her up. But no one came, and the calf showed an inclination to lick her face, so Sophie picked herself up. Shoving the picket stake as far into the earth as she could manage, she marched back up to the house.

Mikal covertly watched the entire display, smiling to himself. Obviously, Sophie's health was improving. The brisk walk back up to the house didn't seem to have left her short of breath.

When he saw Karyn come around the side of the house and head for the well, Mikal set aside the harness and started up toward the soddy. Sophie went inside, but not until she was certain he knew that she was purposely avoiding him.

Karyn was pulling up a bucket of fresh water when Mikal reached from behind her and took over the hoisting of the rope. "It won't be much longer, and I'll have a windmill," he said. "Then I'll build a slurry to carry the water down to the trough at the corral. I'll add a valve so you can collect water without having to hoist it up."

He dipped a tin cup into the bucket and held it out to her. "I hope you won't think I am interfering in the way you manage things, but I suggested that perhaps Sophie could take over the care of Ella."

"Yes." Karyn nodded. "She told me."

"I thought it would be a way for us to help her realize her goal of a shop in Millersburg. That is still her plan, yes?"

Karyn nodded. "I think so."

"Cay mentioned your making shirts for his store. Perhaps Sophie could talk to him about that at tonight's meeting. It would be a good way for her to get started with her own sewing business. She could have her name established before she moves to town."

"It's a good idea. I hate to turn down the work, but I was wondering how I would manage." Karyn set down the tin cup. "The hens should be just about cooked. When do you want to leave?"

Abruptly, Mikal said, "Let Sophie check on the hens. Walk with me."

Karyn walked to the door of the house. "Sophie," she called. "Would you check on the hens, please? Just see if the leg bone is loose like I showed you. Mikal and I"—her heart gave a little jump as she said it—"Mikal and I are going to take a walk together."

Sophie was lying on the bed, panting from the heat. She lifted her head weakly. "Of course, Karyn. In a few moments."

"Don't wait too long. We don't want them to burn." Karyn reached up to push her hair back under her bonnet, hurrying to catch up with Mikal who was already walking toward the creek. When they reached a place where a formation of rocks jutted out over the creek bed, he motioned for Karyn to sit down. Instead of sitting beside her, Mikal walked to the edge of creek. Stooping down, he picked up a flat rock and skipped it across the surface of the water. "I am worried for Sophie. She doesn't seem to be getting much better. Cay is hoping to attract a doctor to Millersburg soon. If it works out, we must take Sophie to see him."

Karyn smiled. "You are very kind to be so concerned,

Mikal. But Sophie has seen many, many doctors. None seemed to be able to find an exact cause for her spells."

Mikal tried to empathize. "Surely she cannot be happy not being able to participate more fully in life. *Arbeit macht Leben suss.*"

Karyn nodded. "Yes, work makes life sweet." She explained, "But from the time when she was very young, it seems that Sophie has always been either just recovering from something or being threatened by a new illness. A little at a time, she withdrew from the daily chores. I think that by the time she was eight Sophie's work had already become entertaining the rest of us while we did the work. She read to us, sang to us, made us laugh. My sisters and I shared her duties. No one seemed to mind." She looked up at him. "I don't think she planned it. It just happened. You know how it is. Every family seems to have one child that everyone enjoys spoiling. For us, it was Sophie."

Mikal sat back on the ground. Resting his elbows on his knees he looked up at her and shook his head. "There were five of us, and we were all expected to work hard. I was six years old when my father decided he was tired of the responsibilities of his family. He left my mother with five small children and a sixth on the way. Without one word of complaint, she took up the farming. Then, she began to take in laundry from the nearby village. My older brothers cared for the livestock; my sisters did the gardening. And I took orders from them all. It didn't matter if we felt sick or not. We all had to work."

Once again, Karyn's attentive listening encouraged him to share more than he had planned. "Mother used to leave us locked in the house when she had to go to the village. We had a big black dog like Celest's Frona to guard us. Unfortunately," he added, chuckling, "our Magda did nothing to guard me from my own brothers. They introduced me to tobacco . . . and entertained themselves by hanging me out the window by my suspenders."

Karyn laughed. "And they no doubt howled with remorse when your mother found out!"

He shook his head. "Oh, Mother was far too busy to know about any of that. And I knew if I said anything it would only get worse the next time she had to be gone." He chuckled. "They weren't cruel. Just normal boys having fun. They tormented me themselves, but if anyone else would have tried to harm me . . ."

Karyn nodded. "That's how we felt about Sophie. Sometimes we suspected she was play-acting. But let anyone else accuse her, and we united in her defense."

Mikal took his hat off and ran his hand through his hair. With a glance toward Karyn, he continued. "The spring after my father left, Mother was trying to harness our horse when he kicked her. She fell back, and her skirt got caught in the plow. That horse dragged her halfway across the field before my brothers could get it back under control. They managed to carry mother in and run for the neighbors. Our little sister was born four days later. She lived one day. My mother was never the same after that."

"Oh, Mikal, I'm so sorry."

Mikal gave a little half-smile. "She had a strong faith in God. She carried on in spirit as though nothing had happened. I never heard her complain of all the work. And I never heard her say a bad word about my father. In fact," he said smiling with the memory, "after every supper, we joined hands to recite a blessing she had taught us. What still amazes me is that Mother never failed to close each of those prayers by asking God to bless our absent father." He stopped short and looked at Karyn. "You know, Karyn, in many ways you remind me of her—always working hard, never complaining."

Karyn blushed. "Your mother sounds like a saint. You can be sure I wouldn't be praying for a man who left me in such a situation."

"It took me a long time to understand that myself. Her

good example didn't rub off on me until I had lost Marie-Louise and spent an entire winter alone with God. I think I understand a little of it now. She used to say over and over again, whenever anything bad happened, that we must simply trust and obey; obey by doing the little thing before us that God had provided to do, and trust in Him for the rest. When Marie-Louise died, the words *trust and obey* came back to me, but they were of no comfort. I did not trust God, and I had no idea why I should obey Him after what He had allowed to happen. It was years before I realized that I had two choices. Either I could trust and obey God, or I could spend the rest of my life being bitter about what had happened. I had had quite enough of bitterness. So I decided to try my mother's way."

"Your mother must have been so happy to know that you found peace, Mikal," Karyn said softly.

He blinked back tears. "Mother died long before I came to America." He stood up, brushing dust off his overalls. "Again, I begin talking, and you are so quiet I go on and on." He returned to the topic of Sophie. "I don't mean to be unkind about Sophie, Karyn. Don't misunderstand. Your entire family is welcome to come to America and to stay with us until they can find a homestead." He had reached out to put his hand on Karyn's shoulder when Sophie screeched, "Help! Help!"

Mikal was the first one to reach the soddy. Smoke was rolling out of the window and the doorway. Inside, Sophie was wrestling the charred remains of three prairie chickens out of the stove. She was covered with soot and crying angry tears.

Karyn came up behind Mikal and shooed him away. "I'll take care of it. You need to get the team hitched."

Mikal backed out of the way. He heard Karyn tease, "Well, Sophie, I think they are cooked now."

At the sound of Karyn's laughter, Sophie spat out, "Don't you dare laugh at me." Mikal heard something slammed down on the stove top with great force. Then, Sophie said, "How could any woman possibly be happy in this hovel? You should have married Hans! You'd be living like a queen on his estate right now, the widow of a war hero. Instead, you work yourself to death in the middle of the Great American Desert!" She burst into tears, unaware that while her words had been directed at Karyn, they had struck Mikal Ritter.

Mikal walked down the slope to hitch up his team, and although he had not done anything particularly tiring that day, his shoulders slumped beneath the weight of a great load of unhappiness and self-doubt.

In July of 1880, Millersburg, Nebraska, was perceived as either a hamlet on its way to becoming the county seat or a sad collection of hovels on its way to oblivion, depending on one's inclination to believe Cay Miller's insistence that the railroad would, indeed, come through Millersburg. He had convinced enough men to believe him that next to his store, along the dirt clearing he referred to as "Miller Street," were a hardware store, a blacksmith shop, and a saloon. Isaac Kruger's harness shop across from his store and a growing number of houses attested to Cay Miller's persuasive talents.

As the community founder, Cay was expected to preside over the Literary Society meetings. Anticipating the arrival of Sophie Ensinger, he took special pains with his preparations that evening. He donned a well-tailored new suit and positioned himself by the door. When Sophie arrived, he ushered her to a seat near the front of the room. Everyone's contribution to supper was arranged on the store counters.

Cay opened the meeting with a brief speech. "You all know that my faith in and hopes for this fine community know no bounds. Later in the evening, after supper is served, I invite you to inspect my new rooms upstairs. I hope to have them rented soon, with at least one business that will be of special interest to the female population." Cay looked meaningfully in Sophie's direction. He went on, "This evening I also want to raise the subject of our need for a social hall."

Celest Delhomme spoke up. "I have some ideas about that, Mr. Miller. She stood and turned to look at the crowd. "In fact, if the women in attendance are in agreement, we can meet upstairs during the refreshment break and form a committee."

Everyone nodded, and Celest sat back down.

Cay introduced the first event of the evening—a debate between Luc Delhomme and Isaac Kruger on the subject "Resolved: That the Capital of the United States Should Be Removed to a More Central Location, i.e., the Great State of Nebraska."

Cay took his seat beside Sophie. The debate was followed by a spelling bee among the men, many of whom were just learning English, and their attempts at spelling made for quite a bit of laughter, even among the contestants themselves.

After the refreshment break, Cay led a group out the front door and up the long outdoor staircase leading upstairs. Sophie ascended the stairs on Luc's arm. Karyn decided to forego Celest's meeting about the social hall in favor of lingering downstairs with Mikal. While some of the men admired Cay's pipe display, others crowded around the table at the back of the store, drinking coffee. Mikal and Karyn made their way outside and sat together on a bench just outside the door.

Karyn said, "I've invited Cay for Sunday dinner."

Mikal nodded. "Good. He and Sophie seemed to enjoy each other's company this evening."

Karyn nodded halfheartedly.

"What's wrong?" Mikal wanted to know. "Did I miss something? Doesn't Sophie like Cay?"

"Of course she does," Karyn said. "Cay is very nice."

"But?" Mikal encouraged her. "Tell me."

Karyn felt awkward. "Oh, it's just that, compared to Luc, Cay isn't very—"

"Compared to Luc." Mikal thought for a moment. "Yes. I see." He said quietly, "But Luc Delhomme wants to be a *musician*. However handsome he may be, he can't offer nearly the future that Cay can. I guess for someone like Sophie it might seem romantic to share a musician's life, but she is just not the kind of woman who can adapt. She'd live to regret such a choice."

Although Karyn had virtually the same opinion as Mikal, she was not prepared to give someone outside the Ensinger family free rein to criticize her little sister—and certainly not when Sophie was not present to defend herself. She stood up. "Well then, Mr. Ritter, since you understand Sophie so well, and since you know the correct future for her, we should hurry upstairs so that you can order her to have feelings for Cay Miller." She folded her arms and added, "Before you do, however, don't forget to remind her to ignore Luc Delhomme's blue eyes and square jawline."

Mikal held up his hands and tried to make peace. "Karyn, I didn't mean—"

But Karyn interrupted him. "You need to realize, Mikal, that most women find it difficult, if not impossible, to simply order themselves to feel a certain way about a certain man." Karyn wished she could pull her words out of the air and stuff them back down her own throat. Mikal looked at her with an odd little smile. To hide the color she could feel creeping up the back of her neck, Karyn wheeled about and headed for the stairs. *You idiot,* she chastised herself. *What do you suppose Mikal thinks now of his little arrangement with you? You just managed to tell him there is little possibility of romantic feeling between the two of you.*

At the foot of the outdoor staircase, Karyn stopped. She wheeled back around, relieved to see that Mikal was following her. She grinned sheepishly. "Remember when I told you how the Ensinger sisters always rallied to defend poor little Sophie? You just got a demonstration. I'm sorry. I know you mean well. Please don't be angry with me. It's just—"

He looked up at her and flashed a smile. "I'm not angry. Just a little confused. But we can discuss that later. At the moment, I'm worried about that." He pointed toward the northwest.

"That little cloud?"

"I don't like the looks of that. If it turns out to be hail—"

"It's just one little cloud, Mikal."

"You're probably right." He smiled at her and turned his back on the clouds. "Can't we at least *try* to help Cay?"

Karyn opened her mouth to answer when a huge clap of thunder made her jump.

Mikal wheeled around and groaned, "Oh, no."

Dark clouds had appeared and were racing to overspread the entire sky to the northwest. In no time, the colors of a beautiful sunset were completely blotted out. Rain began to fall. Mikal and Karyn ducked back inside the store.

A dozen heavy boots clomped down the outside stairs. Men rushed inside the store, each one wanting to be near the window. Mikal put a protecting arm about Karyn. Outside, raindrops changed to small drops of ice. Then marble-size hail began to fall, sending up a chorus of groans from the room.

Just as someone said hopefully, "Maybe it won't be too bad—" a bolt of lightning landed in the street right outside Cay's store. The blinding light made Karyn see stars. She blinked rapidly, rubbing her eyes. When her vision cleared, the first thing she saw was a horse lying dead in the street, smoke rising from its carcass. Hail the size of lemons pounded at the horse's body, slashing its hide.

Mikal pulled Karyn away from the window just as the wind shifted and threw hailstones against Cay's storefront, shattering every one of his new windows.

Karyn heard Sophie scream. Mikal kept her from running out into the storm. "Cay's with Sophie. She'll be all right."

Outside all was chaos. Terrified horses broke away and tore wildly down Miller Street. Men who ran out to try to calm their teams came back inside, cut and bleeding. Luc Delhomme staggered in with a bad gash on the back of his head.

Karyn grabbed a bolt of muslin off of Cay's shelf, ripped off a length, and made a temporary bandage, which she hastily tied around Luc's head. She pulled him toward the back of the store and lit a lamp. Holding the lamp high she demanded, "Let me see." She gently lifted the bandage away from the cut. Blood flowed down the back of Luc's head, staining his shirt collar. Wincing, Karyn looked up at Mikal. "You said Celest does a lot of doctoring. She needs to see this. I can sew it up if I must, but she can probably do a better job."

Mikal grabbed an iron pot off the stove to hold over his head and dashed outside and upstairs. He came back without Celest. "She says just put pressure on it. She's busy with Sophie at the moment." Luc went white and began to weave uncertainly.

"Luc," Karyn ordered, "don't you faint on me. Sit down. Lean your head over on your arms. There. You're going to be fine." She clamped a fresh piece of muslin over the wound, refusing to let herself think about the fact that Luc's skull was showing beneath a jagged piece of flesh. Handing the bolt of muslin to Mikal she ordered, "I'll need more pieces of this ripped off," and then in the same breath asked, "Is Sophie all right?"

"Just a small cut from the broken window. She fainted momentarily. There's a bump on her cheek."

Blood was seeping through the cloth on Luc's head. Karyn pressed down firmly. Luc had fallen asleep. Karyn frowned. "You'd better go get Celest. I'll see to Sophie as soon as Celest gets down here."

It had stopped hailing. Celest came rushing in. When Karyn lifted the bandage from the back of Luc's head, Celest's mouth set in a firm, thin line. "Let's boil some water."

Celest's serious manner banished all thought of Sophie and her little cut from Karyn's mind. She was lighting the stove when Celest said, "I'm going to need another pair of hands. Can you do this? I can't have anyone fainting in the middle of it."

Karyn nodded. "I would have done it myself, but I know you'll leave a neater scar."

Celest looked up at Mikal. "Can you ask Emile to come down? And Cay?"

Mikal left again. Every few moments Celest lifted the bandage to see if the bleeding had stopped enough for her to work.

Emile came in, covered with mud and breathing hard.

"It's all right, dear," Celest said calmly. "Karyn and I will get him sewn up in no time, and then I'm putting him to bed—" She looked at Cay who was standing just behind Emile. "If I can impose?"

"Of course," Cay said.

Celest turned back to Emile. "It's better if we don't move him tonight. Is the team all right?"

"Battered and scared to death, but nothing serious."

"I know you're wondering about the wheat. Why don't you and the boys go on home?"

"Should Remi go for a doctor?"

Celest shook her head. "I don't think so."

Emile called toward the front of the store where Remi and Serge were beginning to pick up shards of glass from Cay's broken windows. "Remi. Stay with your mother

153

and Luc. If there's need for a doctor, you go. Serge and I will drive the team home and check on things."

Mikal came in, a very shaky Sophie leaning on his arm. A length of petticoat had been wrapped around her left forearm. A bump on her left cheek was beginning to turn blue.

"Cay," Celest called out. "I need a needle and thread."

Sophie paled. Her eyes widened as she slumped into the chair across from Luc. She lay her arm on the table and whispered hoarsely, "I thought you said it was just a little cut—"

"The needle and thread are for Luc," Celest said shortly. At that moment, Karyn lifted a kettle of hot water onto the table. Celest replaced the cloth on Luc's head, sliding a bloody one into the hot water.

With a glance at Sophie, Karyn said impatiently, "If you feel faint, Sophie, you'd better move."

Mikal helped Sophie to the front of the store, where she slid gratefully into a rocking chair. There was a conference between himself, the Delhomme men, and Cay. Emile walked back, patted Luc on the shoulder, kissed Celest, and left. Mikal returned to watch Celest and Karyn.

Karyn handed a razor to Celest and sopped up blood while Celest used a tiny pair of sewing scissors to clip blond hair away from the edges of the jagged wound. Once again applying pressure to stop the bleeding, Karyn waited while Celest threaded a needle. Then, as Mikal looked on, she took up a pair of tweezers and pulled the gaping flesh together while Celest stitched. Mikal winced. Luc gave no indication of feeling anything.

"It's good he's asleep," Mikal commented.

Celest tied off her last stitch and stood up. "No. Actually, it isn't. I wish he were awake and yelling. I don't like it." Her hands trembled as she wrapped Luc's head with clean strips of muslin.

Cay came back in. "Use my quarters as an infirmary. I've set up a cot for you, Celest. Remi and I can sleep in here. We'll be nearby if you need anything."

"That doctor you've been trying to get to come," Celest asked. "How far away is he?"

"It's a she. She's in Lincoln."

Celest shook her head. "Too far."

"I can go for Doctor Westerville," Mikal offered.

"If he's been drinking he'll be worthless." Celest sighed and looked down at Luc. "He's a hardheaded boy. Perhaps I'm worrying too much."

Mikal hoisted Luc into his arms and carried him into Cay's quarters. Celest reached for the pot of water, but Karyn pushed her hand away. "Sit. I'll clean up."

Gratefully, Celest sank into her chair. "You're a good assistant, Karyn."

Only after things were cleaned up did anyone think of Sophie. She had curled up in the rocking chair and gone to sleep.

Mikal came back into the store. "What else can I do for Luc?"

"Nothing but pray."

He turned to Remi. "Let's see what we can find to board up the windows."

While Remi and Mikal worked, Karyn lit several lamps and swept up broken glass. When they had done what they could to resurrect Cay's store from the storm, Mikal went to hitch up the team. Sophie woke up. She reached up to touch the bump on her cheek. "Oh, what a headache I have!" she moaned. "Can we go now?"

Mikal drove up outside. Sheltered in Cay's sod stable, his team had escaped injury. All along the street, farmers were tending their cut and bleeding horses. Celest came outside, needle and thread in hand, and went to help where she could. Cay brought a fat feather tick outside and spread it in the wagon for Sophie's comfort. Karyn climbed up beside Mikal, wondering at the four inches of hail that covered the earth as far as she could see.

As they drove out of town, Karyn longed to put her hand in Mikal's, to lay her head on his shoulder, to do something tangible that would say, "It will be all right. We will face it together." But just as she found courage to reach toward him, Sophie bounced up behind them. Seemingly impervious to the tragedy they were about to encounter back at the homestead, she chattered away about the Literary Society meeting. When she finally lay back down, Mikal pulled his hat down so far that Karyn could barely see his eyes. She took it as a sign that he wanted to be left alone.

It was still dark when the interminable ride back to the homestead ended. Mikal left Karyn and Sophie at the door of the soddy and drove off without a word. Sophie half staggered into the soddy and fell into bed without undressing. Karyn lit the lamp and went back outside. She crept along the front of the house and around to the garden where she lifted the lantern high. Shredded vines, broken stems, scattered unripe tomatoes were visible among the mounds of melting hailstones.

The last of the clouds cleared and a full moon came out, illuminating the remains of the garden. As tears of frustration and disappointment pressed against her eyelids, Karyn turned to look toward the dugout. Mikal was coming from the direction of his wheat field, his hands stuffed in the pockets of his overalls, his shoulders slumped.

At times like this, there were no words. At times like this, a woman could only put her arms around a man and hold him. Karyn had taken her first step toward the dugout when Sophie called for her. "Karyn, oh Karyn, my head hurts so . . ."

Karyn looked toward the dugout, sighed, and went in to see about Sophie.

At that moment, Mikal looked up the slope toward the

house. In one day, his world had fallen apart. A few hours ago he had learned that Hans Gilhoff was more than just a boy going off to war. Had she married him, Karyn would at that very moment be living as the mistress of an entire estate. Given that reality, what woman on earth would want a few acres in Nebraska with a ruined wheat field? Why, hadn't Karyn as much as told him that very evening that she couldn't love him? Her words came back to him: "Women find it difficult to order themselves to feel a certain way about a certain man." Was that her way of telling him that she had come to his homestead with good intentions, but she just couldn't make herself care for him?

Mikal sighed. Karyn would have been amazed to learn that his unhappiness had little to do with the loss of his wheat. Standing in the dark, looking up toward his house, Mikal Ritter was praying that in spite of all the obstacles, God would show him how to go about winning the heart of his wife.

The Diary
July 11, 1880
Hail has ruined Mikal's wheat. Everyone was gathered for a pleasant evening in Millersburg when the storm came up, and in moments all was lost. I do not know what we will do. The garden is a complete loss. Worse than all this is that I am unable to comfort Mikal. No, worse than all this is that Mikal does not seek my comfort.

CHAPTER 12

Grains of Wheat

The simple believeth every word:
. . . but the prudent are
crowned with knowledge.
Proverbs 14:15, 18

In the three and a half months since her arrival in
America, Karyn Ritter had learned that no matter what she
expected, both the land and the inhabitants of Custer
County, Nebraska, would surprise her. Her desire to succeed helped her adapt to most surprises. Thus, when an
unexpected hailstorm destroyed her garden and Mikal's
wheat, Karyn summoned strength and prepared to help her
husband. But the morning after the hailstorm presented yet
another surprise for Karyn, for Mikal did not seem to be in
need of comfort.

Karyn made breakfast that morning with an aching
heart. The rising sun revealed the condition of her garden
to be even worse than she had imagined from her brief
inspection by moonlight. *If I feel this way about my little
garden, how must Mikal be feeling? What will I ever say
that can make him feel better?*

When Mikal came up for breakfast Sophie was still
sleeping. He settled by the morning fire and drank a cup
of coffee. When Karyn offered him a second serving of

sausage, he shook his head. "I'm sorry. I'm just not very hungry."

And who could be hungry on such a day? Karyn thought.

Mikal patted his stomach. "I ate far too much at the social last night." Then he looked up at the sky. "It will be hot today. The sun will dry up all this mud in no time." He sipped coffee for a moment before announcing, "I'm going to ride over to Emile's this morning and see what the hail did there. There might be a way to salvage some of the crop. Maybe we can gather some by hand and then dry it in the sun." He grinned. "I may have to change my name to Boaz."

"Boaz?"

"The book of Ruth. Remember?"

Karyn nodded vaguely. "Oh, yes . . . of course."

Mikal went on, "Emile might have much worse damage than I, and with Luc hurt, an extra hand will be welcome." He hesitated. "Of course, they might have been completely spared. In that case, I'll probably meet them on their way to help me. One thing I've learned about the prairie—the weather changes in an instant, and two places five miles apart don't always get the same weather." He stood up and smiled at Karyn. "I'll try to be back by tonight, but if I'm not, don't worry. If there's anything at all to save, it could take longer than just today."

When Karyn still didn't say anything, Mikal said, "I'm sorry, Karyn. I didn't even ask about your garden, did I? Let's have a look."

Karyn shook her head. "There's no need. I checked it when the moon came out last night." She sighed. "The root crops will probably recover. But the tomatoes and vines—"

"Can you replant?" Mikal wanted to know.

Karyn shrugged. "Maybe some things. It depends on when it frosts here in Nebraska."

"Well, if Sophie feels up to it, why don't you two head back to Millersburg later this morning. Cay is a good friend in a crisis. He'll extend enough credit for a few garden seeds. And he can advise you on what's worth trying."

"What about your wheat, Mikal? What will you do?"

He shrugged. "I'll gather up what I can and hope to salvage enough broken heads to replant next spring. Although God might already have done next year's planting for me. Enough might have scattered to give me a good crop next year without planting." He smiled at her. "Don't worry so much, Karyn. As long as there's good *rain*fall instead of good *hail*fall, there will still be some corn. From the twenty acres I could get eight hundred bushels of corn. That's a good mountain of cobs for fuel, which means we'll need fewer chips." He grinned. "I think Celest had a cookbook titled *Thirty-three Ways to Cook Corn.* You may want to borrow it."

"How can you be so—so calm about this? I hardly got a moment's sleep last night worrying about you. Worrying about everything."

Mikal pushed his hat back off his forehead and thought for a moment before answering. "Well, I believe that God knows everything, and that God can do anything. This means He knew it was going to hail. And He could have stopped it. But He didn't." Mikal thought for a moment before continuing, "I don't think God is up in heaven today saying, 'Oh, my goodness, look what happened to Mikal Ritter's wheat! How am I going to get him through the winter?' There is a verse that says all things work together for my good . . . and in many places the Bible assures me that God cares for me. So, I accept that in some way I do not understand, hail on my wheatfield is part of God's plan for my good."

"Where did you get such ideas?" Karyn asked.

"That very long winter in the dugout when I spent a lot of time trying to understand life. I kept asking the same questions and most of my questions involved God. I just kept reading the Bible Celest had given me, looking for answers."

"You seem to have found them," Karyn offered.

Mikal grinned. "Well, I found *some* answers . . . which I had to memorize so that in the face of things like ruined crops, I would be able to remind myself of what I believe!"

Karyn shook her head. "I don't remember our minister at home ever talking about God the way you do. You make Him sound so—personal. I believe He exists, but—"

Mikal interrupted her. "But when the wheat field is smashed"—he looked at her gently—"or the person you love is dead—what really matters is that He is *here*." Mikal patted his chest. He stopped abruptly. "And now I am beginning to preach to you when all you asked was one little question." He poured some water over the fire and turned to go. "Tell Sophie I hope her head is better this morning."

"I will."

"And Karyn . . ." he hesitated momentarily before saying, "Those verses I told you about memorizing. I underlined them in my Bible. If you're interested, you can read them for yourself."

Karyn and Sophie spent the rest of the day trying to resurrect the garden. They picked hundreds of small green tomatoes off the ground, sliced them, and laid them in the sun to dry. Even when the sun came out, Sophie did not complain of the heat. When the two women had finally done all they could in the garden, Karyn mentioned trying to pick up some of the broken wheat.

"We can't possibly glean all those acres by ourselves, Karyn. Mikal will bring back help, and the men will get it done in no time. You said Mikal mentioned our getting more seeds in Millersburg. Wouldn't it be best to do that?"

"And why are you so anxious to go back to Millersburg?

It will be a hot, miserable ride." Karyn smiled knowingly. "So, tell me. Is it Cay or Luc? Because I invited Cay Miller for Sunday."

Sophie didn't try to hide her disappointment. "That will be all right, I guess."

"Only 'all right'?"

"Cay Miller is very nice." Sophie sounded noncommittal.

"Yes, he is," Karyn said. "And he's already quite prosperous."

"Yes."

"But?"

"Why must everyone assume I am looking for a husband?" Sophie complained. "Just because *you* came to America to be married doesn't mean that I want to do that."

"Did you look around on the Fourth of July, Sophie? Or last night? The joke here is that every dance and social is attended by five hundred men and three women. You're a lovely girl, and you can't blame the single men for hoping that you will marry one of them."

Sophie sighed. "But, Karyn, what choices! First, there is Cay Miller. He is prosperous. But he's just not very attractive. Then there's Luc Delhomme. He is handsome enough, but he's going to be a musician. There's no money in that. If Remi and Serge inherit their father's land, they will do all right. But they act like overgrown boys. I want to be taken care of, not mother some fool. That's four of the eligible single men, and there's really not a perfect prospect among them." She added, "And besides that, I don't want to get married for convenience. I want to fall in love first instead of trying to fall in love afterward."

"You never know, Sophie," Karyn replied. "Falling in love afterward might not be so difficult." She blushed in spite of herself. "Celest says that love comes when you act out of love for another."

"That doesn't seem to be working for you," Sophie said bluntly.

"Celest says that it takes time."

"Well just how long does it take? I don't see any evidence of love blossoming between you and Mikal. Does he ever hold your hand? Has he kissed you even once?" Sophie waved her hand. "Oh I know, I know. We aren't supposed to speak of such things. And it isn't any of my business."

Sophie stood up abruptly. "I have to bring Ella in for milking." She had stepped out from beneath the porch when she turned around and said, "But, Karyn, I can assure you that if a man like Mikal Ritter took me home to be his wife, he wouldn't still be sleeping in the barn. Not after one *week*, let alone an entire summer." She laughed nervously and blurted out, "Sometimes I think I should just wait and scoop Mikal up if it doesn't work out between you two. Income and status wouldn't matter much if a woman knew Mikal Ritter loved her."

Karyn rode to Millersburg alone. Sensing that she had said too much, Sophie pleaded a headache, and Karyn was glad to get away from her. All the way to Millersburg she tried to downplay Sophie's comments about Mikal. She was still in turmoil when she put Sugar in Cay's barn and hurried inside the store to ask Cay, "How is Luc?"

From the doorway to Cay's quarters came a shaky answer, "Better, thank you." It was Luc, leaning on his mother's shoulder while Celest helped him to the table at the back of Cay's store.

"No Sophie?" Luc said, looking disappointed.

"No, no Sophie," Karyn said. "She had a headache."

Cay called from the front of the store, "Are you sure she's all right alone?"

"She'll be fine," Karyn assured him.

Luc smiled. "Well, tell her both Cay and I asked for

her." He leaned over and whispered, "Apparently we are to be rivals in the matter of Sophie."

"Your wheat?" Celest asked abruptly.

Karyn shook her head. "The garden, too. All shattered. Mikal sent me to get more seeds. He rode to your place this morning to help Emile."

Celest sighed. "I know that God is in control, but sometimes I am hard-pressed to understand His purpose. Which reminds me of something I wanted to discuss with you." Celest got up and poured Luc a cup of tea. "Drink this, Luc. I want to talk with Karyn about something." She called out, "Cay, when Luc finishes his tea, can you get him back in bed for me?"

With Cay's promise to help Luc, Celest led Karyn outside to a spot of shade on the north side of Cay's barn.

"Karyn, I hope that you won't misunderstand me, but I must broach a rather awkward topic. Luc speaks much of Sophie. I have been observing her." Celest reached out to take Karyn's hands. "Underneath her flirting and her smiles, I don't think Sophie is very happy. Not being able to participate more fully in life would make anyone feel unsettled. Does she *never* feel well enough to work? I wonder, Karyn, if Sophie should see a doctor."

Karyn smiled. "You're very kind to be so concerned, Celest. But, as I have told Mikal, Sophie has seen many, many doctors. None seemed to be able to find the exact cause for her difficulties. Underneath the pouting and her little spells, Sophie is a good girl. She came to America hoping to get well. I think she is better. Perhaps you don't see it, but she is helping more."

Celest nodded. "I'm going to be blunt, Karyn. Luc is going to be a musician. He is very talented and, in time, I think he will do well. But at first he will need a strong woman who can go without fine things, someone who will support him without complaint. Frankly, I don't see Sophie being able to do that."

Karyn tried to reassure Celest. "I don't think she's purposely difficult." She shrugged. "My family spoiled Sophie. But since she's been here, she has taken over the milking, and she helps me with the sewing. Mikal and I have discussed her making shirts for Cay's store." Karyn paused. "She really is trying to do better. She offered to stay at home alone while I came to Millersburg. She even urged me to stay the night—to have a good visit with you. She said not to worry, that if he gets home, she would make Mikal his lunch."

Celest frowned. "Karyn, if Sophie is helping you more, that is good. But she needs to help you more and talk and laugh with Mikal less." She looked at Karyn meaningfully. "Mikal is a good man, but he is a man, and Sophie"—she put her hand on Karyn's shoulder and lowered her voice— "is Mikal still in the dugout—alone?" When Karyn began to redden, Celest scolded, "I'm the mother of five boys, Karyn, and they didn't just sprout up under the cabbages in the garden. So stop blushing and answer me."

Karyn still didn't answer. Celest nodded. "I see." She asked, "You are in love with Mikal, yes?"

Karyn blinked rapidly, then nodded. "Yes, I think so. But he—"

"—he needs to be encouraged. That's all." Celest took a deep breath. "My goodness, child. What is difficult about this? You are already married. What is keeping you from one another?"

"Sophie." Karyn said the word, stifling tears.

"That is easy to solve," Celest said quickly. "If your sewing machine suddenly broke down, Sophie would have to come to my house to borrow my machine. She could stay with us for a while."

"It's not so simple as that," Karyn said. She looked at Celest, finally making herself speak of it. "You know what I mean, or you would not have said that Sophie needs to help me more and laugh with Mikal less." Karyn looked away and swallowed hard before whispering, "As you said, Celest, Mikal is a man . . . and it takes very little wisdom to know which of the two women living in his house is more attractive, more able to make him laugh—"

Gently lifting Karyn's chin, Celest said, "God chose *you* for Mikal's wife, not Sophie. *You* are the one who had the courage to come to America alone. *You* are the one who plastered the walls, and sweeps the floors, and cooks the meals, and tends the garden. That's why God chose you for Mikal. And God does not make mistakes, Karyn!"

Karyn turned away. "You and Mikal. You seem so certain that God has His hand in everything."

"And you aren't?"

Karyn sighed and leaned against the sod wall of the barn. "I don't know. I haven't thought about it very much. We went to church, and I was confirmed. I believe the catechism. But I never thought about applying it all so personally—to everyday things."

"My dear, dear child," Celest soothed, patting Karyn's arm. "Such a good Lutheran girl you are. You know that God loves you so much that His beloved Son died for you, yes? Well, if He loves you so much as that, do you not know that He cares about this little matter with Sophie and Mikal and you? God is the Author of love, dear Karyn. He has given you the love for Mikal that grows in your heart. He means it for your good. You will see."

As Celest had predicted, Karyn soon had opportunity to see how things were. But she didn't see God working to bring herself and Mikal closer together. Instead, she saw Sophie's blue eyes sparkle when she looked at Mikal. She saw Sophie's dimple when she laughed with Mikal. She saw how every night, Sophie seemed to know just when Mikal came around the corner from the corral and started up the slope to join them for supper.

In the evenings, Sophie always had some mending in her

smooth, white hands. There was never any dirt under Sophie's immaculate, smooth fingernails. Karyn saw that her own hands were growing weathered and freckled, her nails cracked and stained with chokecherry juice and elderberry jam.

Karyn saw Mikal's concern for Sophie's comfort. When Sophie mentioned how hot it was outside, Mikal moved the sewing machine inside. He positioned it by the window where there was plenty of light. He even bought screen for the window so that Sophie could enjoy a breeze while she sewed.

When Sophie mentioned missing the regular church services at home, Mikal began to read aloud from his Bible at every supper. He had the three of them hold hands and recite the blessing his own family had recited. It became his habit to ask Sophie and Karyn to sing a hymn together, laughingly excusing himself. "You don't need my off-key bellowing to ruin your music."

On the Sundays Cay Miller joined them for lunch, Karyn saw that Sophie was polite, but she didn't sparkle for Cay as she did for Mikal. Only for Mikal did Sophie turn on all her charms.

Each time Karyn thought that she and Mikal might have time to grow closer, something happened to draw their attention elsewhere. Ella got sick, and Mikal had to go to Emile for advice. The plums ripened, and for several consecutive days Karyn was gone half the morning gathering. One of the horses got a bad gash on its leg. In the midst of all the little crises, there was work and more work.

Sophie's "work," except for tending to Ella, seemed to be staying near the house, sewing and singing to herself. More and more women were bringing in sewing, and Cay Miller asked again for shirts for his store. Sophie could not keep up with all the sewing, let alone help Karyn with other chores. She did manage, however, to make Mikal a straw hat. By plaiting some of the hail-damaged wheat and soaking the long braids in water, she made them soft enough to sew 'round and 'round into a hat.

Karyn labored from dawn until sunset, falling into bed so exhausted she fell immediately asleep. Every time she thought of some little thing she might do for Mikal, she found herself either too busy or too tired to realize her plan.

The second week of August Mikal began to talk of making a trip to the cedar canyons. "Cay Miller wants to stockpile fence posts. He says that once the settlers have built their homes, they will turn their attention to fencing in their property to keep the ranch cattle out of their fields. He will buy all the posts I can cut and pay eleven cents each for them. Luc will probably want to come with me."

Sophie pouted. "You men are always going off somewhere and leaving us alone."

"You won't be alone. Cay will keep an eye on you."

Sophie rolled her eyes and stabbed ferociously at the shirt lying in her lap.

Mikal turned toward Karyn. "Remember when I said that God would provide for us, Karyn? I can earn enough money from this to more than pay for the winter wheat I want to try. And you will be able to stock up on groceries."

On the day that Mikal was to leave, Karyn got up early to get her gardening finished. She had been surprised at her own feelings of dread at the prospect of his leaving. He had said that he and Luc would be gone for at least two weeks. *If it weren't for Sophie, I could have gone along.*

Karyn decided that elderberry sauce would taste delicious poured over the fried cakes they always ate for lunch. It would be a nice treat for Mikal and a nice way to send him off on his trip to the cedar canyons. She set aside the morning of chores she had planned and hurried to a stand of elderberries a quarter of a mile from the soddy.

Mikal's team was already hitched up and waiting outside the soddy when Karyn got back from her berry-picking. *It's a good thing I already rinsed these off in the creek. If I hurry I can still have his surprise ready.* Intending to slip behind the house, Karyn stopped short when she heard Sophie giggling. *I'm not eavesdropping. This is my home. I can enjoy the fresh air for a moment or two if I wish.*

"We can't send you off with a tear in your shirt, Mikal," Sophie was saying. "I can mend it in just a moment. In fact, why not let me get your measurements now, and I can make you a new shirt while you are gone?"

Hearing Sophie's tone of voice, Karyn knew the exact expression that was on her face. She had pursed her lips in a charming little pout. "Come now, Mikal. All seamstresses do fittings for their customers. You don't want a shirt that won't button, do you? Don't be shy. Just take the shirt off so I can get accurate measurements. There's so much sewing to do, and I don't want to waste my time making something that won't fit." She sighed. "There's so little I can do to be of help to Karyn. She works so hard every day. Why, she's ruining her skin while I lounge indoors." She coaxed, "The thought of her growing stooped over like an old woman while I cannot help . . . sewing is a way I can help her, Mikal. Don't you see? If I can take the sewing off her hands, then—"

There was a long pause, and then Sophie said, "Yes. That's it." Sophie cleared her throat. "Chest—123 centimeters. Neck—49 centimeters. Now the sleeve length. Yes, I see. It's a good thing you let me measure, Mikal. I never guessed you were so broad-shouldered."

Karyn finally went to the door. Mikal was standing near the stove with his back to her. Karyn caught her breath as she took in the sight of flawless suntanned skin, broad, muscular shoulders . . . and Sophie's small white hand on Mikal's arm. Sophie noticed Karyn and dropped her hand. "Karyn—you see that I have convinced your shy husband to let me get proper measurements for my sewing."

Mikal wheeled about, grabbed his thermal undershirt, and pulled it quickly over his head.

Sophie broke the awkward silence between them. "And now I will be able to do something to help you even more, dear sister." She clucked her tongue. "We'll have to get extra fabric from Cay. This giant you call your husband is going to require much larger shirts than I anticipated." She flashed an admiring glance up at Mikal.

"I'll ride into Millersburg as soon as Mikal has his lunch," Karyn said mechanically. She swallowed hard. Looking down at the basket of elderberries she whispered hoarsely, "I was going to make something special, but . . ." —she looked at Mikal—"I see that the team is already hitched up. You need to leave. You probably won't want to be bothered with my little surprise." She blinked back tears and pushed by him. Karyn took no notice of the project Sophie had laid out on the makeshift table next to the sewing machine. She set the basket of elderberries down on top of it. Reaching for a covered crockery bowl that stood on the kitchen stove, she mumbled, "I already have the batter mixed. It won't take long to fry some cakes for you. Then you can be on your way."

In only a few moments, Karyn was handing Mikal a plate piled high with fried cakes. She had fresh milk for him to drink and plenty of butter for the cakes. There were even two fried eggs. But Sophie was the only one who truly enjoyed the small feast. Mikal pretended to eat, all the while watching Karyn from under the brim of his hat. Karyn drank cup after cup of strong coffee. She busied herself with tending the fire and a thousand little things that didn't need to be done.

When Mikal finally stood up to go, Sophie stood on tiptoe and demanded that he bend over so that she could kiss him on the cheek. Karyn turned to go to the well for wash water. She had a bucket of water near the top of the well when Mikal reached from behind her and hoisted it up.

"Thank you." She added mechanically, "I hope you

have success these next two weeks. I—" She wanted to say she would miss him, but something held her back.

As she turned to reach for the bucket of water, she felt the pressure of Mikal's hand on the small of her back. Quickly, he leaned down and kissed her on the cheek. He didn't even take off his hat, and the kiss itself was nothing much. It only took an instant. Mikal didn't say a word, and Karyn didn't dare look at him. She stood with her hands on the curbing of the well, listening as he drove away.

The Diary
July 31, 1880
Hot and clear. Mikal is gone to cut fence posts. He says it will yield enough for red wheat and a load of groceries. The wheat lies beneath the snow all winter and ripens in summer. In spite of my efforts here, I begin to think it might be best if I do not expect to see the results of planting this new crop.

CHAPTER 13

A Pocketknife

And call upon me in the day of trouble: I will
deliver thee, and thou shalt glorify me.
Psalm 50:15

The evening that Mikal left, Karyn and Sophie ate a cold supper in relative silence. Knowing she had carried her flirting with Mikal too far, Sophie did not have the courage to reach over the wall she had built between herself and her sister. Karyn had the courage, but she didn't have the energy. So, the two women spoke in half-sentences about things that didn't matter.

After the meal, Sophie insisted that Karyn let her wash the dishes. "And I've already washed the elderberries, so don't worry about them. I think I'll try making some jam tomorrow. And I don't want you to help. I want to try it myself. Why don't you try to sleep late tomorrow, Karyn? You've been working so hard lately. I can feed the sow and get breakfast."

There was the sound of yelping near the corral. Karyn got up. "I'll go check on that. Those coyotes seem bent on getting at Ella's calf. I might walk out toward the ridge. Light the lamp and set it in the window. I don't plan on getting lost, but it never hurts to take precautions." She retrieved Mikal's rifle from inside the soddy and headed down to the corral, where she fired two warning shots in the direction of the coyotes' yelps.

Karyn watched until the lighted lamp appeared in the window. Then she made her way around the edge of the corral and toward the north. She walked in an ever-widening semicircle. Finding no sign of the coyotes, she finally made her way back to the corral. But instead of heading up the slope for bed, she went into the dugout.

Mikal's Bible lay on a table next to the bed. Karyn sat down on the bed, sinking into the feather mattress. She picked up the Bible. In the waning light, she couldn't make out very much, but she could tell that Mikal had, indeed, underlined many, many verses between the worn covers of the book. Resentment and hurt flickered. If he knew so much of this book, then why did he behave as he did with Sophie? Didn't he know it hurt her terribly?

She heard Sophie calling for her. Sighing, Karyn put the Bible down and went to the door of the dugout. "I'm all right, Sophie," she called. "I'm coming." She plodded up the slope.

"I was worried about you," Sophie said. "Come to bed, Karyn. I don't hear any coyotes yelping now."

It wasn't long before Sophie fell asleep. Karyn slipped out of bed, picked up the lantern, and went back down to the dugout where she sat for some time thumbing casually through Mikal's Bible. When she grew sleepy, instead of going back up to the soddy, Karyn stretched out on Mikal's bed.

As shadows flickered on the walls of the dugout, Karyn let her mind go back to the first time she had seen Mikal Ritter. Could it possibly have been four months ago? It seemed like only yesterday. He had half frightened her, with his huge hands and startlingly blue eyes, his mane of wild black hair. *But I never back down from a challenge*, Karyn thought. *So when he asked, I said yes.*

She thought through the ensuing weeks when she had

struggled so to deal with the harsh realities of life in Custer County. What had made her try so hard? Why hadn't she just packed up and left? With her sewing, she could make a living anywhere. *But it wasn't really a living I was looking for.* Finally, Karyn admitted to herself that yes, she had come to America hoping for love. And yes, she had grown to love Mikal Ritter. Just exactly when it had happened, she was not certain. But love him she did. And she could tell a thousand reasons why.

Then, as Karyn thought back over their weeks together, she looked for reasons to be hopeful that, even after being married to someone like Marie-Louise, Mikal Ritter might love someone like herself. *I work hard for him.* But a thousand women would work hard. It was expected. Working hard couldn't make a man love a woman. *I'm not so bad looking.* But even in the poor light in the dugout, Karyn could see the effects of all the hard work on her hands. She could feel that her skin had grown rougher. And she hardly ever had time or energy to put her hair up in that coronet that looked so attractive. *We can have fun at the socials.* But socials in general and dancing in particular didn't seem important to Mikal. Thinking back, Karyn could remember only two times when she had been fairly certain that Mikal felt attracted to her in a way that might end in love. He had been upset when she danced with Luc. And he had squeezed her hand that day when they were alone in the fields. *But lately he hasn't seemed to care much at all. He is much more solicitous of Sophie than of me. He's very concerned for her health . . . and he does so many things to make her life easier.*

No matter how many times Karyn considered the situation, she came to the same conclusion: Mikal Ritter was too honorable a man to admit it, but he had fallen in love with Sophie. As for the little kiss he had given her earlier that day, it wasn't hard to explain. It was only Mikal's way of telling her that he would be true to his marriage vow.

Celest had said that God had chosen her, Karyn, to be Mikal's wife. Celest had said that things would work out. *Well, Celest,* Karyn thought. Then, she raised her heart higher. *Well, God in heaven. I have been patient. I have done what I can. And now, what am I to do? Do I stay here and serve Mikal, all the while knowing that, while he likes me as a friend, he has much deeper feelings for Sophie?* Karyn took a deep breath. *I don't know if I can do that. Celest says that You care about things like this. Celest says that I must trust You and that You will work it out.* Karyn swallowed hard, fighting against the lump in her throat. *If You are the Author of love, then can You not make Mikal love me?* Karyn buried her face in Mikal's pillow and wept.

As Mikal had suspected, Luc was delighted with the idea that he drive an extra wagon and help cut wood. While Luc went to the corral to hitch up a second team, Emile drew Mikal aside. "You boys be careful up there. Fred Smith was by yesterday and said they finally found what happened to the old settler who headed up there last year and never came back. A storm washed what was left of him out of a thirty-foot hole. Fred said the sides of the hole were charred. Lightning must have struck one of the older trees and burned completely down into the roots. The poor old fellow must have slipped into the hole. I'm glad you won't be going alone."

Mikal assured Emile that he and Luc would stay together. He stooped to where his grub box sat waiting to be loaded onto his wagon. Pretending to check over its contents, he said, "I wanted Karyn to go. But I didn't know how to ask her. With Sophie there—"

Emile raised one eyebrow and asked, "Do I detect a little negative feeling toward Sophie's presence?"

Mikal shrugged, closed his grub box and hoisted it to its place under the wagon seat. "Oh, Sophie's all right. I owe it to Karyn to make her feel welcome. It's just that—" He took his hat off and ran his fingers through his hair.

Emile leaned against the wagon. He put his hand on Mikal's shoulder. "You know, Mikal, even the wise patriarch Abraham had difficulty managing a household that included two women."

Mikal wiped his forehead with his sleeve. He nodded agreement. "Yes. But what can I do? She's Karyn's sister."

The men lifted two jugs from the back of the wagon and headed for the well. As Emile pulled a bucket of fresh water up he asked, "Does Karyn know how you feel?"

Mikal shook his head. "I don't know. We were getting along well, but since Sophie arrived there seems to be something between us. I don't know how to get around it. There's never a moment when Karyn and I can just—talk." Mikal shook his head. He filled the two jugs with water. "She's strong-willed. She doesn't back down from a challenge, and I admire her for that. But I can't tell how she feels about me. And this morning I let Sophie talk me into something." He recounted the incident of the shirt-fitting. "I've never claimed to be the most intelligent man in the county, but looking back on that, I can't believe I was so dense. It was totally innocent. I was only thinking that here was another way to encourage Sophie to do something constructive. But then Karyn came in. Seeing it through her eyes, it must have looked terrible. Who knows what it made her think? She just pulled it all inside, made my lunch, and said good-bye. I kissed her on the cheek. I meant it as an apology, but I might as well have been kissing a tree for all the response I got."

Emile frowned and shook his head. "I think you may have to come up with something better than a kiss on the cheek to make up for that one, Mikal. Since you brought this up I will tell you that Celest has been concerned that Sophie is too—familiar—with you."

Mikal nodded. "I know. I've been telling myself not to be vain and think more of it than I should." He shook his head. "But really, Emile. I passed over a dozen girls like Sophie in Grand Island the day I met Karyn. Girls like Marie-Louise. I made that mistake once. I wasn't going to make it again. The more I see of Karyn, the more I like." Hooking a finger through the handle of each water jug he started back toward the wagon. He stopped abruptly and corrected himself. "The more I see of Karyn, the more I love." He looked at Emile. "But then that wall, whatever it is, looms between us. I say the wrong thing, she doesn't say anything." He sighed. "I don't know how to fix it."

Emile followed Mikal back to the wagon where he set the two water jugs behind the wagon seat. Then Emile asked, "Is there something besides Sophie between the two of you?"

Mikal leaned against the wagon box and thought before answering. "Maybe. Karyn told me there was someone in Germany who got killed. She made it sound like it was nothing. But Sophie has let it be known more than once that he was refined, educated, wealthy." He shook his head. "If she's comparing me to him, I don't have much of a chance." He paused. "But I'd sure like to have some time alone with her. Time to talk things out."

"It might take more than talking, Mikal," Emile reminded him.

"I could manage that, too," Mikal said quietly.

"Well, Mikal, here's what I suggest. While you are gone, make it a matter of prayer. Then, if you still feel the same way when you get back, you say something like this: 'Karyn, I am in love with you. Let's send Sophie to the Delhommes' for a visit.'" Emile chuckled. "I'm certain Celest can think of a reason why she needs Sophie's help. By the time you get back, I'll have her convinced. She doesn't approve of Sophie, but if I tell her that it's for

Karyn, she'll be more than willing to help. Luc can bring Sophie here."

Luc walked up. "I only heard the last sentence. But I like the plan, whatever it is." He put one hand on his father's shoulder and one hand on Mikal's. "If Sophie came for a visit, perhaps Mother would change her mind."

Emile defended his wife. "Your Mother—and I—want what is best for you, son. If you are to fulfill your dream of teaching music, you must have a wife who supports you in every way. She must be willing to get by on very little during your years of study."

"How can you be so certain that Sophie would ruin me?" Luc's voice rose a few decibels. "It should be obvious to both of you that she doesn't belong here. She was never meant for this life. If she were living in an apartment in Philadelphia with me, she'd be a different girl. I'm certain of it. Don't be so judgmental."

"And don't be so defensive, Luc," Mikal said. "If you can win Sophie's heart, please do so. And sooner rather than later."

Thanking Emile for his advice, Mikal nodded at Luc. "So let's be going. I'm in a hurry to get home."

All day, every day, for the next week, Luc and Mikal cut wood. While they cut, Mikal prayed about Karyn, and Luc talked about Sophie. A week of praying had made Mikal even more convinced that Karyn was the woman God wanted for him. If only he could convince Karyn of the same thing. Finally, the two men had both wagons filled with fence posts.

"Eleven cents a post," Mikal said as he loaded the last post into his wagon. "That's enough for me to buy that new red wheat I want to try and a few groceries. We should make another haul if we can. I'm hoping Karyn won't have to cook the entire winter with only cornmeal. Another seven dollars would buy a hundred-pound bag of flour."

Luc teased, "I don't know about you, Mikal. One minute you're wondering if Karyn cares about you at all. The next you're assuming she'll be here through the winter."

"She already agreed to stay through the winter," Mikal said.

Luc shook his head. "You better think of something more romantic to buy her than a bag of flour, Mikal. Or have you already decided to spend another winter in that dugout?"

Mikal changed the subject. "I think if I head south across East Table I can get this load to Cay sooner. After you get back to your place, would you ride over and tell Karyn I'll be home in a few days?"

The two wagons headed off, Luc to the southeast toward his own farm, and Mikal into unfamiliar territory. Traversing Pleasant Valley, he made his way across East Table.

Mikal's trouble started after nightfall when the team descended a steep incline and approached the north branch of Mud Creek. There was a full moon, but nowhere did a pinprick of golden light shine through the darkness to lead him to a house. He was lost. On a ridge just ahead, a dark shape loomed up. Hoping to find shelter for the night, Mikal headed up the ridge. The shape proved to be a fallen-in sod house. In the moonlight, Mikal thought he saw a wagon track leading south. *That's it, that's where I should have been all along.* Thinking he had found his way, Mikal turned the team and was heading down the track when Lena faltered. She seemed to have stepped into a hole. She lunged sideways against Grace and stood trembling in the dark.

"Whoa there, Lena," Mikal called out to calm her while he jumped down from the wagon and made his way alongside her. "Maybe we should just camp over near that house and wait until daylight. Let's see, girl—is your leg all—"

Mikal never finished that sentence. As he came even with Lena's flank, he was plunged downward into what he now realized was an old well. Feeling suspended in time, he flung his arms up over his head and slapped his boots together. "God!" The moment he cried out his one-word prayer, Mikal hit the bottom of the well. Several feet of mud and water saved his life.

He was covered with cold water, the entire lower half of his body buried in mud. Choking and sputtering, he managed to flounder about in the mud enough to get his face out of the water. Then, with another prayer for help, he tried to calm himself and get his bearings.

His right knee was twisted, and he suspected his ankle might be broken. Thankfully, his arms were all right, but every breath confirmed that at least one rib had been broken. Looking up, Mikal thought, *It's a miracle I didn't break my neck.* The mouth of the well was barely visible above him. The full moon cast shadows down into the well. When his eyes finally adjusted to the dark, he estimated that at least one hundred feet of earth separated him from escape.

He began to shiver. *I've got to get up out of this water.* The wooden curbing around the bottom of the well was too slimy for him to get hold of, but he managed to break off a loose board. By bracing the board across the top of the curbing, he made a small shelf. As he tried to lift himself onto the shelf, the mud sucked his boots off. With a shout against the pain of the broken rib, he pulled himself onto the little shelf. He leaned against the side of the well until morning.

"Lena—Grace—are you there?" Sunlight was pouring down into the well. Blue sky shone overhead. Mikal called again, "Lena—Grace!" An answering whinny brought a sigh of relief. *God, please send someone this way. Let them see the wagon. Send someone.*

No one came. The mud caked from his waist down had

begun to dry. His stomach growled. Mikal looked up again. In the daylight, it was easier to see how the well was built. There were large sections completely surrounded by wood curbing. Then there would be three or four feet where there was no curbing at all. As far as he could see, everything was in good condition. *At least it's not going to cave in on me.*

Mikal managed to brace himself against the sides of the well and stand up on his good foot. Even with his long arms fully extended he was still at least two feet from the top of the next section of curbing. *Well, Father, what do I do now?* The answer to his prayer came in the form of the pocketknife in his back pocket. *Thank God it didn't disappear into the mud down there.*

Over the next few hours, Mikal laboriously cut wedges into the side of the well. When he was ready to climb up, he removed his socks. Then, he undid his overalls and tied the long straps around the board he had used for a shelf. Tentatively he crept up the side of the well, breathing a sigh of relief when the board was dislodged and dangled below him, held fast by his overall straps. At the top of the next section of curbing, he let go with one hand, worked along the denim straps until he had the board in his hands. Then he positioned it across the top of the curbing. Again he perched on the board.

It was late afternoon. He called again to his horses, rejoicing when Lena's head appeared at the top of the well. She whickered softly. A few stalks of dried grass fell out of her mouth and wafted down the well shaft past Mikal.

"Good girl, Lena, good girl. You stay nearby. God will surely send someone after me."

Mikal rested on the board. His ankle was swollen. His knee hurt worse. Every breath sent sharp pains through his midsection. For the first time, he considered the possibility that he might not have the strength to get out of the well alone. He dozed off, jerked awake by the awful sensation of falling every time his head nodded forward.

During his second night in the well, Mikal listened to coyotes yelping near the abandoned farmstead. In spite of his earnest pleas to God, the coyotes came nearer and nearer. Mikal called out to the team trying in vain to keep them calm. But finally the coyotes sounded right above the mouth of the well. With a shrill whinny, Lena and Grace charged off.

Listening to the crashing sounds as his wagon bounced along behind the terrified team, Mikal realized that there was no chance Lena and Grace would run home. They couldn't possibly know the way. They would run at will, scattering his load of cedar posts across the empty prairie. If they came to a canyon they would plunge to their deaths. Exhausted, Mikal contemplated the loss of his team, the loss of his income, the loss of his own life. Discouraged, wet, and hurting, he brushed angry tears off his face.

Lena and Grace might well have leaped off a canyon ridge had it not been for a wide creek that brought them up short. Foaming at the mouth, their sides heaving, the mares finally stopped running. They drank deeply, lifting their heads to look about them, flicking their ears back and forth. They began to graze. They grazed along the banks of the creek for several hours before Lena lifted her head, pricked her ears, and began to walk east. Grace followed willingly, munching huge mouthfuls of grass. In less than an hour Lena and Grace pulled their empty wagon up to a familiar barn. It was dark. The mares helped themselves to a pile of hay outside the barn.

Daylight finally trickled down into the well, making it easier for Mikal to look around him. He had spent his second night in the well. His strength was waning, and he knew that if he was to survive, this must be the day he reached the top. All day he inched his way up the side of the well, laboriously carving footholds and handholds with his pocketknife. By the end of the day he had made his way to the last curbing. He was only about sixteen feet from the top of the well. But when he examined the last layer of curbing he realized that it would take a miracle for him to make it out. Earth had washed away behind the curbing. If he put his full weight on it, it would hurtle to the bottom of the well and take him with it.

The only way was to burrow behind the curbing, cut toeholds, and pray that by some miracle the earth would hold long enough for him to scramble to safety. Every inch was agony now. He held his breath and reached up, trying to ignore the stabbing pains in his side, his knee, his feet and ankles. He managed to scrape earth away. It took most of the rest of the day for him to hollow out a place big enough for his entire body. *For once I wish I were Cay Miller's size,* he thought grimly.

Within six feet of the top of the well he struck slippery clay. With one last monumental effort, he pulled himself from behind the top of the last curbing. Grimacing with pain he groped upward. He could barely reach the mouth of the well. With a prayer for a miracle, he put the foot that could bear weight on the curbing he had just tunneled behind. He could feel it giving way. With a mighty push, he propelled himself upward, even as the curbing crashed to the bottom of the well. He heard it hit the water just as his upper body cleared the mouth of the well. He dangled there for a moment, unable to force his sore knee to make any more effort.

Finally, with a combination of pulling and scrambling with his knees, Mikal pulled himself up. He was above the ground for the first time in two nights and nearly two full days. He thought of the dead settler whose remains had been washed out of the hole in the cedar canyons. Looking back down into the black hole behind him,

Mikal shuddered. Ignoring his twisted knee, he knelt and thanked God for the miracle of life. Exhausted, he crawled inside the abandoned soddy and fell asleep.

It was almost night when Mikal awoke. He was alive, but his ordeal was far from over. He was thirsty and hungry. He couldn't walk. And he was lost. *If two days and two nights in a well didn't kill me, crawling across the prairie won't, either.* He headed out, following the trail of cedar fence posts left by Lena and Grace's wild dash away from the coyotes.

Celest Delhomme was always the first one up in her household. She prided herself on having her stove fired up and breakfast in progress before the men got up to do their morning chores. It was before dawn when Celest hurried toward the henhouse to gather eggs for breakfast. She rounded the edge of the barn and stopped short at the sight of Lena and Grace and Mikal's empty wagon.

Barely half an hour after Celest found Lena and Grace, the four Delhomme men had saddled horses and were loping across the prairie in the direction they guessed the wagon had come. In the early morning light, it was difficult to follow the trail, but as the sun came up the trail became more evident. They found the spot where the mares had stopped to drink at the creek. From there, a trail of cedar posts led them to where Mikal lay unconscious in the middle of the prairie. He was barefoot and covered with dried mud from his waist down.

Luc knelt over Mikal. "His ankle is broken," he called up to his father.

Together, the men turned him over. Remi pulled Mikal's head into his lap and began to trickle water from a canteen into his mouth. When he finally began to stir, he drank greedily.

"Karyn?" he asked weakly.

The men laughed with relief. "Well, God knows where

he has been in reality, but I guess we all know where he has been in his dreams."

The sound of masculine laughter brought Mikal fully awake. He started to sit up, but Emile pushed him back.

"Whoa there, Mikal, your ankle is broken. Don't move too much until we check you out."

"Just the ankle. Maybe a rib. My knee is twisted. Otherwise, I'm all right."

"What happened?" Luc wanted to know.

"Lena stumbled in a hole in the night. It turned out to be an old well. I got out to check on her and went down the well. The team ran off. Coyotes." He sat up slowly, wincing and laying one hand over his side.

Luc explained, "Mother went out this morning to gather eggs and found them standing by the barn."

Emile broke in, "Can you ride, Mikal? We can go back for the wagon if you need it."

"I can ride. Just get me home."

Emile shook his head. "You are in no condition to go far. Your ankle must be set and Celest must supervise that." Emile looked up. "Luc, you ride to Mikal's and get Karyn and Sophie. We'll meet you at home."

The Diary
August 9, 1880

Mikal still gone. I'm glad Luc is with him. I worry less. Hot and clear. The coyotes are growing more determined to get Ella's calf. I am more determined that they won't. Sophie helps more.

CHAPTER 14

Overall Buttons

For I will pour water upon him that is thirsty,
and floods upon the dry ground.
Isaiah 44:3

Karyn was working in Mikal's ruined wheat field when Luc Delhomme rode up.

"What's happened?" she asked abruptly, trying to keep her voice from shaking.

"He's all right," Luc said. "But he took a bad fall down a well. Then Lena and Grace were frightened by coyotes. By some miracle they came to our house. We found Mikal today. His ankle is broken—"

Karyn reached up. "Pull me up behind you. We'll have to get Sugar. Sophie will want to come." When they reached the corral, Karyn hopped down. "I'll saddle Sugar. You go on up and tell Sophie. Tell her to pack a bag with clean clothes for both of us. I'll get some of Mikal's things from the dugout." She slid down and hurried into the dugout where she collected Mikal's only other pair of overalls and his Bible. With a grim smile, she realized that it was a good thing Sophie had made Mikal a new shirt.

Luc rode up the slope and dismounted at the soddy where Sophie sat under the wide porch sewing. Her bright smile faded the moment she saw Luc's face. She reached out to grab Luc's arm. "What is it? Is it Mikal? Is he—is he dead?" Her voice went up with each word until she sounded nearly hysterical.

"Calm down, Sophie. He's had a bad fall. But by now Mother probably has him bandaged and drinking tea. Karyn said to tell you to pack a bag for the two of you. We'll ride over right away."

Karyn had saddled Sugar, packed Mikal's bag, and ridden up to the house to join Luc when Sophie rushed outside with Karyn's carpetbag.

"Get your bonnet, Sophie," Karyn reminded her. "And Mikal's new shirt. And calm down. Luc says he is all right, and we'll see for ourselves soon enough. He's in good hands."

Karyn urged Sugar forward. Luc extended his hand toward Sophie. "Ride behind me, Sophie."

On the way to the Delhommes', Luc told what he knew of Mikal's adventure.

The moment the trio arrived at the Delhommes', Sophie slid off Luc's horse and started to rush inside. But Celest intercepted her, pulling her back by her sleeve. She spoke to Karyn. "Serge and Remi helped me set the ankle, and I've wrapped his knee. I hope you brought clean clothes. We did what we could, but none of my men's things will fit him. He couldn't even button Serge's shirt."

Karyn held up the bag of Mikal's things. Celest nodded, finally looking at Sophie to include her in the conversation. "Now listen, girls, he looks terrible. He's bruised and scratched, and it hurts every time he moves. Just remember that in spite of appearances and the grimaces and groans, he's come out of this in amazingly good condition. It's a miracle he survived. Emile helped dig that well a few years ago. He said it's at least 140 feet deep."

Celest dropped her hand from Sophie's arm, and she rushed inside ahead of Karyn. "Oh, Mikal," Sophie cried out, falling to her knees beside him. "You poor, poor, thing. What an ordeal!"

Mikal smiled weakly. "I must be a sight." He was patting Sophie on the head, reassuring her, when Karyn and Celest came in.

Karyn froze in the doorway.

Celest frowned. "Sophie, would you come with me? Karyn and Mikal should have some time alone."

Even with Sophie gone, Karyn didn't trust herself to say anything. She was too afraid of embarrassing both herself and Mikal with unwelcome emotion, so she merely leaned against the kitchen table, her hands clasped before her.

Mikal made an attempt at humor. "Some stupid husband you have, Karyn."

"You need to rest," Karyn said. She felt a sudden need to escape lest she succumb to the temptation to engulf Mikal in her arms. "I'll call one of the boys to help you upstairs."

"Karyn," Mikal said softly. "That business at the house with Sophie. And the shirt."

Focusing on Mikal's broken ankle, Karyn forced herself to say calmly, "What is important right now, Mikal, is that you are all right. We can speak of other matters later." She laughed grimly. "It's a good thing Sophie made that shirt." She produced the bag of clean clothing. "I have your other overalls, too. Tomorrow I can go to Millersburg and get new boots."

"But, Karyn—" Mikal cleared his throat, wincing as he shifted his weight in his chair.

"Please, Mikal. Don't speak of it. Not now. We'll talk another time. You must be very tired. I'll get one of the boys to help you upstairs to bed." She hurried out of the room.

Celest and Sophie were coming back from the henhouse. Two plump chickens had met their demise and were dangling from Celest's hands. Luc walked up and began to tease Sophie about her cleaning the chickens for supper.

"Luc," Karyn said shakily, "would you help Mikal upstairs? He needs to rest." Without waiting for Luc to answer her, Karyn turned and walked toward Celest's garden.

Sophie started to follow her, but Celest pulled her back. "No," she said firmly. "You go on inside. Scald the chickens and get them plucked. I'll see to Karyn."

Sophie looked down at the dead birds.

Celest held the chickens out to her. "Just be sure you get all the pinfeathers singed off."

Sophie looked up with pleading eyes. Something in the older woman's expression told her this was not a good time to feel faint. With a grimace, Sophie took the chickens. "Yes, ma'am." She headed for the kitchen.

Smiling to herself, Celest went to look for Karyn. She found her in the garden, sitting where she could lean against the sod wall.

As Celest settled beside her, Karyn smiled weakly and wiped her face on her apron. "I've always been this way. I do very well when the crisis is at hand, but once it's over, I have to sneak away somewhere and have a good cry."

"Ah, but I think this little cry is about more than today's crisis."

Karyn began to cry again. Words tumbled out. "You told me that God had chosen me to be Mikal's wife. You told me to talk to God about it. Well, I have. And the only thing that has happened is that I have had the pleasure of watching my sister throw herself at my husband and my husband succumb to her charms." Karyn described the incident the morning before Mikal left to cut wood. By the end of the story, she had begun to cry again.

Celest said quietly, "Things are not always as they seem, Karyn. It seems to you that Mikal cares for Sophie. It seems to you that God has not answered your prayers. But perhaps Mikal was only trying to humor Sophie into doing something productive." She paused, adding thoughtfully,

"Perhaps God withholds the very thing you want most, so that you will realize that you need Him much more than you need Mikal Ritter."

Celest reached out to take Karyn's hand as she said, "Do you remember the first day we met? I could see that you had been crying when Emile and I rode up. But I could also see that you were determined not to let disappointment beat you down. Since that day, over and over again, I have seen how bright and intelligent and strong you are. You have found a way to overcome every disappointment that has come your way thus far, seemingly without much help from God. But now something has come into your life that has brought you to the end of yourself." She patted the back of Karyn's hand and sighed. "People who depend on other people for their happiness can never be truly happy, Karyn. We poor humans always disappoint one another."

Celest continued. "Let us suppose that Sophie never came. Right away, you and Mikal fell in love." She turned and looked Karyn directly in the eyes. "But one day Mikal goes out to cut wood and is killed in a terrible accident. What then?" Celest could see she was having an impact. She said slowly, "Stop putting Mikal Ritter on the throne of your life, Karyn. Only God belongs there."

Karyn took a deep breath. "I don't see how a relationship with God will solve this mess with Mikal."

Celest answered, "One of my favorite Scripture verses is in the Psalms. It says, 'Delight thyself also in the LORD; and he shall give thee the desires of thine heart. Commit thy way unto the LORD; trust also in him; and he shall bring it to pass.' That does not mean that God gives what we ask, Karyn. It means that He changes our hearts to desire His will."

"But I can't change wanting Mikal."

"And you don't have to. Your part is to delight in the Lord and to commit your way to Him. His promise is to give you right desires and to accomplish the best for you.

Leave your heart and Mikal's heart in God's hands. Only God rules men's and women's hearts."

Finally, Karyn admitted, "I know you're probably right. But I still don't think I can do it."

"A girl as strong-willed and independent as you? I know you, Karyn. You can do anything you set your mind to do. And in this matter, you will have God's help." She put her arm around Karyn's shoulders. "And even with our help you are going to be very busy taking care of things while Mikal's ankle mends."

"How long will that take?"

"I'd like to keep him here for at least two weeks. We could take him home in the wagon, but if he's there, he'll be up trying to do things long before he should. If he stays here, I'll see to it that he behaves himself."

She put her arm through Karyn's. "While you are taking care of Mikal's farm, you can grow your relationship with God. You don't have to be a scholar to understand what God says about Himself. Just pick up that little prayer book you have and read the Psalms. Much of God's character is revealed there."

"Mikal suggested I read his Bible."

Celest chuckled. "Through two different people God has told you that He wants you to get to know Him better, Karyn. Wouldn't you say it's time you listened?" She stood up, pulling Karyn to her feet.

"All right, Celest," Karyn said. "I'll do what you say." She took a deep breath and headed for the house. "Sophie and I will leave in the morning."

Celest shook her head and smiled. "I think you need this time alone with God. Leave Sophie with me. It's time she and I got to know one another better."

"Of course I'm driving the team home," Karyn insisted that evening at supper. "I'll need them. There's still at least one wagonload of wheat to be picked up. And if I'm

191

driving to Millersburg to get your boots, I can take the shirts Sophie finished for Cay's store. There will be more bolts of cloth to bring home. I need the wagon."

It was suppertime, and as the Delhommes, the Ritters, and Sophie sat around the table laden with bowls of fried chicken and baked potatoes, Celest had raised the idea of Mikal and Sophie remaining with her while Karyn carried on at the homestead.

Again, Mikal expressed doubt. "You might get hurt."

"How? There aren't any abandoned wells between here and Millersburg," Karyn joked. "The wagon trail is well beaten down. I can't get lost. What could possibly happen?"

"What if a snake spooks the team? What if someone bothers you? Custer County has its share of horse thieves and bandits."

"I'll take the rifle."

Mikal opened his mouth to say something, but Sophie interrupted him. "Karyn," she said, "I think it's time you let Mikal in on your little secret."

"I wouldn't be defenseless," Karyn said, reaching for a biscuit. "I know something about rifles."

"Don't be so modest, Karyn," Sophie said. Karyn buttered her biscuit while Sophie bragged. "Karyn hunted with Papa from the time she could walk. Last year in Brandenburg she won a shooting contest—in spite of the fact that one of the contestants was a retired military marksman."

Mikal still shook his head. "You've never driven the team. Remi can harness them here, but you'd have to manage at home. It's too much."

Sophie leaned over and patted him lightly on the shoulder. "Dear Mikal, there are many things you have yet to learn about Karyn. At home she drove Papa's delivery wagon. She knows all about harnessing and unhitching."

Serge interjected. "Give it up, Mikal." He raised his glass high. "To Karyn Ritter. Long may she reign."

So it was settled. Karyn would drive the team home, leaving Sugar for Sophie.

Karyn spent the night in a chair in the corner of the bedroom she shared with Mikal. She dozed fitfully, waking to the sound of Mikal groaning every time he moved in bed. Long before dawn, she rose to go downstairs. She had already opened the door when she turned back. She went to the bedside and looked down at Mikal. Impulsively, she reached out to touch his hair. Then, she leaned over to kiss his cheek. When she turned again to go, Mikal grabbed her hand and squeezed it.

"I was just going, Mikal," she whispered. "Go back to sleep." She heard the floor creak behind her. Sophie was standing in the doorway with an odd expression on her face. Karyn brushed by Sophie, pausing to say, "I'll heat water. If he wants some tea, it will be ready."

Karyn was only halfway down the stairs when she heard Celest say, "Good morning, Sophie. I'm so happy to see you feel well this morning. Come. You can help me gather eggs."

Karyn had been home only a few hours when Cay Miller drove up in a new carriage. He was dressed in an impeccably tailored suit and sported a stylish top hat.

"Oh, Cay," Karyn said. "I'm so sorry. Sophie isn't here. Mikal has had an accident. He broke his ankle, and he's staying where Celest can take care of him for a few days." Karyn almost choked on the next words, but she forced herself to sound casual. "I left Sophie there to help."

Cay frowned. His voice was warm with concern as he asked, "Is Mikal all right?"

As quickly as she could, Karyn recounted Mikal's story.

Cay shook his head. "We *must* get a campaign going to get those old wells filled in."

Karyn laughed. "Well, as soon as Mikal's ankle heals, I

know one well that will be filled in. He vowed to personally drag that soddy down and use the sod to fill in the well."

"You tell him to come see me before he does it. I'll get the county to pay him. He'd be doing the community a great service. Imagine if a child had fallen in!" Cay set his top hat on the seat beside him and asked, "What can I do to help you, Karyn?"

Karyn reached into her apron pocket and withdrew a piece of paper on which was traced the shape of a man's foot. She held it up to Cay. "Get Mikal a new pair of boots. His are still at the bottom of the well."

Cay nodded. "Done. What else?"

"Would you take a look at the wheat? Mikal seemed worried about letting it lie any longer."

Immediately Cay jumped down from the carriage. Tying his horse to the post that formed a corner of Karyn's porch, he headed down the hill. Karyn followed, smiling to herself as the little man swaggered ahead.

At the bottom of the hill, Cay waited for Karyn and together they walked to the nearest field. Adjusting his eye patch, Cay bent down and examined the wheat that had been partially shattered and flattened to the earth. Gathering a small bunch of it, he held it up and breathed in deeply. Then, he examined a single stalk closely. Finally, he said, "It's still dry. If you get it picked up and stacked before it rains, you could have a lot of fuel this winter."

"Fuel?" Karyn asked. "I thought that's what we collected chips for. And Mikal still has great hopes for the corn."

"If it's a bad winter, you'll need all the fuel you can get. Wheat straw burns well if you know just how to twist it," Cay offered.

"Can you show me?"

Cay nodded. They walked back to the dugout where Karyn had piled up some straw the previous week. Cay demonstrated, quickly twisting the bundle and tying it with more wheat.

Karyn watched carefully, then tried and failed. She tried again. On her third try, Cay approved. She smiled. "Good. I can work on that. I'll put the tied bundles in the dugout."

"I'll drive back in the morning in my work clothes and help you pick up the last of your wheat. Isaac Kruger will be glad to watch over the store for me. We can probably finish in a day or two."

Karyn smiled at him, her dark eyes glowing with appreciation. "Thank you, Cay. Remi and Serge promised to come by in a couple of days. But with your help perhaps I can have the job nearly finished before they arrive."

Cay frowned. "I suppose Luc will want to stay close to home now that he has Sophie right under his own roof."

"Don't give up so easily," Karyn encouraged him. She asked, "Can I make you an early supper?"

"I don't want to be any trouble," came the reply.

"It's no trouble. Actually, I'd welcome help unharnessing Lena and Grace. At home I drove my father's delivery wagon, but his old mare was barely alive compared to those two giants. They scare me a little. And I think they know it."

Cay smiled. "Draft horses are very gentle, Karyn. You've nothing to fear from them. You're more likely to get bucked off by Sugar than to have Lena or Grace hurt you. You'll see."

Watching Cay handle Lena and Grace helped Karyn relax with them. Cay was fully two inches shorter than Karyn, and yet the mares showed no signs of willfulness when Cay lead them into the corral. He showed Karyn how to undo the massive harness and hang it so that none of the straps tangled. Then, while he worked at cleaning Grace's gigantic feet, Karyn followed suit with Lena. By the time the mares had been curried and bedded down in the stalls inside the dugout, Karyn felt totally at ease handling the horses.

Over supper, Cay regaled Karyn with stories of his war experiences and his plans for Millersburg. When he finally rose to leave, he said, "You tell Mikal that as soon as his ankle heals, if he wants to cut more cedar, I'm paying twenty cents a post right now. I think that's about double what he expected." Cay shook his head. "It's too bad he lost that load."

"Why don't you tell him yourself?" Karyn wanted to know. She looked at Cay meaningfully. "He really could use those boots."

Cay grinned at her. "Well, since you can't take them over, and since he's in such a hurry, I guess I will be forced to deliver them myself."

"That would be really good of you, Cay. And be sure to tell Sophie I send my love." Karyn winked at him.

As Cay drove off, Karyn lit the lamp and put it in the window. Then, she took Celest's advice. Opening the little prayer book that Tilda Stoddard had given her weeks before, she turned to the back and began to read the Psalms. Even though what she read wasn't of any particular significance at first, she felt better knowing that she was fulfilling Celest's wishes. Celest had said that she should read and pray and leave the rest to God. She had determined to try it for at least the two weeks that Mikal and she were apart.

Once in bed, she recited a childhood prayer. But she couldn't sleep. Finally, she spoke into the darkness, "All right, God. I don't want to do this, but I am going to do it anyway. Sophie is a selfish, foolish girl, and I don't want her to have my Mikal. But I'm going to pray for her anyway. Please, God, help Sophie to be happy."

Karyn slept.

Over the next few days, Karyn thought about Mikal, worried over Sophie, and tried her best to trust God. She spent her evenings reading the Psalms. Nothing dramatic happened as a result of her reading. Still, it wasn't long before she began to notice certain themes in what she read. Fulfillment and true happiness were promised to those who turned to God, trusted Him, and served Him first instead of worrying about themselves.

She kept thinking about the cedar logs scattered on the prairie. *Twenty cents a piece. That's the same as if I sold Cay almost ninety pounds of butter.* But even as an idea began to form, she argued with herself. *Don't be ridiculous. You'll never find them.* Then she answered back, *But if I could find them . . . if I could load them . . . it would be a wonderful surprise for Mikal.*

Finally, Karyn tacked a note to the door: *Remi/Serge— Tell Mikal everything is fine. Wheat gathered. Twisted what I could and put in dugout. Gone to Millersburg.*

In Millersburg, Karyn got news from Cay that Mikal was acting like a caged bear.

"And Sophie?" Karyn asked.

Cay smiled. "Sophie is taking cooking lessons from Celest Delhomme. And learning to spin wool and do a million other things." He added happily, "She says she hasn't had a weak spell since she got there."

"That's wonderful!" Karyn said. She didn't ask any more, afraid of what she would hear. Instead, she asked Cay to bring her account up to date and pay her with boots, overalls, a shirt, and a hat. When Cay turned to fill her order, she said, "No, Cay. I think I only need a medium size. And here"—she rummaged in her basket— "I drew around my foot so you can guess at boots while I try on the overalls." She hurried to explain, "I'm going after that load of cedar posts Mikal lost."

"Oh, no, you're not!" Cay insisted. "That's a man's job. Those posts are heavy. You can't possibly—"

Karyn glowered at him. "Cay Miller, if you are going to court my sister, then you had better learn one thing about the Ensinger sisters. One thing you do *not* do is tell us what we cannot do." She added, "And if you are going to be my friend, you had better learn something about me. You can't tell me not to do something 'because it's a man's job.'" She set her basket on Cay's counter and stared at him. "I am going after those logs. I need gloves. And supplies for the grub box. Here's my butter and another shirt for you to sell. Now, you said you knew exactly where that old well is. Draw me a map."

Cay put his hands behind his back. "I can't, Karyn. Mikal would kill me."

"He will not kill you," Karyn said. "He doesn't even have to know, if you're that worried about it. I'll tell him I tricked you into telling me where the abandoned well was. That you didn't know I was planning on going there. That I sneaked the clothes off the shelf when you were back in your own quarters." Just talking about the adventure made her more determined than ever to do it.

"But you're afraid of the team."

"I drove them over here, didn't I?"

"Why don't you ask Remi and Serge to go? How do you know they haven't already gone after that load?"

Karyn shrugged. "I don't." She pleaded, "Please, Cay. I want to surprise Mikal. If I get that load of posts Mikal will be able to pay for both the red wheat and most of the winter's groceries." She leaned across the counter and whispered, "Just draw the map, and you'll have a standing invitation to Sunday dinner."

"Sophie is at the Delhommes'," he grumbled. "I doubt I have much chance with her."

"Why not?" Karyn said, praying that Mikal's name was not about to be mentioned. "Wasn't she nice to you when you took Mikal's boots out?"

"Oh, she was nice enough," he muttered. "But I know where I stand. I may only have one eye, but I can see very well how I compare to the handsome Mr. Delhomme."

"But you can offer a woman a future far better than

Luc's." Karyn reached across the counter and patted Cay's hand. "I said it before, Cay, and I repeat: Don't give up so easily."

Cay grinned. "All right. I won't." He pulled a piece of white paper off the roll bolted to his countertop and began to draw. "Stay on the east side of Muddy Creek. About five miles from here, it branches to the west. Don't follow that. Instead, go up the valley three miles. There will be a long ridge on your left. You'll see the soddy tucked against the ridge just after you pass a boulder the size of your house jutting out of the ridge." He reached behind the counter and collected a pair of overalls, shirt, hat, and gloves. "Try these on in my quarters. I've never fit a woman before."

Karyn walked back to Cay's quarters and reemerged in her stocking feet.

At the sight of her, Cay repeated, "Mikal will kill me if he ever finds out about this."

Karyn laughed. "Well, it's either be killed now by a very angry woman or later by Mikal. Either way, you're dead. Unless, of course, I come back with a full load of cedar fence posts. In which case Mikal will be very, very happy with both of us. Please tell me you have boots that will fit."

Cay tossed a pair of boots to her. "I'll stock the grub box while you put these on."

When Karyn exited his store, Cay followed her out to the wagon. "If you are not back by Friday, I am coming after you."

Karyn nodded. "Good. That way if I fall in a well somewhere, I will be rescued." She laughed. "Don't worry, Cay. I'll be fine." As she clamped on her new hat, she caught sight of Amalia Kruger. The old woman was standing in the doorway of Kruger's Harness Shop squinting at her in disbelief. Karyn called out a greeting, but Amalia pretended not to hear her.

Karyn had no difficulty following Cay Miller's map. She located the homestead, shuddering as she crawled to the edge of the well and peered down into the hole. She could see where Mikal had dug toeholds and handholds near the top. *Thank You, dear God. Whether he belongs to me or not, thank You that Mikal didn't give up.*

Karyn found the first cedar posts about a hundred yards from the well. Pulling the team up, she jumped down and hefted a post into the back of the wagon. After she had loaded only a few, she had to stop to rest. By the end of the day, she was exhausted. She had recovered all sixty-five posts. She unhitched Lena and Grace and walked them to the creek for a drink. As it grew dark, Karyn opened the grub box and ate a hearty meal. She tethered Grace and Lena where they could graze, stretched out under the wagon, and fell instantly asleep.

Dawn found Karyn headed back toward Millersburg with her full load of fence posts. She had barely started the drive along the edge of Mud Creek when two voices shouted, "Hey, you there! Stop! You've got our fence posts!"

Karyn pulled the team up and turned around to see Remi and Serge driving up in an empty wagon. She pulled off her hat, thoroughly enjoying the two young men's open-mouthed amazement.

"Karyn?" Remi sputtered, then broke out laughing. "I don't believe it!"

Karyn blushed. "I wanted to surprise Mikal."

"Well, he's going to be surprised, all right."

"Don't tell him. Please," Karyn pleaded.

"Well, how are we going to explain our empty wagon?"

"Tell him the truth. Someone had already picked up all the fence posts."

Remi nodded. "All right. That's fair." He chuckled. "Are there any more sisters at home like you?"

Karyn laughed. "No. The rest are sweet and charming.

And pretty, like Sophie." She was suddenly serious. "And how is Mikal? Is he mending?"

"He's going crazy. He wants us to make him a crutch. Mother says we're going to have to tie him to the bed before too much longer. His knee is better. And I think he actually managed to get out of bed this morning without sounding like a wounded bull because of that broken rib. He is mending. He misses you, though."

Karyn blushed. "Well, I'm sure Sophie is doing a good job taking care of him."

"Actually," Remi said pointedly, "Mother and Luc are keeping Sophie too busy for her to have much to do with Mikal."

Karyn's heart missed a few beats. Sophie wasn't spending much time with Mikal. Mikal missed her. *Let God handle Mikal's heart, Karyn.*

Serge and Remi escorted Karyn back to Millersburg. As they pulled up in front of Cay's store, Amalia Kruger came to the door of the house across the street. Karyn waved at her again before insisting that she help Remi and Serge unload the fence posts. When the wagon was empty, Cay tried to pay Karyn $13.00. She refused. "I just want Mikal's sack of red wheat. Put the rest on his account. I don't need anything right now."

"I suppose you're going to plant that for him, too," Remi joked.

"Not until I get a good night's rest," Karyn joked back.

At that moment, Amalia Kruger crossed the street. "Mrs. Ritter," she said shortly.

When Karyn turned around, Amalia muttered, "You must be very tired. You are welcome to stay with me tonight. A woman should not be out alone on the prairie after dark."

Karyn looked at her in amazement.

Amalia barked, "You don't want my help, I suppose," and started to shuffle back across the street.

"No, it's not that, Mrs. Kruger. I'm just surprised, that's all."

Amalia looked her up and down. "I have always liked Mikal Ritter. I am glad to see he finally got some sense and picked a woman who would last."

"Go ahead, Karyn," Remi said. "We'll take care of the team. You must be exhausted."

Karyn followed Amalia into her son's immaculate little house.

"My son and his wife are gone to Grand Island. Of course, they did not invite me along. You can have their bed. I put on clean sheets today. And the best quilt."

Karyn undressed wearily. Amalia brought her a cup of tea, but Karyn was already asleep. Peering at Karyn, Amalia smiled in spite of herself.

The Diary
August 16, 1880

Mikal recovers at Celest's from a terrible fall. The tale of it will no doubt be told for some time to come. As Mikal said, it is proof that God can help even when all hope is gone. If only I can apply that to other matters. I have shocked a few people by dressing like a man and retrieving Mikal's lost fence posts. I like knowing that I am helping.

CHAPTER 15

A Butter Stamp

Let my cry come near before thee, O LORD: give
me understanding according to thy word. Let my
supplication come before thee: deliver me
according to thy word.
Psalm 119:169–170

Karyn woke the next morning to the aroma of fresh coffee. She hurried to dress, intending to leave immediately.
When she reached the kitchen, Amalia was standing with
her back to Karyn at the stove. Something in the way the
wizened old woman held her head reminded Karyn
momentarily of her own mother. Amalia moved deliberately, as if she carefully thought out every movement. In
truth, Karyn wondered, looking at Amalia's crooked fingers, perhaps she had to do just that so her arthritic hands
and wrists would obey her.

As Karyn watched, Amalia bent to take a pan of fresh
biscuits from the oven. She grunted softly with the effort of
stooping, reached for the pan of biscuits, and slid it onto
the stove top. Closing the oven door evoked another soft
grunt. When Amalia rested a trembling hand on the top of
a nearby chair for a moment, Karyn's heart softened.

Amalia reached to a shelf near the stove and took down
two plates. When she turned to set them on the table, she

saw Karyn and nodded. Her voice sounded weary. "*Bitte setzen Sie sich*." Before Karyn could cross the large room to obey Amalia and sit down, Amalia was lifting a pot from the back burner of the stove and pouring strong black coffee into a huge brown cup beside Karyn's plate.

While she slathered a biscuit with butter, Karyn considered the room around her. Someone had tacked lace-edged paper along the shelf that held the dishes. There was only one plate and one cup on the shelf, which meant that the entire china supply of the Kruger household amounted to three plates and three cups. But they were china instead of tin like the ones Mikal used. The room was immaculate. From the wood puncheon floor to the rafters, there was not a speck of dust, not a cobweb, in sight. The panes of the window in the far wall sparkled in the morning light.

"You have a nice home, Frau Kruger," Karyn offered while she slathered a biscuit with butter.

"It is not mine. I am reminded of that often by my son's wife." Amalia sighed deeply. "Although she does not seem to mind that I clean it as if it were my own." Without getting up, Amalia reached for the plate of biscuits that she had left warming on the stove. She offered one to Karyn.

Karyn gulped coffee and said, "*Danke*. Having someone cook for me is a nice treat."

Amalia shrugged. "I am not worth much anymore. But I still make good biscuits."

"How long have you been here?" Karyn asked.

"Here? Where here? Here in Nebraska or here in America?"

"America," Karyn said.

"Fifteen years," Amalia said. "Fifteen years of regret and unhappiness." She peered over her tiny oval glasses and blurted out, "Be glad you came to America when you are so young. For young people it is simple. They come to America, they take off their German coat. They put on an American coat. Is done. Just so."

Karyn disagreed. "It has not been that simple for me."

"Already you are speaking English better than I, who have been here for many years." Amalia snorted softly. "Humph. Even that sister of yours speaks better English than I."

"Sophie was always a brilliant student," Karyn said. "I think God gave her that to compensate for her being ill so much. As for me, I had help from some children while their father worked with Mikal." She told Amalia about Tilda and Sten Stoddard.

"The daughter and son were about seven and nine years old—the wagon pulled by a team of skinny white horses?" When Karyn nodded, Amalia said, "I was in Miller's store when they came in. Stoddard was selling everything to go back to—Ohio I think it was." Her expression softened. "Your Mikal bought those children candy." Amalia shook her head. "Tilda Stoddard could have spent an entire year trying to teach me. It would have made no difference. I have no ear for languages." She grimaced. "*Ach*. No matter."

Karyn took another biscuit.

Amalia chuckled. "It is good to see a woman with an appetite." A smile slowly took over the wrinkles on her face, willing them to fold back and transform her usually dour expression into something more pleasant. "As soon as you left yesterday morning, I went over to Cay Miller's. It did not take long to get him to tell me the story of where Karyn Ritter was going dressed like a man." She lowered her voice. "I wish I had been so determined when I was young. I would have had a happier life."

Karyn was wary of Amalia. Still, it was good to be speaking German again. She couldn't resist asking, "What do you wish you had changed?"

"Everything," came the answer. "Everything." Amalia studied Karyn carefully for a moment or two. Then she got up and poured them both another cup of coffee, while she asked, "You are from Brandenburg? Do you know Oelde?" When Karyn shook her head no, Amalia smiled. "*Das schone Oelde.*" She described a charming city over-shadowed by a castle in the midst of thick woods. "My father was mayor of Oelde. When my mother died, I was thirteen." Amalia set the coffeepot back on the stove, but she didn't sit back down. She stared out the window and from her expression Karyn could tell that Amalia was back in Germany. "I was sent to live with my married brother in Munster. He was an independent thinker. So, unlike most German girls of my day, I was educated. We took trips along the Rhine, we attended dances and balls, we participated in musical clubs. We discussed philosophy and art with the same familiarity, the same fervor, as the farmers here discuss what kind of wheat to plant."

"Why did you leave?"

Amalia waved her hand in the air, shook her head, and plopped back in her chair. "For the same reason as you, and a thousand other women like us. Because of a man. My betrothed, Jacob Kruger, was a physician with a good practice and a promising future. I never dreamed he would do anything but practice medicine in Munster. But the fever to emigrate set in." Amalia sighed. "Suddenly, he could speak of nothing but America. Cheap land in America. Future riches. He said he was going to a place called Kansas." Amalia shrugged. "I threatened not to come—to break our engagement. But it was an empty threat. Women could not enter the professions in Germany. My brother would never have supported me. And besides"—Amalia smiled bitterly—"I loved Jacob. So, while my heart was breaking at the thought of leaving, my heart was also breaking at the thought of losing Jacob. He was so determined; so certain that America held the promise of wealth. So we married and came to America."

Amalia grunted. "We lived in a dugout. There was no other woman within ten miles of our little hovel. With his practice, Jacob was gone much of the time—and I was left alone. He learned English readily. But no Tilda Stoddard came along to help me." Amalia clucked her tongue against the roof of her mouth. "And there was no Celest Delhomme with whom I could share my troubles. There were no fences or walls within sight of my one-room house, but I still felt as though I was in prison."

"Such loneliness would be a kind of prison," Karyn empathized. "It must have been dreadful. But at least you knew your husband loved you."

Amalia looked at Karyn. Her eyes narrowed as she said, "Love does not always make the difference in every circumstance. It was still dreadful. There were days when I woke with the determination to take my own life and end my misery. But Jacob always kept his gun with him. And there was not even a tree from which to hang myself." She sighed. "Of course once there were children, I had to stay for them."

Karyn tried to encourage her. "Having children must have been a comfort."

Amalia looked at her keenly. "I thought it would be. Until I had to bury five of my babies there in Kansas."

"Oh, Amalia—I am so sorry." Karyn was beginning to understand why Amalia Kruger was so unhappy. Karyn wondered if she would have fared any better, given Amalia's circumstances.

Amalia shrugged. "It is in the past. Enough talking about me. My Jacob is dead. Ida and Isaac remain. I never hear from Ida, and the woman Isaac married does not really want a difficult old woman like me around." She looked at Karyn. "I understood Marie-Louise Ritter's unhappiness. I wish I could have helped her more."

Amalia sipped coffee while she thought. Then, she said, "I know I do not have pleasant ways like Celest. But that day I met you and told you about Marie-Louise, I *was* trying to help you." Suddenly she reached across and patted

Karyn on the hand. "Learn from my mistakes so that you do not end up like me."

When Karyn was silent, Amalia said, "You do not believe me, do you? You think if only Mikal Ritter loves you, then everything will be wonderful."

Karyn said, "Celest advised me to stop worrying about Mikal so much and to spend my time working on the things I can do something about—the duties at the homestead." She added timidly, "She thinks I am trusting too much in other people and not enough in God."

Amalia looked at Karyn soberly. "If you have a strong faith, so much the better. Perhaps, if I had known God's love years ago, it would have made a difference for me. I do not know. But strong faith or no, a woman must still determine to fight for what she wants. She must not give up." She paused, emphasizing each word of her next sentence. "Even if her own sister succeeds in stealing her husband away from her."

As the meaning of what Amalia was saying sunk in, Karyn protested. "*Was du nicht sagst!*" She wiped her mouth, put both hands on the edge of the table, and started to get up, but Amalia wasn't finished.

She grabbed Karyn by the wrist. "I know what has been going on. I have been watching. " Her voice took on a surprisingly kind tone as she said softly, "*Das Wichtige siehst du nicht.* You are worth a hundred Sophies, Karyn. You remember that. And if Mikal Ritter is such a fool as to fall for another woman like Marie-Louise, he deserves what he gets. You must not allow it to turn you into an unhappy old hag like me. *Sie haben es gut.* In America life can be good for a woman, whether she has a man or not. And Celest's idea about learning to trust God may not be so bad, either." Amalia stood up and shooed Karyn toward the door. "Now, go. You have a cow to milk and a sow to feed. And I have work to do."

Automatically mumbling thanks for Amalia's hospitality, Karyn headed out the door and toward Cay's barn where Lena and Grace had been stabled for the night. She was only a few feet away when Amalia called, "You know, Karyn, here in America a woman can own land. That Herr Stoddard has abandoned his claim. Cay could tell you how to find it." When Karyn turned around to respond, Amalia had already retreated back inside the house.

In spite of Amalia's warnings and implied advice, Karyn had absolutely no intention of looking for Doane Stoddard's homestead. She would return home, work hard to keep things in order for Mikal, and try to trust God.

Her return home found Karyn too busy, too exhausted, too challenged to spend much time worrying over what might be happening between Mikal and Sophie. Weeding and replanting the garden, drawing bucket after bucket of water for the livestock, picking wild fruit and preserving what she could, milking and making butter and cheese, sewing and cleaning, kept her so busy she had not one moment of idle time from sunrise until she collapsed, exhausted, into bed at sundown. It was all she could do to keep her promise to Celest that she would read from the Psalms. Most evenings, she nodded off long before she had read even half a chapter.

Any energy that might have been left after a day of chores was sapped by Nebraska's relentless summer heat. Accustomed to the moderate climate of Brandenburg, where summer temperatures were rarely uncomfortable, Karyn was dismayed when by midmorning sweat was pouring down her face and soaking through the back of her dress. Time and again, she squinted into the distance thinking someone was coming, only to realize that she was being tricked by heat waves.

She began to get up earlier, trying to do as much work as possible before the sun climbed very high in the sky. By noon of the third day of the searing heat, she sought out the shelter offered by the interior of the soddy and began to cut out fabric to make some shirts for Cay's store. She smiled at the fact that thanks to Sophie's flirting she knew Mikal's measurements and could surprise him with another new shirt.

The nights remained so hot Karyn would lie as still as possible, trying to conjure an imaginary breeze. She was grateful she was alone. It meant she didn't have to cover herself with layers of nightgown. One night she took a blanket outside and lay on the ground beneath the porch. The air was slightly cooler there, but mosquitoes and fleas attacked, and she soon fled back inside. The insects followed her. She made a mental note to ask Cay about the cost of a screen door.

The livestock suffered terribly from the unrelenting heat. Karyn watered the seedling trees faithfully, thinking how wonderful it would be if the corral were shaded. She led the mares to the creek and picketed them where one big cottonwood afforded shade. They grazed halfheartedly, their heads hanging down as they munched on the increasingly dried grass. Much of the time they just stood in the shade nose-to-tail, trying unsuccessfully to keep the unrelenting flies away.

Ella grew cross, balking when Karyn tried to move her picket. One morning when Karyn fumbled awkwardly during milking, Ella kicked at her angrily, sending both the milk pail and Karyn flying. Karyn picked herself up out of the dust, tears of frustration stinging her eyes.

The heat presented other challenges—among them finding a way to keep her butter from going rancid. She rode into Millersburg on Saturday to trade, but by the time she arrived, her few pounds of butter were ruined. Before leaving town, she stopped by Amalia's. The old woman welcomed her with surprising friendliness.

Amalia smiled when Karyn mentioned the problem of the butter. "I know how to fix that. Let me tell you what

I did in Kansas. . . ." She described a way for Karyn to save her butter and gave Karyn a small wooden stamp that would leave the design of an acorn and oak leaf in the top of her squares of butter. "I used it all my life," Amalia said. "I want you to have it."

Before leaving town, Karyn returned to Cay's store and asked for four six-gallon crocks. Returning home, she spent the rest of the day creating what Amalia called a "larder" at the back of the dugout. It was after dark before Karyn had dug a trench deep enough to hold the four crocks, but surveying her work by lamplight, Karyn smiled with satisfaction.

As soon as the bucket in the well was filled with blocks of fresh butter, she would salt each block well, then wrap it in muslin and tie it securely with string. Each block of butter would be packed tightly into the crock. When the first crock was full, she would set the lid down on it and cover it with another cloth, tied securely in place. Then, she would cover the crock with several inches of earth to keep it cool. As soon as the heat lifted, she would present Cay with as much butter as he could use. Why, he might pay as much as ten cents a pound for such a fine product!

Karyn stepped outside the dugout and watched the moon appear in the eastern sky. No breeze wafted over the prairie to cool her face. The heat of the night melted her sense of accomplishment, sending rivulets of sweat running down the back of her neck. When she reached up to wipe it away, she could feel grit from her filthy hands scraping against the soft skin at the nape of her neck.

She walked toward the corral, listening for the now-familiar sounds of night on the prairie. But the heat had silenced even the creatures in the tall grass. Leaning against the corral fence, Karyn looked down toward the creek where a few inches of water still flowed, fresh and cool from a spring that bubbled out of the earth less than a mile away. *If Cay Miller ran a hotel I think I would ride all the way to Millersburg by moonlight just to have a real bath*. Articulating the thought gave Karyn an idea. By moonlight she slipped down to the creek and out of her dress and petticoats. She took her hair down and lay in the water. For the first time in what seemed like months she felt cool and clean.

Karyn slept in the dugout that night, waking several times to fire warning shots to keep the increasingly determined coyotes away from Ella's calf. Tomorrow was Sunday. Tomorrow she would ride to the Delhommes'. Mikal would be proud of all she had accomplished. The image of Sophie made her determine to wear her nicest dress. And she would take care with her hair tomorrow morning, as well. In fact, she would take the time to arrange it just the way she had worn it the day she and Mikal met.

Early Sunday morning, Karyn picked the last of the ripe elderberries growing in a thick patch about a half mile from her home. She built a fire, cooking the elderberries and pressing them through a sieve until she had a quart of dark purple juice. Adding water and sugar to the juice, she strained the liquid through cheesecloth. Then, she poured the concoction into a gallon jar and added yeast. While she worked, she pictured herself and Mikal at Christmas, toasting one another with elderberry wine. Sophie was not a factor in her imagined setting.

Karyn had decided not to take the time to hitch up the wagon. She would ride Lena to the Delhommes', surprising Mikal with her early arrival. She would report that things at home were fine, that she had found a way to keep the butter from going rancid, that she had made three shirts for Cay to sell, that Ella and the calf were fine, that the sow was almost big enough to butcher . . . and that for Christmas they would have elderberry wine.

Plodding along astride Lena's broad back, Karyn smiled to herself. Her mother would be shocked to see her own daughter riding a horse like a man instead of perched atop a sidesaddle like a proper lady. But then, everything about life in Custer County would probably shock Mama, who, like Karyn, had imagined Karyn's future in a little cottage "in the countryside."

Bending down to pat Lena on the neck Karyn said aloud, "You know, Lena, Mikal is going to be upset that I'm not bringing the wagon. I'm certain he has it in his mind to insist that he come home today. But I'll tell him he has nothing to worry about, that his ankle must heal . . . and then while he stays at the Delhommes', perhaps you and Grace can help me plant at least one acre of that red wheat." She smiled happily. Surely living in Custer County was difficult, but a woman could do just about anything she set her mind to here. Why, Cay Miller had said they might get a woman doctor in Millersburg. That could never happen in Germany. And Amalia said women could own land. Karyn didn't want a profession. Being Mikal's wife was becoming increasingly fulfilling. And she didn't care to own land—unless Mikal wanted to expand his holdings. Still, it was good to be in a country where even women were free to make choices.

She took a deep breath and began to sing an old German hymn. By the time Lena climbed up the steep incline that led them onto French Table, Karyn was ready to urge her to a canter. "I know it's hot, Lena, but I'll give you plenty of fresh water and hay . . . I just can't wait any longer to see Mikal." *I'm so glad I came to America. I'm not going to let anything ruin today. Not the heat, not doubts about the future—and certainly not Sophie.*

When she arrived at the Delhommes', Karyn led Lena inside the sod barn where she would be cooler. True to her promise to Lena, she pumped a fresh bucket of cool water and forked a mound of hay into the corner of the stall. She reached up to pat the gigantic mare on the neck. "Now, Lena, you enjoy your day of rest in this cool barn."

Next, Karyn turned her attention to readying herself to see her husband. She smoothed her hair and patted her face and the back of her neck with fresh water. She washed her hands, now regretting the morning's session with the elderberries. Hopefully Mikal wouldn't notice the purple stains on her hands. She had just started for the house when Celest came out the front door, dressed in her riding breeches and carrying riding gloves and a crop in her hand.

"I've been watching for you all morning!" Celest said. "I told the family I'd stay behind and make sure Mikal stayed put until you got here. There's to be a church service in Millersburg today. Everyone else has gone on ahead. If I hurry I think I can at least join them for the hymn sing they were planning after lunch." She winked at Karyn and nodded over her shoulder toward the house. "Beware the bear, dear. He's impossible." Celest headed for the barn.

Karyn ran to the house. Then, she stepped across the threshold and forced herself to walk calmly up the stairs to Mikal's room. He was sitting in a chair by the window, his foot propped up on a footstool, his open Bible in his lap.

"Why didn't you bring the wagon?" He was frowning as he closed his Bible and tossed it on the bed.

"Hello to you, too, Mr. Ritter." Karyn felt herself blushing. She had forgotten the exact shade of those blue eyes.

But the blue eyes were glowering at her. "Why didn't you bring the wagon?"

She sat at the foot of the bed and tried to tease him. "If I brought the wagon, you would insist on going home. Celest says you're to stay off the ankle for at least two more weeks. So, unless you can fly, you're going to have to be a good patient."

Mikal would not be humored. He barraged her with questions and warnings. Instead of praising her for her diligent work, he seemed intent on pointing out how she should have done things. It seemed to Karyn that as the moments went by, she steadily lost ground in Mikal's eyes.

Karyn did her best not to overreact to Mikal's criticisms. *After all,* she told herself, *he's had a hard week.* "It's nearly time for lunch," she said when there was a pause in the conversation. "I'll make us something to eat."

She headed downstairs to the kitchen, thankful that Mikal couldn't follow her. Being alone for a few moments would give her time to collect her thoughts and to calm down. Quickly she made biscuits and fried eggs. When the biscuits were finished, Karyn arranged Mikal's and her lunches on a tray. She served him and had barely sat down when he asked abruptly, "So. Tell me. What is it that Remi and Serge have been keeping from me?"

At Karyn's look of surprise, he leaned forward. "Did we lose the calf to the coyotes after all?"

Karyn shook her head. "The calf is fine. I told you that I've slept in the dugout the nights I thought there might be a problem."

"You should take Ella and the calf into the dugout. That's safer."

"All right."

Mikal hadn't eaten yet. He worried, "Well, if it isn't the calf, it must be the sow." Mikal shook his head and looked out the window. "I knew I should have warned you about this heat. They just can't stand heat." He muttered, "She would have given us a good supply of pork—"

"Mikal," Karyn pleaded, "why are you so certain that Remi and Serge's secret news is something bad? The sow is very comfortable—and very, very fat. We'll have to butcher her before long. If you think it should be done now, I'll get Remi and Serge to help." She explained, "I cut branches down at the creek and made a little roof for her pen. She's in the shade, and twice a day I pour a pail of cold water over her to cool her down." Karyn grinned. "She's come to anticipate it. In fact, if I don't get there at the usual hour with her bath, she squeals to get my atten-tion. I think I actually recognize my name in 'pig' now."

Mikal didn't smile. Instead, he raised his voice. "Then what is it? What's happened?"

Karyn sighed. "I wanted it to be a homecoming sur-prise." She paused before finally telling him, "I drove the team out to that abandoned well and followed your trail of cedar fence posts." She smiled. "I found every last one of them and took them to Cay. And he paid twenty cents each for them. That's almost twice what you were expect-ing, isn't it?" She rushed ahead. "So the red wheat— which, by the way, has finally come—is paid for." She chuckled. "Amalia Kruger was so impressed she invited me to rest at her house overnight. She even made me breakfast. I'm not sure which news is more shocking— that your wife dressed in men's clothes and retrieved the posts, or that Amalia Kruger seems to have decided she approves of me."

Mikal glowered at Karyn. He almost shouted, "What possessed you to do such a foolish thing?"

"It wasn't foolish," Karyn retorted. She set her tray of food down on the bed. "It needed to be done, and I did it."

"Maybe you should be a little more like Sophie and a little less anxious to do everything you think needs to be done. You might live longer."

Karyn stood up, biting her lips to retain an angry retort.

Mikal rubbed his forehead briskly. "I'm sorry, Karyn. I shouldn't have said that." He looked out the window. "I don't know how to tell you what this week has been like. I'm afraid I haven't been very successful in handling this. A ruined crop—that I can do something about. But being trapped here, able to do nothing—" He sighed. "Things are a mess. With you. With me. And then there's Sophie—"

The moment Mikal mentioned Sophie, something hap-pened inside Karyn that clicked off whatever Mikal was saying and set her mind to whirling. *Of course. I should have realized. That's why he's so unhappy. Here I am rattling on and on about how well things are going . . . and about the future . . . when he's trying to find a way to tell me about Sophie.* Karyn's dark eyes flashed. *But why didn't Celest warn me?* She reasoned. *Maybe she doesn't know. Maybe it all happened in private . . . while Sophie helped care for him here . . . in this room.*

Karyn interrupted whatever Mikal was saying. "Mikal, I think somewhere in that book you were reading when I arrived that it talks about speaking the truth in love. All you have to do is tell me the truth, Mikal." She backed toward the door. "In fact, since it obviously makes you uncomfortable to talk about it, you don't have to tell me. I'll save you that."

She left Mikal sitting by the window, an odd look of amazement on his face, and hurried down the stairs and outside. As she ran toward the corral, she prayed that Mikal would come after her, that he would tell her she was wrong. But he didn't.

She put the bridle on Lena, climbed up on a hay bale to slip onto the mare's broad back, and rode for the homestead. Once she thought she heard something—she stopped Lena and looked back toward the house, her heart thumping, hoping to see Mikal at the doorway, hoping to hear him calling her name. But whatever it was she had heard, it wasn't Mikal calling for her.

The Diary
August 24, 1880
   Psalm 37—of David, who also knew betrayal
"Fret not thyself because of evildoers, neither be thou envious against the workers of iniquity."
   —But I am so very envious of one tonight.
"Trust in the LORD, and do good";
   —I thought I was trusting. Was my motive impure?

"so shalt thou dwell in the land, and verily thou shalt be fed."

　　—*But not in the land I desire, or so it seems.*
　　　To what land do I go now?

"Delight thyself also in the LORD; and he shall give thee the desires of thine heart."

　　—*Have my desires been so far from His?*

"Commit thy way unto the LORD; trust also in him; and he shall bring it to pass."

　　—*I thought I was committed and trusting.*

"Rest in the LORD, and wait patiently for him":

　　—*I have tried to be patient. What good has it done?*

"fret not thyself because of him who prospereth in his way, because of the man who bringeth wicked devices to pass. Cease from anger, and forsake wrath: fret not thyself in any wise to do evil."

　　—*May God help me to obey, for at this moment I find myself wishing evil on one whom I should love.*

God give me strength to obey. I have read the psalm again and again. But I cannot do what it says. What a poor, pathetic creature I am. Lord, I do believe. Help my unbelief.

Why art thou cast down, O my soul?
and why art thou disquieted in me?
hope thou in God: for I shall yet praise
him for the help of his countenance.
Psalm 42:5

Sitting at the base of the Delhommes' stairs, Mikal looked about him. He rubbed his forehead with the back of his hand. It was no wonder that Karyn had been angry. No wonder that she had gone home. She had done the work of a man and received nothing but criticism in return. It was a wonder that she had not thrown an entire tray of food at him before she left the room that morning. It was little comfort now, realizing that he had intended to apologize. He had grabbed his crutch and tried to follow her . . . he had meant to explain. But she had stormed down the stairs and out of the house so quickly that he couldn't catch her, and when he tried to hurry he had stumbled and fallen headlong down the stairs. Mikal wondered if she had heard the crash.

Slowly, painfully, Mikal inched his way along the floor until he could reach the crutch that had been sent flying halfway across the parlor when he fell. He half crawled across the floor to a chair in the parlor and pulled himself into the chair where he could see outside.

That morning, when the Delhommes' had announced they were going to Millersburg to hear the circuit rider preach, Sophie had volunteered to stay with Mikal, but Luc had talked her out of it.

Mikal smiled grimly at the sudden realization that Celest had finally found a way to allow him and Karyn time alone . . . and he had ruined it. He had finally had the long-awaited opportunity to declare his feelings . . . and instead he had only pushed Karyn farther away.

Once again, Mikal thought back over their short time together that morning. Karyn had ignored his surly mood at first. She had patiently reassured him, had recounted the details of everything she had done in his absence. And she had done so much. Conjuring up the picture of Karyn dressed in overalls loading cedar posts into his wagon made Mikal half angry again. It was too much. That was a man's job. She shouldn't have had to do it. And she didn't have to do it, did she? *She did it because* . . . Mikal wondered, *Perhaps she did it for us.*

The Delhommes and Sophie had taken all the horses. He would have to wait until they all got back from Millersburg before he could go after Karyn.

Mikal sighed, leaning his head back against the high back of the parlor chair. Dusk sprinkled the window ledge with golden light, making the geraniums that bloomed there glow. Karyn would be back at the homestead by now, milking Ella, tending the sow, perhaps baking biscuits for her supper alone. Was she angry or hurt? Had she cried? How would she react when he rode up? He had been waiting for her to show some sign of caring for him . . . but he was finished with waiting. Suddenly, Mikal knew that the time had come for him to convince her that he had held her at arm's length because he wanted so to hold her in his arms.

Taking up his crutch, Mikal hobbled outside and towards the corral, where he sat down on a small pile of hay, facing the direction from which the Delhommes would come. Off to the west the sky glowed with the eerie golden light of fire. It was far enough away that he didn't think it posed a threat. Sitting in the dark, contemplating the odd light in the distance, Mikal spoke with God about the prairie fire, about the heat, making request after request. He realized how fortunate he was that there was a spring-fed creek running through his section. He thanked God that it had never run dry, even in the hottest weather. He mentioned his desire to have a windmill so that Karyn wouldn't have to work so hard to get water. He thanked God for Karyn. Soon he was thanking God for His blessings instead of asking. And then he wasn't talking at all, but rather listening to a still, small voice. And the voice whispered hope, whispered peace, whispered love.

It was about midnight before Emile and Celest broke away from the impromptu social in Millersburg and went outside to stand on the front porch of Cay Miller's store. Emile put his arm around his wife. "I know what you are up to, Madame Delhomme."

"What are you talking about?"

"This little social isn't in the least bit impromptu. You made certain Fred Smith would be here. And that tale about wanting to bring the organ so that we could have a proper hymn sing today? Why, that was shameful bold-faced lying, Celest. That's all it was. You plotted everything so that Karyn and Mikal would be alone tonight."

Celest chuckled and looked up at the sky. "Well, looking at that beautiful, romantic moon, I would say God approves of my little plot. Now if only Karyn and Mikal will cooperate."

"They are probably in each other's arms at this very moment," Emile said, kissing his wife's cheek. They turned to go inside. Emile had seen the golden light to the west, but he didn't think it was anything to be concerned

221

about. At least not tonight. There hadn't been any wind for days. If the glow was still there tomorrow, then they would have to make preparations. But there was time. As long as the air remained still, there would be time.

Karyn took nearly three hours to cover the eight miles between the Delhommes' and home. She let Lena set her own pace while her mind whirled with thoughts of Mikal and Sophie. She loved Mikal Ritter much more completely than she had expected to. She had begun to sense a physical response to his presence that half frightened her. Even now she blushed when she thought about him. The sense of loss that had washed over her when she heard Mikal say that he wished she were more like Sophie had caused an ache deep inside. Her greatest desire and her worst fear had come true all at once. Mikal had finally fallen in love. Only not with her.

She was grateful that she had determined not to be the first to speak of love. What if Mikal had responded out of a sense of duty? Karyn sighed. She had come to Nebraska planning just that kind of partnership—one founded on duty and mutual respect. But Mikal Ritter's blue eyes and strong hands, muscular shoulders and beautiful smile, had changed all that. She had begun wanting those blue eyes to light up when she came into view. Feeling Mikal's hands on her waist had made her long to reach out and put her arms around his broad shoulders.

Karyn imagined what the past week had been like for Mikal. He was an honorable man, and it had probably been hard for him, being more and more attracted to Sophie . . . knowing that on Sunday he would have to face Karyn. Tears stung her eyes as she thought back over the morning. All her cheerful chatter seemed so ridiculous, now that she understood. He had been waiting to speak of Sophie . . . and she had rattled on about how she had kept the sow cool.

Lena had stopped to graze, but Karyn barely noticed. Her mind whirled as the mare nosed her way through the tall grass. Perhaps she should have been more like Sophie, after all. Perhaps she should have flirted more and worked less. She would have had more energy for things like elaborate hairdos. She could have avoided work-worn hands and freckles. Perhaps if Sophie had not come, she and Mikal might have been happy together. Thinking back over the recent months, Karyn was convinced she could have learned to please Mikal. She would have tried with everything in her being to please him. Tears began to flow. Karyn let them stream down her face.

"Lena, let's go." Karyn pulled the mare's head up and urged her forward. She thought of Hans Gilhoff. She had believed that her grief would surely kill her when Hans died. But she had survived. She had even come to believe that she would be happier in the wilderness of America than she would ever have been on an estate just outside of Brandenburg. Was it possible that someday she would realize that her life was better without Mikal Ritter? She doubted it, but she would pray for grace to remember the happy times they had shared without bitterness. There was no use being bitter. No good would come of it. God forbid that she become an unhappy old woman like Amalia Kruger.

Karyn brushed away the last of her tears. Had not Celest warned her against demanding her own way? Had not Celest urged her to love God, to trust Him completely? Karyn smiled sadly. Perhaps Sophie could make Mikal happy. Perhaps things would turn out for the best, after all.

Karyn was brought back to the moment when Lena arched her neck, pricked her ears, and neighed loudly. The mare broke into a canter, quickly covering the ground to the corral where Grace paced up and down the fence, anxious for the return of her partner. Karyn turned Lena into the corral. She took Ella and her calf into the dugout and shut them into a stall.

Looking up the hill toward the soddy, she realized how much she had grown to think of it as home. Taking a deep breath, she forced herself to relinquish her own plans for her future. Slowly, a plan began to form, a plan that would make things easier for Mikal to have what he really wanted. Karyn leaned against the corral fence for a few moments, thinking. Once again, she began to replace her own expectations and hopes with reality. But this time, Karyn prayed for God's help in facing that reality. As she prayed, she grew calmer. God had not granted happiness and love in this place, but certainly He had given her much to be thankful for.

Looking up at her little sod house illuminated by the bright moonlight, Karyn knew what she must do. She went up the slope to the house and inside. She lit the lamp and tore a sheet of paper from her journal. After three failed attempts, she finally managed to write a note that, while not completely satisfactory, expressed some of her thoughts to Mikal. She weighted the note down with the crock that held the elderberry juice. Then, she began to pack. In only a few moments, she was ready. She lay down to rest, grateful for the breeze that stirred the night air. Before dawn she rose and harnessed the team by moonlight.

Mikal fell asleep waiting for the Delhommes and Sophie. Dawn was breaking over the eastern horizon when he started awake at the sound of approaching hoof-beats. He awoke, pushing himself up on his crutch and waving furiously at the approaching riders.

Luc called out, "What is it? What's wrong?" He pulled his horse up next to Mikal.

Grimacing against the pain in his leg, Mikal answered, "I am an idiot, and I have to go after my wife and tell her so."

Sophie had yet to dismount. She looked down at Mikal and scolded, "Don't be absurd, Mikal. You are in no condition to go anywhere."

Mikal looked up at her. "Sophie, you are Karyn's sister, and I have not wanted to say anything, but now I'm telling you. I have let you cause me a lot of trouble. I take the blame. And now I take responsibility to try to right it. I won't say any more as long as you act like the good girl I know you want to be and keep out of my business with Karyn."

Sophie blinked a few times. She looked about her at Remi and Serge and Emile. No one was looking at her. Even Luc was studying the dirt at Mikal's feet.

Emile climbed down from the wagon and said quietly, "Take the team, Mikal. It will be safer." He managed to joke, "Just promise me you won't go on a mad dash across the prairie and end up down another well."

Remi and Serge boosted Mikal up into the wagon seat.

Celest called out, "Give me ten minutes to restock the grub box, Mikal. I'll get some food together."

Luc nodded toward the west. "Make sure there are matches, Mother."

Mikal answered, "Yes, I've been watching." He lowered his voice. "Could you ride over tomorrow and help us burn out the strips between the firebreak?"

Luc nodded.

In moments Celest was back with a basket filled with provisions for the grub box. She laid a hand on Mikal's arm. "Get it right, Mikal. That girl is the best thing that has happened to you in a very long time."

Mikal nodded. "I know. And I will get it right."

Celest lowered her voice. "And Mikal, Cay Miller will be delighted to help Sophie begin a dressmaking business over his store. In fact, I discussed it with him just this afternoon."

Mikal pulled his hat down and slapped the reins across

the backs of Emile's team. It took every ounce of self-control not to send them off in a mad gallop. As the sun came up in the east, Mikal felt a surge of anticipation. He couldn't help but ponder the possibility that he had spent his last night alone in a dugout.

Dear Mikal,

I have done my best to keep things going for you. I hope your ankle heals well. I do not know the laws in America.

Certainly we have plenty of witnesses to the fact that we were married in name only. Hopefully, it will be a simple matter. I will do whatever you wish. Leave word with Amalia Kruger, and I will contact her.

My things are at Amalia's. Grace and Lena and the wagon are with Cay. There is little to worry over in the garden. Don't forget the butter in the dugout.

I should have liked the opportunity to love you, Mikal. But I think I have learned more from not being loved. Perhaps that is what God wanted me to learn. It brought me closer to Him, so it accomplished its purpose in my life. I only write this to assure you that my experience as your wife will not be a cause for my becoming bitter, although I deeply regret that I failed to meet your expectations. Perhaps someday you will believe that I did my best.

The wine will be ready for Christmas. Perhaps you and Sophie will drink a toast to me.

Your ————————
Karyn Ensinger Ritter

She had scratched out part of the closing. Mikal could see that Karyn's trunk was gone. No fresh aprons hung on the post in the center of the house. He hobbled to the door. He lowered the tailgate of the wagon and pulled himself up into the wagon box. Then, he made his way up to the wagon seat. He drove the team down to the dugout where he saw that Karyn had fed the sow. Ella had been milked, and the trough was brimming with fresh water. He let Emile's team eat a little. Then, he drove them back up to the well. Once again, he got down from the wagon, hopped to the well, and drew water. As soon as the team had drunk, he repeated his unusual approach to the wagon seat, took up the reins, and headed for Millersburg.

Early that afternoon, Mikal sat on the wagon seat outside Cay Miller's store, listening as Cay explained, "She's only been gone a couple of hours. She asked how to get to Doane Stoddard's homestead. She made it sound like she had another surprise for you. I thought it was just a matter of her not understanding the land laws—that you have to live on the land to qualify for a preemption." Cay shrugged. "But I wasn't going to argue with her. I tried that when she went after those fence posts."

Cay wiped his hands on his shopkeeper's apron and tried to convince Mikal to come inside the store and rest. "Don't worry about her, Mikal. I made certain the saddlebags were well stocked with food. I loaned a gun to her and she has plenty of ammunition. She proved she knows how to use it by having me toss this in the air." Cay reached into the pocket of his apron and held up a coin with a bullet hole through it. "She should be back in a couple of days. Why don't you stay here until she gets back? Karyn won't want you taking any chances with your leg. That's probably at least part of the reason she slipped away without telling you."

Mikal shook his head. "No, Cay. I can't wait. We have had a misunderstanding, and I must find Karyn and resolve it. Now."

Cay peered at Mikal for a moment before nodding his head briefly. "Well then, at least go inside and let me hitch up Lena and Grace for you. You can leave Emile's team in my barn for now." Cay bustled about like an old maid, helping Mikal down from the wagon and inside his store and heating up coffee and biscuits before leaving to switch teams.

Mikal had practically inhaled two biscuits when the sound of a cane tap-tapping on the store's wood floor filled him with dread.

Amalia Kruger refilled his empty coffee cup. "I am glad to see you, Mikal. You are going after her. Right?"

Mikal looked up and nodded. "Of course."

"I told Karyn she is worth a hundred Sophies. I am glad to see you finally realized that."

Mikal frowned. He resented the fact that Amalia Kruger, of all people, seemed to know details about his relationship with Karyn. Didn't Karyn know this woman was a gossip and the last one she should trust with secrets? He said defensively, "I didn't just realize it, Amalia. I've known it all along."

Amalia thought for a moment. Then, she smiled. "I see. But, Mikal, Karyn does not know that you know." She chuckled. "Mikal, with you and Marie-Louise, it was all passion and no reason. With Karyn, you have been trying it the other way. And if Sophie had not come, I think that by now you would have realized that all reason and no passion does not work very well, either." She laid a hand on Mikal's shoulder and said kindly, "But I know you well enough to know that you will correct that as soon as you catch up with her." Amalia patted Mikal's shoulder. "God bless you, Mikal." Then, she turned to leave.

Mikal was so amazed by Amalia's kindness, he could only nod and mumble his thanks.

Amalia was halfway to the door when she turned around and said, "Karyn told me about reading the Psalms. But I discovered that the Proverbs are good, too. I read one about how lucky a man is who can find a virtuous woman. I think it said something like 'for her price is far above rubies. The heart of her husband doth safely trust in her, . . . she will do him good and not evil all the days of her life.'" Amalia paused a moment and then said, "It has been a hard road for you, Mikal. But you finally have a good woman. See that you do not lose her."

The Diary
August 27, 1880
   I am camping under the stars, like the pioneers who went to the far west only a few years ago. The moon is bright and a breeze is blowing. I cannot say that I am happy, but I am not weeping every moment. That is something. There is a golden light to the west that is very beautiful in an eerie sort of way. I know it is probably a fire of some kind, but I should be able to find the Stoddard homestead by tomorrow, and then I will head back to Millersburg. I have Cay Miller's big bay gelding. If we must, we can outrun a fire. I cannot return to Millersburg before I have a plan for my future.

CHAPTER 17

An Indian Spearhead

Bow down thine ear to me;
deliver me speedily: be thou my strong rock,
for an house of defence to save me. For thou
art my rock and my fortress; therefore for thy
name's sake lead me, and guide me.
Psalm 31:2–3

Cay had warned Karyn that between Millersburg and the Stoddard homestead she would encounter a series of canyons and ridges that had made the area less desirable for homesteading. She was only a few miles from town when she rode down an incline and entered a round, flat valley. Across the valley, she started up a grassy slope to a high hill, finding herself riding along a rim of rock. She stopped the horse and pulled Cay's drawing from her saddlebags. *He said it was a steep descent off this ridge . . . but I didn't real-ize just how steep he meant.* Taking a deep breath, Karyn urged the gelding down the slope. She clung to the saddle horn and gave the horse free rein to pick his own way down. Finally at the bottom, Karyn breathed a sigh of relief. She looked back up behind her, dreading the return ride. *I'll walk up and lead the horse.*

She was at the bottom of the ridge now, and even though it was midmorning, the high bluff cast shadows along her way. From the other side of the bluff a spring bubbled from beneath a huge rock. All along the valley wild hemp and sunflowers grew in profusion.

Karyn was riding toward the mouth of the canyon when she noticed a deeply cut wagon track. Thinking she had found Doane Stoddard's trail, she turned to follow it. A few yards later, she saw a spring from a wagon seat along the trail. Doane Stoddard's wagon seat had been missing a spring. A few feet beyond that, a horse had thrown a shoe. But then the trail led off to her left. She knew now that she was following someone else's trail. According to Cay's directions, the Stoddard place was a few miles to the north and farther west. But Cay had also said it was unlikely she would encounter any signs of civilization en route. Suddenly, she was glad she had decided to wear what she now thought of as her "work clothes." If anyone saw her from a distance they wouldn't know she was a woman.

Descending a low hill, Karyn passed along a ridge of rocks. Suddenly, she came upon a door set flush with the perpendicular bank. Someone had taken great care to camouflage it. From a distance, it would be indiscernible. Her heart beating, Karyn dismounted and tied the gelding's reins to a scrub bush. There were no signs of recent tracks nearby. Still, she cradled Cay's rifle in her arms before trying the door. It opened inward. When her eyes finally adjusted to the dim light, Karyn could see that she was in a room—a rather large room, containing a single sleeping bunk and an old rough board table, fully six feet long. On the table was a copy of *Harper's Weekly* dated June 1879.

At the back of the room there was a huge fireplace, blackened from frequent use. At one side of the fireplace another doorway was cut into the rock. Karyn called out. "Hello. Is anyone here?" There was no answer, so she walked to the doorway and looked into another room larger than the first. This room had feed stalls arranged along one side, and more sleeping bunks. There was corn scattered about.

Karyn went back outside. There were no signs of recent occupancy. The spring-fed creek bubbled along a few yards below the cave, but no paths or tracks led from the cave down to the water. She could have ridden within a few feet of the cave and never known it existed.

Untying the gelding, Karyn walked down to the creek. At the water's edge there was a block of wood about three feet long. It was staked in place with forked stakes. A person could stand upon it and dip water from the brook without getting muddy or wet. Karyn smiled at the ingenuity of the cave dwellers, and made a mental note to do something similar at home. *If I have a creek. Cay said there was a creek on the Stoddard place, didn't he?* She was still thinking of Mikal's place as home. It would probably be some time before she stopped doing that.

Karyn walked back up to untie the gelding and led him down to get a drink. While she waited for him to drink, she looked up to see a gray wolf trotting along the ridge above them. It paused momentarily and looked down at Karyn, then took off toward the east. The sight of the wolf sent a chill down Karyn's spine. She mounted the gelding and headed back to the north and west.

The next landmark Cay had mentioned was easily found. Jutting from the bluff above her was a curiously shaped boulder. Cay had called it "Pawnee Rock." It took little imagination to discern the silhouette of an Indian brave in the rock. She urged the gelding up a narrow trail around the rock and onto the tableland. Expecting to see Doane's soddy any moment, she urged the gelding to a canter.

Doane Stoddard's soddy was a windowless one-room hovel. Two bare sticks planted in the sandy soil of what would have been the front yard testified to Anna Stoddard's unsuccessful attempt with trees. Using one of the dead trees as a hitching post for the gelding, Karyn went to the door. Pushing it open, she peered inside. She didn't step across the threshold. This place could never be home. There was no well, no corral, not even the beginnings of a garden. Of course those things could be added, just as Mikal had. Karyn sighed. *But I don't want to add them. Not out here. Not alone.*

Karyn stepped back outside. Everything she saw made her long for her little soddy nestled against the ridge. Off in the distance, a herd of antelope were trotting along toward the east. It was getting late. She considered starting back, but the image of the wolf that had stared at her from high on the ridge made camping in the shadows of the bluffs less than desirable. She decided to spend the night beside the soddy and head back early in the morning.

As the sun set, Karyn got out matches to start a fire. Looking about her at the dry grass of the tableland, she decided to eat a cold supper. She took off the gelding's saddle and led him across the table to a clump of low bushes where a tiny spring bubbled up out of a rock. *I suppose if a person built a dam down below, you could create a sizable pond.* But Karyn didn't want to build a dam. She wanted to go back home.

Back at the soddy, Karyn hobbled the gelding and turned him loose to graze. Leaning against the front of the shack, she ate bread and cheese, smiling to herself when she discovered that Cay had packed candy for her. *Cay can give you advice of where you might be able to establish a successful dressmaking shop.* Grand Island wasn't such a bad place.

As the sun set, Karyn spread out her bedroll in the shadow of the shack. The wind had come up. Every few moments the gelding lifted his head and looked intently off toward the west. Karyn finally got up and looked around the corner of the soddy. The glow of the prairie fire was brighter. She would need to get an early start for Millersburg.

With a team and wagon, Mikal couldn't descend the steep trail down into the canyon after Karyn. So, while Karyn was investigating the mysteries of the cave in the canyon, Mikal was driving his team along the top of the ridge that edged the canyons. He saw the same wolf that had peered down at Karyn. In fact, he was increasingly seeing wildlife trotting off to the east. It worried him. He reached into the grub box and put the matches in his pocket. Every mile or so he looked about him to locate the place to set a backfire. He decided not to stop for the night, but to continue toward the Stoddard place.

Karyn had no business being in the wake of a prairie fire. Guilt pressed in upon him, and once again he determined that whatever else happened this night, he was going to see to it that Karyn had no further chance to misread his feelings.

Sometime after midnight Karyn woke with a start. What was it? The gelding was standing just to the side of the soddy, his nostrils flared, his eyes wild. He lunged against the hobbles and whinnied. Karyn leaped up and went to his side. She grabbed his halter and tried to soothe him. But as she looked toward the west, her own eyes grew wide. The fire burning far to the west was no longer just a golden light glowing on the distant horizon. She could see flames. The wind was growing stronger, and it carried the scent of burning grass with it.

Karyn ran for the bridle and put it on over the gelding's halter. She pulled the horse to the front of the soddy where he couldn't see the flames, tied his head low, and threw on the blanket and saddle as quickly as possible. She rummaged through the saddlebags for matches. She hesitated for a moment, wondering if she should just set a backfire, or burn off a section of prairie and wait for the fire to go by. But one look at the wall of flames bearing down on her and her heart was gripped with fear. She wouldn't be able to control the gelding. She would have to let him go . . . and then what?

She threw her saddlebags behind the saddle and rammed the rifle in its scabbard. But the gelding wouldn't stand still for her to mount him. Time and again he spun away from her, trotting nervously in a circuitous dance. Finally, she managed to scramble up on his back. Wildlife of every variety was running with them now. A sea of fire was rolling toward them, carrying with it black clouds of suffocating smoke. The horse was wild with fear. Karyn gave him his head. Looking behind her she clung to the saddle horn while the horse charged mindlessly toward the east.

She could hear the roar of the fire behind her. Could it possibly overtake them? The moment the thought occurred, Karyn was being hurtled headlong into the air. The gelding had stumbled and was sliding down the sharp incline that led down into the canyons they had come through before. Karyn rolled down a little hill and landed in a patch of bushes beside the creek. Above her flames were licking at the sides of the canyon, crawling down the ridge from tree to tree, making their way relentlessly toward her. She looked around her, but the horse was gone.

She stumbled out of the bushes and into a creek. Running along the edge of the creek, she wiped smoke from her eyes, looking desperately for a place where the creek would be deep enough that she could immerse herself in water. *Oh, God,* she prayed. *Oh, God, please. God, please. Help!*

In the dark, Karyn stumbled and fell. She had run into something—something hard. A block of wood? Suddenly, she realized she had found the watering place just below the mysterious cave. Could she find it in the dark? The flames were coming closer, sending waves of heat through the air.

A burning tumbleweed flew by. A tree nearby ignited. With another prayer for guidance, Karyn stumbled up the hill toward the rock where she thought the cave door—

Just as a wedge of fire shot down the other side of the creek, she fell into the cave. On all fours she scrambled into the back room, as far as she could get from the flames. She stayed low, huddling in the dark, listening to the roar of the fire just outside the cave door. The door caught on fire, casting an eerie light around the room. In a panic, Karyn rushed forward and pulled with all her might to get the long table away from the door. If it caught on fire, too, then all the bunks . . . the stalls . . . everything would burn.

But the door had burned out. She would be safe. She stumbled back into the room with the stalls and curled up in a corner. Waiting in the dark, she listened to the roar of the fire just outside the cave. When the roar finally stopped, she couldn't bring herself to go outside. Exhausted and sore from her fall from the horse, she stretched out on one of the bunks and fell asleep.

Unlike Karyn, Mikal was not unprepared for the fire. He had watched its relentless approach throughout the night, praying that by some miracle the wind would shift and the flames would take a path other than the one across West Table. Near dawn, he pulled up Lena and Grace, tying them securely to an ancient cedar tree that clung to the edge of the canyon.

With the box of matches in his hand, he hobbled as far away as he dared from his team. Then, he knelt on the ground and opened the box. If he did it right, if the wind held, he could burn a patch of earth large enough to shelter him and the team from the flames. If he could control Lena and Grace, they would all survive, and then he could go after Karyn. His hands shook as he looked off to the west. *God, give Karyn wisdom to know what to do.*

The fire was coming closer. He struck a match. The wind blew it out. Tossing it aside, he struck another. It went out. Match after match failed. The flames were visible in the distance. A bobcat raced by only a few yards away, stretched nearly flat to the earth in its wild run to escape. Lena and Grace were beginning to move about restlessly. Sweat formed on Mikal's brow. There was one match left. *God, please. I have only one match left. You didn't let me die in that well. Save me again.*

His hand trembling, Mikal cupped his huge left hand about the precious last match. It flickered, then smoke rose from the grass. Mikal got up awkwardly and hobbled to where Lena and Grace were tethered. Behind him, he could hear the crackling of the dry grass as a line of small flame and smoke began to appear. Then, the flames grew larger until a row of fire was being blown away toward the east. Mikal and his team were now trapped in a section of dried grass between two fires. He watched as the original fire approached. It would be no use to run away. The flames were ten to twelve feet high and traveling faster than a horse could run. Mikal forced the image of Karyn and the gelding from his mind. He had work to do. First, he must survive. Then, he would find Karyn.

It seemed like hours, but really it was only a few moments before the fire he had set blackened a patch of prairie large enough for the team and wagon. Pulling off his shirt, Mikal tore it in half. He used each half to wrap the horses eyes so they couldn't see the flames. Then, hobbling along in front of them, he awkwardly led them toward the ever-growing width of burned-off grass.

Only moments after the team and wagon reached safety, they were surrounded by a high wall of flames and billowing smoke that threatened to smother them. Grace and Lena whinnied and plunged, trying desperately to escape. Mikal hung on to their harness, trying to calm them. But the mares screamed with fear, plunging and rearing with such force that they lifted Mikal off the ground again and again. He held on grimly, praying for strength to keep his broken ankle from slamming against the earth. Coughing and sputtering, he wondered if he would lose consciousness.

Then, as suddenly as the inferno had raged, it passed. The air cleared. Grace and Lena stopped plunging about, and stood trembling and snorting. Mikal praised them, patted their necks, kissed their soft muzzles with tears of relief running down his cheeks. He waited a few moments to remove the remains of his shirt from their eyes. When he did, the mares snorted and pricked their ears at the strange sight of the smoking prairie, dotted with the whitened bones of long-dead antelope and buffalo.

Mikal bent to pick up his crutch and made his way to the back of the wagon box again. At the back of the wagon he bent to pick up an Indian spearhead that had been hidden in the grass. Shoving it in his pocket, he lifted himself into the wagon box. By the time he reached the seat, he was shaking. He pulled the remnant of his shirt from his pocket and wiped his face. He sat for a few moments before picking up the reins. Then, he turned the team back toward the west, praying aloud to keep himself from thinking about what he might be about to find at Doane Stoddard's abandoned soddy.

CHAPTER 18

A Gold Coin

----

*O LORD, thou hast brought up my soul
from the grave: thou hast kept me alive, that
I should not go down to the pit.*
Psalm 30:3

Dawn illuminated Doane Stoddard's fire-blackened soddy looming in the distance. Approaching it, Mikal fought against the sick feeling in his stomach. He pulled his hat down over his eyes and squinted at the little soddy, hoping against hope that there would be no sign of Karyn. Looking at the black emptiness about him, he groaned with relief. He pushed his hat back on his head, swiped over his face, and sat shaking, taking deep breaths to try to control his emotions. Then he saw something plastered up against the front of the soddy.

Leaving his crutch in the wagon he got down and hopped over, bent down and picked up what appeared to be the charred remains of some kind of blanket. He realized with a shudder that it was part of the bedroll Cay Miller always used on hunting trips. Mikal slumped against the front wall of the soddy. Groping along the wall he shakily pushed the charred door open, thanking God for the empty room inside. Karyn had been here, but she had gotten away before the fire reached the soddy. Gripping the side of the wagon, Mikal looked back toward the east. Would she have run down into the canyons? He couldn't follow. Not with the wagon. Not with his broken ankle.

Tossing the fragment of Cay's bedroll into the back of the wagon, Mikal got back up into the driver's seat. He headed the team for the spring. While they drank, he opened the grub box and pulled out some bread and jerky and set them on the wagon seat. After a quick drink of water for himself, he turned the team east and slapped the reins, urging them to a trot. "Go along, girls, we've got to get some help now. Go along, hup!"

For the first part of his journey back to Millersburg, Mikal stopped every half mile at the edge of the canyon to search below for some sign of Cay's gelding. For a few minutes he would sit on the wagon box and call for Karyn. He grew hoarse from yelling her name.

For a few hours Mikal managed to fight off the specter of Marie-Louise's body lying lifeless on the prairie. Finally, the last time he yelled Karyn's name, he gave in to the dread that had been threatening to overwhelm him all morning. *God . . . not again. I can't go through it again . . . if she isn't alive, then don't let me find her . . . let someone else find her . . . I can't go through that again.* Tears began to flow as Mikal spoke silently to God. *She doesn't even know I love her, God. She doesn't even know I love her . . . give me a chance, God . . . to love her . . .*

While Mikal was driving along the edge of the canyon calling for Karyn, she was curled up in the back room of the cave asleep. When she finally awoke, it was mid-morning and her stomach was growling for breakfast. She stepped outside the cave and into the morning sunshine and caught her breath. Everything in the canyon had been burned off. The air was heavy with the smoke that still rose here and there from felled logs and thick clumps of undergrowth.

Karyn went down to the creek and drank deeply. She splashed her face with water. Finally, she took down her hair. Lying on her back on the charred block of wood at the creek's edge, she leaned back until her entire scalp was in the water. As the cool water flowed through her hair, she looked above her at the blue sky, rejoicing that she was alive. *Thank You, Lord . . . oh, thank You, thank You!* She smiled, wondering who had made the cave that had saved her life. She suspected that he was not one of the more upstanding citizens of Custer County.

She wondered how far the fire had burned. Celest had once told her that a big fire would go on and on for miles . . . maybe half the county . . . and surely this had been a big fire. With a dull ache in her midsection she wondered about Millersburg, the homestead, the Delhommes.

The Delhomme men would have headed east toward the fire—toward Mikal's homestead. They would have set backfires against the main fire, filled wagons with barrels of water, and beat out side fires with wet blankets. Celest had said that sometimes they slaughtered a calf and dragged the carcass behind their horses to smother flames. Karyn shuddered to think about Ella and her calf . . . and the sow . . . Would they have reached the homestead in time? Karyn smiled in spite of herself, thinking of Mikal having to drive a water wagon and watch the others fight the fire. He would be so frustrated. She could see him now, his blue eyes flashing angrily, grumbling about what a bother a little thing like a broken ankle could be.

With a sigh, Karyn sat up. Rivulets of water streamed off her wet hair and down her back. Turning around, she pulled her boots and socks off and soaked her feet in the creek. They would have started a backfire. Surely they started a backfire. And the creek—but Karyn knew that the narrow creek just below her little house would have been an easy thing for the fire to cross. She forced herself to stop thinking about the fire and studied her feet. *I won-der how many blisters I'll have by the time I get to Millersburg. If the fire burned that way, they won't have time to worry about me today, that's for sure.*

She would be out here alone at least one night. Her eyes rose to the edge of the canyon where only yesterday a wolf had stood peering down at her. Except for the gurgling of the water, there was no other sound of life. All the wildlife had fled before the flames. She wouldn't have to worry over coyotes or bobcats or wolves today . . . or tonight, when she slept alone. If the moon was bright, maybe she would just keep walking.

She leaned over and spread her fingers out in the water. It was going to be a long walk home. *Home.* The word brought her thoughts back from the joy of simply being alive to the heartache of the moment. *Well, don't worry about that now. God must have something in mind for you. He certainly could have taken you just a few hours ago. But He didn't. Just do the next thing, Karyn. You've a long walk ahead of you.*

As her hands swished through the water, she reached toward a glint of gold in the sandy bottom of the creek, unearthing a gold coin. She put it in her pocket, pulled her socks and boots back on, tied her still-damp hair back out of her face with a strip of her bandanna. Her hat in her hand, she headed up the canyon toward Millersburg.

On the morning after Mikal had gone home to Karyn, Luc, Remi, and Serge Delhomme rode to his homestead intending to make short work of burning off the firebreak and then head toward the advancing fire and set a back-fire. But instead of finding Karyn and Mikal, they found a deserted homestead.

"They must have gone to Millersburg. I don't know what to think. Karyn's trunk is missing." Luc frowned.

"If they left together, our team and wagon would be here," Remi offered.

"So Karyn must have been gone with Mikal's wagon before he arrived." Luc said, "That's it. Karyn had packed and left. Mikal has gone after her."

"I didn't think things were so bad between them," Remi said.

"Why not?" Serge interrupted. "Don't tell me you've been blind to dear little Sophie's tricks."

"Don't start about Sophie," Luc said angrily.

Remi intervened. "All right, boys. This isn't the time to talk about that. What are we going to do?"

The brothers decided to split up. Remi would take Ella and the calf back to the Delhommes' and report on what had happened while Luc and Serge headed for Millersburg. Without a wagon for transportation, Mikal's sow would have to be left. They let her out of her pen, and she immediately headed for the creek where she sank down into the water with a grunt of satisfaction.

"Could we board her up in the dugout?" Remi wanted to know. "I hate the thought of all that lost sausage."

Before they left Mikal's homestead, the boys drew bucket after bucket of water and sloshed it over the walls and roof of the soddy. They burned off the grass around the house and dugout so that the area around the house appeared as a blackened dot on the tan prairie. Even if the fire burned this far, the house would be saved. Then, they forced the sow out of the creek and into the dugout, boarding her up in one of the stalls with fresh water and straw. "She'll be hungry, but she'll be alive when Mikal gets back."

As they headed off, Luc called out to Remi, "Hopefully we'll meet Mikal and Karyn coming home on our way in. Tell Papa that if the fire still looks threatening, we'll hitch up the team and head off with the other settlers to help fight it here instead of heading for home."

As they covered the miles between the Ritters' and Millersburg and Karyn and Mikal did not come into view, Luc and Serge grew more and more concerned. By the time they galloped into Millersburg several settlers had converged on Cay Miller's store to organize a plan for protecting both the fledgling town and their homesteads.

Cay was helping load empty water barrels into the back of one of the wagons. When Luc and Serge rode up and asked about Mikal and Karyn, Cay explained, ending with, "He is only a few hours behind her. In fact, he has probably caught up with her by now." Cay spoke with more confidence than he felt. "Karyn was on my big gelding, and Mikal knows what he is doing. He will have already set a backfire up ahead. He'll know we are doing the same and keep them out of danger."

Luc nodded. "You're probably right. But after we help set this backfire we're going to head out after them."

"Then make certain you have full barrels in the back of that wagon," Cay urged. "You never know where the wind might carry those flames."

Luc and Serge put their horses in Cay's corral, hitched up their father's team, and pulled into line by Cay's well to fill the barrels in the back of their wagon with water. A settler who had been posted as a lookout about a mile west of Millersburg came thundering into town and reported that the fire appeared to be veering off toward the north. Still, everyone went to work wetting down the section of prairie directly west of town. Then, they set a backfire.

Once a stretch of grass was sufficiently blackened to protect Millersburg from danger, the settlers replenished their supply of water from the town well and headed north and a little east, ready to beat out the onslaught of sidefires with wet sacks and blankets. Luc and Serge filled the barrels in their wagon and headed across the scorched prairie after Mikal. Finally, early in the afternoon, a speck of movement on the horizon caught Serge's attention. He stood up in the wagon, waving his hat and calling out. Luc urged the team to a gallop.

When Mikal saw another team coming toward him, he urged Lena and Grace to run. His hat came off, and with his long hair hanging in his face, he looked half mad. He pulled up alongside Luc and Serge and in short, desperate bursts, and half sobbed, "I can't find her. I know she got away from Stoddard's. Before the fire." He willed himself to take a breath and with a shudder nodded toward the scrap of burned bedroll in the back of the wagon. He wiped his face with his hand, smearing soot across his forehead in a vain attempt to calm himself. "I was hoping she was back in Millersburg."

Luc shook his head. "No. At least not when we left."

Mikal slumped down onto the wagon seat.

Serge broke in. "Look, you two. We're doing Karyn no good standing out here talking. She had a chance if she went down into the canyons. She could have stayed ahead of it."

Mikal choked out the words, "If she had stayed ahead of it, she would be back in Millersburg."

Serge shook his head. "We can't know that. Not until we get some help and search the canyons. Let's head back. When we get to Cay's, I'll ride home and get Papa and Remi. While I'm gone, you and Luc can be packing what we'll need."

Mikal shook his head. "You both need to get home and help fight that fire."

"At the rate that fire was moving, it's already either burned itself out or passed our place. Papa would have burned off the firebreak—maybe the entire yard. Luc and I did that at your place, Mikal. We burned off the whole area inside the firebreak. We wet down the walls, penned up the sow—"

Mikal interrupted him. "Let's get going. You can tell me about all that some other time."

The presence of his friends helped Mikal regain his composure. By the time they rode into Millersburg, he had begun to have hope. He got down from the wagon and reached for his crutch just as Cay came out of the store. Cay had just spoken Mikal's name when Mikal looked across toward the barn and saw Cay's big gelding standing in the corral. Cay said simply, "He came running in about noon, wild-eyed and shaking. The saddlebags are missing, but the rifle's still in the scabbard." Cay paused. "He isn't burned, Mikal. Not one hair singed. That's something. He was able to stay ahead of it."

Mikal sagged against the side of the wagon. Luc and Serge looked at one another and then at Cay. Without a word, they began to unhitch their team.

Mikal spoke up. "Never mind, Luc." His voice cracked. He waited a moment. "There's no need to hurry so much. You boys go on home. See about things." He took a deep breath. "Sophie's probably going mad with worry. Tell her—" He stopped. "Tell her what's happened." He stood up. "I'll stop by Amalia's. I want to get—" He swallowed and let out one desperate sob. "I want to take her trunk home with me." He paused for a moment. Wetting his lips, he looked desperately at Luc. "I don't think I can—I don't think I can ride—"

"It's all right, Mikal," Luc interrupted him. "I understand." Mikal was convinced that they were looking for Karyn's body. And he couldn't face it. Luc said, "We'll take care of it. Go home. Get some rest. We'll start searching first thing in the morning. One of us will come back by nightfall tomorrow and let you know."

Mikal nodded. Then, he started off across the street to ask Amalia for Karyn's trunk.

The fire had burned itself out along Clear Creek just below French Table, leaving the Delhomme homestead and everything east of it untouched. Luc and Serge arrived just as the family was sitting down to supper. They repeated the news Remi had already shared before launching into what they really had to say. They described setting the backfire, and meeting Mikal on his way back from Doane Stoddard's.

Luc paused awkwardly. "When we got back to Cay's," he cleared his throat, "Cay's gelding had come back."

"Thank God," Sophie breathed. "Then Karyn is all right?"

Luc hesitated. "The gelding came back. No rider." He hurried to add, "But he hadn't been in the fire. At least we know he ran clear of it."

"Where is Mikal?" Celest demanded.

"He—uh . . ." Luc swallowed and wet his lips. "He was going to get Karyn's trunk from Amalia's and take it home." Luc looked at his father as he said, "He asked us to let him know."

Emile said softly, "We'll ride to Millersburg tonight so we can start off right away in the morning."

Sophie protested, "But isn't Mikal going to look for her himself?"

"He can't ride into those canyons with a broken ankle," Serge said.

Sophie snorted. "A big, strong man like Mikal? Of course he could. If he wanted to." Sophie looked about her at the Delhommes. They were studying their plates. Her eyes widened. There was no reason why Mikal wouldn't want to look for Karyn. Except one. If Mikal thought Karyn was dead . . . if he thought they were looking for . . . "Oh," Sophie cried out and jumped up. "I've got to go to him. He can't be left alone . . . he needs me . . ."

Celest reached out and grabbed Sophie by the wrist. "No, Sophie. Mikal does not need *you*." Her gray eyes were cold. "He needs his wife. And we are going to find her, if we have to look until snowfall."

Sophie sat back down. "You think she's dead, too, don't you?"

Celest stood up. "What I think is, we need to get these men fed and on their way."

Emile went outside with Remi to saddle up their horses. Celest began to gather supplies. Sophie did her best to help.

When the men had ridden off toward the west, Celest found Sophie sitting in the parlor in the dark, looking out the window. "Are you certain Mikal will be all right alone?" she asked when Celest came in. Then, she hurried to add, "I mean—if you think you should be with him, I can stay here. I would do my best to look after things for you." She laughed sadly. "Although my best is not very satisfactory, sometimes." She began to cry softly. Celest didn't say anything, but she stayed in the room while Sophie cried.

"Could we go to Millersburg tomorrow, Celest? I feel that I should be there for Karyn. For whatever happens."

"Of course."

After a long silence, Sophie murmured, "Something like this makes you stop and consider what is really important in life."

"Yes," Celest answered. "It does."

Sophie rose shakily. "I think I'll be going upstairs now." She paused at the foot of the stairs. "Celest, would you be certain I am awake before you start downstairs in the morning? I know I'm not very good at farmwork, but I will do what I can to help before we leave."

"Thank you, Sophie," Celest said gently. "I appreciate that."

CHAPTER 19

Amalia's Biscuit Recipe

*And be ye kind one to another, tenderhearted,
forgiving one another, even as God for
Christ's sake hath forgiven you.*
Ephesians 4:32

Karyn decided there really was no reason to walk all
night just to get back to Millersburg. The sooner she got
back, the sooner she would have to face Mikal and
Sophie. And she was going to face Mikal and Sophie. She
had mulled over the situation while she walked along and
came to the conclusion that she would not slink away like
a coward. She would be strong enough to face Mikal and
say a proper good-bye. She would ride back to the
Delhommes', and she would wish Sophie well if it killed
her. Then, she could leave and begin a new life somewhere
else, with no regrets.

No regrets. Karen sighed. But there would be so many,
many regrets. Walking through the canyons toward
Millersburg, Karyn thought back over her time in Custer
County. The girl who had stood in a church in Grand Island
looking forward to a little frame cottage in Nebraska had
grown a lot over the past few months. She had taken on a
sod house and almost made it a home. And she had fallen
in love.

Karyn walked for hours. When the sun began to set she had come to the steep incline she had planned to lead the gelding up on the return to Millersburg. She wondered where the horse was. Had he found his way home? Looking about her, Karyn gave a little cry of delight as she saw the saddlebags lying at the side of the trail. Obviously the gelding had run this way, and when he scrambled up the trail, the saddlebags had fallen off. Choosing a flat rock against the canyon wall, Karyn settled down to a cold supper that tasted better than anything she had eaten in a long time. She pulled off her boots and rubbed her tired, aching feet. The saddlebags served as her pillow that night.

Early the next morning, Karyn scrambled up the steep trail onto the tableland. Halfway across the table she came to the last blackened strip of prairie. Someone had set a backfire. *Good. That means Millersburg was saved.* She looked off toward the northeast. As far as she could see, the strip of black extended, but didn't cross where the backfire had been set. Maybe the homestead was saved, too.

Karyn was about to descend into the valley that would lead her to Millersburg when she saw four riders in the distance. She took off her hat and jumped up and down and yelled at the top of her lungs. The distant riders spurred their horses, and in a few moments Karyn was surrounded by exuberant Delhomme men fighting to hug her.

After taking a long drink from Luc's canteen, Karyn stammered, "But how did you know to come after me? I didn't tell anyone but Cay—"

"My dear," Emile said with emotion. "Don't you know that Mikal followed you to the homestead? And when he realized you had left, he set out after you."

Luc nodded. "That's right. He followed you to Millersburg, and then to the Stoddards'. But with a team and wagon he couldn't go down into the canyons."

"Is he all right?" Karyn asked, her hand at her throat. "The fire—"

"Yes, the fire caught him, too. He set a backfire—with the very last match and a good amount of prayer he burned off a place big enough for the team. They're all right. He found part of your bedroll at the Stoddards' . . . and then he knew you'd been there. He spent hours riding along the rim of the canyon calling for you."

Serge broke in. "How did you survive? The gelding arrived back at Cay's yesterday morning. Did he run off?"

Karyn nodded her head. "He threw me right at the edge of the canyon . . . right into a thicket of bushes—and just in front of the advancing fire."

"Then how did you escape?"

Karyn described the cave. "It was a miracle I found it again, but God was with me."

"Be grateful it was empty. And don't tell anyone else that you know where that cave is," Emile warned. "It's been rumored for years that Doc Templeton and his gang of horse thieves have a hideout somewhere in those canyons. I doubt they'd be happy knowing someone had discovered their lair."

Karyn laughed wearily. "Well, I guess I can thank God for the horse thieves. If God hadn't led me to that cave . . ." She looked over her shoulder and shivered.

"Yes," Emile said soberly. "Thank God. And now we have to get you home. Mikal picked up your trunk from Amalia. He's waiting at home to hear from us."

At Karyn's look of surprise, Luc explained, "When we got back to Cay's and saw the gelding we all feared the worst."

The reality of what Luc was saying sunk in. Mikal thought she had died in the fire. Mikal had taken her trunk and gone home. The Delhommes were looking for her. But they were looking for a body.

Serge broke in. "You're a smart girl, Karyn, but you've

been wrong about a lot of things. The most important of which is Mikal's opinion of you."

Remi took Karyn by the arm. "Come on, Karyn. Ride with me." Karyn settled behind Remi, who said gently, "Just put your arms around me and lean your head on my back. I know you're exhausted. Maybe you can get some rest on the way back." Karyn was half asleep before they had gone a mile.

Cay Miller had just ushered Celest and Sophie inside his store when Amalia tap-tapped with her cane across the dusty street and joined them. "They've gone to find Karyn, I see."

Sophie began to cry.

Celest nodded.

Amalia cleared her throat. "May I wait with you?"

"Of course," Celest answered.

The three women made their way to the back corner of the store. Amalia plopped a basket of biscuits on the table. She sat down and sighed heavily. "No one wants to eat at a time like this. I don't know why I always think biscuits are the answer to everything."

Celest smiled. "It's kind of you to think of us, Amalia." She took a biscuit.

"Oh, I was not thinking of you," Amalia said bluntly. "I always bake when I am upset. But my daughter-in-law does not want me heating up her kitchen any more this morning. She saw you both arrive and suggested I come over here." She sighed. "I will get coffee."

"You'll need more firewood," Cay said, excusing himself.

Amalia stirred up the fire in Cay's stove. Celest opened a small French testament and began reading. Sophie sniffed and blew her nose.

When the coffee was ready, Amalia poured each woman a cup before sitting down at the table. Finally, she spoke to Celest. "If what you are reading brings you comfort, Celest, could you perhaps translate a little into German for Sophie and me?"

Celest looked up in surprise. Amalia shrugged and smiled. "I have been reading a little myself. Karyn said she found it helpful. I thought I would try it and see if it could change even a sour old woman like me."

"I was really just reading the same thing over and over again," Celest explained. She began to translate the passage aloud, "'Be careful for nothing; but in everything by prayer and supplication with thanksgiving let your requests be made known unto God. And the peace of God, which passeth all understanding, shall keep your hearts and minds through Christ Jesus.'" She paused to say, "I don't know if my German is good enough to translate it perfectly. Does it sound right?"

Amalia nodded. "Your German is very good." She asked, "So tell me, Celest. At times like this, does the peace of God keep your heart? Do you think the peace of God will keep Mikal's mind? Or will he go half mad with grief again if another wife is found dead on the prairie?"

Sophie began to cry louder. Celest patted her hand and whispered, "Right now I can only cling to the promise and pray that Mikal will do the same."

When Karyn slid off Remi's horse and landed on the boardwalk in front of Cay Miller's store, she was inundated with questions, overwhelmed with kisses and hugs, and almost smothered with attention. Everyone went inside to hear her account of her escape from the fire. When she finished, she pulled the gold coin out of her pocket. "My souvenir of the ordeal," she said. "Don't tell Doc Templeton I have some of his money. I certainly don't want him to come looking for me."

There was an awkward silence. Celest whispered something to Cay, who nodded his head, motioned to Remi and Serge, and left the room. Luc and Emile took one look at

Celest and headed out the front door. When the men were gone, Celest said, "Amalia, I think Sophie has something she needs to say to Karyn in private." With a little shove, she pushed Sophie toward Karyn. "Tell her now, Sophie. You must, or you will never be happy. And neither will she." Celest and Amalia disappeared into Cay's private quarters.

Sophie trembled. Tears began to slide down her cheeks. "Oh, Karyn. Will you ever forgive me? I was so jealous of you. Jealous of everything you had. And I almost—I almost destroyed you." She slumped down into a chair and began to sob.

"Jealous? You were jealous of *me?* Of what? Of my ability to plow and hoe? Of my sunburned skin?" Karyn asked, "Of what is there to be jealous?"

Sophie glanced up at her, her blue eyes brimming with tears. "Mikal."

"Mikal?" The sound of the name sent a pang of regret through her so strong that Karyn had to sit down. The Delhommes had given her reason to hope that Mikal was waiting for her . . . but now the specter of Mikal and Sophie had once again reared its head.

"Oh, Karyn. Can you ever forgive me? I did so many wrong things." Sophie took a deep breath. "I have been such a flirt. Even when I knew Mikal did not care for me . . . I kept on with my flirting. And that day with the shirt-fitting. He was so embarrassed. But I just kept on . . . pretending . . ." She stopped and whispered hoarsely, "And even when I knew it was hurting you terribly, still I did not stop. Yesterday, when Mikal went after you, he told me I had caused so much trouble for him. He said he had tolerated it because I was your sister. But he warned me. I knew I had to apologize to you. I knew I had to stop. I was going to tell you. And then, the fire . . . and I thought you were dead and I would never have a chance. Oh, Karyn, can you ever forgive me?"

Karyn leaned forward in her chair. She reached across the table and clasped Sophie's hands tightly. Giving them a little shake she said, "Tell me what Mikal said, Sophie. Tell me. He was coming for *me*? I mean, because he wanted *me*?"

Sophie nodded her head and murmured, "Of course, Karyn. Mikal never cared for me. He only tolerated me because I was your sister. And—" Sophie ducked her head and confessed, "I kept talking about Hans. About how very different he is from Hans."

Karyn released Sophie's hands and sat back without making any comment. Sophie blurted out, "I won't be in your way anymore, Karyn. I can go home with Celest tonight, and send Luc for my trunk and my things tomorrow. Cay has encouraged me to open my dressmaking shop. He says I can rent the rooms upstairs, and I think the time is right for me to do it. He is going to give my customers a discount when they buy their fabric from him. And Luc has promised to write to me often from Philadelphia."

Celest and Amalia appeared at the doorway leading into Cay's quarters. "Your bath is ready, Karyn. Are you finished here?"

Karyn looked up, surprised. Standing up, she reached out to pat Sophie on the shoulder. "It's all right, Sophie. Thank you for telling me. Even if I had stayed with Mikal, I would always have wondered . . . unless I heard it from you."

Celest called out, "Sophie, Cay said that Karyn was to take whatever she needs. He said he just got three women's dresses in. They are in boxes along the north wall. See what you think."

Amalia put her hand on Karyn's arm and said quietly, "And I will bake fresh biscuits for your wedding breakfast." She leaned over to whisper, "I will even send the recipe home with you." She hurried to make her way to the front of the store and out the door.

CHAPTER 20

A Lace Collar

There be three things which are too wonderful
for me, yea, four which I know not: The way of an
eagle in the air; the way of a serpent upon a rock;
the way of a ship in the midst of the sea;
and the way of a man with a maid.
Proverbs 30:18–19

The afternoon of her rescue, Karyn Ensinger Ritter (in name only) emerged from Cay's store trembling with excitement. She had enjoyed the exquisite opulence of a bath followed by a long nap. Her thick brown hair was done up in an elaborate braid wrapped about her head, and she was dressed in a new, wine-colored calico dress with an ivory lace collar.

Sophie was waiting to hand her Sugar's reins. "I'll ride to the Delhommes' with Luc. You will need Sugar for visiting, and Luc has promised to drive me back to Millersburg as soon as I am ready to move into my new rooms."

Amalia came hurrying across the street and handed up a sack. "Biscuits," she said. "For your wedding breakfast. And I included the recipe." She blew Karyn a kiss.

The Delhommes and Sophie headed out of Millersburg toward the northeast. Remi hung back. "I am to be the escort to ensure that you have an uneventful ride home to Mikal."

The moment the soddy came into view, Remi said, "See you soon, Karyn," and rode off toward home. Karyn watched him ride away before turning to survey her homestead. The earth around the house was black, but she knew that in a short while green shoots would appear, and the grass would be more lush than ever. Tomorrow they would ride to the Delhommes' and get Ella and the calf and bring them home. By the end of the week, they would have the sow slaughtered, and Karyn would make a feast of sausage and ham and invite Sophie and the Delhommes and Cay Miller over. She would embrace Sophie and let her know that all was forgiven.

But that was tomorrow and the days after. Before tomorrow came tonight. She felt a surge of joy at the thought of Mikal waiting for her inside the little house made of dirt. On the footsteps of joy came nervousness. Karyn slid to the ground, aware of a new sensation in her midsection. The sun was setting. A pinprick of golden light shining from the direction of the soddy told her that Mikal had lit the lantern and set it in the window. She walked quietly toward the homestead, her heart beating more and more rapidly as she approached the door. She knocked softly, but there was no answer. Opening the door, she noticed that Mikal had put her trunk back by the bed. But Mikal was not there.

Sugar nudged her from behind. She tied Sugar's reins to a porch post and, taking the bag of Amalia's biscuits, went inside and opened her trunk. She spread her lace tablecloth on the table and arranged the biscuits on a plate. With every addition to the table, she listened for Mikal's footsteps outside. But he didn't come. When she had finished setting the table with her grandmother's tea set, she went back outside and untied Sugar.

"All right, girl, I'll take you down to the barn." Somewhat disappointed that her dramatic entrance had been ruined, Karyn led Sugar down the hill. And then, she saw Mikal. Golden light from a lantern spilled out of the opening to the dugout. He was inside sitting on the bed, his head in his hands.

Karyn turned Sugar into the corral and tiptoed inside to where Mikal sat. Reaching out with a trembling hand, she touched his shoulder. "Mikal."

Mikal looked up at her, blinking in disbelief. His eyes filled with tears. He grabbed her hands, squeezing them so tightly they hurt. "I thought you were Luc coming to tell me—" Finally, he fell to his knees and wrapped his arms around her. Choking back his tears, he said again, "I thought it was Luc—"

Karyn caressed the mane of black hair. "I know. You thought I perished in the fire. But you see, I am here." She put her hands on his shoulders and pushed herself away from him so that she could see his blue eyes when he looked up at her.

He sat back up on the bed. Karyn sat down beside him. Gently he brushed one of her cheeks with his fingertips. Then his fingers traced along her jawline and down her throat to the lace collar of her new dress. He sighed and pulled his hand away. He didn't look at Karyn as he said, "Have I really been so cold and unfeeling that I have driven you away, Karyn?"

Karyn bit her lip. She said as matter-of-factly as possible, "Why would you want me when you could have Sophie?"

Mikal sputtered, "Sophie? What would I want with Sophie?"

"She's so tiny—so ladylike—with soft hands . . ." Karyn looked down at her own work-worn hands. "And I—"

Mikal sounded almost angry. "Was it Sophie who plastered the walls of my house? Was it Sophie who tended a garden all summer, fighting off insects and heat? Was it

Sophie who had the courage to kill a rattlesnake? Did Sophie ever cook over a hot fire to make certain I had a good supper after a day in the fields? Did Sophie wear herself out collecting my lost fence posts? Did Sophie know what to do to survive a prairie fire?" He made a sound of derision. "What would I want with a tiny woman who faints at everything and pleads sickness to avoid hard work?"

Mikal grasped her by both shoulders. "Stop talking about Sophie, Karyn. I have loved you since the day you wore that rose-colored silk gown and sang at the Delhommes'."

"But why didn't you ever tell me?"

He dropped his hands to his sides as he answered. "I didn't want to force myself on you. I am loud and rough—not at all like your Hans Gilhoff, with his refined manners. And I will never be rich enough to give you a great house like his. Comparing my little soddy to an estate in Germany, I began to see I was crazy to think you could ever really care for a hulk of a boy with a few acres planted in corn and a house made of dirt."

"Mikal," Karyn said tenderly, "you think you understand so many things. How is it that you do not understand how very much I love you?" She looked up to see doubt in his blue eyes. Finally, she cried out, "Oh, Mikal. What woman on earth would not want to be held in these arms of yours? How could I not love you?" Karyn reached up to touch his hair. She put a hand on each of his cheeks. Staring intently into his eyes she said, "You listen to me, Mikal Ritter. Hans Gilhoff was a lifetime ago. I was a girl, and he was a boy going off to war. It was all very romantic, and for a while I reveled in the tragedy. But, Mikal, I could never have married Hans Gilhoff." She ran her fingers through his long hair. "I was meant to come to America and to live in a house made of dirt with a raven-haired giant." Impulsively, she kissed him on the cheek.

Mikal turned and engulfed her in his arms, murmuring, "I love you, *mein Schatz.*"

Snuggling against his shoulder, Karyn sighed. "I can hardly believe it yet."

Mikal took a deep breath. Karyn felt his heart begin to beat more quickly. Finally, he leaned down towards her and whispered, "Something tells me that it's time I did more than simply *tell* you that I love you, Mrs.-Ritter-in-name-only. I think it is time that I *show* you."

And he did.

The Diary
August 29, 1880
   Song of Solomon 2:16

Epilogue

The moment she finished reading the translation of Karyn Ritter's diary, Reagan scrambled for her father's Bible to look up Song of Solomon 2:16. "My beloved is mine, and I am his . . ." She sighed and sat back. It was two o'clock in the morning. She had spent the entire night reading the diary, hoping for a fairy-tale ending to the story of two people she had grown to care about. And while the Bible verse that Karyn had referenced hinted at "happily ever after," Reagan was not satisfied. *It wasn't an ending at all. It was only the beginning.*

Karyn and Mikal Ritter had been married for over sixty years. They had raised a family and endured the Dust Bowl. Reagan Bishop did not want to leave them in a one-room soddy at the beginning of their lives together. Indeed, having read the diary, Reagan had more questions than ever. Where had all the beautiful quilts come from? Karyn hadn't mentioned quilting once in her diary. What happened to Sophie? And what about the other sisters? Did they ever come to America? Sighing, Reagan snuggled down into the nest of pillows on her bed. She finally fell asleep to dream of sod houses and prairie fires, buried treasure and a tall, black-haired man with beautiful blue eyes.

When Reagan's phone rang early the next morning, she woke slowly and stretched. Intending to let the answering machine pick up a message, she came instantly awake when she heard Irene's voice say, "I just couldn't wait to ask you—"

"You must be psychic," Reagan said as soon as she snatched up the phone. "I couldn't put it down. I read until 2:00 A.M."

"That means I woke you. I'm sorry."

"No, it's all right." Reagan sat up in bed. "Hold on a minute. Let me switch to the cordless." Reagan pushed the "wait" button on her bedside phone and hurried out to the living room. Once she had her cordless phone she said, "Okay, I'm back. I just want to make coffee while we talk."

"Well, did you enjoy Oma's story?" Irene wanted to know.

"You know I did. Except for one thing," Reagan said. "The end of the diary is really only the beginning. I still have a million questions."

Irene chuckled. "I thought you might. That's why I'm calling so early. Do you have plans for the weekend?"

"Not if you need something."

"Oh, I don't need anything. But I'm driving up to the homestead, and I thought you might want to go along. We can talk about the diary. Who knows? Maybe we'll even drive around a bit. If you're interested."

"I'll be there in half an hour," Reagan said.

Irene cautioned, "Be prepared to 'rough it.' The house is almost empty. I have some neighbors helping with burning off the prairie. I won't want to leave until late tomorrow night."

"Okay, so give me forty-five minutes. I'll locate a sleeping bag and my work boots. Anything else I need?"

Irene laughed. "We can stop at the store on the way up and get food and bottled water. I'll bring an empty cooler. Do you mind driving?"

Less than an hour after Irene called, Reagan pulled up her driveway. In no time they had stowed Irene's camping gear in the back of Reagan's pickup and were cruising down Interstate 80 toward Grand Island.

"What on earth . . . ?" Irene exclaimed.

Reagan's truck had just topped the last rise on the road to the Ritter homestead. Someone had pitched a tent beneath one of the cottonwoods in the front yard. A bright red Dodge Ram pickup was parked next to the barn. Behind the pickup sat a four-wheeler, its tires caked with mud.

Irene was fuming. "How dare they just move in like this, just because the house needs paint, and there's no one around. If they drove that infernal four-wheeler through Opa Mikal's prairie . . ."

Reagan pulled up to the house and hopped out of the truck. "Settle down, Irene," she said. "It's probably just some kids having fun. I'll see if I can find them."

"Having fun?!" Irene was indignant. "Having fun, indeed! Opa Mikal never planted that sixty acres, and he protected it for decades. He knew the prairie would disappear some day. He wanted a piece of it preserved. And if they've put tire tracks through one of the few remaining pieces of virgin prairie in the state . . ." Irene fumbled for the car phone. "I'm going to call the sheriff."

Just as Irene put the phone to her ear Reagan saw someone appear at the top of the ridge behind the house. "Someone's coming. I'll go talk—"

"Get in and lock the door, Reagan," Irene said, locking her own door.

"Don't be ridiculous," Reagan said, laughing. "I'll just go talk to him." She headed up toward the house, calling and waving. The man had seen her and was striding purposefully down the hill. Reagan called out, "You're on private proper—" As the man came closer, the words died in her mouth. He was very tall. With long black hair. And large hands. As he came nearer, Reagan saw the blue eyes and gulped.

The stranger smiled. "Excuse me—I couldn't hear you. Are you lost? This is private property."

"Yes. I know. I just—" Reagan fumbled and turned around and pointed toward her truck. She didn't have to say anything else, because they had finally come around the corner of the house where Irene was watching out the back window of the pickup. The moment the stranger came into view Irene's face lit up. She dropped the phone, pushed open her door, and scrambled out of the truck, exclaiming, "Noah? Noah! It really is you!" She laughed happily and hurried across the lawn.

Noah held out his arms, engulfed Irene in a hug, and then picked her up and swung her around as if she were a child.

Irene patted him on the shoulders. "When did you come? Why didn't you call? How long have you been here?" She was breathless. "How are things in California?"

Noah answered her last question. "As crowded and crime-ridden as ever. I needed to get away for a while."

Irene pulled Reagan over. "This is Reagan Bishop, a friend of mine from Lincoln." Irene turned to Reagan. "Reagan, this is my nephew, Noah. Noah Ritter." Irene took one look at Reagan and laughed. "Yes, I know. It's quite a shock, isn't it? As if Mikal Ritter just came back to life."

Reagan looked up at Noah and smiled, secretly wishing with all her might that she had dark coloring that would possibly hide the crimson she could feel creeping up the back of her neck and onto her cheeks. She couldn't think of anything to say.

Irene saved her further embarrassment. "Since when do you drive a pickup, Noah?" She turned toward Reagan and winked. "The last time he was here he tore the muffler off his little red sports car speeding along one of the back roads."

Noah laughed. "Well, you can see that I came much better prepared this time."

"You look like you're moving in," Irene commented.

"Fact is, I'd like to stay a while, if you don't mind." Noah was suddenly very serious. He looked up toward the roofline of the house. "I thought I might paint the place. Fix a few things."

Irene looked concerned. "Is everything all right with you?"

Reagan cleared her throat. "Look, you two. You probably have a million things to discuss. Irene, if you'll give me the keys, I'll take our things inside."

"Let me help," Noah offered.

Reagan shook her head. "No, thanks. I can manage." She already had the cooler hoisted out of the back of her truck and was headed for the door. She set it down and called, "Just toss the house keys in the bed of the truck, Irene. I'll enjoy looking around inside."

Reagan made several trips back and forth from the pickup to the front door of the house, piling things on the concrete slab that served as a porch. When she finally unlocked the door and went inside, she was disappointed. It was just a half-empty farmhouse. But then, she began to really look about her, and soon she was lost in imagining. She wandered through the rooms on the first floor.

Saddened by the run-down state of the house, Reagan pushed back the musty curtains at the parlor window. Sun streamed into the room. She looked out. Noah was sitting on the tailgate of his truck. Irene was standing at his side, her hand on his knee. Whatever they were talking about, Noah didn't look very happy.

Reagan marveled once again at how closely Noah Ritter resembled his great-grandfather. *Replace the pickup with a farm wagon, and take that ponytail out of his hair . . .* Reagan rubbed the goose bumps from her forearms and stepped away from the window, unaware that God was about to use the legacy of Mikal and Karyn Ritter to mold a future for Reagan Bishop. For the run-down homestead and the fallen-in dugout weren't really an ending at all. They were only the beginning . . .

Behold, I make all things new.
Revelation 21:5

About the Author

STEPHANIE GRACE WHITSON lives in southeast Nebraska with her husband of twenty-five years, four children, and a very spoiled German shepherd. The Whitsons are active in their local Bible-teaching church. Stephanie is the author of the best-selling Prairie Winds Series, *Walks the Fire, Soaring Eagle,* and *Red Bird,* as well as the first book in the Keepsake Legacies series, *Sarah's Patchwork.*

Stephanie can be reached by addressing her at:

Stephanie Grace Whitson
3800 Old Cheney Road #101–178
Lincoln, NE 68516

THE FINESSE

THE FINESSE
How to Win
More Tricks More Often

by Fred L. Karpin

♠   ♡   ◇   ♣

PRENTICE-HALL, INC., Englewood Cliffs, N.J.

The Finesse: How to Win More Tricks
More Often by Fred L. Karpin

Copyright © 1972 by Fred L. Karpin

ISBN: 0-13-317198-1
Library of Congress Catalog Card Number: 75-176403

Printed in the United States of America • 3

Prentice-Hall International, Inc., London
Prentice-Hall of Australia, Pty. Ltd., North Sydney
Prentice-Hall of Canada, Ltd., Toronto
Prentice-Hall of India Private Ltd., New Delhi
Prentice-Hall of Japan, Inc., Tokyo

Introduction

According to the *Official Encyclopedia of Bridge,* a finesse is the attempt to gain power for lower-ranking cards by taking advantage of the favorable position of higher-ranking cards held by the opposition. From abridge viewpoint, this is a much better definition than the one used in *Webster's New International Unabridged Dictionary.*

But the dictionary includes other definitions of the word "finesse" that aptly apply to this book and its author. For example: "Delicate skill; subtle discrimination; refinement." Also: "Cunning; artifice; stratagem."

The finesse is the first bridge play a neophyte learns as a method of increasing the number of tricks he may be able to win. The late self-styled "authority on authorities," Shepard Barclay, once described the finesse as a play from the hand with the low cards toward the hand with the high cards, "sometimes called the Barclay rule of finessing." This would appear to have been inaccurate on two counts. I never heard anybody quote this or any other as "the Barclay rule of finessing." Nor was it truly descriptive of the finesse, which in many cases is a play from either of two hands containing high cards and in others is a play from a hand containing a higher card than the one in the hand led toward.

What I am saying, perhaps in too roundabout a fashion, is that although the finesse is one of the simpler plays in bridge, it is a maneuver of such variety and often of such complexity that it is truly surprising that no author ever before thought to write a book about this single and most often encountered bridge situation. It is *not* surprising that it was Fred Karpin who thought to do it, and that he has done it so well.

Although he is a younger man than Charles Goren, Fred Karpin has been writing about bridge for longer than Mr. Bridge himself; indeed, Karpin's book on point-count bidding was published long before Goren's. It was a large-size paper-cover book, if memory serves me correctly, and it was inspired by the author's great success in teaching his pupils to play better by giving them an easier method of bidding evaluation than the honor trick method that had been popularized by Ely Culbertson.

I am not going to get involved in the controversy over who first invented the point count. I will only tell you that since the time Karpin first espoused it, he has become not only one of the most successful teachers on the Eastern seaboard but also a syndicated bridge columnist and reporter, a prolific writer of many books on the game, and the curator of one of the most extensive collections of bridge hands anyone ever sought to compile. He is also highly esteemed by his fellow bridge-writers not just for his written works but for his readiness to share his research library collection with anyone who cares to ask him to come up with a couple of examples of any play—from a trump coup to the multitudinous examples of finessing situations from which he has culled the material for this complete and completely absorbing book.

If you want to learn how to win more tricks when you play bridge, you can hardly do better than enjoy what Karpin has written here.

—Richard L. Frey

Acknowledgments

I would like to make acknowledgment, and at the same time express my deepest gratitude, to two gentlemen: Thomas M. Smith and Richard L. Frey. Tom, the business manager of the American Contract Bridge League "Bulletin," and one of our nation's top-ranking players, edited this book from A to Z. Not only did he make the necessary corrections and deletions, but, of greater importance, he made many practical recommendations regarding the inclusion of certain finessing positions that I had failed to include.

From an overall viewpoint, I am even more indebted to Richard Frey. Prior to his retirement from active national competition, Dick, Life Master #8, was considered to be one of the world's finest players. Had he not applied continuous pressure on me to write this book on finesses, it would probably still be a gleam in my eye. And when the book had been written, he made valuable contributions to its contents.

To the bridge players of our nation, from the very lowest echelons to the very highest, I also owe a debt of gratitude. Although they had nothing to do with the actual writing, some of the finessing positions that confronted them in combat have been assimilated into this book, thus sparing me the time and effort of creating the deals required to analyze this subject. My appreciation and thanks are hereby recorded.

Fred L. Karpin

Foreword

One of the world's greatest race horses was Native Dancer, who, when he retired, had won twenty-one of twenty-two races. Rumor has it that Native Dancer once played in a bridge tournament. On the very first deal, he reached a grand slam in spades. He went down one trick.

"You should have taken the heart finesse," his partner pointed out. "With the favorable location of the heart king, you couldn't have missed making the slam."

"That's ridiculous!" retorted Native Dancer. "Whoever heard of a horse taking a finesse?"

Without meaning to be disrespectful to a champion, Native Dancer was not well-informed. There are times when horses, as well as people, really have no alternative but to take a finesse. Admittedly, it went against the grain for a horse that had won twenty-one out of twenty-two races to stake his existence on a 50-50 proposition. But, as I'm sure Native Dancer will admit in retrospect, he really had no better alternative available.

It is an undisputed fact that the most recurring type of play in bridge is the finesse. Although no official statistics have been compiled regarding the frequency of occurrence of finesses, reliable sources estimate that the opportunities for the employment of a finesse arise, on the average, about once per deal. Sometimes, in a particular deal, there will be no finesses; but, in other deals, the opportunities for finessing may arise two, three, or even four times.

Generally speaking, the primary objective of a finesse is to gain a vitally needed trick by creating a winner that was not there before. In the hands of the expert player, the finesse has become a most powerful tool, for he has learned how to wield it selectively, and not promiscuously. In the hands of the nonexpert who repeatedly applies the finesse in indiscriminate and automatic fashion, it develops into a play that frequently results in

his destruction (and usually the depletion of his financial resources). Far too often, the nonexpert plays out a hand as though
it were ordained that finesses are compulsory whenever a finessing position exists. As a consequence, he loses many contracts that would have been fulfilled had a little judgment—
instead of wishful thinking—been applied.

This book deals with the trials and tribulations of both
expert and nonexpert players who, through the years, have been
confronted with finessing situations. The hands to be presented
arose in both upper-echelon games (national tournaments and
high-stake rubber-bridge games) and in games of the low, lower,
and lowest echelons (Monday morning duplicates, Thursday
afternoon duplicates, and one-tenth and one-fortieth of a cent
rubber-bridge games). These deals are, in my opinion, a valid
representative sample of the practical question: "To finesse or
not to finesse?"

Fred L. Karpin

Contents

1

Types of Finesses

♠   ♡   ◇   ♣

Defined formally [although in general fashion] a "finesse" might be described as *an attempt to win a trick with a specific card of a suit in which there is a higher card (or cards) outstanding.* In its most recurring form, this is the classic example of the simple, straightforward finesse:

NORTH
♠ 3 2

SOUTH
♠ A Q

The two of spades is led out of the North hand, East follows with the four, and South inserts his queen. Fifty percent of the time East will have been dealt the king of spades and the queen will win the trick. The other 50 percent of the time West will have the king, and the finesse will lose.

In both approach and effect, the finesse is really "wishful thinking" put into action. That is, you figuratively place a key card, which one of your two adversaries possesses, into the hand of the one specific adversary you hope has it—and then proceed to ambush it by encirclement. In other words, you conceive a situation that must exist if your finesse is to succeed—and then attack as though your conception were a reality.

In the example just given, the finesse is strictly a 50-50 proposition, and, as such, might be viewed as a gamble. Admittedly, a person striving to be a winner at the bridge table cannot afford to stake his existence on accepting 50-50 gambles as a steady diet. Actually, however, unless there is a better play available, *the finesse stands to gain everything, and to lose nothing.*

What is the alternative in the preceding example? It would be to play the ace of spades when East follows suit with the four, in the hope of catching the singleton king in the West hand. The mathematical chance of this happening is about 1 in 1500. By finessing the queen, you will make a second spade trick 750 times out of 1500 (50 percent). Is it not true that the gambling play would be to lay down the ace, while the sound play would be to finesse the queen? (And, frankly, if you played the ace, and caught the singleton king in the West hand, the opponents would assume you possessed E.S.P.—or they would view you with deep suspicion.)

If the reader is forming the impression that I am a devotee of the finesse, let me hasten to correct this impression. In espousing the preceding type of simple finesse, I have tried merely to demonstrate that it is not a gamble, but the only correct play. Even among the experts, who spurn finesses whenever possible because they are always on the lookout for a line of play that is less risky, the finesse is their bread-and-butter play. If our experts never took a finesse, they would be losers in every single session in which they played.

The emphasis in this book will be on how to *avoid* finesses whenever possible, since the finesse is not an all-occasion, all-purpose tool of play. It is a "special occasion" tool, to be used only when observation, reinforced by judgment, indicates that it is the most logical way to tackle the situation at hand.

Let us now take a look at the most common varieties of finesses. In each example, it is assumed that *no clues relevant to the distribution of the opponents' cards have been revealed during either the bidding or the play.*

THE DIRECT FINESSE

(1)

NORTH
♠ 3 2

SOUTH
♠ A Q

(2)

NORTH
♠ 4 3 2

SOUTH
♠ A K J

(3)*

NORTH
♠ 3 2

SOUTH
♠ K 5

(4)*

NORTH
♠ 4 3 2

SOUTH
♠ K Q 5

In each of the examples, you lead the deuce of spades from the North hand, East following suit with the six. You are South.

(1)   This combination has already been discussed. You insert the queen and hope East possesses the king.

(2)   You finesse the jack, wishfully thinking East was dealt the queen. Fifty percent of the time, your wishful thinking will materialize.

(3)   You play the king. Half the time East will have the ace and your king will win the trick.

(4)   You put up the king, which will capture the trick the 50 percent of the time that East possesses the ace. If the king wins, you reenter the North hand via some other suit and lead the spade three. With East holding the spade ace, your queen will now become a second winner.

* Technically these examples are indirect finesses (see page 9).

(5)	(6)
NORTH	NORTH
♠ 3 2	♠ 4 3 2
SOUTH	SOUTH
♠ K J	♠ K Q 10

(7)	(8)
NORTH	NORTH
♠ 4 3 2	♠ 4 3 2
SOUTH	SOUTH
♠ K J 10	♠ A Q 10

(5)   You now have a choice of two hopes. If you think (or have a feeling) East possesses the ace, you put up your king when East follows low on your lead of North's spade deuce. If, instead, you assume that East has the queen, you play your jack. If East possesses the queen, the jack will drive out West's (presumed) ace, thereby promoting your king to a winner.

(6)   You finesse your ten of spades, hoping East has the jack. If he does, you have two sure spade tricks when the ten is captured by West's (presumed) ace. An alternative wishful-thinking play would be to put up the king, making the assumption that East was dealt the ace. If he has it, then the king will win, after which the North hand will be reentered via some other suit and another low spade led toward the queen. If East had the ace of spades before, he still has it—and your queen will win a second spade trick for you.

(7)   Play the jack (or ten). You can always win one trick in this suit by giving away the king and jack to the opponents' ace and queen. The idea is to make two tricks, which can be accomplished the half of the time that East was dealt the queen. If the jack is taken by West's ace, you reenter the North hand via some other suit when you regain the lead and play the three of spades. When East follows low, you repeat the finesse against East's queen by inserting the ten.

(8)   You insert the ten of spades. Should this win, you re-enter the North hand and lead another spade, finessing the queen. If East possesses both the king and the jack, you will win three spade tricks. If the initial finesse of the ten loses to the jack, take a second finesse by leading low from the North hand and inserting the queen. If East has the king, the queen will win. If the initial finesse of the ten should lose to the king, the queen of spades becomes a sure winner. This "double finesse" will yield two spade tricks whenever East possesses either the jack or the king (a 75 percent chance).

(9)	(10)
NORTH	NORTH
♡ K 3 2	♡ J 10 2
SOUTH	SOUTH
♡ A J 4	♡ A K 3
(11)	(12)
NORTH	NORTH
♡ K J 2	♡ Q 3 2
SOUTH	SOUTH
♡ A 10 3	♡ K 10 4

(9)   Lead the deuce of hearts, and when East follows low, insert the jack. It will win the trick the 50 percent of the time that East possesses the queen. (Technically, North's king should be played first, on the outside chance that West was dealt the singleton queen.)

(10)   First cash your ace. (West may have a singleton queen.) Then enter the North hand via some side suit and lead the jack of hearts. If East does not produce the queen, let the jack ride in the hope that East was dealt the queen but, correctly, is withholding it.

(11)   This is a pure 50-50 guess. If you think East has the heart queen, then lead North's deuce and finesse the ten. If you think West possesses her ladyship, then lead the three (or the ten) initially, and finesse against West's hoped-for honor. This setup is known as a "two-way" finesse.

(12)   The heart deuce is led out of the North hand, and you put up the ten when East plays low. The half the time when East was dealt the jack, the ten-spot will either win or be captured by West's (presumed) ace.

(13)	(14)
NORTH	**NORTH**
◇ 10 9 2	◇ J 10 9
SOUTH	**SOUTH**
◇ K Q 3	◇ K 3 2

(15)	(16)
NORTH	**NORTH**
◇ 4 3 2	◇ J 2
SOUTH	**SOUTH**
◇ K J 4	◇ K 10

(13)   In order to make two tricks, you can indulge in either of two hopes, both 50-50 chances: (a) The hope that East has the diamond jack. You lead North's ten, and when East plays low, you follow with the three-spot. (b) The hope that East possesses the diamond ace. You lead North's two of diamonds and put up your king. If the king wins, reenter the North hand via some other suit and lead the nine of diamonds to the queen.

(14)   In order to win two tricks, you must hope East has the diamond queen. North's jack is led, and you play the deuce. If the jack wins (or is taken by the ace), lead North's ten on the next diamond lead and take another finesse against East's queen.

(15)   In order to win two tricks in this suit, you must assume East has the ace and the queen. Lead the deuce and insert the jack. If it wins, reenter the North hand and lead the three. Assuming East plays low again, put up the king. If the jack is taken by the ace on the initial diamond lead, the king is now a winner. However, if the jack is taken by the queen, you regain the lead and play a diamond from the North hand to your king. In order to win one diamond trick, it is essential East possesses *either* the act or the queen. If West has both, you can make no tricks in this suit.

(16)   You lead the jack out of the North hand, to entice East into covering with the queen if he has that card. If he covers, you of course put up the king. You now have an automatic diamond winner, whether or not West wins with the ace. If East plays low on the jack, you have to guess whether East has the queen or the ace. If you assume (hope) he possesses the queen, then follow with the ten. If you assume East has the ace, you put up the king. The better play (psychologically, against better players) would be to put up the king on the lead of the jack, since if East had the queen, he might have played it on the jack, having learned to "cover an honor with an honor."

(17)	(18)
NORTH	**NORTH**
♣ 4 3 2	♣ 4 3 2
SOUTH	**SOUTH**
♣ A J 10	♣ A J 9

(19)	(20)
NORTH	**NORTH**
♣ 4 3 2	♣ 4 3 2
SOUTH	**SOUTH**
♣ K 10 9	♣ Q 10 9

In each of these four examples, you lead the deuce from the North hand, East following suit with the five. (You are still South.)

(17)   Play the jack (or ten). Whenever East was dealt the king and queen, the jack will win. Should the jack lose to the king or queen (as it most likely will), when you regain the lead you play North's three. If East follows suit with a low club, you insert your ten.

By playing the suit in this manner, you will win two tricks 75 percent of the time, since mathematically East will have been dealt the queen and/or the king three quarters of the time.

(18)   This finesse is a recurring "book" play. The deuce is led out of the North hand and the nine inserted, in the hope East was dealt either the Q 10 x or K 10 x. If the hoped-for distribution exists, then the nine will be captured by West's queen or king. On the next club lead out of the North hand, play your jack, which will win the trick if East is left with either the queen or king.

The alternative play of inserting your jack on the initial club lead will be the winning play only if East has the king *and* the queen. Mathematically, East is more likely to have been dealt some K 10 or Q 10 combination (Q 10 x x, K 10 x x, Q 10 x x x, K 10 x x x, etc.) than to have been dealt some specific K Q combination (K Q x, K Q x x, K Q x x x, etc.).

(19)   The deuce is led out of the North hand, and you play the ten. Should this drive out the ace, your king has just become a winner. Should the ten lose to the jack or queen (as it most likely will), on the next club lead out of the North hand, insert your nine in the hope that West will have to win the trick with the ace. The "mathematics" involved in this situation are that East figures to have been dealt either the queen or jack of clubs (or both), and, in this case, the recommended line of play will develop a club winner for North-South. However, should the initial play of the ten lose to West's jack or queen, South has some sort of problem on the second club lead out of the North hand: if East has the club ace, the play of the king, instead of the nine, will be the winning one. The play of the nine, in my opinion, is

superior to the king, for if East has the club ace, he will tend to play it on the second club lead, especially if the contract is in a trump suit (for fear that if he didn't take his ace it would get trumped on the next lead, since dummy started with but two clubs).

(20)   Lead the deuce out of the North hand and insert your ten, in the hope that East was dealt the jack. Assuming that the ten is captured by the ace or king, lead the three from the North hand on the second club lead, putting up your nine. Whenever East possesses the jack, you will make one club trick. Barring evidence to the contrary, obviously the chance that East has the jack is far greater than that he was dealt both the ace and the king.

THE INDIRECT FINESSE

In the direct finesse, you mentally place the card you are finessing against in the hand you want it to be, and proceed to encircle or ambush it. In the indirect finesse, instead of surrounding the missing high card, you indulge in long-range wishful thinking, thereby promoting your own high cards into winners.

The most important and most frequently encountered indirect finesse is this one:

NORTH
♠ Q 5 3

SOUTH
♠ A 4 2

If you lead the queen from the North hand, *you can never gain a trick,* no matter whether East or West holds the king. If East has the king, he will play it on the queen. If West has it, and you follow low, then West will capture the queen. Thus, if you lead the queen initially, all you will ever win is your ace. The two relevant distributions are:

(1)
       NORTH
       ♠ Q 5 2

 WEST   EAST
 ♠ J 9 8   ♠ K 10 7 6

       SOUTH
       ♠ A 4 3

(2)
       NORTH
       ♠ Q 5 2

 WEST   EAST
 ♠ K 10 7 6   ♠ J 9 8

       SOUTH
       ♠ A 4 3

In diagram (1), if you lead the queen, East will cover with the king. When you win the trick with your ace, you have just made your first and last spade trick.

In diagram (2), if you lead the queen, East will play the eight. When you then follow with the three, West will capture the queen with the king. You will then win only one spade trick, the ace.

The proper play in the above North-South combination is to start out *by leading the three from the South hand,* with the intention of putting up North's queen if West plays low. In diagram (1), the queen will be captured by East's king, and all you will ever make in the suit will be South's ace. *But in diagram (2), North's queen of spades will become a winner.*

Specifically, it boils down to this: The "indirect" finesse will gain a trick the 50 percent of the time that West possesses the king; whenever East has the king, you will never gain a trick no matter how you attack the suit.

Just as in the case of the direct finesse, the indirect finesse is wishful thinking in action. In this case, you hope that the king lies in front of the queen; if this setup exists—as mathematically it should half of the time—the queen will become a winner. In summary, taking the indirect finesse becomes the practical matter of a 50 percent hope versus no hope.

A recurring standard card combination that the average player often *mistakenly* assumes is an "indirect" finesse is the following:

NORTH
◇ Q 10 9

SOUTH
◇ A 3 2

Sitting South, he lays down the ace of diamonds, then leads the diamond deuce, West playing low. South now has a 50-50 guess on what to play from the North hand. If he assumes (guesses) that West has the diamond king, he will put up dummy's queen; if he assumes West holds the diamond jack, his winning play will be to insert the ten (which, if captured by East's king, promotes the queen to a winner). Basically, South's play is a 50-50 proposition, although he has a little extra going for him in that West may put up the king on his low diamond lead, thus eliminating the need to guess; or West may have been dealt the doubleton K x or J x, in which case he will be forced to play his honor card.

The correct way to eliminate the guesswork in the preceding combination is to lead the ten from the North hand as the initial diamond lead. Assuming that East plays low, South does likewise. If the ten is captured by West's king, North's queen of diamonds is a winner. If, instead, the ten is taken by West's jack, South regains the lead and next leads the nine of diamonds out of the North hand. If East plays low, so does South. If East possesses the diamond king, the nine wins the trick.

Mathematically, this line of play will win 75 percent of the time—whenever East possesses *either* the king or the jack. Admittedly, it will lose whenever *West* possesses both king and jack. But, then, the play of the ace first, followed by the deuce, will lose

whenever *East* has both honors. So these two combinations—the
K J x in the West hand versus the K J x in the East hand—cancel
each other out. The advantage of the two finesses through East
is that it eliminates the necessity for guesswork when the king
and jack are divided in the opponents' hands.

Here is the second most frequently encountered type of indirect finesse:

NORTH
♡ J 5 4

SOUTH
♡ A K 3 2

Leading the jack initially from the North hand will always
be a losing play. If East possesses the queen, he will cover the
jack, forcing South's king. Thus, South's high-card winners will
be the two with which he started: the ace and the king.

If West possesses the heart queen, he will capture the jack
after South plays low. Again, South's only high-card winners
will be the ace and king.

Putting this in diagram form:

(3)   NORTH
                             ♡ J 5 4
       WEST   EAST
       ♡ 8 6   ♡ Q 10 9 7
                             SOUTH
                             ♡ A K 3 2

(4)   NORTH
                             ♡ J 5 4
       WEST   EAST
       ♡ Q 10 9 7   ♡ 8 6
                             SOUTH
                             ♡ A K 3 2

If you take the indirect finesse by leading the deuce of hearts initially out of the South hand, North's jack will win a trick the half of the time that West was dealt the queen. In diagram (3), North's jack will be captured by East's queen, and nothing will have been gained (or lost). But in diagram (4), on the lead of the heart deuce out of the South hand, West's queen will win the trick, thus promoting North's jack of hearts into a third winner for South. (If West does not take his queen, North's jack will win the trick.)

Before presenting the final three types of finesses, I would like to present a deal that occurred some years ago. It features a direct finesse in one suit and an indirect finesse in another suit. The winning play required choosing which finesse to take first. But our South declarer just was not up to it, and he failed to fulfill a slam contract that a better player would have brought home.

Both sides vulnerable. South deals.

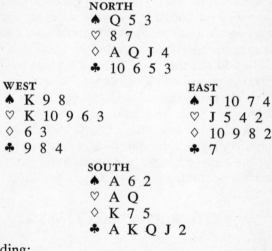

```
                    NORTH
                    ♠ Q 5 3
                    ♡ 8 7
                    ◇ A Q J 4
                    ♣ 10 6 5 3
      WEST                              EAST
      ♠ K 9 8                          ♠ J 10 7 4
      ♡ K 10 9 6 3                     ♡ J 5 4 2
      ◇ 6 3                            ◇ 10 9 8 2
      ♣ 9 8 4                          ♣ 7
                    SOUTH
                    ♠ A 6 2
                    ♡ A Q
                    ◇ K 7 5
                    ♣ A K Q J 2
```

The bidding:

SOUTH	WEST	NORTH	EAST
2 NT	Pass	3 ◇	Pass
4 ♣	Pass	5 ♣	Pass
6 ♣	Pass	Pass	Pass

Opening lead: Four of clubs

After winning the opening lead with his jack, South drew trumps by cashing his ace and king of clubs. Then he entered dummy via the diamond jack, and led the seven of hearts. When East followed suit with the deuce, South inserted his queen, taking the direct finesse.

As is apparent, West captured this trick with his king. He then returned the heart ten, South taking it with his ace. Although South was able to get rid of one of his spades on dummy's fourth diamond, he was unable to prevent West from taking the setting trick with his king of spades.

The success of South's line of play depended exclusively on East having the heart king, a 50-50 proposition. And once this finesse lost, declarer was doomed to defeat. Actually, South could have availed himself of *two* 50-50 chances for the price of one. If his first finesse lost, he could still win his contract if the second finesse were successful.

Going in, South had eleven top tricks. After drawing trumps, he should have led the deuce of spades toward dummy's queen (the indirect finesse). When West put up the king, dummy's spade queen would become declarer's slam-going trick (he would discard his heart queen on dummy's fourth diamond).

If it turned out that East had the king of spades, then declarer, upon regaining the lead, would discard his second spade loser on the fourth diamond and take the heart finesse. Thus, played correctly, declarer would fulfill his contract whenever West possessed the spade king *or* East had the heart king. As South actually played it, he staked the whole hand on East's possession of the king of hearts. In a sense, our declarer "deserved" to go down for not taking full advantage of his assets.

THE BACKWARD FINESSE

The backward finesse is so called because it is taken in an unusual and unnatural way. Various applications of this finesse will be presented in this book. For the present, this finesse arises in two special situations: (1) when "card-reading" proves that the natural, normal way of finessing will lose, and (2) when the finesse can be taken in a manner that will keep a "dangerous" opponent off lead.

Here is an illustration of the standard backward finesse:

NORTH
♣ A 3 2

SOUTH
♣ K J 9

The normal way of attempting to make three club tricks is to lead North's deuce and finesse the jack, on the 50-50 chance that East was dealt the queen. Of course, the jack will win the trick half of the time.

In the backward finesse, the jack is led initially, in the hope that the following distribution exists:

NORTH
♣ A 3 2

WEST
♣ Q 8 7

EAST
♣ 10 6 5 4

SOUTH
♣ K J 9

If West declines to put up his queen on South's jack, the jack wins the trick. If West covers the jack with the queen, North's ace captures the trick. On the return of North's deuce, South inserts his nine, taking a direct finesse against East's hoped-for ten. Thus, the backward finesse gains a trick that otherwise could not have been made.

THE RUFFING FINESSE

This finesse arises only in trump contracts, never at no-trump. As with all finesses, the declarer indulges in the wishful thinking that an adversely-held key card is in a specific oppo-

nent's hand, and he proceeds on the assumption that his wishful
thinking is a fact.

The difference between the normal direct finesse and the
ruffing finesse can be observed in this deal.

Both sides vulnerable. South deals.

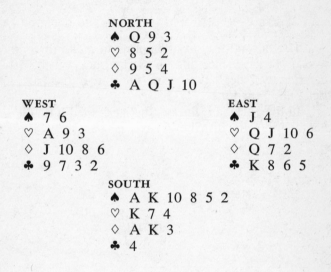

NORTH
♠ Q 9 3
♡ 8 5 2
◇ 9 5 4
♣ A Q J 10

WEST
♠ 7 6
♡ A 9 3
◇ J 10 8 6
♣ 9 7 3 2

EAST
♠ J 4
♡ Q J 10 6
◇ Q 7 2
♣ K 8 6 5

SOUTH
♠ A K 10 8 5 2
♡ K 7 4
◇ A K 3
♣ 4

The bidding:

SOUTH	WEST	NORTH	EAST
1 ♠	Pass	2 ♠	Pass
4 ♠	Pass	Pass	Pass

Opening lead: Jack of diamonds

After declarer captures West's jack of diamonds with his
king, he perceives that he had four potential losers: one in diamonds and three in hearts (if West possessed the heart ace). It

was equally apparent to him that the club suit could be a source of his game-fulfilling trick.

It was a 50-50 proposition whether East or West had been dealt the vital outstanding card—the king of clubs. If West had it, then a successful direct finesse of dummy's queen of clubs would enable South to discard one of his losers on the club ace. But if East possessed the king of clubs, then a direct finesse would result in the queen being captured by East's king. And a heart return by East would be ruinous to declarer (as it would have been) since the defenders might cash three heart tricks. So declarer turned to the ruffing finesse.

At tricks two and three, the ace and king of trumps were cashed. South next led his singleton club to dummy's ace, after which the queen of clubs was led, in the hope that East had the king. East covered the queen with the king, and South ruffed. The North hand was then reentered via the trump queen, and on the jack and ten of clubs, South discarded his three of diamonds and four of hearts. In the end, he lost two heart tricks.

Even if West had possessed the club king (instead of East), the ruffing finesse would have ensured declarer his contract. Had this hypothetical setup existed, on the queen of clubs South would have discarded his losing diamond. West would now have the lead. All the defenders could take would be the ace of hearts, since dummy's established jack and ten of clubs would provide discards for two of South's hearts, and there was no way for East to gain the lead and play through South's king.

Thus, on this deal, the ruffing finesse guaranteed the contract, regardless of whether East or West possessed the club king. The direct finesse, hoping that West had been dealt the club king, would have resulted in declarer's defeat.

THE OBLIGATORY FINESSE

In a purely technical sense, this is not really a finesse. But in the general sense that this play is an attempt to gain a trick by wishful thinking—placing a card where you would like it to be and playing as though your creation were a reality—it is akin to the standard types of finesses.

This is the most recurring type of obligatory finesse:

NORTH
♠ Q 7 6 5

SOUTH
♠ K 4 3 2

Let us say that this is your trump suit, and you would love to lose only one trick in it (to the ace). There are two possible distributions that allow you to achieve this goal:

(1)   *West* possesses the ace of spades as part of a doubleton A x. You lead the deuce of spades, West plays low, and you put up North's queen, which wins. The five of spades is returned and the four is played from the South hand, which West is forced to win with the ace. This would be the setup essential to success:

                          NORTH
                          ♠ Q 7 6 5
WEST   **EAST**
♠ A 8   ♠ J 10 9
                          SOUTH
                          ♠ K 4 3 2

(2)   *East* possesses the doubleton A x of spades. In this case, the North hand is entered via some other suit and the five of spades is led. South inserts his king when East plays low. The deuce of spades is led next, and when West follows suit, North's six is played, which East is forced to win with his ace. This setup would be:

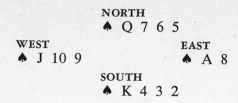

If the opponents' five spades are distributed in any other way than these two illustrations show, South cannot, on his own power, restrict his losers in spades to only one trick. And so, in this obligatory finesse not only must declarer guess which opponent has the ace but, having divined its position, he must indulge in the wishful thinking that the ace is part of a doubleton. If it isn't, South cannot make three spade tricks:

                    NORTH
                    ♠ Q 7 6 5
        WEST   EAST
        ♠ A 10 9   ♠ J 8
                    SOUTH
                    ♠ K 4 3 2

Even if the opponents were to show South their cards, he would have to lose two spade tricks.

2

The Finesse
A Road to Perdition

♠ ♡ ◇ ♣

If bridge players, when confronted with a finessing situation, would pause momentarily to ask themselves "Is this finesse necessary?" their endeavors would be more successful and their pocketbooks enriched. In many types of finessing situations, the answer, upon analysis, would be: "No, it is not necessary." Thus, the finesse would be rejected, and in its place would be substituted a more effective alternative.

The deals in this chapter all arose in low-stake rubber-bridge games: a tenth of a cent a point, a twentieth of a cent, a fortieth of a cent—and one "lunch-hour" game, with no stakes involved. In each deal, our South declarer had a guaranteed contract if he avoided taking an unnecessary finesse. But in each of these deals, the question "Is this finesse necessary?" never even flashed through declarer's thoughts. And so it came to pass that he failed to overcome the lure of the finesse—and he succumbed ingloriously.

Note on the Bidding

The given bidding in each of these deals is not necessarily the way it happened. On occasion, the bidding (as well as the play) left something to be desired. The bidding sequences presented are, in my opinion, the ones that would have developed if the North-South players had been better bidders.

DEAL I

Both sides vulnerable. South deals.

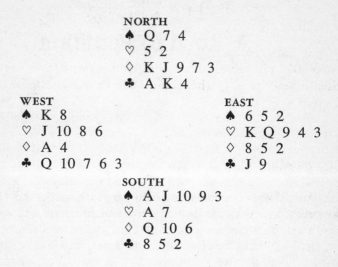

```
                          NORTH
                          ♠ Q 7 4
                          ♡ 5 2
                          ◇ K J 9 7 3
                          ♣ A K 4
        WEST                                   EAST
        ♠ K 8                                  ♠ 6 5 2
        ♡ J 10 8 6                             ♡ K Q 9 4 3
        ◇ A 4                                  ◇ 8 5 2
        ♣ Q 10 7 6 3                           ♣ J 9
                          SOUTH
                          ♠ A J 10 9 3
                          ♡ A 7
                          ◇ Q 10 6
                          ♣ 8 5 2
```

The bidding:

SOUTH	WEST	NORTH	EAST
1 ♠	Pass	2 ◇	Pass
2 ♠	Pass	4 ♠	Pass
Pass	Pass		

Opening lead: Jack of hearts

West opened the jack of hearts, taken by declarer's ace. South entered dummy via the king of clubs and led the queen of trumps. When East followed with a low trump, South did likewise, finessing East for the king.

As luck would have it, the finesse lost to West's king. A heart was returned, East's queen winning. The jack of clubs was now played, driving out dummy's ace. After the trumps were picked up, declarer attacked the diamond suit. West took his ace and cashed the queen of clubs for the setting trick.

After winning the opening heart lead, declarer should have perceived that he had a potential loser in each suit. He also should have realized that the loss of a club trick could be avoided by discarding his losing club on dummy's to-be-established diamond suit. This could have been accomplished easily enough.

At trick two, South should have played the ace and then another trump, West taking his king. A heart would then have been led to East's queen. East would now play a club, dummy's king capturing the trick.

After drawing the outstanding trumps, South would knock out West's ace of diamonds. A club return would be taken by dummy's ace, and on dummy's now-established diamond suit, South would discard his losing club.

As declarer actually played the hand, his thoughts undoubtedly were on avoiding the loss of a trump trick. Had East possessed the king of trumps, South would have accomplished his objective. But in playing the hand as he did, our South declarer jeopardized his contract in order to try for an overtrick. And by leading a club to dummy's king at trick two to take an unnecessary finesse, he lost everything.

DEAL II

Finesses, like death and taxes, will always be with us. But unlike death and taxes, finesses can be avoided. Of course, there are players who choose to live by the finesse—and inevitably they perish by the finesse. Our South declarer was such a "finesser," and received exactly what he deserved.

East-West vulnerable. South deals.

NORTH
♠ K Q 4
♡ J 9
♢ K Q 6 4
♣ 7 5 4 2

WEST
♠ J 10 9 8 3
♡ A K 6
♢ 9
♣ K 10 9 3

EAST
♠ 7 5 2
♡ 8 7 5 2
♢ J 10 8 5 3
♣ 6

SOUTH
♠ A 6
♡ Q 10 4 3
♢ A 7 2
♣ A Q J 8

The bidding:

SOUTH	WEST	NORTH	EAST
1 NT	Pass	3 NT	Pass
Pass	Pass		

Opening lead: Jack of spades

West's opening lead was taken by dummy's king, after which declarer promptly led a low club and finessed his queen. West gathered in the trick with his king and continued spades, South winning his ace.

When declarer next cashed his ace of clubs, he discovered that the 4-1 split would limit him to two club tricks, so he turned his attention to the heart suit, leading a low heart toward dummy's jack. West climbed up with his king and led a third round of spades, driving out dummy's queen. Declarer then tested the diamonds, hoping that the six missing cards were divided 3-3, but to his sorrow this just was not his day. When play ended, South had only eight tricks: three spades, three diamonds, and two clubs.

Had declarer studied the dummy after the opening spade lead, he would have realized that by establishing two heart tricks his contract would be impregnable. After winning the opening spade lead, declarer should have led dummy's jack of hearts. West, upon taking his king, could do no better than to continue spades.

Declarer would win and play a heart to the nine, driving out West's ace. (If West didn't take his ace on this lead, South would reenter his own hand via the diamond ace, to lead the heart queen or ten.) Now South would have nine certain tricks: three spades, two hearts, three diamonds, and one club.

Actually, by finessing clubs first, as he did, declarer had an excellent chance of fulfilling his contract. He would fail only if clubs were badly divided and nothing favorable developed in the diamond suit. But the "excellent chance" afforded by the finesse can never equal an absolute guarantee.

DEAL III

When a finesse fails, declarer loses not only a trick but the lead. This loss of the lead may also result in losing the "timing" of the hand. And, as all experienced players know, when the opponents gain timing, they will use this to further their own cause, not declarer's.

In this deal, our South declarer took an unnecessary finesse; in so doing, he lost a trick, the timing, and his contract.

Both sides vulnerable. South deals.

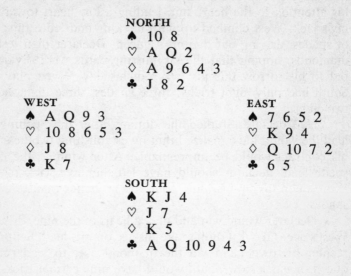

NORTH
♠ 10 8
♡ A Q 2
◇ A 9 6 4 3
♣ J 8 2

WEST
♠ A Q 9 3
♡ 10 8 6 5 3
◇ J 8
♣ K 7

EAST
♠ 7 6 5 2
♡ K 9 4
◇ Q 10 7 2
♣ 6 5

SOUTH
♠ K J 4
♡ J 7
◇ K 5
♣ A Q 10 9 4 3

The bidding:

SOUTH	WEST	NORTH	EAST
1 ♣	Pass	1 ◇	Pass
2 ♣	Pass	3 ♣	Pass
3 NT	Pass	Pass	Pass

Opening lead: Five of hearts

On West's opening heart lead, declarer played low from dummy, hoping West was leading away from the king. But, East captured the opening lead with his heart king and made a nice shift to the spade suit. South played the four. West took the trick with the spade queen, cashed the ace, and then led a third spade. South's king won, but West's nine of spade had now become the highest-ranking spade left in the deck.

Dummy was entered via the heart queen, and the club finesse was attempted, but with no luck. West had the king and cashed the high spade for the setting trick.

Declarer's error came at the very first trick when he elected to take the heart finesse. Had he captured this trick with the board's ace of hearts, he would have had a guaranteed contract.

At trick two, the club finesse would have lost to West's king. Declarer would now have eight top tricks: one heart, two diamonds, and five clubs, and no matter how the defenders twisted and turned, they could not prevent South from setting up a second heart trick. All that would be necessary would be to lead the jack of hearts and concede a trick to East's king.

DEAL IV

This deal is virtually identical to Deal 3, just discussed. The major point of dissimilarity is that our South declarer on this hand happened to be one of America's top-flight mathematicians. After he had gone down a trick at his game contract, he attempted to justify his play by stating, "Well, I knew West was leading his fourth-from-the-highest—and, mathematically, he rated to have the king."

Mathematically speaking, South was right: West figured to have the king of the suit led. But, quite often at the bridge table, the mathematics of a given situation must give way to plain, ordinary common sense. And our South declarer should have recognized that mathematics was not the paramount consideration in the situation at hand.

Both sides vulnerable. South deals.

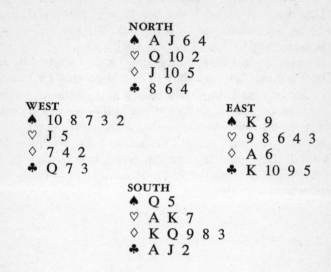

NORTH
♠ A J 6 4
♡ Q 10 2
◇ J 10 5
♣ 8 6 4

WEST
♠ 10 8 7 3 2
♡ J 5
◇ 7 4 2
♣ Q 7 3

EAST
♠ K 9
♡ 9 8 6 4 3
◇ A 6
♣ K 10 9 5

SOUTH
♠ Q 5
♡ A K 7
◇ K Q 9 8 3
♣ A J 2

The bidding:

SOUTH	WEST	NORTH	EAST
1 ◇	Pass	1 ♠	Pass
2 NT	Pass	3 NT	Pass
Pass	Pass		

Opening lead: Three of spades

When dummy came into view after West had led the spade three, there was no question that West (rather than East) figured to have the spade king: West had at least four spades, perhaps five, while East had a maximum of three, and perhaps only two. Hence, the spade king rated to be in the hand that possessed the greater number of spades.

So South, at trick one, finessed against West's presumed king of spades by playing low from dummy. But it was a bad day for mathematicians—East won the trick with his king. Realizing the hopelessness of returning a spade, he led back the ten of clubs. South put up the jack, West took it with the queen, and returned a club to East's king, which was permitted to win. A third club lead drove out South's ace and established East's remaining club as a winner. When declarer next attacked the diamond suit, East took his ace and cashed the thirteenth club, for the setting trick.

All declarer had to do to fulfill his contract was to win the opening lead with the spade ace. He would then knock out the diamond ace, and no matter what the defender returned, wouldn't matter. South could now claim his contract: one spade, three hearts, four diamonds, and one club.

Admittedly, by spurning the spade finesse at trick one, declarer might be throwing away his chances of making an overtrick or two. However, as our declarer would certainly admit, it just couldn't be right—even mathematically—to jeopardize a vulnerable game for the pittance of an overtrick.

DEAL V

The play of many bridge players has become so stereotyped that it is sometimes quite difficult for them to recognize that the specific situation at hand necessitates deviating from habitual technique. This is especially true with regard to the principle of drawing trumps as quickly as possible (a principle all bridge players were weaned upon).

In this uncomplicated deal, our South declarer, without examining the lay of the land, promptly led trumps and took an unnecessary finesse. As soon as he did, he cast himself in a loser's role.

Neither side vulnerable. South deals.

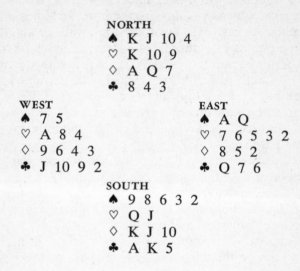

NORTH
♠ K J 10 4
♡ K 10 9
◇ A Q 7
♣ 8 4 3

WEST
♠ 7 5
♡ A 8 4
◇ 9 6 4 3
♣ J 10 9 2

EAST
♠ A Q
♡ 7 6 5 3 2
◇ 8 5 2
♣ Q 7 6

SOUTH
♠ 9 8 6 3 2
♡ Q J
◇ K J 10
♣ A K 5

The bidding:

SOUTH	WEST	NORTH	EAST
1 ♠	Pass	3 ♠	Pass
4 ♠	Pass	Pass	Pass

Opening lead: Jack of clubs

After West's opening club lead had been captured by declarer's king, South promptly led the nine of trumps. It was his intention to finesse West for the queen. If West possessed that card, South would be able to restrict his losers in the trump suit to one trick.

Unfortunately for declarer, East won this trick with his queen. He then played back a club, South's ace winning. At the conclusion of play, South had gone down a trick, losing a club, a heart, and two trump tricks.

South's immediate finesse of the trump suit was ill-advised, to put it mildly, since it was unnecessary to stake the outcome of the hand on a 50-50 chance that West had been dealt the trump queen. Had South focused his sights on the entire hand, rather than on just the trump suit, he would have seen that the loss of a club trick could be averted.

After winning the opening club lead, South should have led the heart queen. West would win his ace and continue clubs, South taking his ace. The jack of hearts would now be overtaken by dummy's king, and South would discard his losing club on the ten of hearts. The location of the trump queen would now become immaterial, for South could afford to lose two trump tricks to the defenders' ace and queen.

If the third lead of hearts were trumped, South, having rid himself of a losing club, could still take a finesse against West's hoped-for queen of trumps. There certainly was no reason to rush into the finesse immediately. After all, if West had been dealt the trump queen, he would still have it later on.

DEAL VI

After South had gone down a trick at his game contract, North criticized him for his bidding. The criticism, I believe, was founded on an emotional basis: North was irked because South had failed to fulfill a vulnerable game contract—and North was in a hurry to get home.

Actually, North's criticism was faulty on two counts: first, South's one and only bid was a reasonable gamble, considering that East had passed West's opening bid; hence, North figured to have some cards to complement and supplement South's holdings. And secondly, if North really had the urge to criticize South, he should have vented his spleen on the latter's play (or, rather, misplay) of the hand.

Both sides vulnerable. West deals.

NORTH
♠ A J 8
♡ J 10 9 2
◇ 8 5 4
♣ 6 4 3

WEST   **EAST**
♠ 6 3   ♠ 7
♡ A K Q 7 4   ♡ 6 5 3
◇ K 10 6   ◇ J 9 7 3
♣ K Q 7   ♣ J 10 9 8 2

SOUTH
♠ K Q 10 9 5 4 2
♡ 8
◇ A Q 2
♣ A 5

The bidding:

WEST	NORTH	EAST	SOUTH
1 ♡	Pass	Pass	4 ♠
Pass	Pass	Pass	

Opening lead: King of hearts

After holding his opening lead, West shifted to the king of
clubs. South won the ace after East followed with the club jack.
The king of trumps was cashed and a trump was led to dummy's
ace.

South then led a low diamond to his queen. East captured this trick with his king and cashed the queen of clubs. Since it was illegal for South to throw his deuce of diamonds under the table, he eventually had to lose a second diamond trick. Thus, he incurred a one-trick set.

For South to have staked his chances on the diamond finesse was thoughtless optimism. Since East was known to possess fewer than six points (and might have had zero points), West certainly rated to have the diamond king.

After winning the second trick with his ace of clubs, South should have entered dummy via the trump eight. The jack of hearts would then be led, South discarding his club five. West would win the trick with the heart queen and return the queen of clubs, South ruffing. Dummy would now be reentered via the trump jack, and the ten of hearts would be led, South tossing away his diamond deuce and allowing West to win this trick with his ace. Thus, dummy's nine of hearts would become the highest-ranking heart outstanding.

After regaining the lead, South would lead a spade to the board's ace, and discard his remaining loser, the diamond queen, on the nine of hearts. Played correctly, declarer's only losers would have been three heart tricks.

By adopting this line of play, declarer would be exchanging two tricks for two other tricks: When he discarded a club on the heart jack, he would be giving the defenders a heart trick instead of a club trick; and in tossing away the diamond deuce on the heart ten, he would be giving them another heart trick instead of a diamond trick. But in the process, he would be establishing the heart nine as a winner and a safe parking place for the diamond queen, instead of giving her highness away to West.

DEAL VII

In this deal, West's opening lead presented South with a trick, which declarer accepted with alacrity. But it turned out to be a rather expensive acceptance, for it cost South a vulnerable game contract.

Both sides vulnerable. North deals.

                              NORTH
                              ♠ A 10 8 4 3
                              ♡ A K 7 2
                              ◇ 10 5
                              ♣ A 4

        WEST   EAST
        ♠ 6 2   ♠ K Q J 9
        ♡ Q 9 8 3   ♡ J 10 5
        ◇ A 4 2   ◇ 8 7 3
        ♣ Q 8 6 5   ♣ 7 3 2

                              SOUTH
                              ♠ 7 5
                              ♡ 6 4
                              ◇ K Q J 9 6
                              ♣ K J 10 9

The bidding:

NORTH	EAST	SOUTH	WEST
1 ♠	Pass	2 ◇	Pass
2 ♡	Pass	2 NT	Pass
3 NT	Pass	Pass	Pass

Opening lead: Five of clubs

West chose to open the five of clubs, the unbid suit. South, appreciating that he was getting a "free finesse," played the four from dummy and captured the trick with his nine. A low diamond was led, and dummy's ten won the trick. A diamond was returned, and South's jack fell to West's ace.

When West played back a club to the board's ace, it suddenly dawned on South that he couldn't return to his own hand to cash either the king of clubs or the established diamonds. So he attempted to establish the spades by leading a low spade from dummy. East won with his nine and shifted to the jack of hearts. When play had ended, declarer had gone down two tricks—and it served him right!

When declarer accepted the "free finesse" by playing dummy's low club on the first trick, he "blew" the entire hand, for he destroyed the king of clubs as the sole future entry to his hand. Had he stopped to count his tricks, he would have seen that he had an unbeatable contract.

All he had to do was capture the opening lead with dummy's ace of clubs. The ten of diamonds would then be led, and diamonds continued until West took his ace.

Whatever West now played back, only an earthquake could prevent declarer from collecting one spade, two hearts, four diamonds, and two clubs. But South probably had his sights exclusively on the club suit, not on the hand as a whole.

DEAL VIII

Here is a less obvious version of the same principle. West opened his fourth-from-the highest spade against South's three no-trump contract in this deal, and South correctly reasoned that West was leading away from the king. He figured he could win a trick cheaply by allowing the opening lead to ride around to his jack.

South was right on both counts, but he lost the contract, for his rush to win the first trick removed a vitally-needed future entry to his own hand.

Both sides vulnerable. North deals.

<pre>
                        NORTH
                        ♠ A 6 2
                        ♡ A K 7 4
                        ◇ A 10 8
                        ♣ A J 3

      WEST   EAST
      ♠ K 10 8 5 4   ♠ 9 7
      ♡ J 8 3   ♡ Q 10 9 5
      ◇ 6 4   ◇ K 7 2
      ♣ Q 7 2   ♣ K 9 8 4

                        SOUTH
                        ♠ Q J 3
                        ♡ 6 2
                        ◇ Q J 9 5 3
                        ♣ 10 6 5
</pre>

The bidding:

NORTH	EAST	SOUTH	WEST
1 ♡	Pass	1 NT	Pass
3 NT	Pass	Pass	Pass

Opening lead: Five of spades

On West's opening lead of the spade five, a low spade was played off the board, and South captured East's nine with his jack. The queen of diamonds was led for a finesse, and East made a nice play when he permitted the queen to win the trick.

Next came a low diamond to dummy's ten. East captured it with the king and returned a spade, which established West's spade suit when South's queen was covered by West's king and taken by dummy's ace. As is evident, South was unable to return to his own hand to cash his remaining diamonds, so he ended up making just seven tricks.

Actually, South took two finesses on this deal. The first came at trick one, when he "finessed" West for the spade king. The second came at trick two, when he finessed for the diamond king. Both these finesses were not only unnecessary, they were suicidal.

Before playing to trick one, South should have realized that he would have no sure entry to his yet-to-be-established diamonds unless he won the opening lead with dummy's ace of spades. Next would come the ace of diamonds, followed by the diamond ten. If East declined to win this trick, a third diamond would be played, forcing out East's king.

Regardless of what East now elected to return, he could not prevent declarer from bringing home nine tricks. In all probability, he would have played back a spade, the suit his partner had led originally. West, after capturing South's jack with the king, would exit with a spade to South's queen. South would now have his nine tricks: two spades, two hearts, four diamonds, and one club.

DEAL IX

As all bridge players know, economy at the bridge table can sometimes turn out to be very expensive. Such was the case in this deal, in which our unthinking declarer elected to win a trick as cheaply as possible. As soon as he did, there was no recovery.

Neither side vulnerable. South deals.

NORTH
♠ 7 6 3
♡ K Q 10 9 7
♢ 5 3
♣ Q 8 6

WEST   EAST
♠ K 4   ♠ Q J 8 5
♡ 8 2   ♡ A 6 4 3
♢ 10 8 7 4   ♢ 9 6 2
♣ K 9 7 5 2   ♣ 10 4

SOUTH
♠ A 10 9 2
♡ J 5
♢ A K Q J
♣ A J 3

The bidding:

SOUTH	WEST	NORTH	EAST
1 ♢	Pass	1 ♡	Pass
2 ♠	Pass	3 ♡	Pass
3 NT	Pass	Pass	Pass

Opening lead: Five of clubs

On West's opening lead of the five of clubs, the eight was played from dummy, covered by East's ten and won by South's jack. The jack of hearts was led, and was allowed to win the trick.

When South played his remaining heart, East took North's king with the ace and returned a club. Declarer played low, and West's king captured the trick. On the club return, dummy's queen and South's ace fell together. Since declarer had no entry to dummy, all he could make were the eight tricks he had on top at the completion of trick two: one spade, one heart, four diamonds, and two clubs.

As so frequently happens, declarer lost his contract at trick one, when he captured the opening lead with the club jack. He should have won it with the *ace*. Then, after establishing dummy's heart suit by driving out East's ace, he could have entered the board via the club queen to cash dummy's established tricks.

Why should declarer have indulged in the extravagance of wasting the club ace on the opening lead? The answer is found in the Rule of Eleven, which was discovered in 1889 by the great whist expert R. F. Foster. This rule comes into play whenever a defender leads the fourth from the highest in his longest suit—the standard lead against no-trump contracts.

West's five of clubs opening figured to be his fourth highest club. That meant, according to the Rule of Eleven, that North, East, and South had amongst them six cards higher than the five-spot (subtracting the denomination of the card led from the number eleven). By observation, declarer, had he been applying the rule should have noted that dummy and South had five of these higher cards. East had played the sixth card, the ten, on the opening lead. Hence, East could have no card higher than the five remaining; therefore, West had to hold the club king, and, by winning the first trick with the club ace, dummy's queen would become a *sure* entry to the board.

DEAL X

One of the characteristics of the expert is his ability to draw the proper inferences from the opponents' bidding—or their silence. The nonexpert, on the other hand, is usually immersed in his own cards, and fails to pay close attention to the significance of the opposition's pronouncements. As a result, the "deaf" player loses many contracts that a "listener" would have brought home safely. This deal is a case in point.

Neither side vulnerable. West deals.

NORTH
- ♠ A J 6 3
- ♡ K J 10 5 2
- ◇ 9 4
- ♣ Q J

WEST
- ♠ 10 4
- ♡ 7 6 3
- ◇ A K 3 2
- ♣ A 8 6 4

EAST
- ♠ K
- ♡ 9 4
- ◇ J 10 8 7 5
- ♣ 10 9 7 5 2

SOUTH
- ♠ Q 9 8 7 5 2
- ♡ A Q 8
- ◇ Q 6
- ♣ K 3

The bidding:

WEST	NORTH	EAST	SOUTH
Pass	1 ♡	Pass	1 ♠
Pass	2 ♠	Pass	4 ♠
Pass	Pass	Pass	

Opening lead: King of diamonds

West cashed the king and ace of diamonds and laid down the ace of clubs. Despite East's discouraging deuce on this lead, West continued with another club (he really had no better lead). South won West's second club lead with his king.

South then led his queen of spades. and when West followed suit with the four, he played the three from dummy. As can be observed, East gathered in the singleton king of trumps for the setting trick.

South's finesse for the king of trumps was—to use a charitable word—naïve. West, as the dealer, had *passed* initially. In the play to the first three tricks, West had revealed the ace and king of diamonds and the ace of clubs. Surely if West had also possessed the K x of spades—which would have given him fourteen prime high-card points—he would have opened the bidding. Hence, West's original pass should have proclaimed, loudly and clearly, that he did not hold the spade king.

Had South drawn this inference, he would have recognized that the finesse for the spade king *had to be a losing play!* The only practical alternative would have been to play the spade ace, hoping that East's marked king was a singleton. As luck (and good diagnosis) would have it, this hope would have materialized.

In conclusion, it should be emphasized that the play of the spade ace did not figure to catch the king, for more often than not East's king would be guarded. But the finesse could *never* be the winning play. And in bridge, as in life, one learns to make the best of what is available.

DEAL XI

This final deal on the "unnecessary finesse" is truly unbelievable—at least it was to me when I saw it played in a tenth-of-a-cent game at a bridge club in Washington, D.C. If there is any reader who doubts its authenticity, I have one reliable witness (North) who will attest to the fact that South played the hand exactly as presented here.

Neither side vulnerable. South deals.

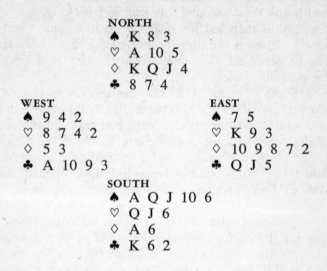

NORTH
♠ K 8 3
♡ A 10 5
◇ K Q J 4
♣ 8 7 4

WEST
♠ 9 4 2
♡ 8 7 4 2
◇ 5 3
♣ A 10 9 3

EAST
♠ 7 5
♡ K 9 3
◇ 10 9 8 7 2
♣ Q J 5

SOUTH
♠ A Q J 10 6
♡ Q J 6
◇ A 6
♣ K 6 2

The bidding:

SOUTH	WEST	NORTH	EAST
1 ♠	Pass	2 ◇	Pass
2 NT	Pass	3 ♠	Pass
4 ♠	Pass	Pass	Pass

Opening lead: Two of hearts

After some deliberation, West opened the deuce of hearts.
From declarer's point of view, West might have been leading
away from the king, so South chose to play a low heart from
dummy. As is evident, East won the trick with his king.

East made the natural shift to the queen of clubs, and before
declarer could take a deep breath, the defenders had rattled off
three club tricks. When declarer got around to winning trick five,

he had been defeated. (With apologies to Sir Walter Scott, he went down "unwept, unhonored, and unsung.")

Of course, West might have been leading away from the heart king, in which case declarer could have made three heart tricks. But to have taken the heart finesse in order to try for a second overtrick was the height of folly.

A simple count of the North-South assets would reveal that South had five sure spade tricks, four diamonds, the ace of hearts and one other heart trick that could always be developed later.

By winning the opening heart lead with the board's ace, South could draw the outstanding trumps in three rounds. Then would come the ace, king, queen, and jack of diamonds, South discarding two of his losing clubs. A heart trick would then be surrendered to whichever of the opponents happened to possess the king, thus promoting South's queen into a winner. Played in this fashion, South's only losers would have been a heart and a club.

That deal was played in 1959, which is a long time ago. Yet whenever I meet North, he still asks me if I remember it. And I always answer: "How could I ever forget it?"

3

Finessing Positions
Most Frequently Misplayed

♠ ♡ ◇ ♣

This chapter presents some finessing positions that are most often misplayed, even by our better players. At the risk of being anticlimactical, I will offer at the outset a classic example of a mismanaged finesse. It has become famous because of the dramatic circumstances surrounding it, and the great names involved in what might be called a tragicomedy.

It was the final deal of the tense semifinal match between the team defending the Spingold Team Championship and the team that went on to win it in 1943 due to this chain of circumstances.

The match was running very late; the kibitzer who had been watching play at the table where defending champs Lee Hazen and Dick Frey had been sitting with the North-South was mistaken in his interpretation of the current state of the match; Frey lived in Great Neck, Long Island, and the match was being played in New York City, and after the 1:42 A.M. train, the Long Island Railroad ran no train between these points until 3:42 A.M. Finally, there was the fact that the fifth member of the team, called in to play this final hand so that Frey could catch the 1:42, did not know how it should have been played. With so many prospective culprits, let's blame the final result on the Long Island Railroad, who by now are accustomed to all such complaints.

At any rate, with just this deal remaining to be played, Dick Frey dashed off for the 1:42. The fifth man, who shall be nameless here, was pressed into service to play the final deal, and the aforementioned kibitzer took it upon himself to advise the in-

coming replacement that things had not been going too well for
Hazen and Frey against the late Sidney Silodor, sitting West, and
John R. Crawford, sitting East. This piece of mistaken judgment
influenced Frey's substitute to bull his way to the grand slam
contract, despite everything Hazen did to sign off. As it turned
out, bidding even a game would have won the match, a small slam
would have guaranteed it, and the grand slam, although unnecessary to his team's success, should have been made.

Both sides vulnerable. West deals.

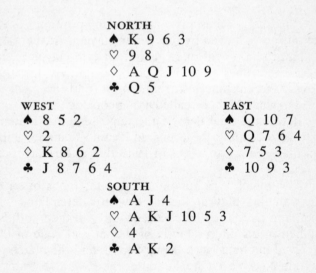

```
                        NORTH
                        ♠ K 9 6 3
                        ♡ 9 8
                        ◇ A Q J 10 9
                        ♣ Q 5
        WEST                              EAST
        ♠ 8 5 2                           ♠ Q 10 7
        ♡ 2                               ♡ Q 7 6 4
        ◇ K 8 6 2                         ◇ 7 5 3
        ♣ J 8 7 6 4                       ♣ 10 9 3
                        SOUTH
                        ♠ A J 4
                        ♡ A K J 10 5 3
                        ◇ 4
                        ♣ A K 2
```

The bidding:

WEST	NORTH	EAST	SOUTH
Pass	1 ◇	Pass	2 ♡
Pass	3 ◇	Pass	4 NT
Pass	5 ◇	Pass	5 NT
Pass	6 ◇	Pass	7 ♡
Pass	Pass	Pass	

Opening lead: Six of clubs

Silodor led the six of clubs against South's grand slam contract, won by the king. Declarer cashed the ace of trumps, entered dummy via the queen of clubs, then led the nine of hearts and let it ride. The finesse won—but East still had the guarded queen of trumps, and subsequently took the setting trick with that card.

Declarer's first play in the trump suit—the ace—was a serious mistake. It was designed to guard against the possibility that West held the singleton queen, on the supposition that the outstanding trumps were divided 4-1. But this play failed to guard against East holding the Q x x x. Assuming that West had a singleton trump, the singleton could be the two, four, six, seven, or queen. Mathematically, the queen would be the singleton only one time out of five. Therefore, in four cases out of five when the trumps were split 4-1, declarer could avoid a trump loser by taking two finesses, and he would need both of dummy's trumps to do so.

The correct play would be to win the opening club lead with dummy's queen, immediately lead the nine of hearts, and finesse. When the nine won, declarer would take a second finesse. Then the ace and king would pick up the queen. Later on, presumably South would have finessed East for the queen of spades, or West for the diamond king. Messrs. Silodor, Crawford, Charles Goren, Howard Schenken, and Edward Hymes, Jr., would then have been eliminated from the National Championship, instead of going on to win it.

There are many finessing combinations that seemingly offer declarer an attractive second choice, but this option is invariably the inferior play. Here is one:

NORTH
♠ 7 6 5 4

SOUTH
♠ A Q J 10 9 8

You lead the four of spades off dummy, East follows with the deuce, and the question is whether you should finesse or play the ace in the hope of catching a singleton king in the West hand.

The correct play is to finesse, as can easily be demonstrated:

```
                    NORTH
                    ♠ 7 6 5 4
    WEST                              EAST
    ―――――                            ♠ K 2
                                     ♠ K 3
                                     ♠ K 3 2
                                     ♠ 3 2
                    SOUTH
                    ♠ A Q J 10 9 8
```

The finesse will be successful whenever East was dealt (1) the K 2, (2) the K 3, or (3) the K 3 2. The ace will be the winning play only when East was dealt the doubleton 3-2 (in which case West was dealt the singleton king). Thus, three times out of four the finesse will avoid the loss of a spade trick.

The following finessing situation appears, superficially, to be a pure guess. Actually, there is only one proper way of handling this combination:

```
                    NORTH
                    ♡ K 3 2

                    SOUTH
                    ♡ A J 10 5 4
```

At first glance, it might seem to be a toss-up whether to finesse West for the heart queen (by leading the jack) or to lead a low heart off dummy and finesse East for the queen. Either could hold that card.

If either opponent holds Q x or Q x x, then it would be a toss of the coin as to which way to finesse. But suppose that one of the opponents holds Q x x x.

(1)

NORTH
♡ K 3 2

WEST   **EAST**
♡ Q 9 8 7   ♡ 6

SOUTH
♡ A J 10 5 4

(2)

NORTH
♡ K 3 2

WEST   **EAST**
♡ 6   ♡ Q 9 8 7

SOUTH
♡ A J 10 5 4

In diagram (1), a heart trick must be lost no matter how declarer tackles the suit. If he leads the jack, West will cover with the queen, and his nine will win a trick on the fourth lead of the suit.

In diagram (2), declarer can avoid the loss of a heart trick by taking the "proper" finesse. He leads a heart to the king and returns a heart to his ten. When the finesse wins, North is re-entered via some other suit and South takes a second finesse by playing a heart to his jack. East's queen will now fall under the ace.

Admittedly, it is a 50-50 proposition as to which opponent holds the missing queen. But by taking the finesse through East, South makes all the tricks whenever East has the Q x, the Q x x, or the Q x x x. He does not have this additional chance if he finesses West for the queen, for West will always make a trick when he holds the Q x x x.

Another finessing situation that is often misplayed is the following:

NORTH
◊ K 5 3 2

SOUTH
◊ A Q 10 9 4

Actually, since the four outstanding cards in the suit usually divide either 2-2 or 3-1, it makes little difference whether South first leads the ace out of his hand or the king from the North hand. In both cases, the top honors will gather in the four missing diamonds.

Nevertheless, the finesse is inherent in this combination, for on occasion one of the opponents will hold all four diamonds:

(1)
NORTH
◊ K 5 3 2

WEST
◊ —

EAST
◊ J 8 7 6

SOUTH
◊ A Q 10 9 4

(2)
NORTH
◊ K 5 3 2

WEST
◊ J 8 7 6

EAST
◊ —

SOUTH
◊ A Q 10 9 4

In diagram (1), if a low diamond is led to North's king, no harm will be done. When West fails to follow suit, South can take the "marked" finesse against East's jack.

But in diagram (2), if the initial diamond lead is to North's king, West's diamond jack will be promoted into a winner.

Declarer can guard against losing a trick no matter how the missing cards are divided by leading the diamond ace first. This is always the winning play. If West fails to follow suit, as in (1), South next leads a diamond to North's king, then finesses his nine on the way back.

If, however, East fails to follow suit, as in (2), declarer next leads the diamond ten and takes the marked finesse against West's jack. The king and queen of diamonds then gather in West's remaining diamonds.

A combination apparently identical to the above, but quite different, is the following:

NORTH
♠ K 9 3 2

SOUTH
♠ A Q 8 5 4

As in the preceding combination, if the missing cards are divided 2-2 or 3-1, South will bring home the entire suit without loss of a trick whether he first plays the ace or the king. The only worry is that one of the opponents holds all four of the outstanding cards in the suit.

(1)
               NORTH
               ♠ K 9 3 2

WEST   **EAST**
♠ J 10 7 6   ♠ —

               SOUTH
               A Q 8 5 4

(2)
               NORTH
               ♠ K 9 3 2

WEST   **EAST**
♠ —   ♠ J 10 7 6

               SOUTH
               ♠ A Q 8 5 4

In diagram (1), South *cannot* make all five spade tricks. Whenever he leads a low spade out of his hand, West will put up the ten, forcing North's king. West's jack of spades cannot be taken away from him, so whether South starts by leading the ace or a low spade to North's king, West is entitled to win a trick.

In diagram (2), if South *incorrectly* plays his ace initially, East, with the tripleton J 10 7 remaining after the first trick, will make a spade trick. But note what happens if South starts by leading a spade to North's king and West fails to follow suit. A second spade lead out of the North hand forces East to put up his ten, which South captures with the queen. Declarer reenters the North hand via some side suit and leads a third spade. East's remaining doubleton J 7 will be trapped by South's A 8 5, and declarer loses no spade tricks.

Hence, with this type of combination (missing the J 10 x x), the right play is to lead a low card toward the single honor (North's king, in this case).

Here is another combination that is frequently mishandled:

NORTH
♠ K J 3 2

SOUTH
♠ A 10

Assuming that you can enter both the North and South hands at will, how do you play this combination to win the maximum number of tricks? At first glance, it may appear to be simply a matter of guessing which opponent to finesse for the spade queen. But this approach is wrong, as is illustrated below:

(1)

NORTH
♠ K J 3 2

WEST   EAST
♠ Q 5 4   ♠ 9 8 7 6

SOUTH
♠ A 10

(2)

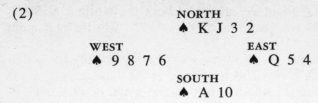

NORTH
♠ K J 3 2

WEST   EAST
♠ 9 8 7 6   ♠ Q 5 4

SOUTH
♠ A 10

In diagram (1), South makes three spade tricks regardless of which opponent he finesses for the queen. If he cashes the ace and leads the ten, West covers with the queen, and South gets his three tricks. East's nine will be the highest-ranking card on the fourth round of the suit.

In diagram (2), declarer can make four tricks if he handles his assets correctly. A low spade is led out of the North hand and South finesses the ten, which wins. After cashing the ace of spades, he enters the North hand via some side suit and cashes the king. East's queen comes tumbling down, so North's jack becomes the fourth spade winner.

Thus, the initial spade lead should be made out of the North hand, and the ten-spot finessed. Whenever East started with either the Q x or the Q x x, South will make four spade tricks. But if the spade ace is led initially, followed by the ten, South can never make more than three tricks, except in the extremely unlikely event that one of the opponents was dealt the singleton queen.

Since it is a pure guess which opponent holds the queen, why not take the 50-50 finesse in such a manner that if it wins, you have a chance of making four tricks in the suit?

This final combination is, in my opinion, mishandled more often than any other type of finesse:

NORTH
♡ Q J 3 2

SOUTH
♡ A 5 4

Assuming unlimited entries to both the North and South hands, how do you play this combination to win the maximum number of tricks?

Most inexperienced players start out by leading the queen from the North hand. This is wrong, for the "finesse" can never gain a trick and is likely to cost one that could be made. To illustrate:

(1)   NORTH
                       ♡ Q J 3 2
       WEST   EAST
       ♡ 7 6   ♡ K 10 9 8
                       SOUTH
                       ♡ A 5 4

(2)   NORTH
                       ♡ Q J 3 2
       WEST   EAST
       ♡ K 10 9 8   ♡ 7 6
                       SOUTH
                       ♡ A 5 4

In diagram (1), if South leads the queen, East will cover with the king. South wins with the ace—and North's jack will be the only heart winner from here in, for a total of two heart tricks.

In diagram (2), if the queen is finessed, West captures it with the king. And again, North's jack and South's ace will win two heart tricks and no more.

Thus, by leading the queen first, declarer can never increase his trick total even if the finesse succeeds. But South is assured of three tricks whenever *West* holds the heart king if he takes an indirect finesse—by leading toward the Q J rather than initially leading one of the honors.

South's proper method of attack is to cash the heart ace (every once in a while East or West will have been dealt the singleton king), then lead a low heart. If West has the king, declarer will take tricks with both of North's heart honors.

With this combination, it can never be the winning play to lead the heart queen initially. By doing so, declarer will limit himself to two tricks if the cards are distributed as in (2), and also if they are distributed in this manner:

NORTH
♡ Q J 3 2

WEST
♡ K 6

EAST
♡ 10 9 8 7

SOUTH
♡ A 5 4

With proper play, he could make three tricks.

4

The Finesse
A Path of Least Resistance

♠　♡　◇　♣

In each of the deals presented in this chapter, our South declarer had alternative methods of play available to him. One option was to take a finesse, which he did in due course. And, in each deal, he lost a contract that would have been fulfilled had the finesse been rejected.

In these eleven deals, our declarers went down a total of 1050 points. Had they played properly, avoiding the appealing finesse, the total points that would have accrued to them would have been 9360! Thus, the "swing" on these deals was a staggering 10,410 points. Nearly a thousand points a finesse is a pretty stiff price for following the path of least resistance.

DEAL I

Every person in this world has impulses, some good, some bad; some legal, some illegal. Most people learn to control those impulses that society decrees should be controlled. Some don't—and pay the penalty.

Bridge players have two impulses that arise frequently: (1) the urge to discard a loser on a trick that dummy is about to win, and (2) the urge to finesse. To become a success at the bridge table, the compulsion to obey these impulses must be overcome, at least to the extent of analyzing whether, in the specific situation, these impulses are "good" or "bad."

This deal embodies both of these temptations.

Both sides vulnerable. North deals.

```
                         NORTH
                         ♠ J 10 8
                         ♡ K J 7 5 3
                         ◇ K Q
                         ♣ A K 7


        WEST                         EAST
        ♠ 7 5 3                      ♠ 6
        ♡ 2                          ♡ Q 10 9 6
        ◇ 9 8 7 6 3                  ◇ A J 10 4 2
        ♣ J 9 4 2                    ♣ Q 10 8


                         SOUTH
                         ♠ A K Q 9 4 2
                         ♡ A 8 4
                         ◇ 5
                         ♣ 6 5 3
```

The bidding:

NORTH	EAST	SOUTH	WEST
1 NT	Pass	3 ♠	Pass
4 ♠	Pass	6 ♠	Pass
Pass	Pass		

Opening lead: Six of diamonds

West opened the diamond six, and East's ace captured the trick. He returned a diamond to dummy's king, as South discarded his losing club.

After picking up the outstanding trumps in three rounds, declarer laid down the ace and four of hearts, with the intention of finessing against West's hoped-for queen. But when West discarded a diamond, South was a dead duck. Eventually, East's queen of hearts took the setting trick.

South made a mistake when he discarded his losing club on dummy's king of diamonds. Instead, he should have discarded a low heart.

The adverse trumps would then be drawn, followed by the ace of hearts and a heart to dummy's king. A third heart would be trumped. Dummy would be reentered via the club king and another heart ruffed, dropping East's queen. The jack of hearts would now be the sole surviving heart in the deck, and it would be an easy matter for declarer to enter dummy with the club ace and discard his losing club.

By discarding a heart instead of a club at trick two, declarer would have increased his chances of fulfilling the slam from 50 percent (the finesse) to almost a certainty. The only distribution that could have defeated him would have been five hearts in East's hand. And had this distribution existed, South would have gone down to defeat no matter how he played the hand.

DEAL II

Abstract mathematics—the knowledge of recurring "percentage" types of situations—can often be useful at the bridge table, for it saves time and effort in determining the superior line of play. But there are frequent occasions when the correct, out-of-context mathematical play must be dispensed with if a line of play can be found that is better suited to the particular occasion. Consider this deal.

Neither side vulnerable. South deals.

                                    NORTH
                                    ♠ 8 3
                                    ♡ Q 9 6
                                    ◇ A K Q 10
                                    ♣ 7 5 4 2

    WEST   **EAST**
    ♠ J 7 4 2   ♠ K Q 5
    ♡ 5 3 2   ♡ A J 10 8 4
    ◇ 9 8 5 3   ◇ 7 4
    ♣ Q 3   ♣ 9 8 6

                                    SOUTH
                                    ♠ A 10 9 6
                                    ♡ K 7
                                    ◇ J 6 2
                                    ♣ A K J 10

The bidding:

SOUTH	WEST	NORTH	EAST
1 ♣	Pass	1 ◇	1 ♡
1 NT	Pass	3 NT	Pass
Pass	Pass		

Opening lead: Five of hearts

The six of hearts was played from dummy on the opening lead of the five-spot, East played the eight, and South won the trick with his king. South next cashed the ace of clubs, then entered dummy via the diamond queen and led a second club. When East followed suit with the eight, South finessed his jack. The finesse lost and West returned another heart, ambushing dummy's Q 9. East quickly cashed four heart tricks, setting declarer.

If one were to consider the club suit alone, the correct mathematical play to make four club tricks would be to first lay down the ace, then finesse the jack and if necessary, the ten.

This deal, however, was a special case, for South did not need four club tricks to fulfill his contract. He needed only *three*. Secondly—and possibly more important—South really could not afford a finesse, for if the finesse lost to West's queen (as it did in the actual play), West's heart return would doom declarer to defeat.

Finally, if *East* had the club queen, South could well afford to lose a *third* club lead to him. The reason is apparent: The board's remaining Q 9 of hearts would effectively prevent *East* from cashing more than his ace of hearts.

Hence, at tricks two and three, South should have banged down his ace and king of clubs. As "luck" would have it, West's queen of clubs would have been caught, and declarer would have ended up with an overtrick instead of incurring a one-trick set.

DEAL III

Every bridge player can make a slam when he holds all the aces, kings, and queens, or when the opponents hand him the slam on a silver platter. The consistent bridge winner, however, is the one who makes a habit of gathering in the "close" slams by taking advantage of all possibilities.

In this deal, South overbid his hand when he contracted for a grand slam. However, as the cards were distributed, the slam was there for the taking—but our declarer overlooked one extra chance and banked everything on a finesse instead. By suffering a one-trick set, not only did he lose a bushelful of points, but (I think) he also incurred the everlasting contempt of his partner who, being materialistically inclined, also lost a bushelful of points.

Both sides vulnerable. South deals.

```
                        NORTH
                        ♠ K J 8 4 2
                        ♡ A
                        ◊ K 7 5 3
                        ♣ 8 6 4
        WEST                                    EAST
        ♠ 6                                     ♠ 9 5
        ♡ 9 8 7 5 3                             ♡ Q J 6
        ◊ Q J 10 8                              ◊ 9 4 2
        ♣ K 10 7                                ♣ J 9 5 3 2
                        SOUTH
                        ♠ A Q 10 7 3
                        ♡ K 10 4 2
                        ◊ A 6
                        ♣ A Q
```

The bidding:

SOUTH	WEST	NORTH	EAST
1 ♠	Pass	3 ♠	Pass
4 NT	Pass	5 ◊	Pass
5 NT	Pass	6 ♡	Pass
7 ♠	Pass	Pass	Pass

Opening lead: Queen of diamonds

Why South elected to bid seven spades knowing that his partnership was lacking a king, I do not know. The fact remains that he did.

West's opening lead of the diamond queen was won by the board's king, after which the ace and king of trumps were cashed. As he viewed the hand, South concluded that the fulfillment of the grand slam contract depended on a successful club finesse—nothing more and nothing less. And so, without further ado or analysis, he led a low club off dummy and finessed his queen. Curtains!

Admittedly, at first glance it would appear that the success of the contract depended solely on a winning club finesse. But a closer look would have revealed that an additional chance existed. While it was not a good chance, it was "on the house." That is, if it failed to materialize, South could always take the club finesse as a last resort.

After dummy's diamond king won the first trick, and trumps were drawn, South should have cashed the ace of hearts. He would then enter his hand via the diamond ace to cash the king of hearts, discarding a club from dummy.

On the king of hearts, East would have dropped the jack. A third heart lead would be ruffed in dummy, East following suit with the queen. South's ten of hearts would now be a winner.

After reentering his hand via the club ace, declarer would cash the ten of hearts, discarding dummy's remaining club. He would then trump the club queen in dummy. Voilà!

Frankly, declarer would have been very lucky in catching East (or it might have been West) with the tripleton Q J x of hearts. But it would have cost nothing to test this possibility before betting all his chips on a successful club finesse.

DEAL IV

Most of the hands that are dealt during the course of any single session of play are relatively simple, routine affairs. On these deals, it makes very little difference how declarer goes about playing them, for they just about play themselves. But on a crucial minority of hands, it requires a bit of savvy to bring the contract home safely.

This is one of those crucial deals that separate the men from the boys. In his handling of it, our declarer, who was a good player although not an expert, must have had a blind spot. I know he was capable of making the winning play.

North-South vulnerable. East deals.

NORTH
♠ A 7 4
♡ 7 5 3
◇ Q 4
♣ Q J 10 8 2

WEST
♠ J 9 6
♡ 9 2
◇ 7 5 3 2
♣ K 7 4 3

EAST
♠ 3
♡ A K Q J 10 6
◇ J 10 9 8
♣ 9 6

SOUTH
♠ K Q 10 8 5 2
♡ 8 4
◇ A K 6
♣ A 5

The bidding:

EAST	SOUTH	WEST	NORTH
3 ♡	3 ♠	Pass	4 ♠
Pass	Pass	Pass	

Opening lead: Nine of hearts

East overtook West's opening lead of the heart nine with the ten, and continued with the ace of hearts at trick two. Then came the king of hearts which, after some deliberation, South ruffed with the ten of trumps. West, of course, overruffed with the jack, then returned a diamond, dummy's queen winning. After cashing the king and ace of trumps, declarer took the club finesse. When it lost, the opponents chalked up 100 points.

It is quite true that when South ruffed East's third heart lead with his ten, it might have won the trick; after all, there is no law that says that West, rather than East, is dealt the jack of spades. However, South was taking a needless gamble in ruffing the trick. All he had to do to virtually ensure his contract was to discard his five of clubs instead, allowing East's king of hearts to capture trick three.

Whatever East now returned, South would win. (If a fourth heart were led, South would ruff, West would overruff, and dummy's ace of trumps would overruff West.) Trumps would then be drawn, and the rest of the tricks would belong to declarer.

Possibly South risked trumping the third heart lead with the ten because he figured that even if it were overtrumped, he would still have the 50-50 club finesse to fall back upon. If so, it was, as a famous jurist once remarked in regard to a nonbridge activity, "the enticing delusion of a thoughtless optimism." Had East possessed the club king, in addition to his known solid six-card heart suit, he surely would have opened the bidding with one heart rather than a preemptive three heart call.

DEAL V

In this next example, declarer did not believe in the maxim "He who fights and runs away, will live to fight another day." And because he persisted in fighting, instead of retreating temporarily, he lost a game that should have been made.

This hand bears a close resemblance to the previous one. However, since its theme is frequently recurring, thoroughly understanding the principle will be of assistance to those who aspire to be better bridge players.

North-South vulnerable. West deals.

NORTH
♠ A 8 6 3
♡ 9 6 4 3
◇ K 4 2
♣ 8 2

WEST
♠ Q 4 2
♡ 5
◇ Q 10 9
♣ K Q J 10 9 6

EAST
♠ J 10 9 7
♡ J 7 2
◇ 8 7 6 3
♣ A 4

SOUTH
♠ K 5
♡ A K Q 10 8
◇ A J 5
♣ 7 5 3

The bidding:

WEST	NORTH	EAST	SOUTH
3 ♣	Pass	Pass	3 ♡
Pass	4 ♡	Pass	Pass
Pass			

Opening lead: King of clubs

The defenders started off perfectly. West opened the king of clubs. East overtook with his ace and returned the four of clubs. West won the nine and continued with the queen.

It was perfectly obvious that East had started with a doubleton club and was prepared to ruff the third lead of the suit. But South was not going to give up without a fight. So, in an attempt to prevent East from winning the trick, he ruffed the third club lead with dummy's nine. This card would have captured the trick *if* West had been dealt the jack of trumps. But, as fate would have it, East had that card and, quite naturally, he overruffed dummy's nine.

Later on, after trumps had been drawn, declarer led a diamond to the board's king and a diamond to his jack. But "fate" again deprived South of his victory, for East took the trick with the queen, for the setting trick. It just was not a day for finesses to be successful.

Had declarer examined his assets more closely, he would have seen that it was unnecessary to wage a battle for the third trick. When West led the club queen, declarer should have discarded dummy's deuce of diamonds, conceding the trick to West. Whatever West played back at trick four, declarer would win.

Three rounds of hearts would gather in the missing trumps, after which would come the king, ace, and jack of diamonds. The jack, of course, would be ruffed with the board's last trump, and declarer could claim his contract.

DEAL VI

When a bridge player can get his opponent to do his work for him, he is admired as a first-class entrepreneur. In this deal, declarer had the perfect opportunity of obtaining an opponent's gratis (albeit involuntary) assistance. Had he done so, he would have fulfilled a contract that he could not (and did not) make on his own power.

Neither side vulnerable. South deals.

NORTH
♠ J 6 3
♡ 9 6 5 2
◊ 8 7 4
♣ A Q 7

WEST   EAST
♠ Q 8 4 2   ♠ 9 7 5
♡ Q 10 8   ♡ J
◊ K Q 10   ◊ A J 6 3 2
♣ 6 5 3   ♣ 9 8 4 2

SOUTH
♠ A K 10
♡ A K 7 4 3
◊ 9 5
♣ K J 10

The bidding:

SOUTH	WEST	NORTH	EAST
1 ♡	Pass	2 ♡	Pass
4 ♡	Pass	Pass	Pass

Opening lead: King of diamonds

West's king of diamonds won the first trick, and he continued with the queen. East overtook with his ace and led the diamond jack, ruffed by South.

The ace and king of trumps were cashed, revealing that West had a sure trump winner. Declarer now played the ace of spades, and entered dummy via the club queen. He next led the jack of spades and let it ride. West's queen of spades and queen of hearts took the next two tricks, and declarer was down one.

Declarer gave a very poor performance. After cashing the ace and king of trumps, he should have recognized that he could put West into the lead with the trump queen any time he wished.

To ensure his contract, declarer should cash the king, queen, and ace of clubs. Clubs would now be eliminated from both the North and South hands. Diamonds had been eliminated from both hands on the first three tricks.

West would then be put on lead with a heart and would, at that moment, become the victim of an end-play. He would have no choice but to lead a spade away from his queen, thus enabling South to avoid the loss of a spade trick.

Even if West still had a club or a diamond to lead, South could ruff with dummy's remaining trump, simultaneously discarding the ten of spades from his own hand.

DEAL VII

It is a distinct pleasure to present a deal where an excellent slam contract was reached by natural bidding methods. In this day and age, too many bridge players make haste to employ ace-showing conventions, such as Blackwood, in their slam bidding.

In making the above statement, I am not belittling the Blackwood Slam Convention, for it has an important niche in slam bidding. The trouble is that it is frequently employed indiscriminately, and leads to many poor slam contracts. After all, aces and kings alone do not make slams. Twelve tricks do.

Although the North-South bidding was very good, it is my unhappy obligation to relate that South's play of the hand was not commensurate with his bidding, resulting in the demise of his contract. The evidence is submitted forthwith.

Neither side vulnerable. South deals.

NORTH
♠ A K Q 2
♡ 7 5
◇ K 10 9 4
♣ 8 6 4

WEST
♠ J 9 7 4
♡ Q J 9 8 2
◇ 3
♣ K 9 7

EAST
♠ 10 8
♡ K 10 6 4 3
◇ 7 6
♣ J 10 5 3

SOUTH
♠ 6 5 3
♡ A
◇ A Q J 8 5 2
♣ A Q 2

The bidding:

SOUTH	WEST	NORTH	EAST
1 ◇	Pass	1 ♠	Pass
3 ◇	Pass	5 ◇	Pass
6 ◇	Pass	Pass	Pass

Opening lead: Queen of hearts

South's six diamond bid was a fine call. He knew that North had a good hand since North could have bid four diamonds (instead of five) without worrying that South might pass. Hence, South reasoned, North's leap to five diamonds denoted an interest in slam.

After South had captured the opening heart lead with his ace, he observed that he had two potential losers in clubs, and that two possibilities existed for the elimination of one of these losers. If the club finesse succeeded, South would be able to restrict his losers to one trick; or if the six missing spades were divided 3-3, then South would be able to get rid of his low club on dummy's fourth spade.

So South drew the outstanding trumps, then proceeded to cash dummy's three top spades. When East failed to follow to the third spade lead, a low club was led and South finessed his queen. West won the trick, and now there was no way to avoid the loss of another club trick.

After drawing trumps, dummy should have been entered via a top spade, in order to ruff North's remaining heart, thus eliminating the hearts from both the North and South hands. Declarer would next cash dummy's high spades. When *East* failed to follow to the third lead, dummy's deuce of spades would be played and South would discard the club deuce.

Forced to win this trick with his jack, West would be end-played. If he returned a heart, dummy would ruff as South simultaneously discarded his queen of clubs. And if, instead, West elected to return a club, South's queen of clubs would become a winner.

The moral of this deal? Well, I do not think it should be that South should pass North's five diamond bid.

DEAL VIII

I am of the opinion that most of America's bridge players, if they were to examine only the North-South hands in this deal, would develop a blind spot: They would assume that the success of South's game contract in diamonds depended on a successful spade finesse. They would be wrong, as was our actual South declarer when the deal came up in real life. The contract could have been fulfilled by normal play, without resorting to the finesse —and the opponents could not have done a thing about it.

Both sides vulnerable. South deals.

NORTH
♠ A Q 6
♡ 8 7 4
◊ J 9 4
♣ J 7 5 2

WEST
♠ 9 7 4 2
♡ J 5 3 2
◊ 8 7
♣ 8 4 3

EAST
♠ K 8 3
♡ A K Q 10 9
◊ 6 2
♣ Q 10 9

SOUTH
♠ J 10 5
♡ 6
◊ A K Q 10 5 3
♣ A K 6

The bidding:

SOUTH	WEST	NORTH	EAST
1 ◊	Pass	1 NT	2 ♡
4 ◊	Pass	5 ◊	Pass
Pass	Pass		

Opening lead: Two of hearts

East won the opening heart lead and tried to cash a second heart, South ruffing. The ace and king of diamonds were then cashed, picking up the outstanding trumps.

South next led the spade jack and took the "obvious" finesse. East captured the trick with his king and returned the king of hearts, which South ruffed. In time, East made a club trick, and declarer went down one, the victim of his own failure to take advantage of good breaks.

After ruffing East's ace of hearts at trick two, South should have cashed his ace of trumps, then led a low trump to the board's jack. Dummy's last heart would now be ruffed in the closed hand.

The ace, king, and a low club would follow, dummy's jack losing to East's queen. At this point, the board's fourth club would be the sole surviving club in the deck, and East would be in the unenviable position of being end-played.

If he returned a heart, South would discard his spade five as the trick was won by dummy's last trump. And South's ten of spades would be discarded on dummy's high club.

If East returned a spade instead of a heart, dummy's queen and ace of spades would both be winners. And, of course, on dummy's established club, South would get rid of his third spade.

Had it developed that the four outstanding trumps were not divided 2-2, or if the missing clubs were not 3-3, then declarer would fall back on the spade finesse as his last resort. But, as things developed, it would have become unnecessary to rely on the spade finesse as a first choice, for the end-play would have achieved the desired result.

DEAL IX

It is said that the novice loves to take finesses because, as a beginner, he is perfectly happy to stake his contract on a 50-50 proposition. The expert, on the other hand, is most unwilling to accept a finesse as a first-choice play, for the simple reason that preservation of his standard of living demands better odds. Hence the expert is continually on the alert for a line of play not dependent on a finesse—and more often than not, he finds one.

In this deal, a novice was sitting in the South seat, and he missed a play that an expert would have spotted instantly.

East-West vulnerable. South deals.

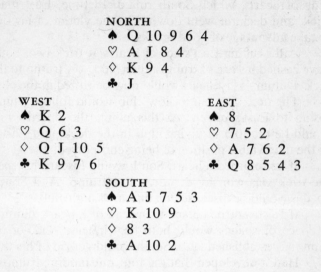

NORTH
♠ Q 10 9 6 4
♡ A J 8 4
◇ K 9 4
♣ J

WEST
♠ K 2
♡ Q 6 3
◇ Q J 10 5
♣ K 9 7 6

EAST
♠ 8
♡ 7 5 2
◇ A 7 6 2
♣ Q 8 5 4 3

SOUTH
♠ A J 7 5 3
♡ K 10 9
◇ 8 3
♣ A 10 2

The bidding:

SOUTH	WEST	NORTH	EAST
1 ♠	Pass	3 ♠	Pass
4 ♠	Pass	Pass	Pass

Opening lead: Queen of diamonds

West's lead of the queen of diamonds was covered by dummy's king and captured by East's ace. A diamond return was taken by West's ten, and South ruffed the third round of diamonds.

Declarer then led the ace of clubs and ruffed a club. The board's queen of trumps came next, and when East followed with the eight, South played his three. West took his king and exited with his remaining trump, which South won with the jack. Declarer then ruffed his remaining club.

Faced with a pure guess as to which way to finesse for the queen of hearts, South guessed wrong. He laid down the ace of hearts and followed up by leading the jack of hearts. When East played low, South finessed. West's queen of hearts now took the setting trick.

Actually, South was quite unlucky. If East had been dealt either the king of spades or the queen of hearts, South would have fulfilled his contract as he played it. But had an expert been sitting South, he would have fulfilled the contract without resorting to either the spade or heart finesse!

After ruffing East's third diamond lead, South would have played the ace of clubs and ruffed a club in dummy. The queen of trumps would be led next—to entice East to cover if he had the king. When East followed suit with the eight, South would go up with his ace. Failure to drop a singleton king would not faze declarer one whit.

South would ruff his remaining club and play a trump. Whoever had the king was most welcome to take it. In the actual case, West would become the victim of an end-play. If he returned a club or a diamond, dummy would ruff it as South discarded the heart nine from his own hand. And if, instead, he led a heart, South would get a free finesse and thus avoid the loss of a heart trick.

South's refusal to take the trump finesse would be a losing decision only if East had been dealt all three of the outstanding trumps. When compared to a 2-1 division, a 3-0 split of the outstanding trumps was most unlikely.

DEAL X

"Statistics" have demonstrated conclusively that one of the most popular plays in bridge is the unnecessary finesse. If someone would undertake to compile additional statistics regarding the frequency of occurrence of all the major types of bridge plays, I am sure that they would reveal that the "unnecessary finesse" results in the loss of more game and slam contracts than does any other type play.

This deal depicts the unnecessary finesse in action—although, in all fairness to our South declarer, his hand was not a simple one to play correctly.

Both sides vulnerable. North deals.

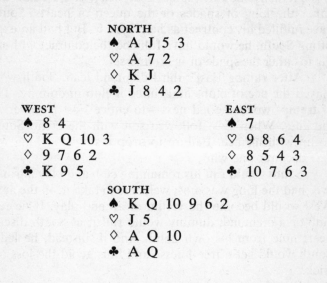

The bidding:

NORTH	EAST	SOUTH	WEST
1 ♣	Pass	2 ♠	Pass
3 ♠	Pass	4 NT	Pass
5 ♡	Pass	6 ♠	Pass
Pass	Pass		

Opening lead: King of hearts

After capturing West's king of hearts opening lead with dummy's ace, declarer cashed the king and ace of trumps. As he viewed the situation, the success of his contract depended on a winning club finesse. So, seeing no good reason to postpone the decision, at trick four he led a low club off dummy and finessed his queen. As is evident, West won this trick and promptly cashed the heart queen to set the slam.

When West made his opening lead of the heart king, declarer should have been absolutely certain of one thing: West possessed the heart queen. Had this knowledge been applied in practical fashion, South would have fulfilled his slam contract.

After drawing trumps, declarer should cash the king, queen, and ace of diamonds, discarding dummy's deuce of hearts on the third round. Next would come the jack of hearts, and since both red suits would have been eliminated from the North and South hands, an unhappy West would be on lead.

If West returned either a heart or a diamond, dummy would trump as South discarded his club queen. And, of course, if West played back a club, South's queen would win the trick.

Even if West had led a trump originally, declarer could have effected the same end-play. He would draw trumps, cash his diamonds, and discard the heart deuce from the North hand. Next would come a heart to the board's ace and a heart to South's jack. West would win this trick with the king—and whatever he led would give South his contract.

Had this hypothetical line of play developed, and it turned out that *East* possessed the heart king or queen, declarer would have been compelled to take the club finesse. But it would have been a last-resort play.

DEAL XI

The concluding deal of this chapter serves as another example of the fact that, at the bridge table, economy can sometimes turn out to be a most expensive luxury. This deal also serves as a sort of catalyst in effecting the transition from the preceding deals, in which the theme was "the improper, or unnecessary, finesse," to the deals contained in the two following chapters, where it will be demonstrated that taking an unusual finesse is frequently the only correct and winning line of play.

In this deal, our South declarer, at trick one, accepted a "free" finesse, which gave him a present of a trick. As a consequence, he discovered that he lacked an entry desperately needed later in order to fulfill his contract.

Neither side vulnerable. South deals.

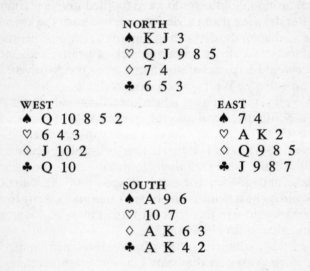

NORTH
♠ K J 3
♡ Q J 9 8 5
◇ 7 4
♣ 6 5 3

WEST
♠ Q 10 8 5 2
♡ 6 4 3
◇ J 10 2
♣ Q 10

EAST
♠ 7 4
♡ A K 2
◇ Q 9 8 5
♣ J 9 8 7

SOUTH
♠ A 9 6
♡ 10 7
◇ A K 6 3
♣ A K 4 2

The bidding:

SOUTH	WEST	NORTH	EAST
1 ◇	Pass	1 ♡	Pass
2 NT	Pass	3 NT	Pass
Pass	Pass		

Opening lead: Five of spades

South's leap to two no-trump was slightly aggressive, but he had no better bid available. A rebid of two clubs would have been more of an underbid than two no-trump was an overbid.

On West's lead of the five of spades, the three was played from dummy, East put up the seven, and South won the trick with his nine. The ten of hearts was led, and East made a very nice play, by allowing the ten to hold the trick.

When South led his remaining heart, East won dummy's queen with his king and returned a spade, South taking his ace. It was now impossible for declarer to both establish and cash dummy's heart suit. He could get to the board via the spade king to lead the heart jack and drive out East's ace, but he could never again reach dummy to cash the two remaining high hearts. And so declarer ended up making just eight tricks.

When East played the spade seven on the opening lead, South should have won it with his ace, and not with the "economical" nine. By applying the Rule of Eleven, South would have known that West *had to hold the queen of spades!* West had led the five of spades. By subtracting the number five from eleven (and, quite naturally, arriving at six), it would be known that North, East, and South had among them exactly six spades higher than the five-spot. North and South had five of those cards in evidence; and East, playing the seven-spot, had shown the sixth higher spade. Therefore East had no spade remaining that was higher than the five.

After capturing the opening lead with the spade ace, South would attack hearts, as he did, East winning the second lead with his king. Assuming that East returned a diamond (no other return could alter the outcome), South would take the trick with his ace. The six of spades would be led next, and when West followed with a low spade, South would insert the board's jack with the "guarantee" that it would win.

East's ace of hearts would now be driven out, thus establishing two heart winners in dummy. When he regained the lead, declarer would play the nine of spades to dummy's king and cash the two high hearts. Ten tricks would now be there for the taking: three spades, three hearts, two diamonds, and two clubs.

5

The Necessary Finesse
Lower-Echelon Games

♠ ♡ ◇ ♣

In each of the nine deals that comprise this chapter our declarer was confronted with optional lines of play, one of which included taking a finesse. In each deal the finesse was the correct, and winning, play. Yet in eight of these nine deals, the finesse was either spurned or mishandled and, as a consequence, the contract defeated.

If, as these deals are examined, the reader feels that declarer's play was naïve and/or absurd, it should be appreciated that our errant players were rank beginners or novices. And if the reader can recall the days when he was a novice, I am sure he will show some compassion for our dubs, who were not skilled enough to withstand the challenge of the situation at hand.

In the majority of these nine deals, I have "doctored up" the bidding to make it logical. If the actual bidding sequences were presented, they would in some instances appear unbelievable (as is frequently the case when a neophyte is partnered by a neophyte). Since the emphasis of this text is on *play*, I trust that the reader will forgive my distortion of the "bidding facts."

DEAL I

This deal occurred in a twentieth-of-a-cent game. The actual bidding is presented here, with North's three spade opening

bid being only slightly out of line. It would be difficult, however,
to criticize South for his leap to six clubs—except if one is prone
to accept the result as the criterion of right or wrong.

Neither side vulnerable. North deals.

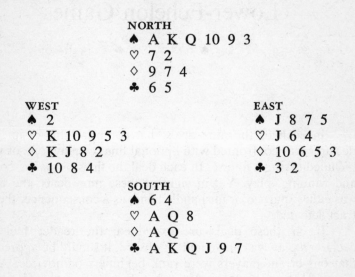

NORTH
♠ A K Q 10 9 3
♡ 7 2
◊ 9 7 4
♣ 6 5

WEST
♠ 2
♡ K 10 9 5 3
◊ K J 8 2
♣ 10 8 4

EAST
♠ J 8 7 5
♡ J 6 4
◊ 10 6 5 3
♣ 3 2

SOUTH
♠ 6 4
♡ A Q 8
◊ A Q
♣ A K Q J 9 7

The bidding:

NORTH	EAST	SOUTH	WEST
3 ♠	Pass	6 ♣	Pass
Pass	Pass		

Opening lead: Four of clubs

If West had opened his singleton spade my story might have
ended then and there, but his actual opening lead of the four of
trumps was taken by South's seven, and two more rounds of
trumps were played. Declarer next cashed the ace, king, and

queen of spades, discarding his eight of hearts. Since the spade suit was not established, South had to resort to a finesse in one of the red suits, so he led a heart off dummy and finessed the queen. West gathered in the king and returned a heart to South's ace. Eventually declarer had to surrender his diamond queen to West's king, thus going down a trick.

Without any doubt, declarer got a tough break on the hand: the jack of spades rated to fall under dummy's ace, king, or queen. And, of course, if the jack had been caught, declarer would have made all 13 tricks. To boot, the red kings were both offside.

Nevertheless, declarer's play was very poor, for he had an absolutely guaranteed twelve tricks that he threw out the window. All he had to do, after drawing trumps, was to lead a spade and insert dummy's nine. If West had the spade jack, South would have at least four sure spade tricks, which are all he needed for his slam.

In the actual case, East would have captured the board's nine of spades with his jack—and South would then have claimed his contract. No matter what East returned, dummy's remaining spades would provide discards for South's three red-suit losers.

South's "crime" (in my opinion, although North will not agree with me), was not that he failed to fulfill an "automatic" contract, but rather that he failed to count his tricks before playing. Had he paused to take stock, he would have realized that he needed only four spade tricks (not six) to emerge victorious. With this knowledge, he would have recognized that finessing the nine on the initial spade lead would assure success.

DEAL II

In bridge, as in most competitive endeavors, timing is a most important element of success. Timing, however, is not mastered overnight, nor can it be learned from books. Its acquisition requires practice, practice, and more practice. And thought.

This deal illustrates how an inexpert declarer completely misjudged the timing.

Both sides vulnerable. North deals.

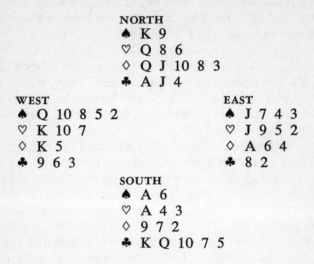

The bidding:

NORTH	EAST	SOUTH	WEST
1 ◇	Pass	2 NT	Pass
3 NT	Pass	Pass	Pass

Opening lead: Five of spades

West's opening lead was the five of spades, won in dummy with the king as East signaled for a continuation of partner's suit by playing the seven-spot. At trick two, declarer led dummy's queen of diamonds; East played low, and West won the trick with his king.

The deuce of spades was returned, East's jack falling to South's ace. Hoping that something fortuitous might happen, declarer led another diamond to establish the suit. When East took this trick with his ace, the board's diamond suit became established—but to no purpose, for East returned a spade and West rattled off three spade tricks. So declarer ended up with the same eight tricks he had from the start.

Declarer was not counting when he attempted to establish the diamond suit. Once West opened a spade, declarer should have recognized that the opponents would establish and cash at least three spade tricks before he could get around to establishing and cashing the board's diamonds. The opponents having beaten him on the timing, his diamond suit was a lost hope.

Had declarer appreciated this position, he would have turned to his only hope: the creation of the ninth trick in the heart suit via an indirect finesse. After winning the opening spade lead, declarer would cash five club tricks, discarding two diamonds from dummy.

A low heart would then be led out of the South hand. As the cards lay, whether West took his king or not was immaterial, for the board's queen of hearts would become declarer's ninth trick.

Admittedly, one does not like to stake success on a 50-50 proposition. Nevertheless, an even chance is infinitely superior to no chance at all. And the latter was the case in the diamond suit.

DEAL III

As has been illustrated in this text, experts shy away from finesses. The obvious reason is that even experts are not going to be consistent winners if they have to gamble on a toss of a coin; hence, they are continually on the lookout for a line of play that offers them better than an even chance.

Nevertheless, there are days when an expert has no alternative but to stake everything on a finesse, and the same goes for the nonexpert. In this deal, a nonexpert was the South declarer, and he acquitted himself nobly when he took the only line of play by which he could have fulfilled his contract. For an expert, the play would have been routine. But for our nonexpert declarer, it was a hazardous undertaking.

Both sides vulnerable. South deals.

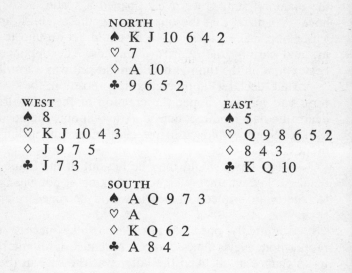

```
                    NORTH
                    ♠ K J 10 6 4 2
                    ♡ 7
                    ◇ A 10
                    ♣ 9 6 5 2
        WEST                        EAST
        ♠ 8                         ♠ 5
        ♡ K J 10 4 3                ♡ Q 9 8 6 5 2
        ◇ J 9 7 5                   ◇ 8 4 3
        ♣ J 7 3                     ♣ K Q 10
                    SOUTH
                    ♠ A Q 9 7 3
                    ♡ A
                    ◇ K Q 6 2
                    ♣ A 8 4
```

The bidding:

SOUTH	WEST	NORTH	EAST
1 ♠	Pass	3 ♠	Pass
6 ♠	Pass	Pass	Pass

Opening lead: Eight of spades

North's jump to three spades was, in a sense, a lesser-of-evils bid. His hand was too good for a direct preemptive raise to four spades, and far too good for a mere single raise to two spades. His three spade response (showing, technically, thirteen to fifteen points, counting distribution) was a compromise call. South, possibly expecting more from North in the way of high-card strength, cannot be criticized for bidding six spades. Of course, South was not enthusiastic about his contract when dummy hit the table.

After winning West's opening trump lead with his queen, South saw two club losers staring him in the face. If he cashed the ace, king, and queen of diamonds, discarding a club from dummy on the third diamond lead, he would gain nothing, since his two club losers would still be there. But if he could make *four* diamond tricks, he would be able to discard two of dummy's clubs.

So, at trick two, with his heart in his mouth, South led the two of diamonds out of his hand and inserted dummy's ten-spot. When the finesse won, the slam contract acquired a 24-carat guarantee.

South cashed the ace of diamonds next and returned to his own hand via the ace of hearts. On the king and queen of diamonds, two of dummy's clubs were discarded. The ace of clubs was played and a club conceded to the opposition. When South regained the lead, he ruffed his remaining club, and was left with nothing but high trumps.

Actually, the finesse of the diamond risked nothing. Even if it lost, declarer would have been down only one. South would still have been able to discard two of dummy's clubs on his king and queen of diamonds, thus losing only one club trick.

DEAL IV

This deal contains a standard recurring book finesse frequently mishandled by the inexperienced player: He takes the same necessary finesse that the experienced player would take, but he does so in the wrong way. As a consequence, although the finesse is successful, he gains nothing. In effect, the operation is successful but the patient dies.

Both sides vulnerable. North deals.

NORTH
♠ A Q 6
♡ A Q 6 3
◊ 9 2
♣ A K 7 3

WEST
♠ 9 4
♡ K 10 7
◊ K Q 10 8 5
♣ 8 6 2

EAST
♠ 8 7 5 3 2
♡ —
◊ A 7 6 4 3
♣ 9 5 4

SOUTH
♠ K J 10
♡ J 9 8 5 4 2
◊ J
♣ Q J 10

The bidding:

NORTH	EAST	SOUTH	WEST
1 ♣	Pass	1 ♡	Pass
4 ♡	Pass	4 NT	Pass
5 ♠	Pass	6 ♡	Pass
Pass	Pass		

Opening lead: King of diamonds

After his king of diamonds had won the first trick, West continued with a low diamond, South ruffing East's ace. The four of trumps was led for a winning finesse of dummy's queen. Although the queen won, West, with the doubleton K 10 of trumps remaining, could not be prevented from taking a trump trick. And so South muffed a slam contract that a more skilled declarer would have fulfilled.

Declarer's finesse against West's hoped-for king of trumps was the correct play. The alternative of banging down the trump ace in the hope of catching a singleton king would be decidedly against the odds. But South's method of taking the finesse left a great deal to be desired.

Declarer's first trump lead should have been the jack. If West played low, so would dummy. If the jack won, it would be a routine matter to lead another trump and finesse the queen.

If West covered the jack with the king, dummy's ace would win. When East failed to follow suit, South would reenter his hand via a spade and lead the nine of trumps. West, with the 10 7 of trumps remaining, would find himself in a hopeless position; he could do nothing to prevent declarer from bringing home the entire trump suit.

Had South led the jack of trumps to start with, he would have taken out insurance against what befell him. As declarer played the hand, he staked everything on West having been dealt either the singleton king, the doubleton K 7, or the doubleton K 10. At no additional cost, he could have protected himself against West possessing the tripleton K 10 7.

DEAL V

Mastery of technical bridge knowledge is, in itself, no guarantee of success. That goal is achieved by the practical application of such knowledge. The serious bridge student en route to his conquest of the game must, of necessity, first learn how to handle certain standard, recurring types of play (as in Deal 4). Then he must learn when not to apply the "book" techniques to the specific situation at hand.

This deal was played by a youngster who was thoroughly familiar with all the standard recurring plays in bridge. As South, he found himself confronted with a book situation that he knew how to handle properly. However, because of a play made by his opponents, he either developed a temporary blind spot or simply panicked.

Neither side vulnerable. North deals.

                                    NORTH
                                    ♠ 5 4 2
                                    ♡ A 4
                                    ◇ 6 5 3
                                    ♣ A K J 10 4

        WEST   EAST
        ♠ 9   ♠ K Q 7
        ♡ K J 10 8 5 2   ♡ 9 6 3
        ◇ Q J 2   ◇ A 10 9 8 7 4
        ♣ 8 7 5   ♣ 2

                                    SOUTH
                                    ♠ A J 10 8 6 3
                                    ♡ Q 7
                                    ◇ K
                                    ♣ Q 9 6 3

The bidding:

NORTH	EAST	SOUTH	WEST
1 ♣	1 ◇	1 ♠	2 ♡
Pass	Pass	3 ♠	Pass
4 ♠	Pass	Pass	Pass

Opening lead: Queen of diamonds

West opened the queen of diamonds, East taking the trick with his ace as South's king fell. East then shifted to the deuce of clubs, which was won by the board's ten. In view of dummy's club holding, declarer was quite certain that East had led a singleton club.

South fully realized that the book play in the trump suit was to lead a low trump and insert his jack. If this lost to the queen or king, and West returned a club for East to trump (as West would surely do), declarer would have clear sailing. There would be but one trump left in the East-West hands, and when South regained the lead, he would pick it up by cashing the ace.

However, South must have developed some overwhelming phobia about East trumping a club, and he was not about to let that happen. So, at trick three, he led the deuce of trumps out of dummy, and when East followed with the seven-spot, South put up his ace. He next led the trump jack, hoping that the missing trumps would fall together. Alas, East won with the queen and shifted to the nine of hearts. Declarer now found it impossible to avoid the loss of a heart trick which, in addition to two spades and one diamond, put him down one trick.

As the cards were actually divided, had declarer finessed his jack of spades on the first trump lead, he would have won the trick. It would then become a simple matter to play the ace and another spade, East's king winning. An overtrick would thus have been scored, since declarer subsequently would have been able to discard his losing heart on the board's fifth club.

DEAL VI

In this deal, our South declarer needed to take two finesses against a guarded king in order to bring home a suit. To accomplish this, two entries to dummy were required. But because of a careless play in a side suit, South failed to create the second entry. His failure proved costly.

Neither side vulnerable. South deals.

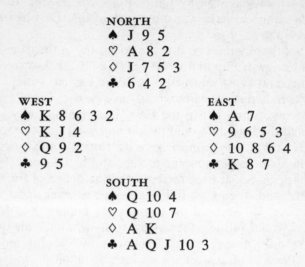

NORTH
♠ J 9 5
♡ A 8 2
◇ J 7 5 3
♣ 6 4 2

WEST
♠ K 8 6 3 2
♡ K J 4
◇ Q 9 2
♣ 9 5

EAST
♠ A 7
♡ 9 6 5 3
◇ 10 8 6 4
♣ K 8 7

SOUTH
♠ Q 10 4
♡ Q 10 7
◇ A K
♣ A Q J 10 3

The bidding:

SOUTH	WEST	NORTH	EAST
1 ♣	Pass	1 ◇	Pass
3 NT	Pass	Pass	Pass

Opening lead: Three of spades

South's rebid of three no-trump was an overbid, but North's response of one diamond was not exactly ironclad. Nevertheless, South's final contract could have been fulfilled with ease by a more experienced declarer.

On West's opening lead of the three of spades, the five was played from dummy, and East won the trick with his ace as South followed suit with the four-spot. On the spade return, South played the ten and West the king. A third spade went to declarer's queen.

Dummy was entered for the first and last time via the heart ace, and South successfully finessed his queen of clubs. Not being able to enter dummy again to repeat the club finesse, South laid down his ace of clubs, hoping to snare the king. No luck. A club had to be conceded to East's king.

East now came back a heart, and West cashed two hearts and two spades. Thus, declarer went down three tricks, losing four spades, two hearts, and one club.

Actually, declarer made quite a few mistakes on this hand. First, he should have played the nine of spades from dummy at trick one, just in case West happened to be leading away from the ace and the king. Had this been the case, the nine-spot would have enabled declarer to win the opening lead in dummy. This technical error, however, did not prove costly.

What did cost dearly was South's failure to drop the queen under East's ace. This play could never cost anything, since declarer still had the jack and ten between the two hands. But it would have provided a virtually sure second entry to dummy.

Assuming East returned a spade, South would play his four. Whether or not West took his king, dummy's jack of spades would provide a second entry to the board. *Two* successful club finesses would enable declarer to bring home five club tricks. Adding this to one spade, one heart, and two diamonds, declarer would chalk up the score for a game bid and made—which, I need hardly point out, is somewhat more profitable than going down three.

DEAL VII

There are occasions when anyone can arrive at a very poor if not almost hopeless contract. When this happens to a good player, he never resigns himself to fate. Instead, he attempts to conceive of a lie of the cards that will allow him to bring home the requisite tricks. Then he proceeds on the assumption that such a distribution exists.

The nonexpert, on the other hand, is not often endowed with this practical faculty of wishful thinking, so he frequently

perishes along the wayside of a route that an experienced player
would have traversed successfully. For example:

Neither side vulnerable. South deals.

```
                         NORTH
                         ♠ A Q 7 5 3 2
                         ♡ 7 4 3
                         ◇ 8 4
                         ♣ A 7
        WEST                              EAST
        ♠ K 10 8                         ♠ J 9
        ♡ K J 9 5                        ♡ Q 6
        ◇ Q 10 9                         ◇ J 6 5 3 2
        ♣ 4 3 2                          ♣ K 9 8 6
                         SOUTH
                         ♠ 6 4
                         ♡ A 10 8 2
                         ◇ A K 7
                         ♣ Q J 10 5
```

The bidding:

SOUTH	WEST	NORTH	EAST
1 ♣	Pass	1 ♠	Pass
1 NT	Pass	3 ♠	Pass
3 NT	Pass	Pass	Pass

Opening lead: Two of clubs

North's three spade rebid might be considered on the aggressive side—but properly so. The perfect rebid, if it were legal, would be 2½ spades. The alternative of two spades would be a distinct underbid.

Despite South's opening one club bid, West elected to lead a club at trick one. Why he picked on the deuce of clubs, I do not know. By doing so, he undoubtedly created the impression in East's mind that the lead was from a four-card club suit.

However, his lead had a serendipitous effect, for when East won the opening lead with the club king, his club return removed dummy's sole entry outside of the spade suit itself.

At trick three, declarer came to his hand with a diamond to his king, then led a spade to dummy's queen. Although the finesse succeeded, all declarer could come to were eight tricks, for it was impossible to both establish and cash the spade suit.

An experienced South would have indulged in the hope, however forlorn, that West had been dealt either K x or K x x in spades. If such were the case, then the entire spade suit could be brought in with the loss of just one trick.

Assuming this hope to be the case, declarer should have led a low spade from dummy at trick three, conceding the trick to East's nine-spot. South would win whatever East played back and lead his remaining spade. When West followed suit with the ten, declarer would close his eyes and play the board's queen. Success! The ace of spades would snare West's king, and that would be that. Declarer could chalk up a game, with two overtricks.

DEAL VIII

You've heard the old wheeze, "Eight ever, nine never." It means that normally, with nine trumps headed by the A K J, the book advises you to cash the ace and king, hoping to catch the queen, as opposed to finessing for the queen by playing the jack. But on this deal, it was wrong to follow the book, as our South declarer learned in the post-mortem.

Both sides vulnerable. East deals.

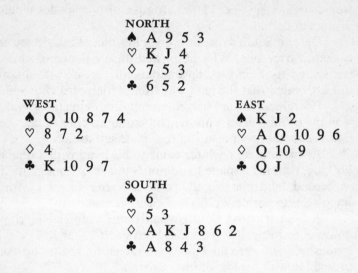

NORTH
♠ A 9 5 3
♡ K J 4
◇ 7 5 3
♣ 6 5 2

WEST
♠ Q 10 8 7 4
♡ 8 7 2
◇ 4
♣ K 10 9 7

EAST
♠ K J 2
♡ A Q 10 9 6
◇ Q 10 9
♣ Q J

SOUTH
♠ 6
♡ 5 3
◇ A K J 8 6 2
♣ A 8 4 3

The bidding:

EAST	SOUTH	WEST	NORTH
1 ♡	2 ◇	Pass	Pass
Pass			

Opening lead: Eight of hearts

West's failure to raise partner to two hearts resulted in South's "stealing" the hand. At a heart contract, East would have made at least eight tricks, and possibly more, depending on how the play went. However, East-West salvaged something, for South managed to incur a one-trick set.

West's opening lead of the heart eight was covered by dummy's jack. East won the queen and shifted to the queen of clubs, which South captured with his ace.

Declarer next laid down his ace and king of trumps, hoping to drop the queen. As is evident, he didn't. As a last resort, South then led a club, in the hope the missing cards were evenly divided or that he would be allowed to ruff a club in dummy. But East was on his toes. He won the club lead, cashed the queen of diamonds, and shifted to a spade. When play ended, declarer had lost three clubs, one diamond, and two hearts, down one.

After winning East's club queen at trick two, declarer could have ensured his contract by laying down the trump ace (as he did), then entering dummy with a spade to the ace and leading a diamond to his jack. In the actual case, the finesse would win and declarer would avoid the loss of a trump trick.

The beauty of finessing the trump jack is that even if it had lost, declarer's contract would still be guaranteed. If West could win with the queen, the defenders' trumps would be exhausted, while dummy still held the trump seven. Declarer could then be sure he could ruff his fourth club for his eighth trick.

In summary, South should have finessed his jack of trumps because the finesse would have been "on the house." Whether it won or lost, declarer would have been home free: If it won, he would make six trump tricks, and if it lost, the board would retain a trump to take care of one of South's losing clubs.

DEAL IX

This final deal features a card combination similar to that illustrated in Deal 8. Declarer again has nine trumps headed by the A K J, and is faced with the same question: Cash the ace and king of trumps in an attempt to drop the queen, or finesse the jack? Here, however, the objective of the finesse (the correct play) was to make certain to keep one of the defenders off lead. If this could be accomplished, then declarer would fulfill his game contract with ease. Whether declarer's actual play was due to thoughtlessness or to lack of proficiency, I do not know; but he, too, succumbed to the book play.

Both sides vulnerable. South deals.

NORTH
♠ 8 6 5 3
♡ K Q 9 6
◇ K 5
♣ 7 4 2

WEST
♠ 9
♡ 8 5 3 2
◇ J 10 9 7
♣ A Q 9 5

EAST
♠ Q 10 4
♡ 7 4
◇ Q 8 6 3 2
♣ J 10 8

SOUTH
♠ A K J 7 2
♡ A J 10
◇ A 4
♣ K 6 3

The bidding:

SOUTH	WEST	NORTH	EAST
1 ♠	Pass	2 ♠	Pass
4 ♠	Pass	Pass	Pass

Opening led: Jack of diamonds

South won the diamond opening with his ace. Declarer next
cashed the ace and king of trumps—and his contract was irre-
trievably lost.

Hoping to discard a losing club on dummy's fourth heart
(as he could have done had East been dealt three or more
hearts), South cashed the ace and jack of hearts, then overtook

the ten with dummy's queen. But East ruffed this third heart lead and plunked down the jack of clubs. The defenders inevitably cashed three club tricks, pinning a one-trick set on declarer.

As the score was being recorded, South moaned to North: "Boy, did I get bad breaks! Not only didn't I catch the queen of trumps, but East had only two hearts. Even so, if East had the ace of clubs, I would have made my contract anyway."

Admittedly, declarer did get bad breaks. But a pessimistic expert in the South seat would have made the play look easy as pie.

After winning the opening diamond lead and cashing the ace of trumps, South would recognize that the only danger to his contract was that East might gain the lead with the trump queen, to play a club through South's king. To overcome this possibility, South should have led a diamond to the king and a trump off dummy. When East followed, declarer would put in his jack. On this deal, the jack would win, and South would wind up with an overtrick.

But even if the "antibook" finesse lost, the contract would be guaranteed no matter what West returned. When South regained the lead, he would simply run four heart tricks, discarding a losing club from his own hand.

6

The Necessary Finesse
Better-Than-Average Games

♠ ♡ ◇ ♣

The ten deals in this chapter occurred in games where all of the players could be considered, on past performances, as better-than average. In two of the deals, our declarers demonstrated that they were worthy of their designation. But eight of the ten failed in their missions; and based on their performances, I would have to demote them to "lower-echelon" better-than-average players. So do not be concerned if you miss the vital play. The two successful declarers would, naturally, be promoted to "upper-echelon" better-than-average players. I hope you join them.

DEAL I

One vital element in the play of the hand is to maintain lines of communication between dummy and the closed hand. These lines of communication are generally referred to as *entries*.

In this deal, our South declarer was able to make an over-trick only because he found a hidden entry that enabled him to take a needed finesse. The hand came up in a duplicate game, where an overtrick can be worth its weight in uranium.

Neither side vulnerable. South deals.

NORTH
- ♠ 6 4 3
- ♡ 9 7 5
- ◇ A 7 4
- ♣ K 5 3 2

WEST
- ♠ J 10 7 5 2
- ♡ 6 4
- ◇ Q J 10 8
- ♣ 10 8

EAST
- ♠ 9 8
- ♡ K 8 3 2
- ◇ 6 5 3 2
- ♣ 9 7 6

SOUTH
- ♠ A K Q
- ♡ A Q J 10
- ◇ K 9
- ♣ A Q J 4

The bidding:

SOUTH	WEST	NORTH	EAST
3 NT	Pass	4 NT	Pass
6 NT	Pass	Pass	Pass

Opening lead: Queen of diamonds

North's raise to four no-trump invited South to bid the small slam if he possessed more than his announced minimum (twenty-six or twenty-seven points, rather than twenty-five). South, of course, happily accepted the invitation.

West opened the queen of diamonds. Declarer won in dummy with the ace and took the heart finesse. Actually, declarer was sure of his slam whether the finesse won or lost, for he had twelve top tricks: three spades, three hearts, two diamonds, and four clubs.

When the finesse won, South scented the making of all 13 tricks. He laid down the ace and queen of clubs, noting with satisfaction that both opponents twice followed suit.

Now the jack of clubs was overtaken by the board's king, and hearts were again successfully finessed. South's remaining club, the carefully preserved four-spot, was then led to dummy's five—the "hidden" entry. When the third heart finesse also succeeded, declarer was able to claim all thirteen tricks.

Of course, if one of the defenders failed to follow to the second round of clubs, South could not afford to overtake the jack of clubs, and would have been unable to pick up the heart king. But with the actual distribution, he was able to make maximum use of all of the assets of the two hands, entirely without risk.

DEAL II

One of the dominant characteristics of an experienced player is a cautious degree of pessimism in the play. However, when it was dealt in a rubber-bridge game, an expert was not at the helm. Unfortunately, our actual declarer was looking at things through rose-tinted glasses. As a result, when play ended, he found himself in the red.

Both sides vulnerable. North deals.

NORTH
- ♠ A Q J 8 4
- ♡ A J 6
- ◊ Q 10
- ♣ A 7 2

WEST
- ♠ 9 6 3 2
- ♡ K 10 7 4
- ◊ 8 5
- ♣ J 10 8

EAST
- ♠ 10 7 5
- ♡ 2
- ◊ 9 6 4 3 2
- ♣ Q 9 5 3

SOUTH
- ♠ K
- ♡ Q 9 8 5 3
- ◊ A K J 7
- ♣ K 6 4

The bidding:

NORTH	EAST	SOUTH	WEST
1 ♠	Pass	2 ♡	Pass
4 ♡	Pass	4 NT	Pass
5 ♠	Pass	5 NT	Pass
6 ♣	Pass	6 ♡	Pass
Pass	Pass		

Opening lead: Jack of clubs

After capturing West's club jack with his king, South led a low trump and finessed dummy's jack, which won the trick. Assuming that the outstanding trumps would split normally, declarer next cashed the board's ace of trumps. When East discarded the deuce of diamonds, South was a goner; West now had two trump tricks.

In a sense, South could attribute his defeat to a tough break, since the actual trump division was abnormal. But South's defeat was exclusively his own fault, for after the finesse of dummy's jack succeeded, he failed to take into consideration the possibility that West might have begun with four trumps. Had he played with appropriate pessimism, he could have taken the necessary precautions.

Once the jack of hearts had won the initial trump lead, declarer should have reentered his hand via the king of spades and led the nine of trumps. Assuming that West followed suit with the seven, declarer would play dummy's six. In this deal, the nine would have won the trick, and after the trump ace had been cashed, West would be left with the high king of trumps. That card would be the defenders' only trick.

If *East* were able to win the second trump lead with the ten-spot, declarer would still have cinched his contract. In this case, the only outstanding trump would be the king, and that would fall under the ace when South next gained the lead. South's losing club would later be discarded on the board's ace of spades.

The moral of this deal? Why assume good breaks when it is such a simple matter to overcome bad ones?

DEAL III

It is an accepted principle of play that at no-trump contracts the declarer's longest suit is attacked first, in an effort to make winners out of the long cards in that suit. But, as with all principles, there are exceptions.

In this deal, our South declarer did "what comes naturally": He attacked his longest suit first. Subsequent events proved he did the wrong thing. It cost him a vulnerable game.

Both sides vulnerable. South deals.

NORTH
♠ Q 7 4 2
♡ K
◇ Q 6 5
♣ K J 10 8 4

WEST
♠ K 10
♡ Q 10 8 3 2
◇ 9 8 2
♣ 6 5 3

EAST
♠ 9 8 6 5 3
♡ 9 7 6 4
◇ K J 4
♣ A

SOUTH
♠ A J
♡ A J 5
◇ A 10 7 3
♣ Q 9 7 2

The bidding:

SOUTH	WEST	NORTH	EAST
1 NT	Pass	2 ♣	Pass
2 ◇	Pass	3 NT	Pass
Pass	Pass		

Opening lead: Three of hearts

West's heart opening lead was won in dummy with the singleton king, and at trick two, the king of clubs was played. East took the ace perforce and returned a heart, South finessing the jack. This lost to the queen. West returned a heart, knocking out South's ace. Declarer then entered dummy with the jack of clubs and tried the spade finesse. But West won the king and cashed two heart tricks to defeat the contract one trick.

After he had won the opening heart lead, declarer should have studied the hand with more care. Had South done so, he would have realized that it might prove costly if East obtained the lead before he had the hand under control. And attacking clubs first ran just that risk.

The winning line of play is to lead a spade off dummy at trick two, finessing the jack. In the actual setup, West would have won with his king—and he would have found himself in a hopeless position.

If he played back a heart, he would give South a present of the heart jack. If he chose to return a spade or a diamond instead, declarer would win the trick, then drive out the club ace. Thus, declarer would come to nine tricks: two spades, two hearts, one diamond, and four clubs.

By attacking the shorter spade suit first, declarer would have kept East off lead until a second spade trick had been assured. South just did not look far enough ahead to visualize the possible consequences of his club lead at trick two.

DEAL IV

Although I cannot prove it, South was probably sorry that he was not in slam after the dummy came down. But when play had ended, he was probably sorry that he had climbed as high as game. However, our better-than-average South deserves no sympathy, for he mishandled his assets.

Both sides vulnerable. South deals.

NORTH
♠ K 10 6
♡ —
♢ 9 7 5 4
♣ K Q J 9 5 2

WEST
♠ J 7 4 3
♡ K Q 10 5
♢ K 10 6
♣ 7 4

EAST
♠ 5
♡ A J 9 8 4
♢ Q J 3 2
♣ 8 6 3

SOUTH
♠ A Q 9 8 2
♡ 7 6 3 2
♢ A 8
♣ A 10

The bidding:

SOUTH	WEST	NORTH	EAST
1 ♠	Pass	2 ♣	Pass
2 ♠	Pass	3 ♠	Pass
4 ♠	Pass	Pass	Pass

Opening lead: King of hearts

As soon as the opening lead had been made and the dummy came into view, South saw that he could make all thirteen tricks if the five outstanding trumps were divided 3-2. If such were the case (as it rated to be), South could ruff West's king of hearts and draw the missing trumps. All of South's losers would then be discarded on dummy's clubs.

So South ruffed the opening heart lead in dummy and cashed the king of trumps. He then led the trump ten to his queen, but East awakened declarer to reality when he discarded a club. South next cashed the ace of trumps, leaving West's high jack outstanding.

In the hope that West possessed three or more clubs—so that South could get rid of a couple of his losing hearts—declarer then played the ace, king, and queen of clubs, discarding a low heart. West ruffed the third club lead, after which the defenders cashed two heart tricks. Since dummy could not be reached, declarer eventually had to lose a diamond as well, so he went down a trick.

Basically, declarer's error in play was placing his contract in jeopardy by failing to give any consideration to the not inconsiderable (28 percent) possibility that the missing trumps might be divided 4-1.

After ruffing the opening heart lead, declarer should have led dummy's ten of trumps and played low from his own hand, ostensibly finessing East for the jack. The finesse would have lost, but declarer would now be home safely, with two overtricks.

Assuming West returned a heart (no other return could alter the outcome), dummy would ruff with the singleton king. South would reenter his hand via the diamond ace and pick up West's remaining trumps. The rest of the tricks would now belong to South. By playing correctly, declarer would have made twelve tricks even though the outstanding trumps were divided 4-1.

DEAL V

One of the interesting features of many deals is the race that develops between declarer and the defenders, with declarer trying to build up tricks and the defenders doing their best to prevent him from doing so.

In this deal, there were two races. The first race declarer had to lose, and he should have conceded it. He would then have devoted his energies to the crucial second race, which would have made him the victor. But he stubbornly refused to concede the first race, and so lost both of them.

Neither side vulnerable. South deals.

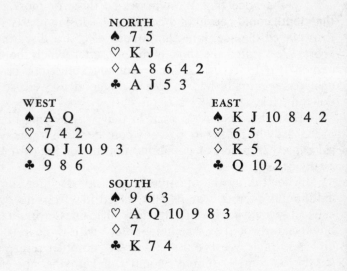

NORTH
♠ 7 5
♡ K J
♢ A 8 6 4 2
♣ A J 5 3

WEST
♠ A Q
♡ 7 4 2
♢ Q J 10 9 3
♣ 9 8 6

EAST
♠ K J 10 8 4 2
♡ 6 5
♢ K 5
♣ Q 10 2

SOUTH
♠ 9 6 3
♡ A Q 10 9 8 3
♢ 7
♣ K 7 4

The bidding:

SOUTH	WEST	NORTH	EAST
2 ♡	Pass	4 ♡	Pass
Pass	Pass		

Opening lead: Queen of diamonds

South's two heart opening call was the modern "weak" two bid, showing a good six-card suit and a hand that contained six to twelve high-card points. North's raise to four hearts was an overbid, and was probably based on the hope that South's outside strength—if any—was in clubs or diamonds.

West opened the diamond queen, captured by dummy's ace. A spade was led off the board and West's queen won. Since it was apparent that declarer was planning to ruff a spade in dummy, West shifted to the trump deuce, the board's king taking the trick.

Obstinately, South persisted by leading another spade. West won the ace, continuing with a trump. South overtook dummy's jack with the ace and drew the outstanding trump with his queen. Since he had no other recourse, declarer next cashed the club king and finessed dummy's jack. A split second after East had won his queen, he cashed the king of spades for the setting trick.

When West returned a trump after winning the initial spade lead (at trick two), it should have been rather apparent to declarer that the opponents were not about to allow him to ruff his third spade. Hence, he should have abandoned this plan. The alternate, and successful, line would have been to overtake dummy's king of trumps with his ace and lead a club, finessing dummy's jack. As is evident, East would have captured this trick with his queen.

When declarer regained the lead, he would draw the missing trumps with his queen and ten, then cash the king and ace of clubs, noting with delight that both of the opponents followed suit. Dummy's fourth club would now provide a parking place for one of South's spade losers.

There was, of course, no guarantee that the six outstanding clubs would be divided 3-3 (a 36 percent chance), but once the opponents led a trump at trick three, South really had no practical choice other than to rely on the club suit "behaving nicely." As he actually played the hand, he never gave himself the opportunity of testing the club suit.

(Since the opponents were bound to prevent the spade ruff, declarer could have given himself an extra chance—that the dia-

monds would split—by ruffing a diamond at trick two. He would
then return to dummy with a trump and ruff another diamond.
When that plan proved hopeless, there would still be time to play
the clubs while the heart king remained in dummy to prevent the
loss of three fast tricks in spades.)

DEAL VI

When I first saw this deal played some years ago, I felt that
it really was a thing of beauty. My opinion has not changed. At
first glance, it might appear that whatever South played from
dummy at trick one did not matter. But on closer examination, it
will be observed that it made all the difference in the world.

Neither side vulnerable. South deals.

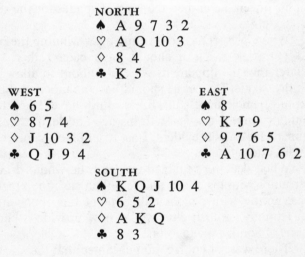

```
                        NORTH
                        ♠ A 9 7 3 2
                        ♡ A Q 10 3
                        ◇ 8 4
                        ♣ K 5
        WEST                            EAST
        ♠ 6 5                           ♠ 8
        ♡ 8 7 4                         ♡ K J 9
        ◇ J 10 3 2                      ◇ 9 7 6 5
        ♣ Q J 9 4                       ♣ A 10 7 6 2
                        SOUTH
                        ♠ K Q J 10 4
                        ♡ 6 5 2
                        ◇ A K Q
                        ♣ 8 3
```

The bidding:

SOUTH	WEST	NORTH	EAST
1 ♠	Pass	3 ♠	Pass
4 ♠	Pass	Pass	Pass

Opening lead: Queen of clubs

West led the queen of clubs and declarer, adhering slavishly to the principle of "covering an honor with an honor," mechanically put up dummy's king. After taking his ace, East returned a low club, West's nine winning. West now shifted to the eight of hearts, and declarer finessed dummy's ten, losing to East's jack. Eventually East made his heart king, for the setting trick.

South was truly unlucky in finding the defenders' honor cards distributed as they were. If West had possessed any one of three cards—the ace of clubs, or the jack of hearts, or the king of hearts—South would have fulfilled his contract easily. Nonetheless, despite the terrible distribution, the contract was unbeatable from the moment that the opening lead was made.

Although dummy's king of clubs was obviously trapped on the opening lead, declarer nevertheless should have played low from dummy. If West then shifted to, let us say, a heart, South would put up dummy's ace. Trumps would be drawn, after which declarer would cash his top diamonds, discarding the king of clubs. From here in, he could lose only two hearts.

If, at trick two, West continued with a club, East would win the ace, then probably shift to a diamond, South's queen winning. After trumps were drawn, declarer would cash the king and ace of diamonds, discarding a heart from dummy.

With both clubs and diamonds eliminated from the North-South hands, it would be safe to lead a heart to the ten. Though the finesse lost, East would find himself in an impossible position. If he played back a club or a diamond, South would discard his five of hearts as he ruffed in dummy. And if East returned a heart, dummy would have two heart winners.

By not playing the club king at trick one, declarer would have broken the East-West line of communication, preventing *West* from leading a heart *after* East-West had cashed two club tricks.

DEAL VII

In this deal, South arrived at the inferior game contract of three no-trump. However, it is difficult to fault either North or

South for their bidding, for there really was no acceptable opening bid with the North hand. Actually, five diamonds would have been the ideal contract, but I doubt any pair in the world would have reached that spot.

Nevertheless, despite North's "stab-in-the-dark" raise to three no-trump, South could (and should) have brought the game home. His failure to do so, in my opinion, can be attributed only to a desire to make sure that he would not go down more than one trick.

Neither side vulnerable. North deals.

```
                    NORTH
                    ♠ 6 5 2
                    ♡ A K Q
                    ◇ A Q 4
                    ♣ A K Q 5
      WEST                          EAST
      ♠ J 10 9 7 4 3               ♠ K Q 8
      ♡ 8 4                        ♡ J 10 6 2
      ◇ K J 10                     ◇ 9 3
      ♣ J 8                        ♣ 10 9 7 4
                    SOUTH
                    ♠ A
                    ♡ 9 7 5 3
                    ◇ 8 7 6 5 2
                    ♣ 6 3 2
```

The bidding:

NORTH	EAST	SOUTH	WEST
2 ♣ (!)	Pass	2 NT	Pass
3 NT (!)	Pass	Pass	Pass

Opening lead: Jack of spades

On West's opening lead of the spade jack, East unblocked with the queen, and South won the trick with his ace. He then cashed dummy's three top clubs, hoping, of course, that the six missing clubs were divided 3-3. When that failed to materialize, declarer ended up with the same eight tricks he had started with.

As soon as dummy came into view, declarer could count eight tricks. The ninth trick, if it could be made at all, had to come from either the diamond suit (by taking the finesse) or the club suit (if the outstanding clubs were divided 3-3). It was equally obvious that once South led to trick two, he could never again return to his hand. The issue—which could not be deferred —was whether to take the diamond finesse or go after the clubs.

The diamond finesse offered a 50-50 chance of success. The chance that the clubs would divide 3-3, however, was only a 36 percent proposition. Hence, at trick two, South should have taken the diamond finesse instead of staking everything on an even division of the missing clubs.

It is agreed that no one enjoys risking everything on a 50-50 chance. But, being realistic, when the choice is between a 50 percent chance and a 36 percent chance, one must accept the better of what is available.

Admittedly, if the diamond finesse had failed, the normal spade return would have resulted in South suffering a two-trick set. But as a principle of sound play, one should not allow the potential loss of an extra trick influence him to take an inferior, penny-saving line of play.

DEAL VIII

In this deal, as in the preceding one, knowledge of the "percentages" of a standard, recurring situation was the key to the winning line of play. At the table, South took a "wrong view" —and he dropped a rung in the hierarchy of better-than-average players.

Neither side vulnerable. North deals.

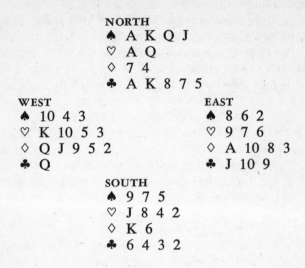

NORTH
♠ A K Q J
♡ A Q
♢ 7 4
♣ A K 8 7 5

WEST
♠ 10 4 3
♡ K 10 5 3
♢ Q J 9 5 2
♣ Q

EAST
♠ 8 6 2
♡ 9 7 6
♢ A 10 8 3
♣ J 10 9

SOUTH
♠ 9 7 5
♡ J 8 4 2
♢ K 6
♣ 6 4 3 2

The bidding:

NORTH	EAST	SOUTH	WEST
2 ♣	Pass	2 NT	Pass
3 ♠	Pass	3 NT	Pass
Pass	Pass		

Opening lead: Queen of diamonds

North's game-forcing two club opening bid was a marginal call at best, but there was nothing wrong with the three no-trump contract except the final result.

After West opened the queen of diamonds, East put up the ace and returned a diamond to South's king. Trusting that the four outstanding clubs were divided 2-2 (which would give declarer five club tricks), South cashed the ace and king of clubs.

When West failed to follow suit to the second club lead, it was revealed simultaneously that East had a sure club winner and that the three no-trump contract was no longer makable. Declarer chose to concede a club, and East's diamond return enabled the defenders to cash sufficient diamond tricks to defeat the contract.

At trick two, South knew that once he played to trick three, he would be unable to get back to his hand unless the defenders' clubs were evenly divided. Thus, he had to make a decision as to whether to attack the club suit or take the heart finesse. As a player who had been around for many years, he should have known that it was wrong to tackle the clubs.

When there are four cards of a suit outstanding, mathematics predict they will divide 2-2 only 40 percent of the time. And everybody knows, without having obtained a Ph.D. in math, that a straightforward finesse offers a 50 percent chance of success.

Therefore, at trick three, South should have led a low heart out of his hand and finessed the board's queen. As "luck" would have it, dummy's queen of hearts would have become declarer's ninth trick.

Had the finesse lost, South *might* have gone down an extra trick (if West had started with six diamonds). But South should have considered the extra 10 percent chance of success well worth the payment of a 50-point premium.

DEAL IX

In this deal, it was obvious from the start that the success or failure of declarer's slam contract would depend on a finesse. As things developed, declarer actually took two finesses, one of which had to be successful if the contract were to be fulfilled. But both of them lost.

At the conclusion of play, it was noted that declarer had played the hand poorly, for the slam was there from the word "go"—and it was there without relying on one of two finesses.

North-South vulnerable. South deals.

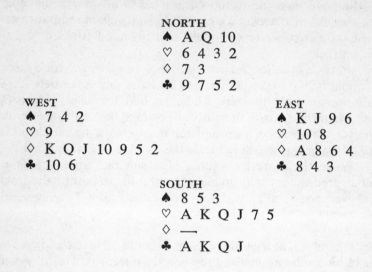

NORTH
♠ A Q 10
♡ 6 4 3 2
◇ 7 3
♣ 9 7 5 2

WEST
♠ 7 4 2
♡ 9
◇ K Q J 10 9 5 2
♣ 10 6

EAST
♠ K J 9 6
♡ 10 8
◇ A 8 6 4
♣ 8 4 3

SOUTH
♠ 8 5 3
♡ A K Q J 7 5
◇ —
♣ A K Q J

The bidding:

SOUTH	WEST	NORTH	EAST
2 ♡	4 ◇	4 ♡	5 ◇
6 ♡	Pass	Pass	Pass

Opening lead: King of diamonds

The bidding may appear wild and woolly, but it makes sense. West's nonvulnerable jump to four diamonds was an attempt to throw North-South off balance (after all, South had announced a game-going hand), and East was quite willing to continue this tactic by raising to five diamonds. (In fact, East-West would have gone down only two tricks at five diamonds.) Actually, however, the East-West bidding helped South make his dramatic leap to six hearts. North figured to have no strength in diamonds, and it was known to South that North had no high-card points in either hearts or clubs, so he rated to have a couple of high cards in spades to justify his free bid of four hearts.

South ruffed West's king of diamonds opening lead with the five-spot and drew trumps in two rounds. After cashing his four clubs, declarer led a spade to dummy's ten. East won the jack and came back a diamond, which declarer ruffed. Now a second spade finesse was tried. When this also lost, South voiced a complaint about his "tough luck," pointing out that if West had been dealt either the jack or king of spades, the slam contract would have been fulfilled.

How about it? Did the cards play a dirty trick on South?

Once West opened a diamond, South had a guaranteed contract, regardless of the location of the king and jack of spades. All he had to do was ruff the opening lead with the seven, not with the five!

The two top trumps would then be played, followed by the four high clubs. Declarer would enter dummy by leading the five hearts to the six, in order to ruff the board's remaining diamond, thereby eliminating diamonds from the North and South hands.

Now the finesse of the spade ten could be taken without a care. East would win the jack—and would be end-played. If he returned a diamond, declarer would discard his losing spade as he ruffed the trick with the board's last trump. And if East played back a spade, dummy's queen would become declarer's twelfth trick.

DEAL X

Most finesses are purely and simply 50-50 propositions. However, clues often develop in either the bidding or the play that point the way to a winning finesse. This deal is a case in point, and South handled the play with consummate ease.

Both sides vulnerable. South deals.

```
                        NORTH
                        ♠ K 9 6 3
                        ♡ 6
                        ◇ J 8 6 2
                        ♣ Q 10 8 3
        WEST                                EAST
        ♠ 5                                 ♠ Q 7 4 2
        ♡ K Q J 10 9 8                      ♡ 7 5 4 2
        ◇ 7 4                               ◇ 9 5 3
        ♣ A K J 5                           ♣ 9 2
                        SOUTH
                        ♠ A J 10 8
                        ♡ A 3
                        ◇ A K Q 10
                        ♣ 7 6 4
```

The bidding:

SOUTH	WEST	NORTH	EAST
1 ◇	1 ♡	2 ◇	Pass
2 ♠	3 ♡	3 ♠	Pass
4 ♠	Pass	Pass	Pass

Opening lead: King of clubs

On West's opening lead of the king of clubs, East initiated a high-low signal by dropping the nine-spot. The ace of clubs was continued, followed by a third club, which East ruffed. East exited with a heart, won by South's ace.

Superficially, perhaps, the location of the trump queen might appear to be a 50-50 guess. But our South declarer had no problem in ascertaining its whereabouts. Here are the factors that led him to his conclusion.

First, West was known to have started with four clubs, since East had ruffed the third lead of that suit. Secondly, West had bid up to three hearts, vulnerable, all by himself. Surely West rated to have a minimum of six hearts, especially since he was missing the ace of his suit. Thus, ten of West's original cards were accounted for.

By subtraction, West therefore had only three cards in spades and diamonds. East, on the other hand, rated to have four hearts and, of course, exactly two clubs (by observation). Consequently, East had been dealt seven cards in spades and diamonds.

Since West had three unknown cards in spades and diamonds, while East possessed seven cards in these two suits, the odds were that the spade queen had been dealt to East. (When there are two "piles" to pick from, any card that one is looking for figures to be in the bigger pile.)

So, at trick five, South led a spade to dummy's king and returned a spade. When East followed low, South inserted the ten. Success! The ace of spades captured the queen, and it was an easy matter for declarer to ruff his losing heart in dummy and claim the contract.

7

The Necessary Finesse
Top-Echelon Games

♠   ♡   ◇   ♣

The eleven deals in this chapter were all played in top-level games. In eight of these deals, South came up with the performances you'd expect of expert players. But three of the eleven declarers committed errors, either of omission or commission, thus demonstrating that no bridge player is infallible.

DEAL I

Usually, when one indulges in wishful thinking, it is with the hope that something nice will happen. But, on occasion, a bridge player indulges in the wishful thinking that something bad will happen!

In this deal, which was played in a team-of-four match, declarer was not exuberant when he saw the dummy. If the opponents' trumps were divided 2-2, a slam would be there for the taking. And it was not beyond the realm of possibility that the South on the opposing team might bid a slam when the deal was replayed. So our declarer indulged in the wishful thinking that the trumps would be divided evilly rather than evenly. This abnormal approach served him well.

Both sides vulnerable. South deals.

NORTH
- ♠ K 10 5 2
- ♡ A Q 6 3
- ◇ A K 4
- ♣ 8 5

WEST
- ♠ 8 4
- ♡ 9 2
- ◇ Q J 10 3
- ♣ Q J 9 7 4

EAST
- ♠ 9 7 6 3
- ♡ J 10 8 5 4
- ◇ —
- ♣ A 10 6 2

SOUTH
- ♠ A Q J
- ♡ K 7
- ◇ 9 8 7 6 5 2
- ♣ K 3

The bidding:

SOUTH	WEST	NORTH	EAST
1 ◇	Pass	1 ♡	Pass
2 ◇	Pass	2 ♠	Pass
2 NT	Pass	3 ◇	Pass
4 ◇	Pass	5 ◇	Pass
Pass	Pass		

Opening lead: Queen of clubs

In retrospect, South might have bid three no-trump over North's three diamond call. This contract would have been laydown—with an overtrick if West led a club. However, since North's bidding showed not only a very good hand but also a lack of interest in playing at no-trump, North-South reached a reasonable contract of five diamonds.

East won the opening lead of the queen of clubs with his ace, and returned a club to South's king. At trick three, South led the deuce of trumps, and when West followed with the three, declarer took a deep finesse by playing dummy's four!

To declarer's surprise, the four-spot won the trick—and he smiled at the "terrible break." Obviously, not only was a small slam unmakable, but the slightest carelessness might cost a game! The ace and king of trumps were cashed next, and in time West made his trump queen. Declarer's only losers were a club and a trump.

In both a team game and in rubber bridge, finessing the board's four of diamonds on the original trump lead had to be the correct play. It was a safety play to guard against West's admittedly unlikely but not impossible possession of the four outstanding trumps. It is obvious, of course, that had declarer played dummy's king on the first trump lead, he would have been compelled to lose two trump tricks.

For the record, when the deal was replayed, the second South declarer also arrived at a five diamond contract. But he, too, utilized the same safety play to bring home eleven tricks, so the result was a standoff.

DEAL II

It is my belief that if all of the world's nonexpert players found themselves sitting in the South seat on this deal, the great majority of them would fail to fulfill their game contract. The reason would be that their thoughts would be centered on making the maximum number of tricks.

When this deal occurred, an expert occupied the South seat. He played the hand to make sure of fulfilling his ten-trick contract, and ended up making all thirteen tricks!

East-West vulnerable. West deals.

NORTH
♠ 9 7 4
♡ —
◇ A K J 10 3 2
♣ 7 6 3 2

WEST
♠ 2
♡ K Q J 10 5
◇ 8 6 4
♣ A Q J 10

EAST
♠ J 6 5 3
♡ A 9 8 7 4
◇ 7
♣ 9 8 5

SOUTH
♠ A K Q 10 8
♡ 6 3 2
◇ Q 9 5
♣ K 4

The bidding:

WEST	NORTH	EAST	SOUTH
1 ♡	2 ◇	3 ♡	3 ♠
4 ♡	4 ♠	Pass	Pass
Pass			

Opening lead: King of hearts

West's king of hearts opening lead was ruffed in dummy. The seven of trumps was led to South's eight, followed by another heart, ruffed with the board's last trump.

South then returned to his hand via the diamond queen and drew the missing three trumps. Dummy's diamond suit now provided a convenient parking spot for declarer's last heart and two clubs. The rest of the tricks were his.

How different the result would have been if declarer cashed the ace and king of trumps at tricks two and three (on the assumption that the five outstanding trumps figured to be divided 3-2 about 68 percent of the time). When West failed to follow suit to the second trump lead, declarer would have ended up losing one spade, two hearts, and two clubs, thus suffering a two-trick defeat.

The beauty of South's first-round finesse against the trump jack was that even if it lost to West's jack, all the defenders could make from here in would be their ace of clubs.

There are probably those who feel that declarer took a risk in playing for all thirteen tricks. Why should he ruff a heart in dummy at trick three and risk coming back to his hand with a diamond? Suppose East were void of diamonds, and ruffed the diamond lead?

But if one examines the hand closely, this was really a remote possibility. Had East been void of diamonds, he probably would have (1) bid four hearts (instead of three) on his first response or (2) not sold out to South at four spades.

Incidentally, it might be noted that East-West could have made eleven tricks at hearts, thanks to the favorable location of the club king.

DEAL III

In the two preceding deals, "evidence" was presented to illustrate the extreme extent to which an expert will go to assure the safety of a game contract by taking a finesse. Here is another example of the same philosophy, this time at a slam contract. The deal occurred in a high-stake rubber-bridge game.

Both sides vulnerable. South deals.

NORTH
- ♠ A 4 2
- ♡ Q 7
- ◇ A K 3
- ♣ K Q 10 6 3

WEST
- ♠ Q 9
- ♡ J 10 9
- ◇ 7 6 2
- ♣ J 9 8 7 4

EAST
- ♠ J 10 8 6
- ♡ 8 5 4 3
- ◇ 10 9 5 4
- ♣ 2

SOUTH
- ♠ K 7 5 3
- ♡ A K 6 2
- ◇ Q J 8
- ♣ A 5

The bidding:

SOUTH	WEST	NORTH	EAST
1 NT	Pass	6 NT	Pass
Pass	Pass		

Opening lead: Jack of hearts

West's opening lead of the heart jack was won by dummy's queen, and declarer led the three of clubs to her ace (yes, it was a *she* declarer). She then played her remaining club, and when West followed suit with the seven-spot, inserted dummy's ten. The ten won, so twelve tricks were now guaranteed.

Actually, when the hand ended, declarer had taken all thirteen tricks, for East found himself a victim of a squeeze. On the ten, king, and queen of clubs, declarer threw two spades and East discarded three diamonds. But when South next cashed the queen, king, and ace of diamonds, East had problems finding two discards. He could safely let go a spade on the second round of diamonds, but if he discarded another spade, dummy's third spade would become established. Alternatively, if he threw a heart, declarer would take the last trick with her fourth heart.

What motivated declarer to finesse the board's ten of clubs at trick three? Basically, it was the natural desire to fulfill the slam contract. If West had the jack of clubs, the finesse guaranteed success. And if the ten of clubs lost to East's jack, the opponent's clubs could be divided no worse than 4-2. Thus, when declarer regained the lead, she would cash the king and queen of clubs, and dummy's fifth club would be the slam-going trick.

Some readers will point out that declarer could have fulfilled her contract via a squeeze even if she had not finessed dummy's ten of clubs. That is quite true. But, in all seriousness, anyone who would not finesse the ten of clubs would probably not be familiar with squeezes.

DEAL IV

If a good player had unlimited time at the bridge table, he could almost always work out the pros and cons of alternative lines of play. But, of course, a player does not have this time; frequently he must make relatively hurried decisions as to his next play.

This deal occurred in a top-level game in Sweden. Declarer was a victim of a bad break in his trump suit; however, as he

himself apologetically pointed out later, had he taken a little more
time to look ahead, he would have come up with the winning line
of play. But he felt that he had already taken up too much time
before playing to trick two.

Both sides vulnerable. South deals.

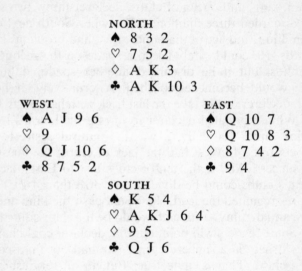

NORTH
♠ 8 3 2
♡ 7 5 2
◇ A K 3
♣ A K 10 3

WEST
♠ A J 9 6
♡ 9
◇ Q J 10 6
♣ 8 7 5 2

EAST
♠ Q 10 7
♡ Q 10 8 3
◇ 8 7 4 2
♣ 9 4

SOUTH
♠ K 5 4
♡ A K J 6 4
◇ 9 5
♣ Q J 6

The bidding:

SOUTH	WEST	NORTH	EAST
1 ♡	Pass	2 ♣	Pass
2 ♡	Pass	4 ♡	Pass
Pass	Pass		

Opening lead: Queen of diamonds

After West's queen of diamonds opening lead had been
taken by dummy's king, a low trump was led off the board. When

East followed suit with the three, South inserted his jack, which won the trick when West played the nine.

The bad trump break was revealed on the ace of trumps as West discarded the six of spades. The trump king was cashed next, leaving East with the high queen.

In the hope of discarding a spade on dummy's fourth club (which he could do if East started with three or more clubs), South now cashed the queen and jack of clubs, followed by a club to dummy's king. But, alas, East ruffed the king. He now shifted to the spade ten, and the defenders collected three spade tricks to set the contract one trick.

From the outset, it was quite apparent to South that his play had to be geared toward keeping East out of the lead, to prevent him from leading a spade through South's king. His finesse of the trump jack was a move in the right direction; had the five outstanding trumps been divided 3-2, he would have fulfilled his contract. But a better line of play was available to him.

When East played the trump three on the first round of trumps, South should have inserted his six-spot! West would have won with his nine and presumably returned a diamond to dummy's ace. A trump lead to South's ace would now have revealed that East still had the doubleton Q 10 remaining, but declarer would have been in complete control. He would reenter dummy via the club ten, and on the third round of trumps, East's Q 10 would be trapped. After trumps had been picked up, South would discard one of his spades on the board's fourth club. From here in, his only losers would have been two spade tricks.

DEAL V

When declarer and dummy hold eleven trumps between them, and the two outstanding trumps consist of the king and a low card, the mathematicians tell us that the two will be divided 1-1 about 52 percent of the time. Thus, the abstract, out-of-context percentages tell us to play the ace, hoping to fell the king, rather than to finesse for the king.

In many real-life situations, however, the correct play is to finesse for the king. Such was the case in this deal.

East-West vulnerable. South deals.

NORTH
♠ K 9 3
♡ J 9
◇ J 6 2
♣ A 8 6 5 4

WEST
♠ J 8 2
♡ 7 5
◇ A K Q 10 8 4
♣ K 2

EAST
♠ A Q 10 6
♡ 8 6 4 3 2
◇ 9 7 5 3
♣ —

SOUTH
♠ 7 5 4
♡ A K Q 10
◇ —
♣ Q J 10 9 7 3

The bidding:

SOUTH	WEST	NORTH	EAST
1 ♣	1 ◇	3 ♣	3 ◇
5 ♣	Pass	Pass	Pass

Opening lead: King of diamonds

Had West guessed to lead the jack of spades, the defenders would have defeated the five club contract immediately by cashing three spade tricks. However, West, quite naturally, opened the king of diamonds, which South ruffed. Declarer then led his queen of trumps, and West followed suit with the deuce.

The question, of course, was whether the two outstanding trumps were divided 1-1, or did West have both of them. If the latter, then the finesse would be the winning play. If they were split 1-1, then dummy's ace would fell East's singleton king.

Our declarer had no problem—he followed suit with dummy's four-spot, finessing against West's hoped-for king. The play now became routine. A trump to dummy's ace picked up West's king, after which four rounds of hearts allowed declarer to discard two of dummy's spades. A spade trick was conceded to East's ace, and in time, South ruffed out his two remaining spades to score an overtrick.

Why did South take the trump finesse? The answer is simple: He could not afford to run the risk of West obtaining the lead. If this happened, then a spade shift through dummy's king might have given the defenders enough tricks to defeat the contract (as would have been the case).

But suppose the finesse had lost. In that case, the best the defenders could have done after that would have been to cash the ace of spades. South would always be able to discard two of dummy's spades on his high hearts, so the finesse, whether it won or lost, guaranteed the contract.

DEAL VI

In this deal, South reached a stage in the play where it was perfectly obvious that he had to take a finesse. But South had played carelessly to the previous tricks, so even if the finesse were successful, it would not help him one iota. An inglorious one-trick defeat was the result.

Both sides vulnerable. North deals.

<pre>
                          NORTH
                          ♠ Q 10 6
                          ♡ 3
                          ◇ A Q 8 5 3 2
                          ♣ A J 4
        WEST   EAST
        ♠ A 7 4 2   ♠ 9 8 5
        ♡ K J 9 5 2   ♡ Q 8 6 4
        ◇ 4   ◇ J 10 9 6
        ♣ Q 10 9   ♣ 7 5
                          SOUTH
                          ♠ K J 3
                          ♡ A 10 7
                          ◇ K 7
                          ♣ K 8 6 3 2
</pre>

The bidding:

NORTH	EAST	SOUTH	WEST
1 ◇	Pass	2 NT	Pass
3 ◇	Pass	3 NT	Pass
Pass	Pass		

Opening lead: Five of hearts

On West's five of hearts opening lead, East put up the queen, which was permitted to win the trick. East returned the four of hearts, South inserted his ten, and West took it with the jack. The king of hearts lead then drove out South's ace and established West's heart suit. On the second and third heart leads, two spades were discarded from dummy.

From declarer's view of the hand, prospects seemed bright, for the five outstanding diamonds figured to be divided 3-2. So he promptly laid down the king of diamonds, followed by a diamond to dummy's ace. When West discarded a spade on the second diamond lead, South had just become a most unhappy fella.

At this point declarer could have returned to his hand via the club king to lead another club and finesse dummy's jack successfully. The ace would then fell West's queen, but South would have no way of getting to his own hand to cash his two remaining clubs.

South therefore resigned himself to defeat. He led the queen of spades. West won with the ace and cashed two heart tricks, and declarer was down one.

Had declarer played the hand properly, he could have had two chances for the price of one—and the second chance would have netted him his contract.

After winning the third heart lead, declarer should have led a low diamond to the board's ace, then a diamond back to his king. If both opponents followed suit to the two leads, South would reenter the board via the club ace and cash the rest of the diamonds. Thus, he would make one heart, six diamonds, and two clubs.

But, in the actual setup, when West failed to follow suit to the second diamond lead, South would be in position to lead a low club to dummy's jack, successfully finessing West for the queen. Now would follow the club ace and the diamond queen, after which a third club would be taken by South's king, West's queen falling. South would now have his nine tricks: one heart, three diamonds, and five clubs.

DEAL VII

Most finesses are taken against kings and queens. Much less frequently, finesses are taken against jacks. And it is rare indeed that a finesse against a jack is taken at trick two. However, this was the case in this deal, and the early finesse against a jack was the only correct play.

Neither side vulnerable. South deals.

                        NORTH
                        ♠ 7 5
                        ♡ Q 10 4
                        ◇ A K 10 9 5
                        ♣ 9 7 2

WEST   EAST
♠ 10 9 6 2   ♠ K Q J
♡ 5   ♡ K 9 8 7 2
◇ J 7 4 2   ◇ 6 3
♣ K Q 6 3   ♣ 8 5 4

                        SOUTH
                        ♠ A 8 4 3
                        ♡ A J 6 3
                        ◇ Q 8
                        ♣ A J 10

The bidding:

SOUTH	WEST	NORTH	EAST
1 ♣	Pass	1 ◇	1 ♡
1 NT	Pass	2 NT	Pass
3 NT	Pass	Pass	Pass

Opening lead: Five of hearts

Declarer made a nice play when he followed with the four of hearts from dummy on West's opening lead of the heart five. Had he put up the ten or queen, East would have played low, and South would have been unable to reach the board later to cash the soon-to-be-established diamonds.

After winning West's opening lead with his jack of hearts, South promptly led the eight of diamonds. West followed with the deuce and South played the five from dummy! When the eight won the trick, the three no-trump contract was now there for the taking.

South next cashed the diamond queen, then led a low heart to dummy's queen. East took this with his king and shifted to the king of spades. South won his ace, entered dummy via the ten of hearts, and cashed three more diamonds. At the conclusion of play, South had ten tricks: one spade, three hearts, five diamonds, and one club.

The brilliance of South's finesse against the diamond jack at trick two becomes apparent when it is recognized that if East had (theoretically) won this trick with the jack, South would still be assured of nine tricks!

Let's suppose that East won the diamond jack, then shifted to the king of spades, let us say, which South would have taken with his ace. The queen of diamonds would have been led next, and overtaken by dummy's king. After cashing dummy's remaining diamonds, the queen of hearts would have been led, and the finesse taken against East's "marked" king (East had bid hearts). In this hypothetical sequence, South would have come home with one spade, three hearts, four diamonds, and the ace of clubs.

Had South played the diamond suit "normally," by playing the queen, king, and ace of diamonds at tricks two, three, and four (hoping to catch the jack), he would have gone down. Although he could establish dummy's fifth diamond by conceding a trick to the jack, West would shift to a spade. With proper de-defense, East-West could then gather five tricks before declarer had time to take his nine.

DEAL VIII

It is an undisputed fact that of the thirteen tricks played in each deal, the most critical is trick one. Quite often, if the wrong card is played to this all-important trick, the contract is doomed automatically. Alternatively, by playing the right card, declarer can guarantee himself a happy future—or at least create an opportunity for its possible procurement.

In this deal, our South declarer made a simple play—for a good player—at trick one, and it enabled him to fulfill his contract. Had it not been made, the hand would have slipped out of control.

Neither side vulnerable. South deals.

```
                        NORTH
                        ♠ Q 9 5 3 2
                        ♡ 3
                        ◇ 8 7 4
                        ♣ A 10 7 3
        WEST                                EAST
        ♠ A J 7 4                           ♠ K 10 6
        ♡ 10 6                              ♡ 9 7 5
        ◇ K J 9                             ◇ Q 10 6 2
        ♣ J 8 6 5                           ♣ K 9 2
                        SOUTH
                        ♠ 8
                        ♡ A K Q J 8 4 2
                        ◇ A 5 3
                        ♣ Q 4
```

The bidding:

SOUTH	WEST	NORTH	EAST
1 ♡	Pass	1 ♠	Pass
4 ♡	Pass	Pass	Pass

Opening lead: Five of clubs

Had South known North's exact hand, he would have bid three no-trump because nine tricks are there for the taking. But, not being clairvoyant, he elected to make the slight overbid of four hearts. If the result can serve as the criterion of right or wrong, no one can criticize his selection.

On West's opening lead of the five of clubs, South naturally played low from dummy, hoping that West was leading away from the king. But East produced this card—and South made his imaginative play when he tossed away the queen under the king.

At trick two, East shifted to a low diamond. South won with his ace and drew trumps in three rounds. Next came the four of clubs, and when West followed suit with the six, South inserted the board's ten. When the finesse won, South breathed a sigh of relief. The ace of clubs provided a parking place for one of declarer's losers, so he could claim ten tricks.

Had South not played the club queen on the opening lead, he would have made only one club trick (either the ace or queen, but not both) and would have been compelled to lose two diamonds and a spade, in addition to the club trick already lost. But by "unblocking" the club queen, South put himself in a position to finesse West for the jack of clubs. As luck would have it, West had that key card, for which both South and North were grateful.

Of course, if East held the club jack, South's finesse of the ten-spot would have lost. South would then have gone down two tricks instead of one, since the club ace would have languished in dummy for the duration of the play. If this had come to pass, South would have lost an extra fifty points—a worthwhile investment since game was at stake.

DEAL IX

Of the deals included in this chapter, this one is probably the most difficult to play correctly. When it came up in a high-stake game a few years ago, one of our nation's top-ranking players was the South declarer. He demonstrated that his reputation was not based on just hearsay.

Both sides vulnerable. South deals.

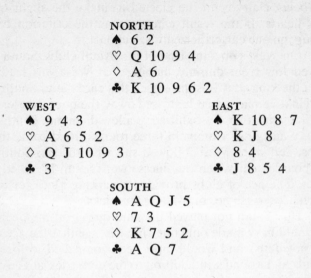

NORTH
♠ 6 2
♡ Q 10 9 4
◇ A 6
♣ K 10 9 6 2

WEST
♠ 9 4 3
♡ A 6 5 2
◇ Q J 10 9 3
♣ 3

EAST
♠ K 10 8 7
♡ K J 8
◇ 8 4
♣ J 8 5 4

SOUTH
♠ A Q J 5
♡ 7 3
◇ K 7 5 2
♣ A Q 7

The bidding:

SOUTH	WEST	NORTH	EAST
1 NT	Pass	2 ♣	Pass
2 ♠	Pass	3 NT	Pass
Pass	Pass		

Opening lead: Queen of diamonds

North's two club call was the Stayman Convention. It asked
South to bid a four-card major suit, if he had one. When South
bid two spades, North (who hoped South might have four
hearts), bid the no-trump game.

West's opening diamond lead was taken by South's king.
At first glance, the contract appeared to be a cinch, since five club
tricks looked like they were in the bag, plus two diamonds and a
minimum of two spades. At tricks two and three, the ace and

queen of clubs were cashed. When West discarded a heart on the second club lead, South was temporarily jolted and took time out for contemplation.

Since four club tricks were now the maximum declarer could make in this suit, it became apparent that *three* spade tricks were needed to fulfill the contract. Hence South had to assume that East possessed the spade king. And further, South had to take two finesses in order to make winners out of the queen and jack of spades.

At trick three, South overtook the queen of clubs with dummy's king. A low spade was led, and declarer successfully finessed his queen. South now conceded a club to East's jack, and East returned a diamond to dummy's king.

After cashing the nine and six of clubs, South led a spade and finessed his jack. He then claimed his contract: three spades, two diamonds, and four clubs.

I doubt that an "average" player would have played the hand in this manner. He probably would not have overtaken the club queen with the king (at trick three), but would have allowed the queen to win, after which a third club lead would have been captured by dummy's king.

A fourth lead of clubs would be won by East's jack. A diamond return would then be taken by the board's ace, and dummy's fifth club would be cashed. Declarer would now finesse his queen of spades, which would win the trick. But then declarer could not get back to dummy to take another spade finesse. He would thus end up making just eight tricks: two spades, two diamonds, and four clubs.

DEAL X

The theme embodied in this deal is old hat to the experienced bridge player, for he has encountered it many times in the past. But the player who has not come across it is quite apt to go wrong when he encounters it for the first time. If you wish to check out my thesis, try it out on some of your nonexpert friends. Let them sit South and play out the hand (without looking at the East-West hands).

Neither side vulnerable. North deals.

```
                        NORTH
                        ♠ A 7 2
                        ♡ J 4
                        ◇ A K 6 4 2
                        ♣ K 8 5
        WEST                            EAST
        ♠ K                             ♠ 9 8 5 4
        ♡ K 10 8 5 3                    ♡ A 9 6
        ◇ J 9 7                         ◇ Q 10
        ♣ Q 9 4 2                       ♣ J 10 7 3
                        SOUTH
                        ♠ Q J 10 6 3
                        ♡ Q 7 2
                        ◇ 8 5 3
                        ♣ A 6
```

The bidding:

NORTH	EAST	SOUTH	WEST
1 ◇	Pass	1 ♠	Pass
2 ♠	Pass	3 ♠	Pass
4 ♠	Pass	Pass	Pass

Opening lead: Five of hearts

West's opening lead of the heart five was won by East's ace. East returned a heart, West's king winning. West then shifted to a club and East's ten was taken by South's ace.

Declarer now led the ten of spades; West put up the king (what else?) and dummy's ace won the trick. The seven of spades was played back, and when East followed with the five-spot, South played his three!

The rest of the play was routine: South's queen and jack of spades picked up East's remaining trumps. Eventually the defenders made a diamond trick. Thus, declarer's only losers were two hearts and a diamond.

When South led the trump ten at trick four and West put up the king, there was a strong suspicion that the king was a singleton. Surely if West had been dealt K x or K x x of trumps, he would not have played the king on the ten.

Hence, when dummy's ace took West's king, South assumed that East had started with the 9 8 5 4 of trumps originally. So when South led the seven off the board, he had the courage of his convictions and "finessed" against East's presumed nine and eight of trumps.

Had South made the "normal" lead of the spade *queen* on his initial trump lead, he almost surely would have ended up losing a trump trick (and his contract). In this case, East would have covered the queen with the king (what else?), dummy's ace taking the trick.

But now declarer would not even vaguely suspect that West's king was a singleton, for West would have just as surely covered the queen if he had held the K x of trumps. And so South most certainly would have won the second trump lead with his ten, on the assumption that the defenders' trumps were divided 3-2. East would now have himself a trump trick—and 50 points for inflicting a one-trick set on declarer.

DEAL XI

This deal features inferior play by our top-level South declarer and superior play by our expert West defender. As befits such circumstances, justice was served, for our West defender emerged as the victor.

In the analysis that followed the deal, it was demonstrated that declarer's inexpert play gave West a chance to be a hero—and he made the grade. It was also pointed out that if declarer had played imaginatively, *he* would have earned the plaudits of the onlookers, while West would have had no opportunity to excel.

North-South vulnerable. South deals.

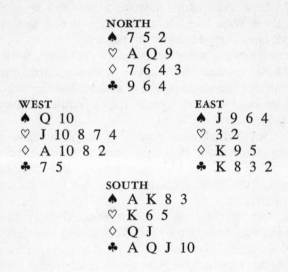

NORTH
♠ 7 5 2
♡ A Q 9
◇ 7 6 4 3
♣ 9 6 4

WEST
♠ Q 10
♡ J 10 8 7 4
◇ A 10 8 2
♣ 7 5

EAST
♠ J 9 6 4
♡ 3 2
◇ K 9 5
♣ K 8 3 2

SOUTH
♠ A K 8 3
♡ K 6 5
◇ Q J
♣ A Q J 10

The bidding:

SOUTH	WEST	NORTH	EAST
1 ♣	Pass	1 ◇	Pass
3 NT	Pass	Pass	Pass

Opening lead: Jack of hearts

After West had opened the jack of hearts, South noted immediately that he needed four club tricks to bring home his contract. So he won the opening lead with the board's queen of hearts, then led a club and finessed his queen.

Since he had to get to dummy two more times in order to take two additional club finesses, South intended to lead the six of hearts out of his hand and finesse dummy's nine-spot. The nine would be certain to win the trick, since West's opening lead of the heart jack virtually guaranteed possession of the ten of hearts. Later, in order to enter dummy a third time, South would lead his heart king and overtake it with the board's ace.

But West spiked declarer's plan. When South led the six of hearts, West put up the ten! This forced declarer to win the trick with the board's ace. Another club successfully finessed, but as is apparent, South could not enter dummy again to take a third club finesse, since it is illegal (and the opponents were watching) to lead the king of hearts and overtake it with the nine of hearts. In desperation, South laid down the club ace, hoping East's king would fall. When it did not, he ended up with eight tricks, one short of his contract.

Had South looked ahead far enough after the opening lead of the heart jack, he would have seen the possible necessity of reaching dummy three times to take three club finesses. He could have accomplished this objective in simple fashion once he appreciated that West's lead of the jack of hearts indicated the possession of the heart ten.

The opening heart lead should have been taken by the board's ace, with South dropping the *king* on this trick! Dummy would now have the doubleton Q 9 of hearts and declarer the 6-5, so it would become a routine matter to get to dummy two more times by finessing against West's ten of hearts. South would now be assured of the opportunity of taking three club finesses, and when they succeeded, his contract would be fulfilled.

8

Which Finesse to Take?

♠ ♡ ◇ ♣

We have seen in the preceding chapters that there are "un-necessary" finesses and "necessary" ones. In some deals, declarer was confronted with two finesses, one of which was a mistake to take while the other was a necessity.

Actually, the problem of which of two finesses to take occurs often enough to warrant more than merely a passing "look-see." Therefore, this chapter on "which finesse to take." All of these deals were played in better-than-average or top-echelon games.

DEAL I

This deal is an excellent test for determining playing apti-tude. If you have some friends who are considered good players, you might ask them to take the helm on this hand from a rubber-bridge game.

Both sides vulnerable. North deals.

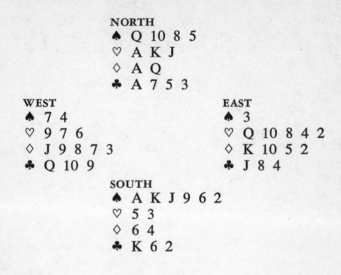

NORTH
♠ Q 10 8 5
♡ A K J
♢ A Q
♣ A 7 5 3

WEST
♠ 7 4
♡ 9 7 6
♢ J 9 8 7 3
♣ Q 10 9

EAST
♠ 3
♡ Q 10 8 4 2
♢ K 10 5 2
♣ J 8 4

SOUTH
♠ A K J 9 6 2
♡ 5 3
♢ 6 4
♣ K 6 2

The bidding:

NORTH	EAST	SOUTH	WEST
1 ♣	Pass	1 ♠	Pass
4 ♠	Pass	4 NT	Pass
5 ♠	Pass	6 ♠	Pass
Pass	Pass		

Opening lead: Seven of spades

The bidding was letter perfect. North's jump to four spades showed at least twenty points in support of spades. South, with thirteen points of his own, then employed the Blackwood Convention to find out about his partner's three aces en route to the slam.

Let us analyze the play objectively. South wins the opening trump lead and plays a second round, drawing West's last trump.

From the moment the opening lead was made, declarer had eleven top tricks.

The twelfth trick can come from one of three sources: (1) a diamond finesse; (2) a heart finesse; or (3) a 3-3 division of the six outstanding clubs, in which case dummy's fourth club will become a winner.

Declarer should disregard the club suit for the moment, since the six outstanding clubs will be divided 3-3 only a little more than one third of the time (36 percent). Thus, both the heart and the diamond finesses are available. If either one succeeds (a 75 percent chance), declarer has his twelfth trick.

That's good enough, you might say. But which finesse should be taken first? It doesn't matter, you might answer. Ah, but you're wrong! It matters very much.

Let's say that declarer took the diamond finesse first, and it happens to lose (as it would on this deal). There is then little choice but to finesse West for the queen of hearts. And when that also loses (as it does), the contract is set.

But defeat would have been entirely declarer's fault, not blamable on the lie of the cards. Declarer should have taken the heart finesse first. This would have lost to the queen. When South regained the lead at the next trick, he would cash the board's ace and king of hearts, discarding the deuce of clubs from his hand. Next would come a club to the king, a club to the ace, and a ruff of a third round of clubs. When clubs split 3-3, dummy's fourth club would be a winner, and the diamond finesse would no longer be necessary.

If clubs were not divided 3-3, then, as a last resort, declarer would still have the diamond finesse available. In short, by taking the heart finesse first, South would have enjoyed a third and winning chance at no extra cost.

DEAL II

With a superficial glance at the North-South cards in this deal, it might appear that after an opening heart lead by West, fulfilling the small slam contract depends on the king of diamonds being in the West hand. Actually, it does not, as South demonstrated in his play of the hand.

Both sides vulnerable. South deals.

                          NORTH
                          ♠ J 8 6 3
                          ♡ Q 10 8 4
                          ◇ A Q J
                          ♣ K 6

      WEST   EAST
      ♠ 9 7   ♠ 5
      ♡ 5 3 2   ♡ 9 7 6
      ◇ 9 7 6 5   ◇ K 8 4 2
      ♣ A 10 4 2   ♣ Q J 9 7 3

                          SOUTH
                          ♠ A K Q 10 4 2
                          ♡ A K J
                          ◇ 10 3
                          ♣ 8 5

The bidding:

      SOUTH   WEST   NORTH   EAST
      1 ♠   Pass   3 ♠   Pass
      6 ♠   Pass   Pass   Pass

Opening lead: Five of hearts

South's leap to six spades might be categorized as "barging into a slam." His justification was the hope that opponents would be unable to cash the first two tricks. If such were the case, South felt he would have a reasonable chance to collect twelve tricks.

Declarer won West's opening heart lead with his king and drew the opponents' trumps in two rounds. He next cashed the ace of hearts, followed by the jack of hearts, which was overtaken by dummy's queen. On the ten of hearts, South discarded his five of clubs.

Declarer reentered his hand with a trump and led his remaining club. When West went up with his ace, South had no further problem. All he had to do was discard a diamond on dummy's king of clubs.

It was a 50-50 proposition whether East or West possessed the club ace. If West held it, then everything would be fine, since dummy's king would then become declarer's twelfth trick. But if East had that card, then precautions had to be taken to avoid losing two club tricks. That is, if South had failed to discard a club on dummy's ten of hearts before leading a club, the defenders might have taken two quick club tricks.

As South played the hand, if East had the club ace, he would have taken dummy's king and returned a club, but South would have ruffed. Declarer would now still have the opportunity of making his contract if the diamond finesse succeeded.

Declarer's play of the hand gave him two 50-50 chances to fulfill his contract: if West had either the ace of clubs on the king of diamonds. And, as all who are familiar with higher mathematics know, two chances are twice as good as one.

DEAL III

In principle, when playing a suit contract, declarer normally draws the outstanding trumps as soon as he obtains the lead. However, there are many situations where the drawing of trumps must be deferred. One of these occurs when declarer simply does not know how to play the trump suit—and the answer cannot

become known until some other suit has been tested first. This
deal is a case in point.

East-West vulnerable. North deals.

```
                              NORTH
                              ♠ Q 7 4
                              ♡ A Q 3
                              ◇ K 8 7
                              ♣ A Q 6 4
        WEST                                        EAST
        ♠ K                                         ♠ 10 9 8 6
        ♡ J 10 9 7 4                                ♡ 8 2
        ◇ 10 9 5 2                                  ◇ 6 4 3
        ♣ K 8 2                                     ♣ 9 7 5 3
                              SOUTH
                              ♠ A J 5 3 2
                              ♡ K 6 5
                              ◇ A Q J
                              ♣ J 10
```

The bidding:

NORTH	EAST	SOUTH	WEST
1 NT	Pass	3 ♠	Pass
4 ♠	Pass	6 ♠	Pass
Pass	Pass		

Opening lead: Jack of hearts

When the dummy came down after West had opened the
jack of hearts, South was not overly enthusiastic about his slam
contract. He had an almost certain loser in trumps, and a 50-50
chance of losing a club.

A less-skilled declarer would probably have won the opening heart lead with the queen and led a low spade to his jack. The loss of another trump trick to East would now become unavoidable.

But our declarer saw that it would be wrong to tackle the trump suit first. An examination of the combined assets revealed that sooner or later the club finesse would have to be taken. If that lost, then he would have to finesse the jack of trumps in the hope that East had been dealt the doubleton king. However, if the club finesse won, then declarer could play the trump suit in such a manner as to minimize the danger of losing two trump tricks.

So declarer won the opening heart lead with his king and promptly led the jack of clubs. He breathed a sigh of relief when West covered with the king, for his potential club loser had just disappeared.

The four of trumps was now led off the board, and South put up his ace. When the king of trumps luckily fell on this trick, South was safely home. Eventually East made a trump trick, for the defenders' only winner. Had the trump king not fallen, declarer would have led another trump, playing for the normal 3-2 division of the five outstanding trumps.

The key play, of course, was the immediate finesse of the club suit. Once the club loser had been eliminated, declarer was able to avail himself of the safety play in the trump suit, which was designed to guard against West having the singleton king.

DEAL IV

This deal was played in a rubber-bridge game in London, England. It serves as a good illustration of expert technique in the play of a hand.

If one examines the North-South hands, there appear to be two straightforward 50-50 finesses in each of the red suits. However, by fine play, declarer put himself in the position where he was able to take one of the finesses "on the house." As a result, he fulfilled his contract without being forced to guess which finesse to take.

East-West vulnerable. North deals.

NORTH
♠ 7 6 2
♡ A 6 2
♢ A Q
♣ A Q 8 6 4

WEST
♠ Q J 10
♡ Q 10 8
♢ K 10 7 6 5 2
♣ 9

EAST
♠ 9
♡ 9 7 4
♢ J 9 8 4
♣ J 10 7 5 3

SOUTH
♠ A K 8 5 4 3
♡ K J 5 3
♢ 3
♣ K 2

The bidding:

NORTH	EAST	SOUTH	WEST
1 NT	Pass	3 ♠	Pass
4 ♠	Pass	4 NT	Pass
5 ♠	Pass	6 ♠	Pass
Pass	Pass		

Opening lead: Queen of spades

West opened the queen of trumps, won by declarer's ace. South then cashed the king of trumps, East discarding a diamond. With a certain trump loser staring him in the face. South now planned to get rid of his losing hearts on dummy's clubs (one of the hearts would be discarded on the board's queen of clubs, and the other on dummy's fifth club, assuming, of course, that the missing clubs were divided no worse than 4-2).

At trick three, the club king was played, followed by a low club, West discarding a diamond. Had West ruffed this lead, the board's ace and queen of clubs would have provided declarer with two winners, on which he would have subsequently discarded his two low hearts.

South won the second club with the ace and continued with the club queen. Many players probably would have discarded a heart on this lead. Our actual declarer, however, made a superior discard: He tossed away his singleton diamond.

The beauty of this discard quickly became apparent. If West ruffed this lead, he would have been compelled to lead either a heart or a diamond. If he chose to lead a diamond, South would finesse the board's queen "on the house." If the queen won, the slam was guaranteed; and if East had the diamond king, South would ruff and would still be able to fall back on the finesse of the jack of hearts. Had South discarded a heart on the club queen, and West, after ruffing, led a diamond, South would have to guess whether or not to finesse the queen.

However, West elected not to ruff, but this merely postponed the moment of truth. Declarer's next play was a trump, forcing West into the lead. West now had no choice but to lead a red suit. In practice, he returned a diamond. South discarded two hearts on the queen and ace of diamonds, and claimed his slam contract.

DEAL V

This deal presents a recurring situation: Declarer is faced with both a direct finesse and an indirect finesse. One of them is right, one is wrong. Our actual South declarer had no problem in finding the "right" finesse first. Even if this had lost, he would still have had the other finesse available as a last resort. But if the wrong finesse had been taken first, and it lost (as it would have), there would have been no tomorrow.

Both sides vulnerable. South deals.

NORTH
- ♠ K J
- ♡ A K 7 2
- ♢ A Q 10 8
- ♣ 6 4 3

WEST
- ♠ 9 8 7 3
- ♡ 8 5 4 3
- ♢ 5 2
- ♣ K J 10

EAST
- ♠ 6 5 2
- ♡ Q 10 9
- ♢ 9 6 4 3
- ♣ 9 8 2

SOUTH
- ♠ A Q 10 4
- ♡ J 6
- ♢ K J 7
- ♣ A Q 7 5

The bidding:

SOUTH	WEST	NORTH	EAST
1 NT	Pass	6 NT	Pass
Pass	Pass		

Opening lead: Nine of spades

The bidding was simple, direct, and to the point (no pun intended). North added his seventeen high-card points to the minimum of sixteen announced by South, and bid the small slam.

West's opening lead was the nine of spades. When the dummy came into view, South counted eleven top tricks. A successful club finesse would yield his twelfth trick. However, he recognized also that if the club finesse lost, there would be no other chance of making his slam-going trick (unless one of the opponents had been dealt the singleton queen of hearts).

On closer scrutiny, declarer saw another possibility for the twelfth trick, a possibility that did not preclude taking the club finesse if it became necessary to do so.

After taking West's opening lead of the spade nine with dummy's king, declarer led the deuce of hearts off the board. East, quite naturally, won the trick with his queen. Declarer now spread his hand and claimed his slam: four spades, three hearts, four diamonds, and one club.

As South played the hand (by taking the indirect finesse first), he had two 50-50 chances going for him: (1) that East had the heart queen, which would promote South's jack to winning rank; (2) if that possibility failed to materialize, there would be available the 50-50 chance offered by the club finesse.

If declarer elected to take the club finesse first, and it lost (as it would have), he would have been unable to attack the heart suit without giving the defenders the setting trick.

DEAL VI

In virtually all finessing situations, a finesse is taken in the hope that it will win. On occasion, however, a finesse is taken with the fervent hope that it will lose.

This deal is the story of two finesses, one of which declarer was rooting for to win, and the other to lose. Although only half of his wishes materialized, the story had a happy ending.

Both sides vulnerable. South deals.

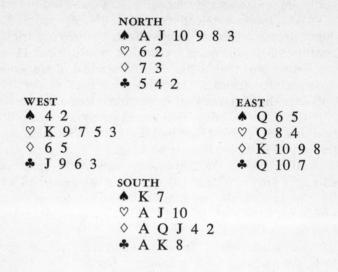

NORTH
♠ A J 10 9 8 3
♡ 6 2
◇ 7 3
♣ 5 4 2

WEST
♠ 4 2
♡ K 9 7 5 3
◇ 6 5
♣ J 9 6 3

EAST
♠ Q 6 5
♡ Q 8 4
◇ K 10 9 8
♣ Q 10 7

SOUTH
♠ K 7
♡ A J 10
◇ A Q J 4 2
♣ A K 8

The bidding:

SOUTH	WEST	NORTH	EAST
2 NT	Pass	3 ♠	Pass
3 NT	Pass	Pass	Pass

Opening lead: Five of hearts

On West's opening lead of the five of hearts, East put up the queen and South took his ace. The seven of spades was led next, and when West followed with a low spade, dummy's jack was inserted. South would have liked nothing better than to have the finesse lose. Had this happened, declarer would have been able to make five spade tricks by overtaking his own king with dummy's ace.

But East allowed the jack to win the trick! It was a nice bit of thinking on his part. He was sure South possessed the king of spades for his two no-trump opening bid. And, reasoned East, if South had the K x x of spades, he would have led the king first. So, concluded East, South wanted to give the jack away to establish the board's spade suit. East was not about to oblige him.

Thwarted with this plan, South then led a diamond off dummy and finessed his queen. This finesse he wanted to win. When the queen held the trick, he led his king of spades and overtook it with the board's ace. When the queen of spades did not drop, another diamond was led off the board, and South successfully finessed the jack.

Nine tricks were now in the bag, whether declarer surrendered the jack of hearts to West's king or established his fifth diamond. Declarer chose to lead the diamond ace, hoping, of course, that he might catch East's king. When this did not materialize, he conceded a fourth diamond to East. East then cashed the spade queen, after which he returned a heart. Thus, declarer made an overtrick.

Declarer played the hand very well. Either of two alternatives would have failed. One was to cash the king and ace of spades, hoping that one of the opponents had been dealt the doubleton Q x. The other alternative was to first cash the king of spades and then finesse West for the queen, hoping he had been dealt the tripleton Q x x. But South, who had once been a dairy farmer, had learned not to put all his eggs into one basket.

DEAL VII

In this deal, declarer was confronted with the problem of which of *three* finesses to take (in one of the finessing suits, he had an option of which of two finesses to take). In retrospect, whichever of the three finesses he elected to take would have lost. Nevertheless, there was a "right" finesse and a "wrong" finesse—and our declarer found the "right" one.

Both sides vulnerable. South deals.

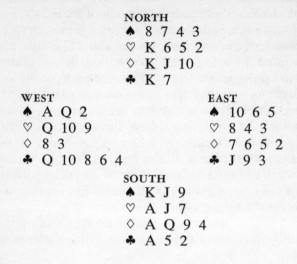

                              NORTH
                              ♠ 8 7 4 3
                              ♡ K 6 5 2
                              ◇ K J 10
                              ♣ K 7
            WEST   EAST
            ♠ A Q 2   ♠ 10 6 5
            ♡ Q 10 9   ♡ 8 4 3
            ◇ 8 3   ◇ 7 6 5 2
            ♣ Q 10 8 6 4   ♣ J 9 3
                              SOUTH
                              ♠ K J 9
                              ♡ A J 7
                              ◇ A Q 9 4
                              ♣ A 5 2

The bidding:

SOUTH	WEST	NORTH	EAST
1 ◇	Pass	1 ♡	Pass
2 NT	Pass	3 NT	Pass
Pass	Pass		

Opening lead: Six of clubs

On West's opening lead of the club six, the seven was played
from dummy, East put up the jack, and South permitted East to
hold the trick. A club was returned, taken by dummy's king.

From the moment that the opening lead was made, South
could count eight top tricks. He could make his ninth from any
of three sources: (1) he could finesse the jack of hearts, (2) he
could lead a spade to his jack in the hope that this would win or
drive out the ace, or (3) he could lead a spade to his king, playing
East for the ace.

Of course, declarer was fully aware that if he took the heart finesse and it lost, West would return a club to establish that suit for his side. West's club suit would also become established if South took the spade finesse and either (1) the jack lost to the queen or (2) the king lost to the ace. In these three situations, if West subsequently regained the lead, South would be at his mercy.

At trick three, a low heart was led off dummy and declarer finessed his jack, which lost to West's queen. West returned a club, South's ace winning, as a spade was discarded from dummy.

After cashing four diamond tricks (another spade was thrown from dummy on the fourth diamond), South laid down his ace of hearts. Next came South's remaining heart to dummy's king. When both of the opponents followed suit, dummy's thirteenth heart became declarer's game-going trick.

Why did South choose to take the 50-50 heart finesse rather than either of the two possible finesses in the spade suit? For two reasons: The heart finesse offered something extra in that if it lost, the board's fourth heart might develop into a winner. The spade suit offered no such extra chance. In addition, if the hearts did not break, declarer would still have one last hope. When he won his eighth trick with the king of hearts, he could lead a spade off dummy. If East had the ace of spades and no more clubs, South could not have been prevented from making his spade king at the end.

DEAL VIII

In the final deal of this chapter, another illustration is presented on how the bidding by the defenders steered declarer to the winning line of play. Had our defender not made his bid (a penalty double), South almost surely would have failed to fulfill his contract.

This deal also illustrates that there are many occasions in bridge when one must be content with a minimum profit rather than attempt to secure the maximum. This approach becomes ingrained after sad and bitter experiences, when the quest for the maximum profit results in destruction.

North-South vulnerable. South deals.

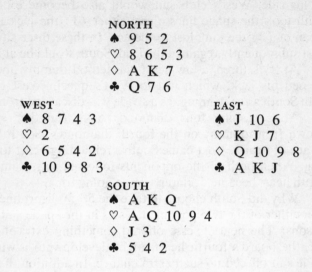

NORTH
♠ 9 5 2
♡ 8 6 5 3
◇ A K 7
♣ Q 7 6

WEST
♠ 8 7 4 3
♡ 2
◇ 6 5 4 2
♣ 10 9 8 3

EAST
♠ J 10 6
♡ K J 7
◇ Q 10 9 8
♣ A K J

SOUTH
♠ A K Q
♡ A Q 10 9 4
◇ J 3
♣ 5 4 2

The bidding:

SOUTH	WEST	NORTH	EAST
1 ♡	Pass	2 ♡	Pass
3 ♡	Pass	4 ♡	Double
Pass	Pass	Pass	

Opening lead: Ten of clubs

West opened the ten of clubs, and East promptly cashed
three club tricks. He then shifted to the jack of spades, which
South won with the queen. Dummy was entered via the diamond
ace, and the eight of trumps was led. When East followed suit
with the seven, South played the four. As can be observed, the
eight won the trick.

A second trump lead fetched East's jack and South's queen,
and the ace of trumps picked up East's king. Declarer now

chalked up 990 points: 700 for the rubber, 240 for the doubled trick score, and 50 as an "insult" bonus for fulfilling a doubled contract.

Full "credit" for the fulfillment of declarer's game contract can be placed squarely on East's shoulders. Whether he doubled the four heart contract because he did not like the sound of the North-South bidding or because he wanted to pick up an extra 100 points is, frankly, conjectural. But I would venture a guess that his fifteen high-card points made him feel that he had a sure thing—and he probably never gave even a passing thought that perhaps his double might guide declarer to the winning line of play.

Had East not doubled, declarer would have had to be clairvoyant to diagnose the position of the missing trumps. In all probability, he would have made the normal play of leading a low trump off the dummy and finessing his queen (hoping East had been dealt either the K x or the K x x of hearts). The queen, in this case, would have won the trick, but East would still retain the K J, and a sure trump trick.

But when East made his double, he just about told declarer where the outstanding high trumps were located. And so instead of gaining 100 points, East-West lost 990.

9

Which Way to Finesse?

♠   ♡   ◇   ♣

Mathematically speaking, a finesse is strictly a 50-50 proposition. At the bridge table, however, there are almost always clues divulged in either the bidding or play that point to one defender, rather than the other, having some key card. And these clues, in the hands of an expert, point the way to taking a successful finesse.

Each of the declarers of the deals that comprise this chapter was confronted with the problem of "which way to finesse for a specific queen or jack." In nine of the hands, the winning solution was based on a complete or partial clue. In the remainder of the deals, declarer failed to find the clue that would have snatched victory from the jaws of defeat.

DEAL I

This deal is "as old as the hills," and is employed by just about every bridge teacher in the world to check the "counting-out-of-a-hand" aptitude of their pupils. It came up in a rubber-bridge game in the early 1930's.

Both sides vulnerable. South deals.

NORTH
♠ K Q 3
♡ K Q 7 5
◇ K 10 9
♣ Q J 4

WEST
♠ 8 4 2
♡ 6 4 3
◇ 7
♣ 10 9 8 6 5 2

EAST
♠ 9 7 6 5
♡ 10 8
◇ Q 8 6 5 3 2
♣ 7

SOUTH
♠ A J 10
♡ A J 9 2
◇ A J 4
♣ A K 3

The bidding:

SOUTH	WEST	NORTH	EAST
2 NT	Pass	7 NT	Pass
Pass	Pass		

Opening lead: Ten of clubs

Despite the fact that the North-South hands contain only twelve winners, the bidding was quite sound. It will not happen once in a thousand times that a partnership, possessing thirty-eight high-card points, does not have thirteen tricks "off the top." Thus, from North's point of view, he was looking at sixteen high-card points opposite a partner who had guaranteed a minimum of twenty-two. Hence his direct leap to seven no-trump.

West opened the ten of clubs, and when dummy came into view, it was rather obvious to declarer that his thirteenth trick could come only from the diamond suit. His sole problem was determining whether East or West had the queen of diamonds.

Since the fate of the deal depends on which opponent declarer finesses for the diamond queen—a 50-50 proposition at trick one—declarer should save the finesse until the end, by which time he might have gathered some significant information as to the location of that vital card.

South won the opening club lead with his king and cashed the ace of clubs. On this trick, East discarded the deuce of diamonds—and South had his first bit of practical information: West was known to have been dealt six clubs.

South now focused his attention on an attempt to reconstruct the remainder of West's thirteen cards. The ace, king, and queen of spades were cashed next, and West followed suit to all three spade leads. West was now known to have started with six clubs and three spades.

Then come the king, queen, and ace of hearts, and again West followed to all three leads. South now knew that West was dealt six clubs, three spades, and three hearts. At most, he could have only one diamond.

South next led a diamond to dummy's king. When West followed suit with the seven of diamonds, his hand had become an open book: All of his original thirteen cards were known—and the diamond queen was not one of them.

So declarer then played a diamond to his jack with the absolute assurance that it would win the trick. When it did, South chalked up the score for a vulnerable grand slam, bid and made.

DEAL II

An inexperienced South was at the controls in this deal, and either through inertia, inability, or a reluctance to "waste time," he failed to gather in the evidence that would have enabled him to fulfill a slam contract.

Neither side vulnerable. South deals.

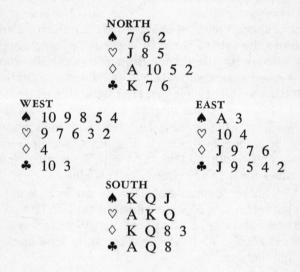

NORTH
♠ 7 6 2
♡ J 8 5
◊ A 10 5 2
♣ K 7 6

WEST
♠ 10 9 8 5 4
♡ 9 7 6 3 2
◊ 4
♣ 10 3

EAST
♠ A 3
♡ 10 4
◊ J 9 7 6
♣ J 9 5 4 2

SOUTH
♠ K Q J
♡ A K Q
◊ K Q 8 3
♣ A Q 8

The bidding:

SOUTH	WEST	NORTH	EAST
3 NT	Pass	6 NT	Pass
Pass	Pass		

Opening lead: Ten of spades

East won the opening spade lead with his ace and returned a spade, South's king winning the trick. A count of declarer's assets revealed that he had eleven top winners—and the twelfth figured to be a cinch, since the five outstanding diamonds rated to be divided 3-2.

So, without studying the situation any further, declarer laid down his diamond king and queen. When West discarded a spade, the slam was doomed because there was no longer any way to make four diamond tricks. South was in too great a hurry to test the diamonds. Had he played the hand correctly, he would have discovered that the normal play in the diamond suit had to fail.

After winning East's spade return at trick two, declarer should have cashed the spade Queen. When East failed to follow suit to the third spade lead, West would be known to have five spades.

Next would come the ace, king, and queen of hearts, East discarding on the third heart lead. Declarer would now know that West had both five spades and five hearts. To complete his count of West's hand, declarer should then play the ace and queen of clubs, noting that West followed suit to both leads. Thus, it would become obvious that West had, at most, one diamond.

A diamond would then be led to the board's ace, West following suit with the four. All of West's original thirteen cards would now be accounted for—and, simultaneously, it would be absolutely certain that East had the tripleton J 9 7 of diamonds remaining.

The ten of diamonds would be led next, East covering with the jack and South winning with the queen. Dummy would be reentered via the club king, and a third diamond led. Since East's remaining diamonds would be the 9 7, while declarer had the K 8, South could not now be prevented from making two more diamond tricks—and his slam contract.

DEAL III

It is my feeling that Mr. Average Player, had he been sitting in the South seat, might well have gone down in this slam contract by misguessing the location of a vital queen. The actual South

declarer had no such problem in his play, for he ascertained with
absolute certainty where the queen was located.

Both sides vulnerable. South deals.

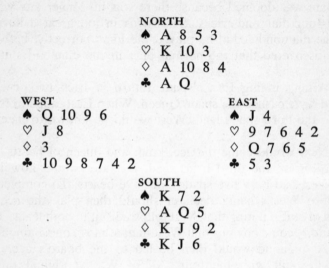

NORTH
♠ A 8 5 3
♡ K 10 3
◊ A 10 8 4
♣ A Q

WEST
♠ Q 10 9 6
♡ J 8
◊ 3
♣ 10 9 8 7 4 2

EAST
♠ J 4
♡ 9 7 6 4 2
◊ Q 7 6 5
♣ 5 3

SOUTH
♠ K 7 2
♡ A Q 5
◊ K J 9 2
♣ K J 6

The bidding:

SOUTH	WEST	NORTH	EAST
1 NT	Pass	6 NT	Pass
Pass	Pass		

Opening lead: Ten of clubs

After winning the opening lead with dummy's ace of clubs,
South counted ten top tricks. If he could determine which opponent possessed the queen of diamonds, it would become a
routine matter to finesse against that card and bring home four
diamond tricks.

In an attempt to get a count of the defenders' distribution, declarer led a low spade off dummy at trick two. When East followed with the four, South inserted his seven-spot.

West won with the nine and made the safe exit of a club, dummy winning the trick with the queen. The ace of spades was cashed next, followed by a spade to South's king. When East discarded a heart on the spade lead, West was known to have started with four spades.

South now cashed his king of clubs, discarding dummy's remaining spade, as East let go of another low heart. At this point, things started to shape up, for West was known to have started with six clubs and four spades. The hand became an open book when declarer next cashed his king, ace, and queen of hearts and West discarded a club on the third lead.

South's "count" was now complete. West had been dealt exactly four spades, six clubs, and two hearts. The diamond suit had been isolated: West had started with just one diamond.

The deuce of diamonds was then led to the board's ace, West following suit with the three. All of West's original thirteen cards were now known to South—and the queen of diamonds was not one of them. Hence, East had to harbor the diamond queen.

After winning the diamond lead with the board's ace, declarer returned the ten of diamonds, and when East followed suit with the six, inserted his nine. The ten won as it had to, and a third diamond lead off dummy allowed South to finesse his jack successfully. Thus, South made two spade tricks, three hearts, four diamonds, and three clubs. In all systems of mathematics, this added up to twelve tricks.

DEAL IV

After the first three tricks had been played, it appeared that the success of South's contract depended purely and simply on a straightforward finesse. But initial appearances can sometimes be quite deceiving, as our expert South declarer demonstrated in his play. The deal arose in a top-flight, high-stake rubber-bridge game.

Both sides vulnerable. South deals.

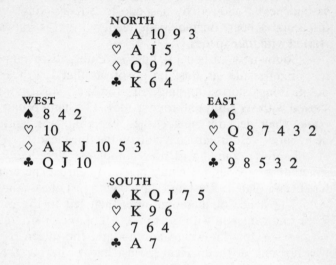

NORTH
♠ A 10 9 3
♡ A J 5
◇ Q 9 2
♣ K 6 4

WEST
♠ 8 4 2
♡ 10
◇ A K J 10 5 3
♣ Q J 10

EAST
♠ 6
♡ Q 8 7 4 3 2
◇ 8
♣ 9 8 5 3 2

SOUTH
♠ K Q J 7 5
♡ K 9 6
◇ 7 6 4
♣ A 7

The bidding:

SOUTH	WEST	NORTH	EAST
1 ♠	2 ◇	3 ♠	Pass
4 ♠	Pass	Pass	Pass

Opening lead: King of diamonds

West cashed the king and ace of diamonds, then led a third round for partner to ruff. East exited with a club, South winning the trick with his ace. Declarer now paused to examine the layout.

If one were to look at the North-South cards only, it would appear the success of South's contract depended on a finesse through West for the queen of hearts. Actually, if it came to this, South had no violent objection to finessing, since it did offer him a 50-50 chance. When play had ended, however, declarer had fulfilled his contract without resorting to this particular finesse.

After capturing the club return with his ace, South drew the outstanding trumps in three rounds. Then he led a club to dummy's king and ruffed dummy's remaining club. And, once again, he paused for reflection.

Since East had failed to follow to the second diamond lead, West was known to have started with six diamonds. And West had followed suit to both three trump leads and three club leads. So West possessed, at most, one heart. Hence, the thought of finessing West for the queen of hearts had to be eliminated from consideration.

The only chance was that West had either a singleton queen or ten of hearts. So South led a heart to the ace, sighing with relief when West followed with the ten. The five of hearts was played back. East followed with a low heart and South confidently inserted the nine-spot, which, of course, won the trick.

This deal, in my opinion, illustrates quite clearly one of the predominant attributes of the expert: his appreciation that no hand is ever to be played mechanically. From this attitude develops the ability to salvage many games and slams that would otherwise be lost.

DEAL V

When contract bridge was in its infancy some four decades ago, the technique of counting out a hand was considered too difficult for the average player to absorb, and was reserved for those in the expert class. But, in the words of Tennyson, just as "the old order changeth, yielding place to new," so counting out a hand is now a part of the public domain.

In each of the four preceding deals of this chapter, the theme was counting out a hand, by which is meant the attempt to reconstruct the original suit distribution of the opponents'

cards. Usually the purpose of such counting is to locate a missing
key card.

In this deal, we have another illustration of "counting." The
hand came up in the Vanderbilt Cup Championships of 1968.

North-South vulnerable. East deals.

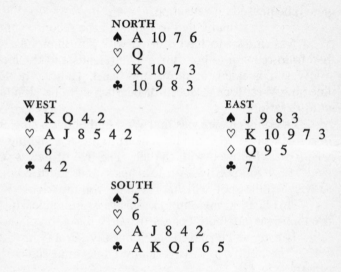

NORTH
♠ A 10 7 6
♡ Q
◇ K 10 7 3
♣ 10 9 8 3

WEST
♠ K Q 4 2
♡ A J 8 5 4 2
◇ 6
♣ 4 2

EAST
♠ J 9 8 3
♡ K 10 9 7 3
◇ Q 9 5
♣ 7

SOUTH
♠ 5
♡ 6
◇ A J 8 4 2
♣ A K Q J 6 5

The bidding:

EAST	SOUTH	WEST	NORTH
Pass	1 ♣	1 ♡	1 ♠
3 ♡	5 ♣	Pass	6 ♣
Pass	Pass	Pass	

Opening lead: King of spades

West's opening lead of the spade king was won by dummy's
ace, after which declarer ruffed a spade with the jack of trumps.

The North hand was entered via the club ten, and spade was ruffed with the club queen. Dummy was entered once again, via the club nine, and its last spade was ruffed in the closed hand. Declarer now took a time out to study the situation at hand.

From the very beginning, it was quite apparent that the success of South's slam contract was going to depend on his play of the diamond suit: to cash the ace and king, hoping to catch the queen, or to finesse either East or West for the diamond queen?

West was known to have started with exactly four spades, since both he and East had followed suit to four spade leads. West had also shown up with two clubs. After some thought, declarer concluded that West probably had six hearts rather than five for his overcall, since if East had six hearts he probably would have bid four hearts (not vulnerable) instead of three hearts.

And so, proceeding on the assumption that West held six hearts, four spades, and two clubs for a total of twelve cards, it did not require a tremendous knowledge of mathematics to figure out that West would therefore have just one diamond. Declarer led a diamond to dummy's king, then played the diamond ten and finessed against East's (presumed) queen. As can be observed, the ten won the trick. The ace of diamonds felled the queen, and that was that. Actually, declarer made an overtrick, for on his fifth diamond he was able to discard dummy's queen of hearts. But that was simply a bonus for a well-played hand.

DEAL VI

Ingrained in every expert's thoughts is the appreciation that on each deal he must give consideration to counting out the opponents' cards. Admittedly, in a large proportion of deals, it will be impossible to obtain any count of the hands. And also, on many deals, the count will turn out to be only a partial one. Yet, even in these "partial" situations, the expert will frequently unearth a line of play that gives him an edge that a noncounting player would not have.

In this deal, only a partial count of a defender's hand was obtained. But it was sufficient to enable declarer to come up with the winning "percentage" play. The reader will note the similarity between this deal and Deal 10 of Chapter 6.

East-West vulnerable. South deals.

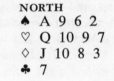

NORTH
♠ A 9 6 2
♡ Q 10 9 7
◇ J 10 8 3
♣ 7

WEST
♠ 7
♡ 8 5
◇ A K 6 2
♣ K Q 10 9 8 2

EAST
♠ Q 5 4 3
♡ 6 4 2
◇ 9 5
♣ J 6 4 3

SOUTH
♠ K J 10 8
♡ A K J 3
◇ Q 7 4
♣ A 5

The bidding:

SOUTH	WEST	NORTH	EAST
1 ♠	2 ♣	2 ♠	Pass
3 ♡	Pass	4 ♡	Pass
Pass	Pass		

Opening lead: King of diamonds

On West's opening lead of the diamond king, East initiated a high-low signal by dropping the nine. West dutifully continued with the ace of diamonds and a third round was ruffed by East.

East exited with a club to South's ace. Trumps were drawn in three rounds, after which came a pause for deliberation and counting. The purpose of the reflection was, of course, to ascertain if any clues could be put together that might guide declarer in determining which way to finesse for the queen of spades.

Since East had ruffed the third diamond lead, West was known to have started with four diamonds. West had also followed suit to two trump leads. And since West had made a vulnerable two club overcall, he certainly had at least a five-card suit, and in all probability six of the suit. That left room in his hand for a theoretical maximum of two spades. Since East had started with more spades than West, East rather than West figured to possess the queen of spades.

So South led the jack of spades to dummy's ace, West following suit. The nine of spades was then returned. East played the four-spot, and South followed suit with the eight. A third spade allowed declarer to finesse his ten, and all that remained to do was to ruff a club in dummy and claim ten tricks.

DEAL VII

This deal occurred in a team-of-four match. Both South declarers arrived at the identical game contract, via the same sequence of bidding, and both fulfilled this contract by "guessing" the location of the queen of trumps. In the post-mortem discussion of the hand, each South declarer pointed out that there really was no guess as to how to play the trump suit, for the "correct play was automatic."

To the objective observer, a trace of vanity might have been detected in their voices. If it were there, I, for one, would excuse it, for they had every reason to be proud of their analysis.

Neither side vulnerable. North deals.

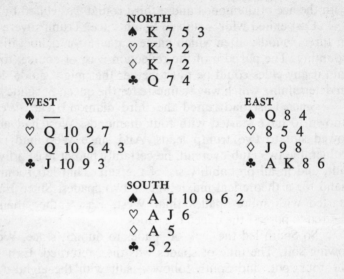

NORTH
♠ K 7 5 3
♡ K 3 2
◇ K 7 2
♣ Q 7 4

WEST
♠ —
♡ Q 10 9 7
◇ Q 10 6 4 3
♣ J 10 9 3

EAST
♠ Q 8 4
♡ 8 5 4
◇ J 9 8
♣ A K 8 6

SOUTH
♠ A J 10 9 6 2
♡ A J 6
◇ A 5
♣ 5 2

The bidding:

NORTH	EAST	SOUTH	WEST
Pass	Pass	1 ♠	Pass
3 ♠	Pass	4 ♠	Pass
Pass	Pass		

Opening lead: Jack of clubs

North's jump to three spades on his 4 3 3 3 hand was a slight
overbid, despite the fact he had passed originally. But, then, he
was not permitted to bid 2½ spades, which is what he would have
liked to do.

West opened the jack of clubs, which won the trick when
everybody followed suit with low clubs. He then continued with
the club ten, which also won, and a third club that was ruffed by
South.

A trump was next played to dummy's king. When West failed to follow suit to this lead, it became a routine matter to finesse East for the marked queen. Declarer eventually lost a heart trick to West, but the game contract was fulfilled.

It should be noted that had declarer led the trump ace first, the contract would have been defeated, since the loss of both a trump trick and a heart would now have been unavoidable.

On the face of it, it appears to be a pure guess as to which of the opponents might have the three outstanding trumps (and it is highly unlikely that either does). But, actually, no guess is necessary.

Let's suppose that when declarer led a trump to dummy's king, *East* had failed to follow suit. West would now have a sure trump trick. South would proceed by cashing the ace of trumps, the ace of diamonds, and dummy's diamond king, followed by a ruff of the board's remaining diamond.

West would then be put on lead with his trump queen—and would be end-played. If he led either a club or a diamond, declarer would ruff in dummy while tossing away the losing heart from his own hand. And if West returned a heart instead, South's jack would become a winner. Thus, the initial lead of a low trump from the South hand could not be a losing play regardless of which hand held the trump queen.

DEAL VIII

It has always been a moot question—even amongst experts —as to whether, in the long run, the bidding by the eventual defending pair is more beneficial to the defenders or to the declarer.

Unquestionably, defensive bidding very often paves the way to winning defense; without it, they would be groping in the dark. Yet, quite frequently, the opponents' bidding guides declarer to a successful line of play that would not have been found had the defenders remained quiet.

In this deal, the bidding of the West defender virtually told declarer how to play the hand. Declarer listened and obeyed.

Both sides vulnerable. South deals.

NORTH
♠ 8 6 5 3
♡ J 7
◊ 8 7 3
♣ K Q J 2

WEST
♠ K Q 7
♡ K 10 5 3
◊ Q J 9 6 2
♣ 6

EAST
♠ J 10 2
♡ 9 8 4
◊ A K 10 5 4
♣ 8 4

SOUTH
♠ A 9 4
♡ A Q 6 2
◊ —
♣ A 10 9 7 5 3

The bidding:

SOUTH	WEST	NORTH	EAST
1 ♣	1 ◊	2 ♣	3 ◊
3 ♡	Pass	4 ♣	Pass
5 ♣	Pass	Pass	Pass

Opening lead: Queen of diamonds

Had West hit upon a spade opening, declarer would have gone down, losing two spade tricks and one heart. But in view of East's support of diamonds, West elected to play it safe by opening the queen of diamonds.

Declarer ruffed West's lead, then looked over the lay of the land. Considering West's lead, East was marked with the ace and king of diamonds—West would not have led the queen from either K Q or A Q.

Since West had made a vulnerable overcall on a queen-high suit, and had no strength whatsoever in clubs, he figured to have strength in the major suits. In all probability, deduced South, West possessed the heart king.

At trick two, South played a trump to dummy's king and a trump to his ace. He then led a heart toward the board's jack. West took his king and shifted—belatedly—to the spade king. Declarer won the trick with his ace, led a low heart to dummy's jack, and ruffed a diamond. On the ace and queen of hearts, two of dummy's spades were discarded.

It was now a routine matter for declarer to concede a spade trick and subsequently ruff his third spade in dummy. His only losers were a spade and a heart.

Had West not overcalled, declarer would have had a tough guess as to whether to play the heart suit as he actually did (by taking an indirect finesse), or to lead a heart off dummy and take a direct finesse (hoping that East had been dealt the king of hearts). Unfortunately for the defenders, West's overcall steered South to the winning path.

DEAL IX

It is an extremely rare case when, at trick two, a declarer must determine which of his opponents possesses the ace of trumps. In this deal, declarer was confronted with this problem. And when he resolved it, his play of the hand became a routine affair.

Both sides vulnerable. East deals.

NORTH
♠ Q 9 6 2
♡ K J 10
♢ K J 9 4
♣ A 6

WEST   EAST
♠ —   ♠ A 10 8 4
♡ 9 7 5 4 3 2   ♡ A 6
♢ 8 5 3   ♢ 7 2
♣ 9 7 4 2   ♣ K Q 10 8 3

SOUTH
♠ K J 7 5 3
♡ Q 8
♢ A Q 10 6
♣ J 5

The bidding:

EAST	SOUTH	WEST	NORTH
1 ♣	1 ♠	Pass	4 ♠
Pass	Pass	Pass	

Opening lead: Two of clubs

West's deuce of clubs opening lead was taken by dummy's ace, after which declarer paused for reflection. An examination of his assets revealed that a minimum of three tricks would have to be lost: a trump, a heart, and a club. And, viewing his possibilities pessimistically, declarer recognized that if one of the opponents happened to have the four outstanding trumps, a second trump trick might also be lost.

Since one of the four outstanding trumps was the ace, it would not be illogical to state that if either of the opponents happened to possess all four of the outstanding trumps, it would be the one who possessed the ace. As South viewed his hand and the dummy, which between them contained twenty-seven high-card points, he concluded that East just about had to have the spade ace. Without it, he would not have had the slightest semblance of an opening bid.

And so, at trick two, South played dummy's queen of trumps, East's ace winning as West discarded a heart. East cashed his king of clubs and ace of hearts, then led a diamond, which was won in dummy.

The nine of trumps was led; East covered with the ten and South won with the jack. Dummy was reentered via the heart king, and the six of trumps was played. East, with the 8 4 remaining in front of South's K 7, could not prevent South from bringing home the trump suit.

It should be noted that had declarer, at trick two, led a low trump off dummy instead of the queen, and put up his jack when East followed with the four-spot, he would have lost two trump tricks and his contract. East, with the A 10 8 of trumps remaining, would now have two certain trump winners.

Admittedly, the four outstanding trumps did not figure to be divided 4-0; and had they been divided either 3-1 or 2-2, any South declarer would have fulfilled his contract whether he led a low trump or the queen off dummy at trick two. Thus, once again, it is apparent how important a pessimistic approach can be if one hopes to be a winner.

DEAL X

There is no sure way of playing the majority of deals to guarantee the fulfillment of the contract. Nevertheless, in virtually every deal, there is a superior line of play available, and one or more inferior lines of play. This deal, which occurred in a rubber-bridge game, illustrates this theme.

Both sides vulnerable. South deals.

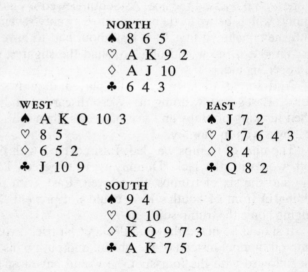

```
                        NORTH
                        ♠ 8 6 5
                        ♡ A K 9 2
                        ◊ A J 10
                        ♣ 6 4 3
        WEST                                EAST
        ♠ A K Q 10 3                        ♠ J 7 2
        ♡ 8 5                               ♡ J 7 6 4 3
        ◊ 6 5 2                             ◊ 8 4
        ♣ J 10 9                            ♣ Q 8 2
                        SOUTH
                        ♠ 9 4
                        ♡ Q 10
                        ◊ K Q 9 7 3
                        ♣ A K 7 5
```

The bidding:

SOUTH	WEST	NORTH	EAST
1 ◊	1 ♠	2 ♡	Pass
3 ♣	Pass	4 ◊	Pass
5 ◊	Pass	Pass	Pass

Opening lead: King of spades

West won the first two tricks with the king and ace of spades, and South ruffed the third round of spades. Declarer next cashed the king and ace of trumps, noting East's play of the eight-spot on the second trump lead. He then pushed his chair back a bit and paused to contemplate.

In order to fulfill his contract, South had to bring home four heart tricks (so that he could discard his two losing clubs). To play the queen, king, and ace of hearts, hoping that one of the defenders had been dealt the tripleton J x x, was definitely against the odds. But if declarer could guess which way to finesse against the jack of hearts, he could guarantee four heart tricks. The question was whether to finesse East or West.

West's spade overcall, combined with the fall of East's spade jack on the third round of that suit, indicated that West figured to have started with five spades. And East's play of the trump eight on the second trump lead suggested that East had no more trumps.

Thus, eight of West's original thirteen cards were "known": five spades and three trumps. Five of East's cards were known: three spades and two trumps. East had eight unknown cards, while West had five unknown cards. Thus, the jack of hearts rated to be in East's hand, rather than West's.

So, at trick six, a low heart was led off dummy, and declarer finessed his ten. As is evident, it won the trick. After cashing the queen of hearts, declarer entered dummy via the jack of trumps (picking up West's remaining trump en route) and discarded his two losing clubs on the ace and king of hearts.

DEAL XI

The final deal of this chapter is a tough one. As a change of pace, I would like to present it as a bridge "mystery." You are to serve as both judge and jury. Your task is to determine whether South was guilty or not guilty of "conduct unbecoming an expert" in his play of the slam contract.

North-South vulnerable. South deals.

NORTH
♠ A 10 7 4 3
♡ A J 9 2
♢ Q
♣ A 6 3

WEST
♠ —
♡ Q 7 6
♢ 9 8 7 4 3
♣ K Q J 9 2

EAST
♠ J 9 8 5
♡ 4
♢ K J 10 2
♣ 10 8 7 5

SOUTH
♠ K Q 6 2
♡ K 10 8 5 3
♢ A 6 5
♣ 4

The bidding:

SOUTH	WEST	NORTH	EAST
1 ♡	Pass	2 ♠	Pass
3 ♠	Pass	4 NT	Pass
5 ♢	Pass	6 ♡	Pass
Pass	Pass		

Opening lead: King of clubs

West's opening lead of the king of clubs was captured by the board's ace. South cashed the trump ace and led a heart to his king, as East discarded a club. Declarer then laid down his king of spades—and West ruffed. Eventually, South had to lose a trick to East's jack of spades, to incur a one-trick set. As the score was being recorded, South commented: "If I had known that West had no spades, I would have finessed him for the queen of hearts."

South was correct in his statement. If West had no spades, he would probably be long in hearts, and therefore would be more likely to possess the queen of hearts than East. Did South commit any wrongdoing in his play of the hand?

On the evidence, no judge or jury would convict South of any transgression. And yet, a lingering doubt persists that perhaps South should have fulfilled the slam.

First, it should be pointed out that if the heart suit were taken out of context, it would be a pure guess as to how to play it to avoid losing a heart trick. On this point, South would be adjudged "not guilty" for his initial lead of the trump ace.

Since he could afford to misguess the hearts, South's only worry on the hand should have been that East had the four missing spades (if West had them, South would be able to bring home the entire suit by finessing against West's jack). Therefore should not South have *assumed*—pessimistically—that East had the four missing spades? And, if such were the case, did not West, rather than East, figure to have the trump queen?

In this light, should not South have led a trump to his king at trick two, then returned a trump to dummy's jack? The trump ace would have felled the queen, and South's only loser would have been a spade trick to East's jack.

Was South guilty or not? And if guilty, of what?

10

The Defenders Thwart the Finesser

♠   ♡   ◇   ♣

This chapter presents ten deals in which the key issue was a finessing situation. These deals feature defensive techniques, stratagems, and bits of chicanery which either (1) "talked" declarer into taking a losing finesse, (2) *forced* him to take a losing finesse, (3) prevented him from taking a winning finesse, or (4) created in declarer's mind the conviction that a mirage was a reality. In each deal, the contract was defeated, and the defenders should be saluted with a "Well done!" for their excellent, imaginative defense.

DEAL I

This deal, and the four that follow, are concerned with different types of *falsecards* that were employed by the defenders. A falsecard is the play of a card, by either a defender or the declarer, *with the deliberate intention of deceiving or misleading his opponent*. The falsecard can be a very potent weapon if applied judiciously, but a very dangerous one if used indiscriminately.

This is especially true for a defender. Where the falsecard is apt to mislead partner, it can develop into a Frankenstein monster (although, as will be observed, on occasion it can be used in practical fashion to *deliberately* mislead partner). But where it will tend to deceive only declarer, it can become a most effective tool.

Declarer can falsecard to his heart's content, since his partner is a non-participant and it does not matter if he is deceived.

In this deal, a defender came up with a neat bit of falsecarding that achieved the desired effect.

Both sides vulnerable. East deals.

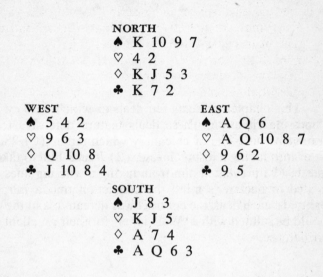

NORTH
♠ K 10 9 7
♡ 4 2
♢ K J 5 3
♣ K 7 2

WEST
♠ 5 4 2
♡ 9 6 3
♢ Q 10 8
♣ J 10 8 4

EAST
♠ A Q 6
♡ A Q 10 8 7
♢ 9 6 2
♣ 9 5

SOUTH
♠ J 8 3
♡ K J 5
♢ A 7 4
♣ A Q 6 3

The bidding:

EAST	SOUTH	WEST	NORTH
1 ♡	Double	Pass	2 ♠
Pass	2 NT	Pass	3 NT
Pass	Pass	Pass	

Opening lead: Three of hearts

West's opening heart lead was taken by East's ace, and the seven of hearts was played back, South's jack winning. Hoping that West had been dealt the spade queen, declarer played his jack of spades and let it ride. East calmly won the trick with his *ace!* He then returned a heart, driving out South's king and establishing his heart suit.

South was now convinced that West had the spade queen, so he led another spade and inserted dummy's ten-spot. Great was his dismay when East produced the queen and rattled off two more heart tricks to put the contract down one.

Had East won the first spade trick with his queen—the normal play—declarer would have been *forced* to fulfill his contract. He would abandon the spade suit. For his opening bid, East was certain to possess the ace of spades; and as soon as he regained the lead, he would cash his hearts.

South would now really have no chance but to swing over to diamonds. He would lay down his diamond ace and then lead another diamond, finessing dummy's jack successfully. When the outstanding diamonds fell under the diamond king, dummy's fourth diamond would become declarer's ninth trick.

East's falsecard of the spade ace was, as he could almost be certain, the only way to set the contract.

DEAL II

As a governing principle, "honesty is the best policy." At the bridge table, however, utter honesty can often by the worst policy.

In this deal, declarer had a problem deciding how to play the trump suit. Had he been left to his own resources, he *might* have come up with the right answer. But a "dishonest" defender made it virtually impossible for declarer to emerge victorious.

North-South vulnerable. South deals.

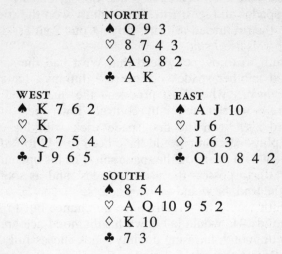

NORTH
♠ Q 9 3
♡ 8 7 4 3
◇ A 9 8 2
♣ A K

WEST
♠ K 7 6 2
♡ K
◇ Q 7 5 4
♣ J 9 6 5

EAST
♠ A J 10
♡ J 6
◇ J 6 3
♣ Q 10 8 4 2

SOUTH
♠ 8 5 4
♡ A Q 10 9 5 2
◇ K 10
♣ 7 3

The bidding:

SOUTH	WEST	NORTH	EAST
2 ♡	Pass	4 ♡	Pass
Pass	Pass		

Opening lead: Two of spades

South's two heart opening bid was a weak two-bid, showing a good six-card suit within a hand that contained from six to twelve high-card points. North's raise to four hearts was an overbid, since South could have had far less for his opening. However, there was nothing wrong with the final contract.

On West's opening lead of the spade deuce, the three was played from dummy, and East finessed his ten, which won the trick. The ace of spades was cashed next, followed by the spade jack to West's king. West then exited with a club, won by dummy's king.

Exactly how declarer was going to play the trump suit, I do not know. Perhaps he intended to lead a low trump off the board and make the normal, standard book play of finessing his queen. Or, perhaps, a little bird had whispered in his ear and told him that West had been dealt the singleton king. But East came up with a play that shattered whatever thoughts declarer might have had.

When declarer led a low trump off the board, East put up the jack! Assuming the jack to be an honest play, West just could not possess the singleton king of trumps—the little bird notwithstanding—for the six of trumps then had to be in West's hand. So declarer finessed his queen, and West's singleton king took the setting trick.

Had East followed suit with the heart six instead of the jack, declarer *might* have put up his ace of hearts. But the false-card of the jack made it appear declarer's best hope was that East had started with the doubleton K J. (If the jack were truly a singleton, then West could not be prevented from winning a trick with his guarded king.)

East's play of the trump jack was well-calculated. He knew that South, for his weak two heart opening bid, had a six-card suit, so it was a definite possibility that West might have had the singleton king of trumps.

DEAL III

The most practical weapon possessed by the defensive side is the high-low signal, that is, playing a higher card first, then a lower one, to indicate a very positive interest in that suit.

In this deal, our East defender utilized this signal to deliberately mislead his partner. Paradoxically, this deceptive play by East, and its acceptance by West as the truth, the whole truth, and nothing but the truth, was the only way South's contract could be defeated.

Neither side vulnerable. North deals.

NORTH
♠ A K Q 7 2
♡ 8 7 4 3
◇ 9 8
♣ 8 5

WEST
♠ 9 8 6 4
♡ Q 10 5
◇ 5
♣ A K Q 10 7

EAST
♠ J 10 3
♡ J 9 6 2
◇ K 6 4
♣ 9 3 2

SOUTH
♠ 5
♡ A K
◇ A Q J 10 7 3 2
♣ J 6 4

The bidding:

NORTH	EAST	SOUTH	WEST
Pass	Pass	5 ◇	Pass
Pass	Pass		

Opening lead: King of clubs

Technically, in terms of high-card strength, South's hand was too good for an opening bid of five diamonds; and, had he been sitting in either first or second position, he would have opened with one diamond. However, in third position, opposite a partner who had passed, South felt that the chances of a North-South slam were negligible, and that a high-level preemptive bid would be the best way to describe his hand. North might have enough strength to give the partnership a reasonable play for game.

At tricks one and two, West cashed the king and ace of clubs. Had East played normally to these leads—first the discouraging deuce of clubs and then the three—West would almost certainly have shifted to some other suit and declarer would have fulfilled his contract.

South would have won West's presumed heart shift, entered dummy via the spade ace, and discarded the jack of clubs on the king of spades. Now it would have been a simple matter to take repeated diamond finesses and thus avoid the loss of a trump trick.

But East was alive to this possibility, so on the first round of clubs, he initiated a high-low signal by playing the nine. On the ace of clubs, he completed his signal by following with the deuce. West, assuming East could ruff the third round, continued with the queen of clubs.

Declarer had no choice but to ruff the third club lead in dummy. Since the board now had but one trump left, he could take only one successful finesse against East's king of trumps, and East ultimately won his trump king, for the setting trick.

DEAL IV

Had this hand been dealt in the average home rubber-bridge game, South would probably have fulfilled his game contract. But when the deal occurred, it was in an all-expert game, and our East defender was presented with the opportunity of becoming a hero by applying a rare "book" play. He rose to the occasion . . . to hand declarer a one-trick set.

North-South vulnerable. South deals.

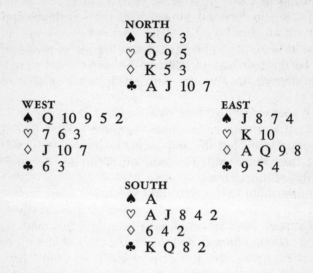

NORTH
♠ K 6 3
♡ Q 9 5
♢ K 5 3
♣ A J 10 7

WEST
♠ Q 10 9 5 2
♡ 7 6 3
♢ J 10 7
♣ 6 3

EAST
♠ J 8 7 4
♡ K 10
♢ A Q 9 8
♣ 9 5 4

SOUTH
♠ A
♡ A J 8 4 2
♢ 6 4 2
♣ K Q 8 2

The bidding:

SOUTH	WEST	NORTH	EAST
1 ♡	Pass	2 NT	Pass
3 ♣	Pass	3 ♡	Pass
4 ♡	Pass	Pass	Pass

Opening lead: Jack of diamonds

West opened the diamond jack, which won the trick. He continued with the ten. East overtook with the queen, cashed the ace, and exited with a spade to declarer's ace.

With all four hands in view, it would appear that declarer should make the rest of the tricks without any difficulty whatsoever. He enters dummy via the ten of clubs and leads a low trump. When East follows suit with the ten-spot, South finesses his queen successfully. He returns to dummy with another club, and when the king of hearts appears on the next round of trumps, South claims his contract.

But, at the table, it did not work out quite that way, for East indulged in a bit of trickery that South did not diagnose. When a low trump was led off the board at trick six, East did not follow suit with the ten. Instead, he played the king!

It seemed perfectly "obvious" that East had been dealt the singleton king. Why else would he have played it?

Of course, South knew East might be falsecarding. But, on balance, it is always better to treat such cards as if they were honest plays. And so, if East had been dealt the singleton king, West had been dealt the 10 7 6 3 and had 10 7 6 remaining.

After winning the king with his ace, South therefore led a low trump out of his hand to dummy's nine. East, as is evident, took home the ten, for the setting trick. East's falsecard of the king had paid a handsome dividend.

If there are those who would criticize declarer for his play, it should be appreciated that *if* East had been dealt the singleton king of trumps, he would perforce have played it on the initial trump lead. And, had such been the case, South's only play to land the contract would have been to finesse against West's ten-spot.

DEAL V

Since self-preservation is the first law of bridge as well as nature, the rubber-bridge player's guiding philosophy is never to jeopardize his contract for the sake of an overtrick. In this deal, South "forgot" this philosophy—and his contract perished ignominiously. No tears should be wasted sympathizing with South, for he was an expert and should have known better.

Actually, declarer went down to defeat because of a nervy falsecard by the East defender. In a restricted sense, East's play might not be deemed to be a falsecard. But in a technical sense, if one defines a falsecard as a play in which one does not play his natural and normal card, East made a falsecard of the highest order.

North-South vulnerable. South deals.

NORTH
♠ 7 5
♡ A K J 10 6
◊ 8 3 2
♣ 8 5 3

WEST
♠ Q J 10 6 4
♡ 7 5 4 2
◊ Q 5
♣ J 7

EAST
♠ 9 8 2
♡ Q 8
◊ J 10 9 6
♣ Q 10 9 4

SOUTH
♠ A K 3
♡ 9 3
◊ A K 7 4
♣ A K 6 2

The bidding:

SOUTH	WEST	NORTH	EAST
1 ◊	Pass	1 ♡	Pass
3 NT	Pass	Pass	Pass

Opening lead: Queen of spades

After taking West's opening lead of the spade queen with his ace, South promptly led the nine of hearts and played low from dummy when West followed suit with the deuce. East made an excellent play when he nonchalantly followed suit with the eight, thus permitting South's nine to win the trick.

From East's point of view, if he had captured this trick with his queen, he would be giving declarer four heart tricks. And, based on South's leap to three no-trump (showing twenty or more points), he realized that four heart tricks would be more than sufficient to give declarer his contract.

When the nine of hearts won the trick, the three no-trump contract was there for the taking: two spades, three hearts, two diamonds, and two clubs. But the combination of the successful heart finesse and the fall of the eight of hearts from the East hand ((which could have been a singleton)) led declarer to believe West had the queen of hearts.

So it came to pass that declarer led his remaining heart and repeated his "successful" finesse. When East pounced on this with his queen, dummy's three remaining hearts were doomed to languish on the board for the duration of the play. Declarer could now make only seven tricks.

Had declarer not taken the second heart finesse, he would have made eleven tricks, and would have scored 700 for the game, 100 for the trick score, and 60 points for two overtricks. By taking the second heart finesse, South went down two tricks, for a loss of 200 points. Thus, the "swing" on the hand was 1060 points—all for the pittance of an overtrick worth 30 points.

DEAL VI

In all echelons of play, there are times when such seemingly irrational things happen at the bridge table that it causes one to speculate on why he ever spent so much time learning the technical aspects of the game.

To illustrate: If one were to look at all four hands in this deal, it would be most difficult to comprehend how South contrived to go down at his four heart contract. But, in fact, he was set. His downfall was brought about by an almost unbelievable bit of sleight of hand by the East defender.

North-South vulnerable. South deals.

```
                        NORTH
                        ♠ 7 5
                        ♡ K 5 3
                        ◇ K 8 2
                        ♣ K Q J 10 6
     WEST                                    EAST
     ♠ K Q 10 9 3                            ♠ A J 6
     ♡ Q                                     ♡ 9 7 6
     ◇ J 7 5 4                               ◇ 10 9 6 3
     ♣ 9 5 2                                 ♣ A 8 4
                        SOUTH
                        ♠ 8 4 2
                        ♡ A J 10 8 4 2
                        ◇ A Q
                        ♣ 7 3
```

The bidding:

SOUTH	WEST	NORTH	EAST
1 ♡	1 ♠	2 ♣	2 ♠
3 ♡	Pass	4 ♡	Pass
Pass	Pass		

Opening lead: King of spades

West's opening lead was the king of spades. East went up with the ace and returned the jack of spades, which West over-took with his queen.

It seemed likely to West, and to South, that East had started with the doubleton A J of spades (which would have been sufficient trump support to have raised West's overcall, provided that East had some outside strength). And it seemed equally possible that East could ruff a third round of spades.

So West, quite naturally, led the ten of spades. Declarer, just as naturally (from the viewpoint of self-preservation) was not going to allow East to ruff this trick with a low trump, for if he did, the defenders' ace of clubs would defeat the contract for sure. If East had the queen of hearts, declarer had an alternative line that would bring home the contract.

South ruffed the third spade lead with the board's king of hearts, then led a low heart and finessed his jack. Thus, West made his singleton queen, and eventually East took the setting trick with the club ace.

Had declarer been gifted with extrasensory perception, he would have played his ace of hearts (instead of finessing) to drop West's queen. But if declarer had possessed E.S.P., he would have ruffed West's third spade lead with a low heart, not with the king.

As for East's motivation in defending as he did, there is no rational justification that I can think of. If his plays had turned out badly for his side, they probably would have been referred to as the "caprices of an unstable mind." But, on this deal, they culminated in a strategic triumph for the defenders.

DEAL VII

In this deal, South was neither outfoxed nor outplayed. As a matter of fact, South played his slam contract very well in order to avoid taking a finesse. But West came up with a couple of superb plays that left declarer no choice but to finesse. Although the ending turned out to be a happy one for the defenders, declarer had no cause for any self-criticism.

Both sides vulnerable. South deals.

NORTH
♠ Q 9 7 5
♡ K 3 2
◊ 8 3
♣ K 6 4 2

WEST
♠ 3 2
♡ Q J 6
◊ K J 10 5 2
♣ 9 7 3

EAST
♠ 6
♡ 10 9 8 5
◊ 9 7 6 4
♣ Q J 10 8

SOUTH
♠ A K J 10 8 4
♡ A 7 4
◊ A Q
♣ A 5

The bidding:

SOUTH	WEST	NORTH	EAST
2 ♠	Pass	3 ♠	Pass
6 ♠	Pass	Pass	Pass

Opening lead: Two of spades

West's opening lead of the deuce of trumps was taken by South's eight-spot, after which the king of trumps was cashed. It was perfectly obvious that the success of the slam contract hinged on a successful diamond finesse or on forcing West to lead a diamond. (The loss of a heart trick could not be avoided.)

South's first maneuver was to cash the ace and king of clubs and ruff a club. He then led the four of hearts toward the king. West could have played the six-spot to force dummy's king, but he saw through declarer's plot and "unblocked" by putting up the jack. After taking the king, South ruffed dummy's last club and laid down the ace of hearts. On this trick, West tossed away his queen!

Now a third heart was led. If West had won this trick, he would have had no choice but to lead a diamond into South's A Q or a heart, which South would ruff in dummy while simultaneously discarding his queen of diamonds.

But, because of West's unblock, *East* captured the third heart lead. When he then returned a diamond, South had no option whatsoever but to take the finesse. West's king of diamonds now took the setting trick.

If South happened to possess the ten of hearts (instead of, let us say, the seven), West's unblocking of both the jack and queen of hearts would have promoted South's ten-spot into a winner. But if South had had the ten of hearts, the slam would have been fulfilled no matter what West played on the first two heart leads.

DEAL VIII

Had declarer been left to his own resources in this deal, he would have had no problem in fulfilling his game contract. Unfortunately for him, the East defender was a highly imaginative sort of fellow who came up with a play that steered declarer to another line of play. The result was costly for North-South, yet it is difficult to censure South for his play.

Both sides vulnerable. South deals.

NORTH
♠ K 10 7 3
♡ 5 2
♦ A K J 9 2
♣ Q J

WEST
♠ Q J 8 4 2
♡ 7
♦ Q 10 3
♣ 9 8 6 5

EAST
♠ 9 6 5
♡ Q J 8 4
♦ 8 6
♣ A K 7 4

SOUTH
♠ A
♡ A K 10 9 6 3
♦ 7 5 4
♣ 10 3 2

The bidding:

SOUTH	WEST	NORTH	EAST
1 ♡	Pass	2 ♦	Pass
2 ♡	Pass	2 ♠	Pass
3 ♡	Pass	4 ♡	Pass
Pass	Pass		

Opening lead: Five of clubs

West opened the five of clubs, and East quickly cashed two club tricks. Had East led either a spade or a club at this point, declarer, in all probability would have fulfilled his contract.

He would have won East's return and cashed his ace of trumps. After entering dummy via the diamond ace, he would have returned the board's remaining trump. When East followed with the eight-spot, South would play his ten.

This would be a safety play designed to guard against East having been dealt the Q J x x of trumps. If the ten lost, declarer would draw the outstanding trump when he regained the lead. As the cards lay, the ten would win, so declarer's only loses would be a heart and two clubs.

But an enterprising East, after winning the first two tricks with his king and ace of clubs, led the six of diamonds into the jaws of dummy's A K J 9 2. West put up the queen, and the trick was captured by the board's king.

South led a trump to his ace, but now he was afraid to lead a second diamond to dummy's ace (in order to make a second trump lead off dummy) for fear East would ruff this lead. After all, did not East, for his unorthodox lead of a diamond at trick three, figure to have started with just a singleton diamond?

So declarer cashed his king of trumps, hoping that the five missing trumps were divided 3-2. When this failed to materialize, East had two sure trump tricks, and his imagination had earned his side a 100-point set.

DEAL IX

Possibly the most risky opening lead in bridge is the under-lead of an ace against a suit contract. One of the dangers inherent in this lead is that either dummy or declarer might have a single-ton king of the suit led. Thus, not only does the king win the trick, but the ace gets trumped when the suit is led later.

However, there are occasional situations when the under-lead of the ace at trick one works out beautifully, primarily because declarer can never bring himself to believe that this dangerous lead is being made against him. And, in these circumstances, the defenders are able to capitalize on declarer's incredulity.

Neither side vulnerable. East deals.

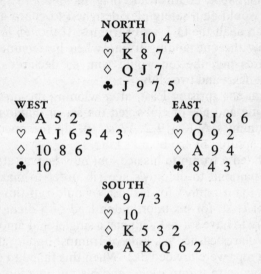

NORTH
♠ K 10 4
♡ K 8 7
♢ Q J 7
♣ J 9 7 5

WEST
♠ A 5 2
♡ A J 6 5 4 3
♢ 10 8 6
♣ 10

EAST
♠ Q J 8 6
♡ Q 9 2
♢ A 9 4
♣ 8 4 3

SOUTH
♠ 9 7 3
♡ 10
♢ K 5 3 2
♣ A K Q 6 2

The bidding:

EAST	SOUTH	WEST	NORTH
Pass	1 ♣	2 ♡	2 NT
Pass	3 ♣	Pass	Pass
Pass			

Opening lead: Two of spades

West's two heart jump overcall was supposed to be of the "weak" variety, showing a respectable six-card suit with little or no outside high-card strength. According to prevailing standards, West's hand was a trifle too good for a weak jump overcall—but it turned out to be a gorgeous bid because it caused South to misjudge the situation and go down to defeat.

At trick one, West elected to open the deuce of spades, away from his ace. The four was played from dummy, and East put up the jack, which won the trick. East now knew West possessed the spade ace, for if South had held that card he would have surely won the first trick.

A low heart was now returned to West's ace. West recognized that East held the queen of spades, for if South had held that card, he would have captured East's jack at trick one. So at trick three, West returned the five of spades, once again underleading his ace.

From the very beginning, declarer gave West credit for something like a six-card heart suit, headed by perhaps the A Q J. It was possible that West also possessed the *queen* of spades. But he certainly did not figure to have the ace of spades, for with that card he would have had a solid *one* heart overcall. So, placing East with the spade ace, and hoping that West had the queen of that suit, declarer followed with dummy's ten of spades. Curtains!

East won this lead with his queen and made haste to return a spade to his partner's ace. Thus, the defenders took the first four tricks, and eventually East made his ace of diamonds, to hand declarer a one-trick set. Two nervy underleads of an ace had defeated the contract.

DEAL X

As stated at the outset of this chapter, the potential danger inherent in a deceptive play by a defender is that the play is apt to mislead partner, and thereby result in misdefense.

However, on occasions, situations arise where a deceptive play by a defender can be utilized to deceive only the declarer, with no risk that the deception will have a harmful effect on partner. This deal, which occurred in a rubber-bridge game, illustrates the theme of *safe deception* by a defender.

Both sides vulnerable. South deals.

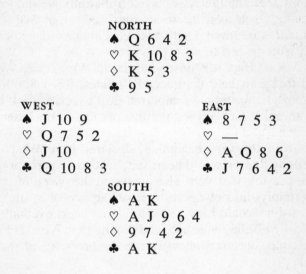

NORTH
♠ Q 6 4 2
♡ K 10 8 3
♢ K 5 3
♣ 9 5

WEST
♠ J 10 9
♡ Q 7 5 2
♢ J 10
♣ Q 10 8 3

EAST
♠ 8 7 5 3
♡ —
♢ A Q 8 6
♣ J 7 6 4 2

SOUTH
♠ A K
♡ A J 9 6 4
♢ 9 7 4 2
♣ A K

The bidding:

SOUTH	WEST	NORTH	EAST
1 ♡	Pass	2 ♡	Pass
4 ♡	Pass	Pass	Pass

Opening lead: Jack of diamonds

West's opening lead of the diamond jack won the first trick when everybody followed suit with low diamonds. He continued with the ten of diamonds, covered by dummy's king. East won his ace and returned the queen of diamonds.

West now made a startling play: He trumped his partner's queen of diamonds, despite the fact that everybody knew that the diamond queen would win the trick. West shifted to the jack of spades, and after South had won with the king, he paused for reflection.

As South analyzed the situation, *East* certainly possessed the queen of trumps, for if West had held that vital card, he would have been interested in guarding it with as many low trumps as possible. Therefore, West's needless expenditure of a low trump to ruff his partner's high queen of diamonds "surely" indicated that West did not have the queen of trumps.

So, at trick five, South led a low trump to the board's king, intending to finesse East for the trump queen on the next round if it became necessary. He was rudely jolted when East failed to follow suit. Now West could not be prevented from eventually making his trump queen for the setting trick.

Had West not ruffed East's queen of diamonds at trick three, it is conceivable declarer might still have played the trump suit exactly as he did. But West's play made it virtually impossible for declarer to diagnose the true state of affairs.

It is axiomatic to state that if South's initial trump lead had been the ace, West would have been exposed as the possessor of the trump queen, and by taking the finesse in trumps, South would have avoided the loss of a trump trick. But one cannot really fault South for going wrong with all that dust West had thrown into declarer's eyes.

11

Championship Play
The Defenders Thwart the Finesser

♠   ♡   ◇   ♣

In this chapter, as in Chapter 10, the defenders outmaneuvered the declarers in diverse types of finessing situations. The fundamental, or perhaps materialistic, difference between the deals contained herein, and those in the preceding chapter, is that these deals were played for "glory" in top-level championship tournament play; the deals in Chapter 10 were played in top-level, usually high-stake "money" games.

DEAL I

This deal occurred in the National Championships of 1942. The West defender, at trick two, made what may appear to the inexpert, untrained eye to be a completely irrational lead. In the post-mortem analysis of the deal, however, it was revealed that West's lead was the only one that could have defeated South's contract. Alvin Roth of New York City, one of the world's top players, was sitting in the West chair. What motivated him to make his winning lead at trick two was his partner's play at trick one.

East-West vulnerable. North deals.

NORTH
♠ 10 5 3
♡ 7 4 2
◇ 9 6
♣ A K Q 8 3

WEST
♠ A K Q J 6 4
♡ 9 8 5
◇ —
♣ 9 7 5 2

EAST
♠ 9 7 2
♡ A 10 3
◇ J 7 5 4
♣ J 10 6

SOUTH
♠ 8
♡ K Q J 6
◇ A K Q 10 8 3 2
♣ 4

The bidding:

NORTH	EAST	SOUTH	WEST
Pass	Pass	5 ◇	Pass
Pass	Pass		

Opening lead: King of spades

Against the five diamond contract, Roth opened the king of spades; East played the deuce, and South followed with the eight-spot. West then led a low club, dummy's queen winning. The ace of clubs was cashed, South discarding the six of hearts.

When declarer next led a trump to his ace and West discarded a spade, it was impossible to prevent East from making his guarded jack of trumps. And, of course, South also had to lose a trick to East's ace of hearts. Thus, declarer suffered a one-trick set.

Had Roth made the natural and normal lead of the spade ace at trick two, declarer would have fulfilled his contract with ease. He would have ruffed this lead and laid down the trump ace, West failing to follow suit.

Dummy would be entered via the club ace. Declarer would discard his losing heart on the king of clubs and then take the "marked" finesse against East's jack of trumps. In this case, he would avoid the loss of a trump trick, and his only losers would be a spade and a heart.

Roth's decision not to lead another top spade at trick two was based directly on East's play of the spade deuce at trick one. If East held the doubleton 9-7 or 9-2 of spades, he would have begun a high-low signal by playing his higher spade first. Hence, Roth concluded, East figured to have three spades originally, and South a singleton. Roth's club lead at trick two "killed" dummy's sole entry, preventing declarer from reaching dummy later once he learned that East had all four outstanding trumps.

Of course, East's deuce of spades might have been a singleton. But Roth correctly concluded that South, who had opened the bidding with five diamonds, did not figure to have three little spades in his hand.

DEAL II

Another of the world's top-ranking players is Eric Murray, of Canada. His ability (or perhaps "guts") can be observed in this deal, in which he was partnered by Douglas Drury. The hand

arose in the National Men's Pair Championship of 1954, which
was won, not unsurprisingly, by Murray and Drury. The deal
was the final hand of the tournament, and it was Murray's defensive play that enabled this duo to win the event. He was sitting
East.

Both sides vulnerable. West deals.

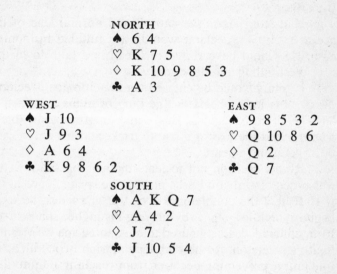

NORTH
♠ 6 4
♡ K 7 5
♢ K 10 9 8 5 3
♣ A 3

WEST
♠ J 10
♡ J 9 3
♢ A 6 4
♣ K 9 8 6 2

EAST
♠ 9 8 5 3 2
♡ Q 10 8 6
♢ Q 2
♣ Q 7

SOUTH
♠ A K Q 7
♡ A 4 2
♢ J 7
♣ J 10 5 4

The bidding:

WEST	NORTH	EAST	SOUTH
Pass	1 ♢	Pass	1 ♠
Pass	2 ♢	Pass	3 NT
Pass	Pass	Pass	

Opening lead: Six of clubs

West made the normal opening lead of the six of clubs. The three was played from dummy and Murray won the queen. He returned a club to dummy's ace.

Declarer then entered the South hand via a spade to his queen, and led the jack of diamonds. West followed with the four-spot, the three was played from dummy—and Murray non-chalantly followed suit with the deuce!

As is evident, all declarer had to do at this point was lead his remaining diamond and (assuming West played low) put up dummy's king. When the queen fell, a diamond would then be conceded to West's ace, and declarer would romp home with an overtrick.

But our declarer (even as you and I) was not endowed with E.S.P. From his view, West surely had the diamond queen. So he next led the seven of diamonds and overtook it with the board's eight. Murray produced the card he "could not" have— the queen—and returned a spade.

With just one outside entry to dummy—the heart king—it was now impossible for declarer to *both* establish *and* cash the diamond suit. Eventually he went down a trick.

Had Murray won the first diamond trick with his queen (at trick four), declarer would have had smooth sailing en route to the fulfillment of the contract. He would have won East's spade or heart return and driven out the diamond ace. Dummy's re-maining diamonds would now all be winners, with the king of hearts as an entry to cash them. But, unfortunately for declarer, Eric Murray happened to be sitting in the East seat.

DEAL III

This deal is unique in perhaps a novel way. In 1968, it was acclaimed by all who saw it as the "hard-luck tournament hand" of that year. It came up in the National Championships held in Coronado, Calif. Sympathy is hereby extended to the South declarer.

Both sides vulnerable. South deals.

```
                        NORTH
                        ♠ K Q J 8 4
                        ♡ K Q 5 4
                        ◇ A Q 5
                        ♣ A

WEST                                        EAST
♠ 9 5 3                                     ♠ 10 7 6
♡ J                                         ♡ 10 9 6
◇ K 3                                       ◇ 9 8 6
♣ K J 9 8 7 6 2                             ♣ Q 10 4 3

                        SOUTH
                        ♠ A 2
                        ♡ A 8 7 3 2
                        ◇ J 10 7 4 2
                        ♣ 5
```

The bidding:

SOUTH	WEST	NORTH	EAST
Pass	3 ♣	4 ♣	Pass
5 ♡	Pass	6 ♡	Pass
Pass	Pass		

Opening lead: Three of of diamonds

This deal was replayed thirteen times during the afternoon, and all of the North-South pairs arrived at some slam contract, most often six hearts. At two tables, the optimistic contract of seven hearts was reached. At every table but one, thirteen tricks were made via a successful diamond finesse. At one table, only twelve tricks were taken. Here is the story of what happened at this one table, where the above bidding sequence took place.

Against the six heart contract, West got off to the devilish lead of the three of diamonds, and declarer was confronted immediately with a problem that could not be deferred: to finesse or not to finesse. Based on the bidding, West figured to hold seven clubs, so his opening diamond lead might well be a singleton. If the finesse were taken, and it lost, the certain diamond return by East would be ruffed by West for the setting trick.

So declarer, not wishing to jeopardize his contract to try for an improbable overtrick, won the opening lead with the board's ace of diamonds. Since there was no possible way of preventing West from eventually making his diamond king, South ended up with just twelve tricks.

When all of the scores were posted at the end of the session of play, North-South learned to their sorrow that they had the lowest score on this deal. At no other table was a low diamond opened; and, of course, at no other table did the South declarer have any problem.

With any opening lead other than a low diamond, declarer makes all thirteen tricks without even breathing hard. But our declarer felt he just could not afford to take the finesse. The result notwithstanding, I think he was right; and I am reasonably certain that most bridge players would agree.

DEAL IV

This deal occurred in a team-of-four match in London, England. It is a tale about how a defender talked a declarer out of taking a winning finesse and, simultaneously, talked him into taking a losing finesse. The hand also serves as a good example of how top-level matches are won and lost.

North-South vulnerable. South deals.

<pre>
                          NORTH
                          ♠ K 5 3
                          ♡ 8 5
                          ◇ Q J 5
                          ♣ A Q 10 9 4

      WEST   EAST
      ♠ J 9 6   ♠ 10 8 7 4 2
      ♡ A Q 9 7 4 2   ♡ J 6
      ◇ 7 3   ◇ K 6 2
      ♣ 6 5   ♣ K J 7

                          SOUTH
                          ♠ A Q
                          ♡ K 10 3
                          ◇ A 10 9 8 4
                          ♣ 8 3 2
</pre>

The bidding:

SOUTH	WEST	NORTH	EAST
1 ◇	1 ♡	2 ♣	Pass
2 NT	Pass	3 NT	Pass
Pass	Pass		

Opening lead: Six of hearts

At both tables the bidding was identical, as was the opening lead of the six of hearts and the play of East's jack and South's king. It was readily apparent to both declarers that if the opponents ever obtained the lead, the three no-trump contract would be defeated.

Both declarers came to the proper conclusion that the diamond suit offered the best chance of bringing home the contract. So each of them cashed the ace and queen of spades, then entered dummy via the ace of clubs. But, as will be observed in a moment, now came a parting of the ways.

At the first table, declarer led the board's queen of diamonds. When it won the trick, he cashed dummy's king of spades. Next came the jack of diamonds. East covered with the king, so South had ten tricks: three spades, one heart, five diamonds, and one club. This declarer had smooth sailing except possibly for the temporary aggravation he suffered wondering whether his diamond finesse was going to win or lose.

When the deal was replayed at the second table, something spectacular happened at trick four. When declarer led a club to the board's ace, East played the king of clubs!

Although declarer had entered dummy with every intention of taking the diamond finesse, he now changed his mind (perhaps "his mind was changed" would be a better way of putting it). After all, there seemed to be no question that East's king of clubs was a singleton. Thus, West must have started with the J x x x of clubs, and at this point had the tripleton J x x remaining. By finessing West out of the jack of clubs, declarer would make an identical ten tricks: five clubs, three spades, one heart, and one diamond.

So declarer led a diamond to his ace and laid down the eight of clubs. When West played low, declarer took the "marked" finesse for the jack of clubs. East, naturally, captured the eight-spot with the jack, cashed the diamond king, and returned a heart to his partner. West then proceeded to rattle off five heart tricks, and declarer suffered a three-trick set.

DEAL V

In this deal, which came up in the Life Masters' Pairs Championship of 1948, every one of the North-South pairs arrived at a four spade contract. At each table but one, this contract was fulfilled. Where it was defeated, S. Garton Churchill was the West defender and Cecil Head was East. Churchill's inspired defense certainly contributed to the duo's victory in this blue-ribbon championship event.

Neither side vulnerable. South deals.

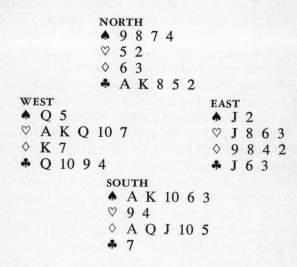

```
                    NORTH
                    ♠ 9 8 7 4
                    ♡ 5 2
                    ◇ 6 3
                    ♣ A K 8 5 2
     WEST                              EAST
     ♠ Q 5                            ♠ J 2
     ♡ A K Q 10 7                     ♡ J 8 6 3
     ◇ K 7                            ◇ 9 8 4 2
     ♣ Q 10 9 4                       ♣ J 6 3
                    SOUTH
                    ♠ A K 10 6 3
                    ♡ 9 4
                    ◇ A Q J 10 5
                    ♣ 7
```

The bidding:

SOUTH	WEST	NORTH	EAST
1 ♠	2 ♡	2 ♠	Pass
3 ◇	Pass	4 ♠	Pass
Pass	Pass		

Opening lead: King of hearts

This was the bidding sequence at Churchill's table. I do not know how the play developed at the other tables, but I imagine that virtually all of the West defenders, after cashing the two top hearts, shifted to a club. But not Churchill. After playing the king and ace of hearts at tricks one and two, he led the five of spades! East put up the jack, and declarer won the trick with his king.

Had West led any card except a low spade at trick three, declarer would have had no problem whatsoever. He would have cashed the king and ace of trumps, dropping both the jack and queen, thus avoiding the loss of a trump trick. His only other loser would have been a diamond to West's king.

But when East's jack fell to South's king at trick three, declarer became fixed with the idea that East's original trump holding was the Q J 12. West surely would not have led a spade away from the queen.

So instead of trying to split the trumps 2-2, declarer entered dummy via the king of clubs and returned the nine of trumps. When East followed with the deuce, declarer played his three-spot, finessing against East's presumed queen.

West, quite naturally, won this trick with his queen, and exited with the queen of clubs. Eventually he made his king of diamonds, to hand declarer a one-trick set.

It is easy enough to criticize South for being taken in by West's low trump lead. But the fact of the matter is that West conceivably might have had a singleton trump, in which case declarer's subsequent finesse for the trump queen would have been the only winning play.

Whether declarer played correctly is, in a sense, immaterial, for the point under discussion is West's deceptive lead of a trump, which implanted in South's mind the thought that the lead was a singleton. I am certain that the beauty of Churchill's lead would not be denied by anyone.

DEAL VI

Through the years, whenever somebody has discussed an excellent play made by a defender, the word used to describe the

play has usually been "brilliant," or "gorgeous," or "imaginative."

In this deal, it is my opinion that an apt one-word descrip-
tion of East-West's defensive play would be "diabolical." The
hand arose in 1951, and the West defender was the brilliant in-
ternationalist Jean Besse, of Switzerland.

Both sides vulnerable. North deals.

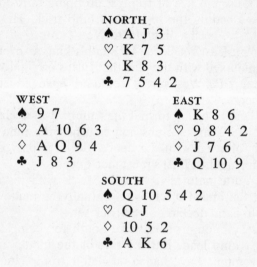

```
                          NORTH
                          ♠ A J 3
                          ♡ K 7 5
                          ◇ K 8 3
                          ♣ 7 5 4 2
        WEST                                EAST
        ♠ 9 7                               ♠ K 8 6
        ♡ A 10 6 3                          ♡ 9 8 4 2
        ◇ A Q 9 4                           ◇ J 7 6
        ♣ J 8 3                             ♣ Q 10 9
                          SOUTH
                          ♠ Q 10 5 4 2
                          ♡ Q J
                          ◇ 10 5 2
                          ♣ A K 6
```

The bidding:

NORTH	EAST	SOUTH	WEST
1 NT	Pass	2 ♠	Pass
Pass	Pass		

Opening lead: Queen of diamonds

North-South were using weak one no-trump opening bids (eleven to thirteen points) and South's slightly pessimistic two spade response was probably a hunch that his side had no chance of making game. As subsequent events demonstrated, he was quite right.

A few seconds after the bidding had been completed, West opened the queen of diamonds! Declarer, without any problem, played the three of diamonds off the board. This was a perfectly normal play, since West figured to be leading away from some Q J combination, and South saw no reason to put up dummy's king.

At trick two, West led the diamond four, and declarer, working on the assumption West had the diamond jack, again played a low diamond from dummy. East won his jack and returned his remaining diamond to Besse's ace.

West then shifted to the seven of spades. When dummy followed with the three-spot, East nonchalantly put up the eight, South's ten capturing the trick. Declarer next led the jack of hearts. Besse grabbed his ace and returned the nine of spades.

South naturally took the finesse and, of course, East won this trick with his king. He then played back his remaining spade to dummy's ace.

Suddenly it dawned on South that he had two heart winners—but only one of them was cashable. He had the singleton queen (in his hand), while dummy had the doubleton K 7. Unfortunately, there was no entry to the dummy, so eventually he lost a club trick, incurring a one-trick set.

Had declarer been clairvoyant, he would have made an overtrick. He would have put up dummy's king on the opening diamond lead, and then attacked the hearts, surrendering the jack to West's ace. After subsequently cashing the heart queen, he would have discarded his losing club on the board's king of hearts. His only losers would have been a spade, two diamonds, and a heart. To have accomplished this, though, he would have had to play like the devil himself to overcome the diabolical defense.

DEAL VII

In the "trials" held in Paris, France, to select the French team that would represent that nation in the 1969 World Championships, the quality of play was exceedingly high. This deal is an illustration. The West defender came up with a beautiful bit of deception, thereby luring declarer to his doom.

East-West vulnerable. South deals.

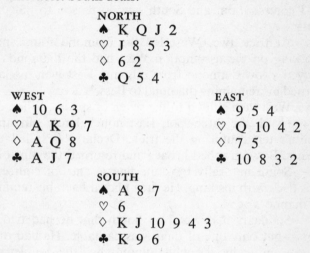

```
                          NORTH
                          ♠ K Q J 2
                          ♡ J 8 5 3
                          ◇ 6 2
                          ♣ Q 5 4
        WEST                                        EAST
        ♠ 10 6 3                                    ♠ 9 5 4
        ♡ A K 9 7                                   ♡ Q 10 4 2
        ◇ A Q 8                                     ◇ 7 5
        ♣ A J 7                                     ♣ 10 8 3 2
                          SOUTH
                          ♠ A 8 7
                          ♡ 6
                          ◇ K J 10 9 4 3
                          ♣ K 9 6
```

The bidding:

SOUTH	WEST	NORTH	EAST
1 ◇	Double	1 NT	Pass
2 ◇	Pass	2 ♠	Pass
3 ◇	Pass	Pass	Pass

Opening lead: King of hearts

West won the opening lead with the heart king and continued with the ace of hearts, which South ruffed. Dummy was then entered via the jack of spades and a low trump was led, declarer inserting his jack.

After winning the trick with his queen, West paused briefly to analyze the situation. He came to the conclusion that the contract was unbeatable, since South, for his bidding, figured to have a good six-card diamond suit, plus the spade ace and the club king. Nevertheless, he found a way to get two club tricks, to defeat the contract.

At trick four, West led the jack of clubs, which South captured with his king. He then laid down the king of trumps. West took his ace and returned the seven of clubs!

Now put yourself in South's shoes as you attempt to diagnose West's two club leads. Wouldn't you assume, as declarer did, that West's original lead of the jack figured to be from some J 10 combination; and, consequently, that East rated to possess the ace of clubs?

Thus, it came to pass that declarer played a low club from the board, on the assumption that East could win the trick only with his ace. But, as is evident, East captured the trick with his ten-spot, and returned a club to West's ace for the setting trick.

Had West not shifted to a club at trick five, South would have fulfilled his contract automatically. After drawing trumps, he would have discarded his six of clubs on dummy's fourth spade. For West, deception had paid a nice dividend.

In this deal, as in the preceding one, South could have fulfilled his contract had he diagnosed the true situation. But it was almost impossible for him to have done so. West, who made an original take-out double and then stopped bidding, had been revealed to hold the ace and king of hearts, the ace and queen of diamonds, and the jack of clubs. To have given West credit for also possessing the ace of clubs was a little too much. West would then have had an eighteen-point hand, and he did not figure to remain quiet over South's two diamond rebid.

DEAL VIII

One of the old-timers of bridge is Meyer Schleifer, West
Coast bridge luminary. He is still not only an excellent techni-
cian but an expert with a most vivid practical imagination.

In this deal, which came up in the Summer National
Championships held in Los Angeles in 1969, a bit of razzle-
dazzle by both East and West brought about the defeat of South's
game contract. Schleifer was sitting West.

Both sides vulnerable. South deals.

```
                        NORTH
                        ♠ Q 10 8 5
                        ♡ A K J
                        ◇ Q 9 2
                        ♣ 7 6 3
        WEST                            EAST
        ♠ A K 4 3                       ♠ J 9 6
        ♡ 7 2                           ♡ 6 5 4 3
        ◇ 8 5 3                         ◇ 10 7 4
        ♣ Q 10 8 5                      ♣ A 9 2
                        SOUTH
                        ♠ 7 2
                        ♡ Q 10 9 8
                        ◇ A K J 6
                        ♣ K J 4
```

The bidding:

SOUTH	WEST	NORTH	EAST
1 ♡	Pass	1 ♠	Pass
1 NT	Pass	3 NT	Pass
Pass	Pass		

Opening lead: Three of spades

When this deal was played thirteen times, at virtually every table South became the declarer at a three no-trump contract. Usually, the various West defenders elected to open a club; East won with the ace and returned a club. South now had his nine tricks: four hearts, four diamonds, and one club.

Schleifer, however, elected to open the three of spades, and South played the eight-spot from dummy. East, after winning the trick with his nine, returned the nine of clubs. Declarer pondered the situation and decided to put up the jack. West captured this trick with his queen.

West now made the daring lead of the four of spades. However, this was almost completely safe, for he knew his partner had the jack of spades and declarer would almost certainly misguess. Declarer, little dreaming that Schleifer was underleading the A K, did just that. He played the ten from dummy, and East's jack captured the trick.

East next cashed his ace of clubs, after which he played his remaining spade. West then cashed his two top spades. The defenders thus took the first six tricks, inflicting a two-trick set on declarer.

In retrospect, South could have guessed correctly at either trick one, trick two, or trick three, and made his contract. If, at trick one, he had put up the board's queen of spades, he would have had his ninth trick.

Having misguessed the winning play at trick one, he could have recovered at trick two by playing his king of clubs when East returned the club nine. But, once again, he misguessed.

South's third opportunity to be a good guesser came at trick three, when West returned the four of spades. Again he misguessed the true situation. And, as they say in baseball, three strikes and you're out.

DEAL IX

At times, a top-flight expert will make a simple, automatic, and technically correct play that will not even be thought of by the nonexpert player and will pass by unnoticed by the average observer or kibitzer. Such was the case in this deal, which came up in the National Mixed Pairs Championship of 1969. This hand, incidently, bears a marked resemblance in type to Deal 2 of Chapter 10.

Sitting East was Peggy Parker; West was her husband, Steve. The Parkers, whose combined ages totaled fifty-three years, captured this four-session championship event. In the twenty-four-year history of this event, they are the youngest pair to have won this title.

For the record, and to emphasize that little things mean a lot, it should be stated that if it were not for Mrs. Parker's defensive play on this deal, the Parkers might not have become the 1969 National Mixed Pairs champions.

Both sides vulnerable. South deals.

NORTH
♠ Q 8 7 5 3
♡ A J 5
◇ J 9
♣ A J 10

WEST   EAST
♠ K   ♠ 9 2
♡ 10 9 8 7 4   ♡ 6 3 2
◇ 8 5 2   ◇ 7 6 4 3
♣ Q 9 6 3   ♣ 8 5 4 2

SOUTH
♠ A J 10 6 4
♡ K Q
◇ A K Q 10
♣ K 7

The bidding:

SOUTH	WEST	NORTH	EAST
1 ♠	Pass	3 ♠	Pass
4 NT	Pass	5 ♡	Pass
7 ♠	Pass	Pass	Pass

Opening lead: Ten of hearts

South's seven spade bid was ambitious, and needlessly so. Had he stopped off en route to the slam to employ the Blackwood Slam Convention to check for kings, he would have discovered that North had none. In the light of this knowledge—that the opponents possessed the king of trumps—he would then almost surely have settled for a small slam.

West opened the ten of hearts, and the trick was won by dummy's ace. South then promptly led the queen of trumps off the board, and Mrs. Parker, without undue haste or undue deliberation, followed suit with the nine-spot. After huddling for perhaps fifteen seconds, declarer let the queen ride. And so Mr. Parker's singleton king took the setting trick.

What is so excellent about Mrs. Parker's play of the nine (the highest card in her hand!) you might ask? Well, as we all know from having been down this road before, there are times when a declarer, holding ten trumps, has a hunch there is a singleton king offside. And if he listens to and obeys his hunch, he plays the ace in the hope of felling the king.

Had Mrs. Parker played the trump deuce, South *might* have played the ace—and fulfilled his grand slam contract. But, from declarer's point of view, if the nine were a true play, then East had started with either the singleton nine or the doubleton K 9. Hence, if East were an honest lady, then it was impossible for West to possess the singleton king (since West would be known to have the deuce). And so declarer, to his sorrow, took the trump finesse.

12

The Defenders Err in
Finessing Situations

♠ ♡ ◇ ♣

It is an accepted fact of life that a declarer will often fulfill a contract not on his own power but, rather, because the opponents slip in their defense. Conversely, it is equally true that the defenders will be, almost as often, the beneficiaries of a mistake in play by a declarer, thus enabling them to defeat a contract that correct play would have brought home safely.

This chapter deals with defensive errors in both judgment and technical execution. More specifically, the defenders erred in finessing situations. As a consequence, in each case declarer fulfilled a contract that more astute defense would have defeated.

DEAL

If statistics were ever compiled, it would be revealed that the vast majority of the world's bridge players do not make sufficient penalty doubles. Whether this is due to their inability to evaluate correctly the trick-taking capacity of their defending hands, or to their understandable reluctance to tip off declarer as to the location of the outstanding high cards, or to their unwillingness to gamble for double stakes, will probably never be known.

At the other extreme, there are those eternal optimists who make penalty doubles on a wing and a prayer. When their accounts are totaled at the end of each year, each of them discovers he is in the red. The only thing that varies in their individual accounts is the amount they have paid out to the winners.

This deal is an example of the "trigger-happy doubler" in action. His double forewarned declarer that a finesse which would normally be taken would lose. Declarer needed the warning, and ended up collecting a staggering amount of points.

North-South vulnerable. South deals.

```
                        NORTH
                        ♠ Q 9 7 3
                        ♡ A Q 4
                        ◇ K 8 2
                        ♣ A 6 4
        WEST                            EAST
        ♠ K 6                           ♠ 5
        ♡ J 10 9 8                      ♡ 7 5 3 2
        ◇ 10 9 7 6                      ◇ Q J 4 3
        ♣ K J 7                         ♣ 9 8 5 2
                        SOUTH
                        ♠ A J 10 8 4 2
                        ♡ K 6
                        ◇ A 5
                        ♣ Q 10 3
```

The bidding:

SOUTH	WEST	NORTH	EAST
1 ♠	Pass	2 NT	Pass
3 ♠	Pass	4 ♠	Pass
4 NT	Pass	5 ♡	Pass
6 ♠	Double	Redouble	Pass
Pass	Pass		

Opening lead: Jack of hearts

After West had opened the jack of hearts, and the dummy came into view, declarer concluded that West, for his double, was a cinch to possess both the spade and club kings. Hence the trump finesse was bound to be a losing play.

The opening lead was captured by South's king, after which the ace of trumps was cashed, both opponents following suit. Next came the ace and queen of hearts, South discarding a club. The ace and king of diamonds were then played, followed by a diamond ruff in the closed hand.

West was now put on lead with a trump. He saw that if he led either a heart or a diamond, declarer would ruff it in dummy while simultaneously discarding a losing club from his own hand. So, hoping that his partner had the club queen, West returned the seven of clubs. Declarer played low from dummy and won the trick with his ten-spot. The rest of the tricks were his.

Had West not doubled, declarer almost surely would have taken the trump finesse—and lost his contract. East-West would then have scored 100 points. But West's double and North's redouble enabled North-South to score 2220 points: 750 for the small slam, 700 for the rubber, 720 for the redoubled trick score, and a 50-point bonus for fulfilling a doubled contract. The word "double" cost West (and his unfortunate partner) 2320 points.

DEAL II

One of the most difficult urges for a nonexpert to repress is the desire to win a trick whenever the opportunity presents itself. In this deal, a defender played unthinkingly when he elected to win a trick. In so doing, he actually left declarer with no choice but to come up with the winning line of play. Had our defender not played mechanically, declarer might well have failed to diagnose the true situation.

North-South vulnerable. South deals.

NORTH
♠ K Q 10
♡ 9 5 3
♢ K 8 2
♣ K J 6 2

WEST
♠ J 9 8 5
♡ 10 7 4 2
♢ 7 6 4 3
♣ 9

EAST
♠ A 7 2
♡ Q J 6
♢ J 9 5
♣ Q 10 8 4

SOUTH
♠ 6 4 3
♡ A K 8
♢ A Q 10
♣ A 7 5 3

The bidding:

SOUTH	WEST	NORTH	EAST
1 NT	Pass	3 NT	Pass
Pass	Pass		

Opening lead: Five of spades

West opened the five of spades; declarer put up dummy's king, and East took the trick with his ace. The queen of hearts was returned, South's ace winning.

In the hope that West had the queen of clubs or that the five outstanding clubs were divided 3-2 (in which case a long-suit winner could be created in clubs), declarer next cashed his ace of clubs. He then led another club, and won dummy's king when West discarded a diamond. It was now quite obvious that South had just made all the club tricks he was ever going to make.

Declarer returned to his own hand via the diamond queen and led a low spade. When West followed suit with the eight-spot, declarer inserted the board's ten. When it won, declarer had his ninth trick.

On the face of it, the result may appear to be perfectly normal, but it was not. East made a mistake when he won the opening lead with his ace of spades. He should have allowed dummy's king to hold the first trick.

Had the king been permitted to win, declarer would undoubtedly have cashed his ace and king of clubs (as he did in actual practice). When he found that he could not make his ninth trick in the club suit, he would have had no choice but to turn to the spade suit. He would then have returned to the South hand via a heart or a diamond and led a spade.

With West following suit with a low spade, South would be faced with a pure 50-50 guess whether to play the queen of spades (hoping West possessed the ace) or the ten (hoping West had been dealt the spade jack). If he guessed wrong, he would go down, since all he could make would be one spade, two hearts, three diamonds, and two clubs.

But, as is apparent, East's premature winning of his spade ace at trick one left South with no alternative but to finesse West for the jack of spades.

DEAL III

In bridge, as in many avenues of competitive endeavor, players commit errors of commission and errors of omission. The former category consists of things done incorrectly, technically speaking; the latter includes mistakes made because somebody "forgot" to do something that he should have done. Both types of errors can, of course, be equally costly to the wrongdoer.

In this deal, one of the defenders committed an error of omission, thereby making it relatively simple for South to fulfill his contract. Had the error not been made, it is possible the contract would have been defeated.

Both sides vulnerable. South deals.

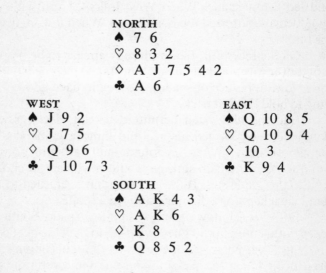

```
                        NORTH
                        ♠ 7 6
                        ♡ 8 3 2
                        ◊ A J 7 5 4 2
                        ♣ A 6
        WEST                            EAST
        ♠ J 9 2                         ♠ Q 10 8 5
        ♡ J 7 5                         ♡ Q 10 9 4
        ◊ Q 9 6                         ◊ 10 3
        ♣ J 10 7 3                      ♣ K 9 4
                        SOUTH
                        ♠ A K 4 3
                        ♡ A K 6
                        ◊ K 8
                        ♣ Q 8 5 2
```

The bidding:

SOUTH	WEST	NORTH	EAST
1 ♣	Pass	2 ◊	Pass
2 NT	Pass	3 NT	Pass
Pass	Pass		

Opening lead: Three of clubs

On West's opening lead of the club three, dummy's six was played and East captured the trick with his king. He returned a club to dummy's ace, thereby removing the board's only entry outside the diamond suit.

Declarer then led a diamond to his king, East following with the three-spot and West the six. South's remaining diamond was led and, with his heart in his mouth, he inserted dummy's jack. When East followed suit with the ten, South breathed a sign of relief.

From here in, the play was routine. The ace of diamonds dropped West's queen, and declarer ended up making twelve tricks. Had the defense been perfect, he *might* have made only eight tricks.

When South played a diamond to his king, East should have followed suit with the ten-spot, not the three. Had he done so, declarer would have been confronted with a real dilemma: Was the ten-spot an "honest" play or not?

If the ten were an honest play, then either it was a singleton or a doubleton Q 10. Declarer would now have to decide whether to finesse dummy's jack on the second lead of diamonds (the winning play if the ten were a singleton) or to go up with dummy's ace instead, hoping to catch East's queen (the winning play if East had started with the doubleton Q 10).

How he would have decided will never be known, of course. If he guessed wrong by putting up dummy's ace, all he would ever make would be eight tricks, two in each suit. However, East gave South no opportunity to make an incorrect decision, so South ended up with three overtricks.

DEAL IV

In this deal, as in the preceding one, a defender committed an error of omission, thereby eliminating any guesswork that declarer might have had under more trying circumstances. From a purely technical point of view, a jury of his peers would probably acquit the defender of any wrongdoing. But the defender was guilty of a crime against winning bridge.

Both sides vulnerable. South deals.

NORTH
♠ J 9 3
♡ A 5 2
◇ A J 6
♣ Q 8 7 3

WEST
♠ 6 5 4
♡ J 10 9 7
◇ 8 7 3
♣ 10 9 5

EAST
♠ Q 10 8 2
♡ 8 6 4
◇ 9 5 4 2
♣ K 2

SOUTH
♠ A K 7
♡ K Q 3
◇ K Q 10
♣ A J 6 4

The bidding:

SOUTH	WEST	NORTH	EAST
2 NT	Pass	6 NT	Pass
Pass	Pass		

Opening lead: Jack of hearts

After West had opened the jack of hearts, declarer was not enamoured with the dummy. Unless one of the opponents had the doubleton Q x of spades (which would give declarer three spade tricks), he would have to bring home four club tricks in order to fulfill his slam contract. And the prospects of making four club tricks were not good.

South won the opening lead with the board's ace and led the three of clubs. When East followed with the deuce, South inserted his jack, which won the trick as West played the five-spot. The ace of clubs was cashed, dropping East's king, and South chalked up the score for a vulnerable small slam bid and made.

The West defender committed an error of omission at trick two, when South finessed his jack of clubs. He could have created a problem for declarer by following suit with the nine of clubs instead of the five-spot.

Let's assume West had dropped the club nine. From declarer's point of view, he might have concluded that West had started with the doubleton 10 9. And if such were the case, then it meant East had started with the tripleton K 5 2.

If this distribution existed, then declarer's winning play would be to reenter dummy and lead the queen of clubs. If East covered with the king, South would win it with his ace, dropping West's ten-spot. In the process, the board's eight and seven would be promoted into winners. It would have made no difference if East did not cover with the king.

In this deal, had West dropped the club nine and declarer led the queen of clubs on the second round, it is readily apparent that the contract would have failed because South would have had to lose a club trick. But in the actual play, declarer had no option in playing the club suit. His only hope was to drop the king, and when he did, it was curtains for the defense.

DEAL V

This deal is presented as a bridge mystery. You are informed that as a result of a defensive error, declarer was per-

mitted to fulfill a game contract that should have been defeated.
It is your job, as a bridge sleuth, to bring the defensive misplay
to light, and introduce evidence that will convict the defender of
the crime of "conduct unbecoming a good bridge player."

Neither side vulnerable. South deals.

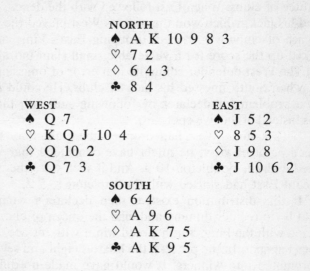

NORTH
♠ A K 10 9 8 3
♡ 7 2
♢ 6 4 3
♣ 8 4

WEST
♠ Q 7
♡ K Q J 10 4
♢ Q 10 2
♣ Q 7 3

EAST
♠ J 5 2
♡ 8 5 3
♢ J 9 8
♣ J 10 6 2

SOUTH
♠ 6 4
♡ A 9 6
♢ A K 7 5
♣ A K 9 5

The bidding:

SOUTH	WEST	NORTH	EAST
1 ♢	1 ♡	1 ♠	Pass
2 NT	Pass	3 ♠	Pass
3 NT	Pass	Pass	Pass

Opening lead: King of hearts

North, with no outside entries to his hand, made an inferior
call when he passed three no-trump. He should have bid four
spades. At that contract, all he would have lost would have been
a spade, a heart, and a diamond.

West was permitted to win the first two tricks with the king and queen of hearts, and a third heart lead was captured by South's ace.

It was rather apparent to declarer that in order to fulfill his contract he had to bring home the spade suit. It was equally apparent that West, with his two established hearts, had to be kept out of the lead.

At trick four, South led a low spade, and when West followed with the seven, the board's eight-spot was inserted. East won this trick with his jack—and whatever he returned, declarer could not be prevented from taking the rest of the tricks. Where did the defenders slip?

At trick four, when South led a low spade, West should have played the queen. Had he done so, South would have had no choice but to win the trick. If he did not, West would cash two heart tricks. And once West played the queen, declarer would be limited to two spade tricks, the ace and king, since he would be unable to establish the suit.

This play was completely safe, regardless of who had the jack of spades. If South had that jack, then he would always make six spade tricks (even if he were the world's worst player), whether West played the spade seven or the spade queen on the initial spade lead.

West had to presume that East possessed the spade jack, for this was the only condition whereby declarer could be prevented from setting up dummy's spade suit.

But, unfortunately for his side, the West defender played mechanically in refusing to "sacrifice" his queen—and in so doing he relegated himself to a loser's role.

DEAL VI

As has been stated elsewhere in this book, one of the oldest "rules" in bridge is the "Rule of Eleven." The rule states, in part: "When partner opens the fourth from the highest in his longest suit, and dummy comes into view, subtract the number of pips (spots) on the card led from the number eleven. The result gives the number of higher cards (above the one led) in the other three hands (exclusive of the leader)."

This deal illustrates the Rule of Eleven, in possibly negative fashion.

Neither side vulnerable. North deals.

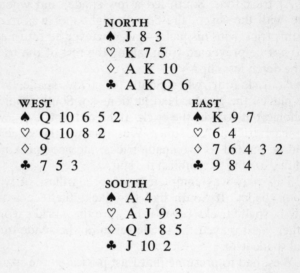

The bidding:

NORTH	EAST	SOUTH	WEST
1 ♣	Pass	2 NT	Pass
6 NT	Pass	Pass	Pass

Opening lead: Five of spades

The bidding was more or less routine, South's response of two no-trump showing thirteen to fifteen points. North, counting to at least thirty-three points in high cards, promptly contracted for the small slam.

West made a good choice when he elected to open a spade. Had he chosen to lead a heart instead, declarer would have won the trick with his jack and would have had twelve tricks off the top.

On West's five of spades opening lead, the eight was played from dummy, East put up the king, and South won the trick with his ace. From South's view, West certainly possessed the queen of spades, for if East had held both the queen and king, he would have played the queen, the lower of touching honors.

At trick two, declarer led his remaining spade toward the jack. West went up with the queen, so dummy's jack became South's slam-going trick.

When West opened the five of spades, and the eight was played from dummy, East should have applied the Rule of Eleven (as he undoubtedly would have done had he been familiar with it). By subtracting five (the denomination of West's lead) from the number eleven, East would have arrived at the number six. That would have meant that in the North, East, and South hands, there were six spades higher than the five-spot. Dummy had two cards higher and East himself had three cards higher.

Thus, declarer could have only one card that was higher than West's five. Surely that card was the ace, for, on the given bidding, no West defender would have underled the ace against South's slam contract.

East, therefore, should have played the spade nine, instead of the king, at trick one. The only place where South would now have any hope of making his twelfth trick would be hearts. In all probability, somewhere along the line, declarer would have taken the heart finesse. West would win his queen, and declarer would go down.

DEAL VII

In all areas of competitive endeavor, the combination of luck and skill is the "winningest" asset to possess. This also holds true, of course, at the bridge table, where both skill and luck play a major role in determining the destiny of any given contract.

Our South declarer in this deal was both skillful and lucky, and as a result he fulfilled his contract. Yet, without taking any credit away from South, the defenders are entitled to a slight "assist" for declarer's success, for they pointed the way to the winning line of play.

Both sides vulnerable. North deals.

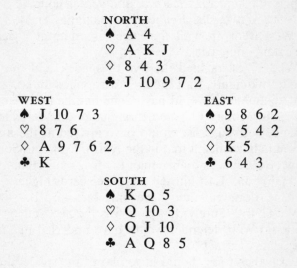

```
                    NORTH
                    ♠ A 4
                    ♡ A K J
                    ◇ 8 4 3
                    ♣ J 10 9 7 2
        WEST                        EAST
        ♠ J 10 7 3                  ♠ 9 8 6 2
        ♡ 8 7 6                     ♡ 9 5 4 2
        ◇ A 9 7 6 2                 ◇ K 5
        ♣ K                         ♣ 6 4 3
                    SOUTH
                    ♠ K Q 5
                    ♡ Q 10 3
                    ◇ Q J 10
                    ♣ A Q 8 5
```

The bidding:

NORTH	EAST	SOUTH	WEST
1 ♣	Pass	3 NT	Pass
Pass	Pass		

Opening lead: Six of diamonds

West made the normal opening lead of the six of diamonds. East won the trick with his king and returned a diamond, South's jack being taken by West's ace. A third diamond went to South's queen, as East discarded a heart.

After a few moments reflection, declarer laid down his ace of clubs—and caught West's king. The rest of the tricks were now his.

There is no doubt that South was lucky when he dropped the club king. With four clubs outstanding, the king did not figure to be a singleton. But South's luck was intertwined with skill.

South's approach to the play had to be geared toward keeping West out of the lead. If West obtained the lead, he would cash his two high diamonds. If the club king had not fallen under the ace, South would have led another club. Had *East* held the king of clubs, everything would be lovely, for East was known to have no diamonds. And if West had the club king, then South would go down, for West would now cash his two established diamonds.

By playing the club ace first, instead of finessing, South would not lose to a singleton king in either hand. . . . And if West had the guarded king of clubs, he would win a trick with that card whether or not South finessed. Thus, the initial play of the club ace was "on the house."

The outcome might have been different had West refused to win the second diamond trick. It is conceivable (although not likely) that declarer might now decide that the seven outstanding diamonds were originally divided 4-3. With this distribution, the club finesse could be taken safely, for even if it lost, the defenders could cash no more than two additional diamond tricks.

If declarer did take the club finesse he would have gone down. But, then, we'll never know what might have happened if West had defended as suggested.

DEAL VIII

It has been reiterated in this text that, in expert circles, deceptive plays by the defenders are very rare. The reason, again, is that far too often a defensive deceptive play will mislead one's partner, and thereby result in misdefense. But, on occasion, a bit of trickery by a defender is necessary.

Such was the case in this deal, which arose in a team-of-four match. At one table, there was no deception. When the deal

was replayed, deception was applied, with a most beneficial result.

Both sides vulnerable. North deals.

                    NORTH
                    ♠ A J 6 2
                    ♡ K J 7
                    ◇ A K 10 5 2
                    ♣ 7

WEST   EAST
♠ K 10 7 4   ♠ 9 8 5
♡ 8 5 3   ♡ 9 6 4 2
◇ 3   ◇ 8 6
♣ J 9 8 4 2   ♣ A K 6 3

                    SOUTH
                    ♠ Q 3
                    ♡ A Q 10
                    ◇ Q J 9 7 4
                    ♣ Q 10 5

The bidding:

NORTH	EAST	SOUTH	WEST
1 ◇	Pass	2 NT	Pass
3 ♠	Pass	3 NT	Pass
Pass	Pass		

Opening lead: Four of clubs

The bidding was identical at both tables—and is subject to criticism. With five-card support for North's diamond suit, South certainly should have supported diamonds on his second bid. A five diamond contract would have been there for the taking, with an overtrick thanks to the favorable location of the spade king.

When the deal was played originally, West opened the four of clubs. East won with the king, cashed the ace of clubs, then led a third club to South's queen. South now rattled off nine tricks (a club, five diamonds, and three hearts), and took the spade finesse. Thus, he made two overtricks.

In the replay, East did not win the opening lead with the club king. Instead, he won it with the ace, and then played back the club three! South was now confronted with a problem.

The problem, of course, was whether to put up the ten or queen. As South reflected on the situation, he came to the conclusion that West probably had the club king. After all, if East held that card, he would have tended to play it at trick one (a defender, in third position, usually plays the lower of touching honors). Of course, if West had both the king and jack, South's cause was hopeless no matter what he played.

And so, accepting East's play of the club ace at face value, South inserted the ten of clubs at trick two. East took this with his jack and played back a club. In less time than one can say "you guessed wrong," the defenders took three more club tricks, and declarer was down one.

DEAL IX

This deal came up a few years ago in a "social" bridge game in Washington, D.C., at the home of one of the members of our diplomatic corps. South was a good player; East was not, as became evident when play had ended. I have frequently speculated on what might have developed had East been a good player, and have concluded that the struggle would have been a fascinating battle of wits, with South probably emerging as the winner.

Neither side vulnerable. East deals.

NORTH
- ♠ K Q J 7 3
- ♡ 8 5 4
- ◇ 6
- ♣ K 10 4 2

WEST
- ♠ 9 6 5
- ♡ 9 7
- ◇ Q 10 8 5 4 3
- ♣ 7 6

EAST
- ♠ A 10 4
- ♡ K J 10 6 3
- ◇ A J 9
- ♣ 9 5

SOUTH
- ♠ 8 2
- ♡ A Q 2
- ◇ K 7 2
- ♣ A Q J 8 3

The bidding:

EAST	SOUTH	WEST	NORTH
1 ♡	2 ♣	Pass	2 ♠
Pass	2 NT	Pass	3 ♣
Pass	3 NT	Pass	Pass
Pass			

Opening lead: Five of diamonds

On West's opening lead of the diamond five, East put up the ace and returned the diamond jack, which was allowed to win. East persisted with the diamond nine, and South took his king.

Because declarer could not make nine tricks without at least one spade trick, he now led a low spade to dummy's jack. East won his ace, and since he had no more diamonds, declarer took the rest of the tricks. All of dummy's spades were winners.

Suppose East had been a good player. On the bidding, East should have realized that South would surely hold the diamond king. Based on this information, East should have played the jack of diamonds (instead of the ace) on the opening lead.

If South now made the mistake of winning this trick with his king, he would be in bad shape. When East subsequently obtained the lead with the spade ace, he would cash the diamond ace and then lead the diamond nine. West would then cash all of his diamonds.

But if a "good" East defender had put up the diamond jack at trick one, an equally good South declarer should have allowed the jack to capture the trick. After all, East had opened the bidding, and he surely had the diamond ace as part of his opening bid (South was looking at twenty-five high-card points in the North-South hands).

If East were permitted to win the diamond jack, he could not make any return that would prevent South from fulfilling his contract. In real life, however, South's sailing was smooth and pleasurable.

DEAL X

Before presenting the concluding deal of this chapter, I would like to make an observation. It is, in a sense, unfair that in the scoring the defenders share their profit on a 50-50 basis when they defeat a contract. For example, in this deal one of the defenders made a poor play. The other, however, came up with an excellent play to negate his partner's boner, and it resulted in declarer's defeat. Yet each defender received the identical reward. In my opinion, it was a gross miscarriage of justice, since the errant defender was really entitled to nothing.

Both sides vulnerable. South deals.

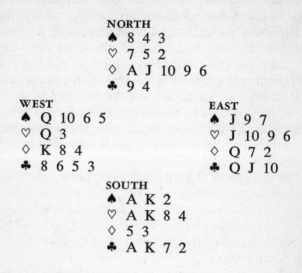

NORTH
♠ 8 4 3
♡ 7 5 2
◇ A J 10 9 6
♣ 9 4

WEST
♠ Q 10 6 5
♡ Q 3
◇ K 8 4
♣ 8 6 5 3

EAST
♠ J 9 7
♡ J 10 9 6
◇ Q 7 2
♣ Q J 10

SOUTH
♠ A K 2
♡ A K 8 4
◇ 5 3
♣ A K 7 2

The bidding:

SOUTH	WEST	NORTH	EAST
1 ♣	Pass	1 ◇	Pass
3 NT	Pass	Pass	Pass

Opening lead: Five of spades

On West's opening lead of the spade five, East put up the jack and South won the trick with his king. It was rather apparent to declarer that he had to attack the diamond suit. If he could bring in three diamond tricks, his contract would be fulfilled.

So, at trick two, he led the three of diamonds, and when West followed suit with the four-spot, dummy's nine was inserted. Had East won this trick with his queen, the defenders would have been hors de combat: When declarer regained the lead, he would have taken a second diamond finesse. With the king onside and the missing diamonds evenly divided, South would have made four diamond tricks.

However, East refused to win the first diamond trick with his queen! Declarer was now a doomed man, for all he could make from here in was the diamond ace. He then attacked the heart suit, in the hope that the outstanding hearts were divided 3-3, in which case South's fourth heart would become his ninth trick. When this failed to materialize, South went down one.

What motivated East to decline to take his diamond queen, I do not know, but he saved the day for the defenders. West, on the other hand, made an unthinking play when he mechanically followed with the four of diamonds on the first round of the suit. Surely, if South had held the diamond queen, he would have led it first. Hence, from West's vantage point, East certainly figured to have the queen of diamonds.

Had West "sacrificed" his king of diamonds at trick two, declarer could not have brought home three diamond tricks no matter how he played (he could not have made even two diamond tricks) and East would not have been called on to make a brilliant play. But West just was not on his toes. Fortunately, East was. And so West (parasitically) obtained his 50 percent of the profits.

13

Celebrities and the Finesse

♠　♡　◇　♣

The distinguished personalities whose "finessing exploits" constitute the contents of this chapter all reached the top in their chosen professions or vocations: authors, actors, actresses, musicians, industrialists, physicists, and statesmen. None of them reached the same pinnacle in bridge. Their pressure-packed life pursuits left them too little time. However, our individuals were fortunate to have available an interest, or avocation, that enabled them to combine both their recreation and their relaxation into one healthful capsule. That interest was contract bridge.

In each of the ten deals in this chapter, our famous personalities did the right thing: They finessed when they were supposed to finesse, and they did not finesse when they were not supposed to. In a bridge sense, I may have glorified these celebrities, selecting only those deals where they have "looked good." I have done this because they are all amateurs—dilettantes at the game —and I have ignored the Shakespearian observation that "the evil that men do lives after them; the good is oft interred with their bones."

And so, with apologies to the Bard for the inversion, I have interred the evil and brought out the good. After all, being practical about it, someday *I* may need a favor from them.

DEAL I

The late W. Somerset Maugham, England's famous novelist and playwright, once stated: "If I had my way, I would have children taught bridge as a matter of course, just as they are taught dancing. In the end, it will be more useful to them. In fact, when all else fails—sports, love, ambition—bridge remains a solace and an entertainment. . . ."

Such was his conviction. He was not an expert player, but he was a good one. In his later years, failing eyesight forced him to give up not only reading but also bridge. In earlier years, however, he made his presence felt whenever he sat down at a bridge table. Here is an example of his ability. He was sitting South.

North-South vulnerable. South deals.

```
                        NORTH
                        ♠ Q 5
                        ♡ Q 9 8 2
                        ◊ A 7 2
                        ♣ 7 6 5 4

        WEST                            EAST
        ♠ K 7 4                         ♠ J 10 9 6 3
        ♡ K 4                           ♡ 6 3
        ◊ Q J 10 8                      ◊ 9 5 3
        ♣ K J 8 3                       ♣ Q 10 9

                        SOUTH
                        ♠ A 8 2
                        ♡ A J 10 7 5
                        ◊ K 6 4
                        ♣ A 2
```

The bidding:

SOUTH	WEST	NORTH	EAST
1 ♡	Pass	2 ♡	Pass
3 ♡	Pass	4 ♡	Pass
Pass	Pass		

Opening lead: Queen of diamonds

After West had opened the queen of diamonds, Maugham surveyed the scene. The instinctive tendency would have been to win the queen with the ace and take the trump finesse. When this lost, a diamond continuation would doom declarer to defeat; he would end up losing a trick in each suit.

Maugham realized, however, that if the trump finesse were going to be successful now, it would also be successful later on. So he was in no hurry to take that finesse, especially since there was more pressing business at hand, to wit, the creation of a needed trick on which to discard a losing diamond.

He won the opening lead with his king and promptly led a low spade toward dummy's queen. West took his king and continued diamonds, the board's ace winning. The queen of spades was cashed next, after which South reentered his hand via the club ace and discarded dummy's last diamond on the ace of spades.

Maugham now followed with his remaining diamond, which he ruffed with the board's eight of hearts (to make sure that East, if he started with only two diamonds, would not overruff with a low trump). The queen of trumps was led next, and the finesse taken (as a luxury), losing to West's king. West then cashed the club king, for the defender's last trick. Declarer's only losers were a spade, a heart, and a club.

If East held the king of spades, he would have captured dummy's queen at trick two, and a diamond loser would have been inevitable. Maugham would then have been compelled to stake the fate of his contract on a successful trump finesse. On this particular day, however, it was unnecessary to do so.

DEAL II

One of the better players in the theatrical world was the late Tallulah Bankhead. From a technical point of view, she was not a good bidder, primarily because she felt that life was too brief to spend time mastering the many types of specialized bids which, in her opinion, arose all too infrequently. However, she was an excellent player of the cards, as this deal demonstrates. Miss Bankhead was, appropriately, in the South seat.

Neither side vulnerable. South deals.

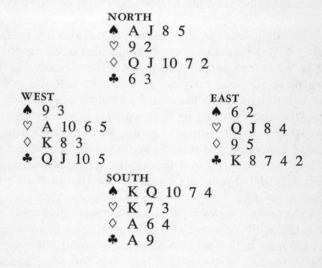

```
                    NORTH
                    ♠ A J 8 5
                    ♡ 9 2
                    ◇ Q J 10 7 2
                    ♣ 6 3
        WEST                        EAST
        ♠ 9 3                       ♠ 6 2
        ♡ A 10 6 5                  ♡ Q J 8 4
        ◇ K 8 3                     ◇ 9 5
        ♣ Q J 10 5                  ♣ K 8 7 4 2
                    SOUTH
                    ♠ K Q 10 7 4
                    ♡ K 7 3
                    ◇ A 6 4
                    ♣ A 9
```

The bidding:

SOUTH	WEST	NORTH	EAST
1 ♠	Pass	2 ♠	Pass
4 ♠	Pass	Pass	Pass

Opening lead: Queen of clubs

South's four spade call was an overbid, but Miss Bankhead felt that life was too short to waste time on "delicate" bids such as, for example, three spades, to find out whether her partner had a minimum or a maximum raise. In fact, North would have raised three to game, so the final contract was not affected.

When West's queen of clubs opening lead rode around to Miss Bankhead in the South seat, she did not win the trick and then pause for reflection. Instead, she reflected *before* playing to trick one.

It was readily apparent that if either the king of diamonds or the ace of hearts were favorably located, fulfilling the contract would be a cinch. But Miss Bankhead assumed, in the pessimistic fashion that is characteristic of the expert approach, that West possessed both of these key cards.

If the heart ace were located in West's hand, reasoned Miss Bankhead, it was imperative that East be kept out of the lead, since a heart shift by him would enable the defenders to cash two heart tricks. And so Miss Bankhead geared her play to keeping East out of the lead. She permitted West's club queen to win the first trick.

West continued with a low club, East's king falling to South's ace. The king of trumps was followed by a trump to dummy's ace. Next came the queen of diamonds, and declarer finessed, losing to West's king. In the hope that his partner held the heart king, West now cashed the ace of hearts. As is evident, South took the rest of the tricks.

Had Miss Bankhead won the opening lead with her ace of clubs, the opponents would surely have defeated the four spade contract. In this case, when West won the diamond king, he would have led a low club to East's king. East would have made the automatic shift to the queen of hearts, and the defenders would have cashed two heart tricks.

But Miss Bankhead's foresight at trick one prevented East from ever gaining the lead, and "sewed up" her contract.

DEAL III

The late Harold S. Vanderbilt was most widely known as a yachtsman. He successfully defended the America's Cup three

times, and never lost an important race. Nevertheless, his lasting
fame is more likely to come from his contributions to the game
of bridge.

To bridge players, he is known primarily as the father of
contract bridge. Back in 1925, on a cruise from California to
Havana, he invented the scoring system that launched the game.
He also devised the first unified system of bidding, known as the
Vanderbilt Club.

Vanderbilt retired from active competition a good many
years before his death in 1970, but in his day he was truly a great
player. As an example of his ability, here is a deal played in the
annual tournament that has borne his name ever since 1928: the
Vanderbilt Cup Championship.

Both sides vulnerable. South deals.

```
                        NORTH
                        ♠ J 10 3 2
                        ♡ Q 10 9
                        ◇ A Q J
                        ♣ 5 4 2
        WEST                                EAST
        ♠ Q 9 6 5                           ♠ 8 7 4
        ♡ 4                                 ♡ 6 3 2
        ◇ 10 9 8 4                          ◇ K 6 5 3
        ♣ A 9 8 6                           ♣ Q J 10
                        SOUTH
                        ♠ A K
                        ♡ A K J 8 7 5
                        ◇ 7 2
                        ♣ K 7 3
```

The bidding:

SOUTH	WEST	NORTH	EAST
1 ♡	Pass	2 ♡	Pass
4 ♡	Pass	Pass	Pass

Opening lead: Ten of diamonds

When West opened the ten of diamonds, Vanderbilt quickly recognized that the danger to his contract lay in East obtaining the lead with the diamond king and leading a club through South's king. If that happened, the defenders might collect three club tricks to defeat the contract.

Spurning the diamond finesse, Vanderbilt won the opening lead with dummy's ace of diamonds and cashed the ace and king of spades. Next came a low trump to dummy's nine, and this was followed by the jack of spades. When East followed with a low spade, Vanderbilt discarded his losing diamond.

West won the queen of spades, and correctly played back a spade, which East ruffed and South overruffed. Dummy was now reentered via the trump ten (picking up East's outstanding trump en route), and the diamond queen was led.

When East covered the queen with the king, South ruffed with the trump ace (had East not covered with the king, South would have discarded one of his low clubs). Dummy was entered with the queen of trumps, and on the established jack of diamonds, Vanderbilt discarded a club. From here in, his only losers were two club tricks.

It made no difference which defender held the diamond king. If West held that card, he would have captured dummy's queen, as South discarded a club. The defenders could now make only the club ace, since South would have been able to discard his second low club on dummy's jack of diamonds.

As you've seen, success often depends on which finesse you *lose*. By losing the spade finesse instead of the diamond finesse, Vanderbilt performed a "scissors coup" that cut the opponents' communications and ensured his contract.

DEAL IV

While he was the Chinese Ambassador to the United States from 1946 to 1956, Wellington Koo derived much enjoyment from the game of bridge. In this deal, which arose in a social rubber-bridge game about twenty years ago, Mr. Koo, in the West

seat, "swindled" our South declarer out of a slam contract. Had
an expert been sitting South, it is doubtful whether he would
have allowed himself to be swindled even by so accomplished a
diplomat—but, then again, he might have been.

Neither side vulnerable. North deals.

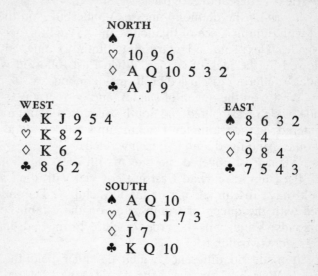

```
                    NORTH
                    ♠ 7
                    ♡ 10 9 6
                    ◇ A Q 10 5 3 2
                    ♣ A J 9
    WEST                            EAST
    ♠ K J 9 5 4                     ♠ 8 6 3 2
    ♡ K 8 2                         ♡ 5 4
    ◇ K 6                           ◇ 9 8 4
    ♣ 8 6 2                         ♣ 7 5 4 3
                    SOUTH
                    ♠ A Q 10
                    ♡ A Q J 7 3
                    ◇ J 7
                    ♣ K Q 10
```

The bidding:

NORTH	EAST	SOUTH	WEST
1 ◇	Pass	2 ♡	Pass
3 ◇	Pass	3 ♡	Pass
4 ♡	Pass	6 ♡	Pass
Pass	Pass		

Opening lead: Six of diamonds

Having heard the opponents bid aggressively to a slam in hearts, and looking at his own hand, Mr. Koo realized that his partner did not figure to have even one jack in his hand. (How right he was!) Most defenders, had they been sitting in the West seat, would probably have led a club, since this figured to be the safest lead.

However, as Dr. Koo looked at his doubleton king of diamonds, he did not like its position. North had bid diamonds twice, and it was therefore quite likely that North possessed a diamond suit headed by the A Q. If such were the case, then South would have no trouble in establishing that suit via a successful finesse against the king.

On the brighter side of things, Mr. Koo appreciated that his trump king would probably win a trick, since South rated to have the ace of hearts.

After some deliberation, Mr. Koo decided that his best hope for the setting trick was to try to talk declarer out of taking the diamond finesse. Thus, at trick one, he opened the six of diamonds!

When the dummy came down, South was not overly enthusiastic about what he saw. Actually, he was probably a bit scared, for if West's six of diamonds were a singleton, which it could easily have been, then by taking a losing finesse at trick one, declarer would go down when East returned a diamond for West to ruff at trick two.

So, rightly or wrongly (in retrospect, wrongly), declarer rejected the finesse in diamonds. He won the trick with the board's ace and led the ten of hearts, thus staking everything on the location of the king of trumps. When East played low, South did likewise. As is evident, Mr. Koo's king captured the trick, and, in time, West's king of diamonds took the setting trick.

It is obvious, of course, that if West had led anything but a low diamond, declarer's slam contract would have been a shoo-in. After losing the trump finesse, declarer would automatically have taken the diamond finesse, and would have avoided the loss of a trick in that suit.

DEAL V

The late Christian A. Herter, Secretary of State under President Eisenhower, was a good bridge player. Owing to the importance of his various governmental positions through the years, he never had time to play in tournaments, or even in duplicate games. But he kept abreast of theoretical developments in the fields of both duplicate and rubber bridge by studying the literature.

In this rubber-bridge deal, Mr. Herter gave a simple, practical demonstration of expert play. He was sitting South.

Both sides vulnerable. South deals.

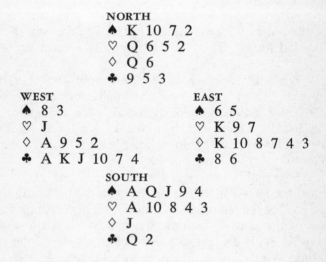

NORTH
♠ K 10 7 2
♡ Q 6 5 2
◊ Q 6
♣ 9 5 3

WEST
♠ 8 3
♡ J
◊ A 9 5 2
♣ A K J 10 7 4

EAST
♠ 6 5
♡ K 9 7
◊ K 10 8 7 4 3
♣ 8 6

SOUTH
♠ A Q J 9 4
♡ A 10 8 4 3
◊ J
♣ Q 2

The bidding:

SOUTH	WEST	NORTH	EAST
1 ♠	2 ♣	2 ♠	Pass
4 ♠	Pass	Pass	Pass

Opening lead: King of clubs

After West had cashed the king and ace of clubs, he laid down the ace of diamonds followed by another diamond. East covered dummy's queen with the king, and South, of course, ruffed.

Declarer's prospects of fulfilling his contract were bleak since the chances of avoiding a heart loser were not good. Just one distribution of the opponents' hearts would enable declarer to make his game—and Mr. Herter found it quickly.

At trick five, he cashed the ace of trumps and led the trump queen to dummy's king. Next came the queen of hearts—and whether East covered with the king or not, South was home.

If East played low, South would do likewise, as West's jack fell on this trick. If East put up the king—as he actually did—South would win it with his ace. Dummy would then be reentered via the trump ten and another heart led, South finessing his eight-spot when East followed suit with the seven. East's nine would fall under the ten, and victory would be attained.

If one examines the heart suit closely, he will conclude that the only combination where South could avoid the loss of a heart trick was the one that actually existed: West held the singleton jack. If, instead, Mr. Herter cashed the ace of hearts in the hope of dropping a singleton king, it could not possibly have helped him even if the king did fall. In this case, the other defender would have started with the tripleton J 9 7, and declarer could not have prevented him from winning a heart trick.

DEAL VI

One of bridge's most ardent enthusiasts was the late Karl T. Compton, world-renowned physicist and former president of the Massachusetts Institute of Technology. In this deal, Dr. Compton was sitting in the East seat, defending against South's game contract. His imaginative defense was expert in the full sense of the word.

Neither side vulnerable. East deals.

NORTH
- ♠ J 9 3 2
- ♡ A Q 6 5
- ◇ 4
- ♣ Q J 10 9

WEST
- ♠ 7 4
- ♡ J 9 7
- ◇ J 10 6 2
- ♣ 8 6 4 3

EAST
- ♠ 8 6
- ♡ K 10 2
- ◇ A Q 9 8 5
- ♣ A K 5

SOUTH
- ♠ A K Q 10 5
- ♡ 8 4 3
- ◇ K 7 3
- ♣ 7 2

The bidding:

EAST	SOUTH	WEST	NORTH
1 ◇	1 ♠	Pass	3 ♠
Pass	4 ♠	Pass	Pass
Pass			

Opening lead: Jack of diamonds

After winning West's opening lead of the diamond jack with his ace, it was obvious to Dr. Compton from the bidding that South had just about every outstanding high card. On further examination, it was equally obvious that if South had any losers in hearts, he figured to discard them on dummy's club suit once the ace and king were driven out.

From Dr. Compton's view, the defenders' sole hope of defeating the contract was to set up a heart trick before dummy's club suit became established. With this as his objective, Dr. Compton shifted to the deuce of hearts, at trick two, away from his king and right into the jaws of dummy's A Q!

Declarer won the queen, drew the outstanding trumps in two rounds, then led a club. East won the king and returned the ten of hearts, which drove out the board's ace. When declarer led the jack of clubs, East took his ace, and cashed the king of hearts for the setting trick. Dr. Compton had beaten declarer on the "timing"; he had established his king of hearts before declarer was able to set up the board's club suit. It was a neat bit of defense, don't you agree?

Had East played back any suit but hearts at trick two, declarer would have fulfilled his contract with ease. After drawing trumps, he would have conceded two tricks to East's ace and king of clubs. Dummy's two remaining clubs would then provide convenient discards for South's two losing hearts.

DEAL VII

One of the greatest cellists in the world is Gregor Piatigorsky. He is also a pretty fair amateur bridge player, as is illustrated by his handling of this part-score contract. By expert standards, his play would not be considered extraordinary. But Piatigorsky is an expert cellist, not an expert bridge player.

This deal was played many years ago, at about 3:00 A.M., after a concert Piatigorsky had given in Wichita, Kansas. He had also played *seven* encores! He should have been a very tired man, but if he were, I would hate to have to play against him when he was rested. The cellist was in the South seat.

Neither side vulnerable. West deals.

NORTH
♠ 9 7 5
♡ 8 6 4
◇ 6 3 2
♣ Q J 7 2

WEST
♠ K Q J 10 3
♡ K 7 2
◇ K 10 5
♣ 8 4

EAST
♠ 6 4
♡ J 10 9 5
◇ J 9 8 4
♣ 9 6 5

SOUTH
♠ A 8 2
♡ A Q 3
◇ A Q 7
♣ A K 10 3

The bidding:

WEST	NORTH	EAST	SOUTH
1 ♠	Pass	Pass	2 NT
Pass	Pass	Pass	

Opening lead: King of spades

The bidding was quite normal. West's opening bid was a marginal one. When East passed, South jumped to two no-trump in an attempt to portray a hand that would have been opened with two no-trump (twenty-two to twenty-four high-card points). As it turned out, North, with his three high-card points, made the winning bid when he elected not to push on to game.

When the dummy came into view after West had opened the king of spades, Piatigorsky deduced that West, for his opening bid, had to have both red-suit kings. Hence, taking either the heart or diamond finesse had to be a losing play. Piatigorsky's solution was simple and effective.

The king of spades was permitted to win the first trick, and Piatigorsky won the spade queen continuation with his ace. He next cashed the queen, jack, ace, and king of clubs. Now he exited with his remaining spade, forcing West into the lead with the spade ten.

After West was through taking his spade tricks, he had no option but to lead a red suit away from either his king of hearts or king of diamonds. Whichever suit he led, he would give Piatigorsky his eighth trick. At the table, West chose to lead a low heart.

And so Piatigorsky fulfilled his contract via an end-play. At trick thirteen, he surrendered his diamond queen to West's king. And, it should be mentioned, despite the late hour and his exhausting concert performance, Piatigorsky did not forget to score up the 150 bonus for holding four aces.

DEAL VIII

A screen celebrity who plays excellent bridge is actor Burt Lancaster. Back in 1960, Lancaster won the "best actor" Oscar for his performance in *Elmer Gantry*. If Academy Awards were given for best performances at the bridge table, Lancaster would probably have been nominated one on his role as the South declarer in this deal.

Both sides vulnerable. South deals.

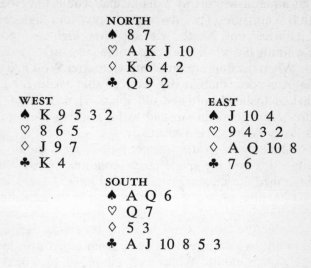

NORTH
♠ 8 7
♡ A K J 10
◇ K 6 4 2
♣ Q 9 2

WEST
♠ K 9 5 3 2
♡ 8 6 5
◇ J 9 7
♣ K 4

EAST
♠ J 10 4
♡ 9 4 3 2
◇ A Q 10 8
♣ 7 6

SOUTH
♠ A Q 6
♡ Q 7
◇ 5 3
♣ A J 10 8 5 3

The bidding:

SOUTH	WEST	NORTH	EAST
1 ♣	Pass	1 ◇	Pass
2 ♣	Pass	2 ♡	Pass
3 NT	Pass	Pass	Pass

Opening lead: Three of spades

On West's opening lead of the three of spades, East put up the ten, and Lancaster won the trick—with his ace! He then led the seven of hearts to the king and returned the queen of clubs, finessing against East's hoped-for king. West, of course, won this trick—and returned a low spade! Lancaster gathered in this trick with his queen, and scampered home with eleven tricks.

Superficially, it might appear that both Lancaster and the West defender were performing in some surreal Hollywood script. First of all, South could have taken the opening lead with his queen, instead of with the ace. And West, when he won his king of clubs, could have shifted to a high diamond instead of returning a low spade. Had he done so, the defense could have collected four diamond tricks, four spades, and the king of clubs, thus inflicting a five-trick set on declarer. Let's examine the motivation behind the plays by South and West.

First, why did South win the opening lead with the spade ace rather than the queen? If East had the club king, then South would bring home six club tricks, four hearts, and one spade. In this case, the overtrick which he "threw away" (the spade queen) would be of little import.

But if West had the club king, Lancaster did not want West to shift to a diamond. And Lancaster felt that if he captured the opening lead with the queen of spades, and West had the club king, West would tend not to continue spades, and might, in desperation, shift to a diamond. So he "falsecarded" with the spade ace at trick one, trying to take out some insurance against a diamond shift by West.

From West's point of view, when South won East's spade ten with the ace, it certainly appeared that he had hit East with the Q J 10 of spades—otherwise, why would South have won the trick with the ace instead of the queen or jack? Thus, West assumed that East would win the second spade lead and return a spade. West could then overtake with the king and cash his remaining spades. But it did not quite work out that way for the defenders.

DEAL IX

One of the great statesmen of this century was England's Winston Churchill. He was also a most enthusiastic bridge player.

During the early 1950's, while visiting in New York City, Mr. Churchill played bridge a few times. Whether he was a winning bridge player, I do not know. But if one accepts this deal as an indication of his ability, I would say that he figured to be a winner. He was sitting in the South seat.

North-South vulnerable. South deals.

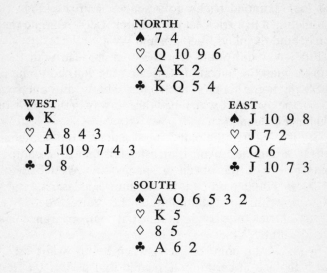

NORTH
♠ 7 4
♡ Q 10 9 6
♢ A K 2
♣ K Q 5 4

WEST
♠ K
♡ A 8 4 3
♢ J 10 9 7 4 3
♣ 9 8

EAST
♠ J 10 9 8
♡ J 7 2
♢ Q 6
♣ J 10 7 3

SOUTH
♠ A Q 6 5 3 2
♡ K 5
♢ 8 5
♣ A 6 2

The bidding:

SOUTH	WEST	NORTH	EAST
1 ♠	Pass	2 NT	Pass
4 ♠	Pass	Pass	Pass

Opening lead: Jack of diamonds

After winning West's opening lead of the jack of diamonds with the king, Churchill led a low trump off dummy. When East followed suit with the eight-spot, Churchill unhesitatingly put up his ace. West's king dropped, so Churchill's only losers were two trump tricks and a heart.

It is apparent that had South finessed his queen of trumps at trick two, he would have gone down, because he would have lost three trump tricks and a heart. Why did Churchill spurn the trump finesse? Elementary, my dear Winston.

If East had the trump king, South could not lose more than two trump tricks (unless East had all five of the outstanding trumps, in which case three trump tricks would be lost even if East showed South his cards). Alternatively, if West had the K J 10 9 of trumps, then South would be operating under circumstances beyond his control.

Let's suppose that when Churchill cashed the trump ace at trick two, West had followed suit with the eight-spot. Dummy would then have been entered via the diamond ace, and the remaining trump would have been led. Assuming that East followed with the ten, South would insert his queen. If East had the king, the queen would win; and if West had the king, then the opponents' trumps had to divide 3-2, so all South would lose would be two tricks in the trump suit beside the ace of hearts.

Had an expert been sitting in the South seat, he would have recognized immediately that the play of the spade ace at trick two was a simple, "book-type" safety play designed to restrict the losses in the suit to a maximum of two tricks. It should be appreciated that Churchill probably did not have too much time to study bridge techniques and therefore, in my opinion, his instinctive play of the ace is entitled to more applause than if it had been made by an expert.

DEAL X

Among the accomplishments of the late leader of India, Jawaharlal Nehru, was the acquisition of a master's touch at bridge. Although he played rarely, he frequently referred to the game to illustrate the difference between free will and determinism.

"Determinism is like the cards that are dealt you," he once said. "Free will is how you play them. The interaction between the two determines what you are as a person—or even a nation."

I have grave doubts that Nehru ever lectured on "determinism" and "free will" to a conference of bridge players, but if he had, he might well have used this deal, in which he was the declarer, to illustrate his beliefs on determinism and free will. It is a rather easy deal, but it hits the bull's-eye.

Neither side vulnerable. South deals.

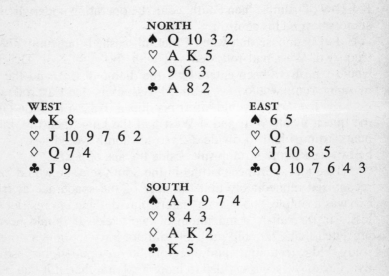

```
                        NORTH
                        ♠ Q 10 3 2
                        ♡ A K 5
                        ◇ 9 6 3
                        ♣ A 8 2
        WEST                                EAST
        ♠ K 8                               ♠ 6 5
        ♡ J 10 9 7 6 2                      ♡ Q
        ◇ Q 7 4                             ◇ J 10 8 5
        ♣ J 9                               ♣ Q 10 7 6 4 3
                        SOUTH
                        ♠ A J 9 7 4
                        ♡ 8 4 3
                        ◇ A K 2
                        ♣ K 5
```

The bidding:

SOUTH	WEST	NORTH	EAST
1 ♠	Pass	3 ♠	Pass
4 ♠	Pass	Pass	Pass

Opening lead: Jack of hearts

West opened the heart jack, dummy's king was played, and East dropped the queen. It appeared reasonable to assume that the queen was a singleton.

Had Nehru taken the trump finesse, he would have gone down. West, when he won with the trump king, would have returned the ten of hearts, and East would have ruffed away the ace. Eventually the defenders would have collected two more tricks, a heart and a diamond.

But Nehru saw that he had ten sure tricks, provided the defenders did not score a ruff. And he certainly was not going to finesse for the trump king in an attempt to gain an overtrick.

So, at trick two, he led the board's queen of trumps, to entice East into covering with the king if he had that card (Nehru had no objection to making an overtrick if he could do it without jeopardizing his contract). But when East followed suit with the deuce, Nehru promptly went up with the ace.

He then shot back a trump, West's king taking the trick as East's remaining trump fell. With the adverse trumps now removed from circulation, nothing could prevent declarer from fulfilling his contract.

Again, this deal is a rather simple one to play correctly. Aren't they all—provided declarer knows when and how to finesse . . . and when *not* to!